SERVICE

ANSWER THE CALL

THE LAST DAYS SAGA
BOOK 1

ERIC MALDONADO

D1528748

This book is dedicated to both the living,
and the dead.

ALSO BY ERIC MALDONADO...

In the Last Days Saga...

CATCH OR KILL - *Prequel*

SERVICE - I

THE PATH OF HEAVEN - II

(Coming Soon)

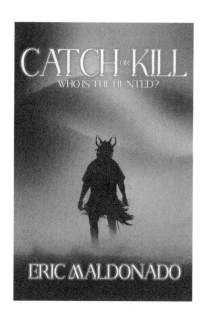

Get The Last Days Saga Prequel
Catch Or Kill

FOR FREE

Sign up for the no-spam newsletter and get Eric Maldonado's
exclusive give away, absolutely free.

Go To
www.ericmaldonadoauthor.com
And Sign Up!

SERVICE

ANSWER THE CALL

ERIC MALDONADO

1

PASSING

Today was the greatest day of Gerald's life because today he died.

He had lived a good life, he recalled, a life filled with great friends, family, some tragedy, a little bit of sadness, and a lot of happiness. He wasn't much of a thinker, he mused, but he accomplished a lot, and he always tried to help where he could. The only regret he had was that he didn't have his wife Lia with him, but he knew eventually she would come but hopefully not too soon because their son George would need her with him gone now.

Passing away wasn't painful. He felt himself detach from his body like a loose tooth, with that last little bit finally coming free afterlife had worked at him until his body couldn't go on anymore. The sweet release he felt as he started to float upwards was negated when he stopped to look back and say goodbye. Emotion welled up within him as he tried to get their attention but no one saw or heard him and, from his perspective, they all looked far away and muffled. He took one last look at his wife and son and then he felt himself being pulled upwards.

He passed through the walls and timber of the home he had

been born in without feeling anything and could see through them. Though it was only a nanosecond in passing, he could see the distinct layers of the wood grain that made up his roof timber and the roof itself. The change from the timber to the roof shingles was immediate as the texture changed from various hues of the wood browns to the stark and solid layer of grainy gray-black that made up the roof shingles.

Up higher and higher Gerald floated, feeling neither the breeze nor the liquid patter of the rain coming down. It was a strange thought, but he liked to think this was good luck; he died on a rainy day, kind of like getting married on one.

As Gerald went up higher and higher past the rain clouds, he saw the sun shining as bright as a golden coin on a blue sea. With a pang of sadness, he knew this was the last time he would ever see that sun again and tried to frame it in his mind so he could remember it wherever he went. He had floated past the blue sky and slowly saw the utter blackness of space dotted with countless stars scattered about like a child's marbles on the blacktop. As he reached the end of the Earth's troposphere, he felt a tearing that pained him as he was severed from the Earth. It was as if he had lost a limb, and the ghost pain of that lost limb lingered. He trembled with the certain knowledge that he was connected to Mother Earth even after death. He reached back and stretched his arm out to somehow touch the blue giant quickly being pulled away from him.

This hollow feeling lingered as he approached the behemoth of golden fire that is the Sun. He had never felt so insignificant as he did now, moving closer and closer to it, the sheer size beyond comprehension, and before long all he could see was a never-ending wall of fire that soon surrounded him.

As he passed into the Sun, he could see the vast oceans of solar activity seething and churning in on itself. The range of reds and oranges that burned through these vast oceans of nuclear fire seemed to suddenly shift and ripple as if his presence, as insignificant as it was, sent ripples and reacted to him as if he were a small dinghy sliding across a burning ocean.

The swirling masses began to follow Gerald as he moved through the Sun's mass. A shape faded in and out of his vision, and it seemed a trick of the senses when the flickering outline seemed to stretch out its shimmering arms. As he tried to make sense of this flickering behemoth, it started to shimmer, lose shape, and scatter in a roiling mass of fire and energy.

2

PURGATUM

Gerald watched as a great flare flashed out and sped toward him. Instinctively he put his hands up to shield his face, but no pain or heat bore down upon him. Instead, some unseen force lifted him and pushed him out of the Sun. He quickly pulled away from the burning surface into the black depths of space. He stopped moving for a few seconds and then, with a lurch of vertigo-inducing speed, shot forward into the abyss.

In a blink he blew past the Moons of Jupiter. He blinked again, and he was past the solar system and beyond the cradle of mankind. Rocketing into the unknown faster and faster, the stars were going by so fast they were lines of light rather than dots in the black canvas of space. Planets, asteroids, and meteors all flashed by or through in a blink.

Gerald did not feel or see the layers when he sped through a solid object. Zooming so fast that color and light blurred, he started to feel a growing sense of panic as he sped faster and faster into the void. He felt the panic rise as he sped up even more and he felt the edges of a blackout threatening to overtake him. As he fought to stay conscious, he began to make out a haze in the distance. The colors from this distance were grayish and seemed to swirl and move.

As he approached the haze, it grew larger and larger until it filled his field of vision. The color wasn't gray but a pearlescent white which shined so brightly that it hurt to look at. It appeared to be a large wall of cloud that stretched out forever in every direction.

As he approached the wall of cloud, he could see shapes moving within the swirls and eddies. He didn't slow as he impacted the wall, but his forward momentum completely stopped. The force of it caused him to see spots in front of his eyes, but as the black spots cleared, he realized that he could physically feel the essence of whatever this thing was.

He could feel the mist of it on every surface of his being like a warm cloth. He could see the whirls of the mist extend and retract as it reached out and touched him. It was as if it was smelling his scent and testing whether he was a friend or foe. It was at once welcoming yet cautious, and as he began to move through the mist, he would see flashes of faces go by him. Each one he did see had its mouth open as if singing.

He began to pick up on a sound. It started like a buzzing but then he realized it was more like they were holding a note, a long, loud clear note of the purest sound he ever heard. He could make out now the individual voices that made up that clear, perfect note. It was a chorus of all and one, together and separate, interwoven to perfection. Choking back emotionally to hear something so beautiful. He wanted to laugh and cry at the same time.

The note gradually became louder and louder as he made his way through the mist until the sound of it was vibrating through him and threatening to shake him loose. The vibration continued to build, and he panicked because he could feel himself coming apart down to a molecular level. He tried to scream but it was drowned out by the chorus. His very scream was pulled into it and he felt himself being separated like a thread from a sweater that kept being pulled, in this cacophony, he started to make out a jumbled word.

As he threatened to become undone by the noise, he struggled against it until he could focus on the word, but it kept slipping from his mind. Not slipped, he realized, but pulled from his mind. Gerald fought against the noise. He fought the chorus around him as he focused on what they were trying to say even as the noise rose like a thunderous wave building and building on itself and crashing down on Gerald to scatter him against the shores of his consciousness.

His sanity started to fray as he knew that he was powerless to stop it and then...it stopped, and they all spoke, not just a word he realized and it was directed at him. "It is time." One voice for all grumbled like thunder throughout his very being. Gerald felt a cold feeling of dread flow down his spine and spread through his soul. The weight of millennia was a tangible thing that exuded from the mist that held him now. The mist tightened around Gerald and, without warning, he felt his thoughts pulled out of his very being to be absorbed by the constricting miasma. Gerald felt cold panic overtake him as he fought against this invasion. The flow was similar to a small stream of salmon beating the upward surge of the stream. They shivered ever so slightly in his mind, and they spoke again to Gerald: "Rest easy," the thunderous voice said.

Gerald couldn't rest easy, though. He knew he had come to it, the point in time all of us fear, and he was afraid to be found wanting. He wanted to scream but he couldn't. He tried to weep, and no tears would come. He struggled against nothing and everything.

A warmth spread over Gerald. It washed over him and brought a soothing calm. It also brought just a smidgeon of the things they had seen: snatches of lives, glimpses of mountains, deserts, plains, faces, and tastes, they all blew around and through him like a deck of scattered cards, and then he understood what they knew already: "Judgment comes to us all" They and he said.

A thought jumped into his mind. "Are you God?" Gerald asked, knowing somehow that this being wasn't. The rumbling laugh echoing through Gerald to his core was his answer, and he accepted his fate.

His life was laid bare. Like small drizzles of smoke, he could see instances of it flash through his mind's eye. He saw himself as a young boy of no more than ten fly-fishing with his father in the river near his home, just one instance in about a thousand instances they had fly-fished in that river together. The memory brought back the old ache he had whenever he remembered his father and how much he missed him when he was gone.

Another image came unbidden to him, an image of smoke, heat, and fire. He remembered the bitter cold biting into him, suffocating him with its hungry embrace even in late spring in the Black Forest of Germany. He remembered the dead as well. The bodies were everywhere. Many were twisted and bent into unnatural angles while others were mangled as if by some mad butcher.

Anger swelled within him. Even after all these years and all the good things he had done and built with his life, that time, that place still festered in his psyche like a wound that never fully healed. Gerald screamed out his rage and pushed those memories away. He could see the force of that memory spread around him and the fiery waves of it dispersed.

The mist seemed to look Gerald in the eye for what seemed like an eternity before continuing their work. Gerald felt embarrassed by his outburst and apologized to them. A mental nod was thrown his way before it continued.

Other memories came rushing up and out of his consciousness into the flaming ether such as hearing "Hey Gerald" from his brother Chance as he greeted him. Chance looked just as handsome as ever on that late summer day when they were walking into their family church. Gerald's heart swelled as he went to take his place next to his best friend Charlie who looked as nervous as a groom should as he stretched out his hand to Gerald and then hugged him then Chance. "Glad you could make it." Gerald jibed Charlie. The sweet memory of that day dissolved as fast as it came.

Lia, his wife, his everything, appeared before him. The first time he saw her on Main Street. The smile she gave him. Also, the frown her brother shot him with soon after. Trying to find ways to see her in 1950s Georgia where a white man wooing a woman of color was more than frowned upon. Skip to their wedding day, the trials and tribulations, and the love. All worth it.

Lia faded but George swelled up in front of him as he watched his only son being used as a tackling dummy by his teammates at the University of Georgia. Gerald chuckled as he remembered how much George loved playing football and how much it meant to be a Georgia Bulldog. Never cared that he never saw a sniff of playing time, only that he was part of that Georgia team. Pride came and went with the memory, and before Gerald knew it, all his memories were whipping up faster and faster like a tornado, spiraling up into the mist that surrounded him.

The whispering stopped. Gerald looked up anxiously for what would happen next. He could feel with a growing sense of dread that they were communicating with someone or something. A chill started to work its way down his spine even though he still felt the warmth they had given him. He could feel them communing with whatever it was, and the worst part was that he knew with a growing certainty that he was being allowed to know that he was being judged.

Fear like nothing he ever faced before pounced upon him like a hungry beast. It tore into every fiber of his immortal soul. This was it. *Whatever I had done in my life that had just passed, whatever good, whatever evil I have done was now on trial.*

Have I done enough? Gerald thought as the fear continued to chew away at his resolve like a termite in wood. *Does any man know?* he thought as the fear overwhelmed him, drowning him in a sea of what-ifs and what could have been. Even in despair, he thought back to the things he had done, both good and bad, and he remembered his father's voice breaking through like a beacon. "Whatever you do or try, do the right thing, most times it's the hard thing," he recalled looking down at his father's deathbed. "A man couldn't be prouder of his family."

His father's face displayed the wrinkles and lines that traversed over it like a broken road, weathered to the nub. With that, the fear racing through every fiber of his being like a plague was gone and replaced by a cold certainty. *Yes, I have done enough,* Gerald thought. His father was the best man he ever knew, and if he thought he was a good man then that was enough for him, come what may. And then he blacked out.

WHEN GERALD AWOKE, he was standing in a field. He stood there for a little while and when nothing happened he began to walk. He didn't have a particular destination but he knew where he was going. A dirt road appeared, and he started down it at a nice, easy pace. He smelled the ferns and the rich soil as he walked. Everything smelled so rich. He could make out the light smell of roses growing wild on the side of the road and then traces of morning dew right before the sun burned it off the grass.

Gerald walked by a pond where he could hear the fish disturbing the surface of the water to feed on mosquitoes, and when he looked up, the morning sun had suddenly moved to the top of its zenith, meaning it was now noon. He could have sworn he wasn't walking more than twenty minutes. Time was moving much faster than he thought; he hurried his pace a bit, and after another half hour of walking, it was dark and he could hear the cicadas singing in the background.

Eventually, he came upon a wooden gate. *It isn't a pearly gate, that's for sure*, he thought as he looked it over. The wood used for the gate he couldn't identify. It was very smooth and seemed to be mixed with some kind of metal like it was melted down with metal and wood and it hardened to this unique structure.

Without thinking, he touched the side of the gate post. He could feel a hum; sort of like the singing echoes from the cloud choir he had heard so vociferously before. He placed his cheek against the wood post, and the rushing sound grew louder and louder as if a dam had burst and was now breaking free to rush down the mountain that was Gerald's being.

Fear clutched him as he realized that he couldn't break contact with the post. The sound was bearing down on him like an avalanche. The sound began to build back up to the level it had before when it began to shake his very soul apart. Gerald fought with all his might to wrench himself free of the post. He pushed and pushed twisted and turned but nothing worked and still, the sound was relentless, suffocating. He could feel his being starting to break apart.

Exhausted, Gerald gave into the sound, the knowledge that it was futile to resist it, and just as suddenly, the noise stopped and Gerald found himself sitting on his ass in front of the gate. It no longer issued a sound, and the gate looked just as inert as it had before. Slowly he got back on his feet, knocked the road dust off his jeans, and stood before the gate once more. He sure as hell wasn't going to touch the gate again, but he was going to walk right through that son of a gun if it was the last thing he did. For whatever reason, he felt like the gate was toying with him. Of course, it sounded nuts, but for a second he could have sworn that the gate seemed to know what he was thinking.

"Hello." The voice startled Gerald and when he turned around, a man was standing right behind him. The first thing Gerald noticed was that the man seemed to glow. He radiated a vitality and goodness that made him instantly likable. This inner light flowed through the handsome cut of his features. He looked like an older man in his mid-fifties with long, dark hair tied into a ponytail. He was dressed in what looked like a toga spun from a material that seemed to shimmer with various shades of white, and on his feet were a pair of simple brown sandals. His height only seemed to add to his presence as he towered over Gerald by at least a foot.

"You just popped up," Gerald responded.

"Sorry about that. It's a bad habit." The stranger smiled. "My name is Kerael. I'm your guide," he said with a wave of his hands.

"Nice to meet you." Gerald reached out his hand and they shook.

"Nice to meet you as well." They stood there for a few moments before Kerael broke the uncomfortable silence. "So, as you've gathered by now, you've died."

Gerald smiled. "Feel great." He spread his arms and laughed.

"Being rid of your mortal coil is very freeing from what I hear, but seeing as I'm an angel, I am immortal."

"You're an angel?" Gerald asked. "I thought you would look different, you know?" He motioned behind him for where the wings would be. He felt kind of silly and a little worried that maybe he would offend his guide.

Two large, feathery, pearl-white wings spread out behind

Kerael, and with a quick flip of his wings floating in the air in front of Gerald. Kerael also seemed to grow with internal light and seemed to expand his own gravity at the same time. Kerael was limiting himself so Gerald wasn't overwhelmed he realized but didn't know how he knew that. He still felt awed at being in front of an honest-to-God angel. Unable to speak, his mind having difficulty comprehending the angel in front of him. The stories a person reads still do not prepare you for seeing a large humanoid being flapping his pearly white wings in front of you.

Kerael floated back down and folded his wings back so they weren't visible again. "They never fail to impress," he said as he with a smile that dropped from his face, replaced by a grim set to his lips. Without warning, the nimbus of light around Kerael increased. He reached out his hand to Gerald and he grew again in size until all other things were pushed aside by Kerael's presence. "Come, it's time." His voice emanated the power he had been holding back until now.

Alternating feelings of awe and fear collided, trembling, he took the angel's hand. As soon as their hands touched a sudden sense of vertigo swept over Gerald as everything went black and he was pulled out of the place he was and into another. The effect was immediate. They came from a place of life or a semblance of life that felt familiar and grounded. Now, they were in a void, the void. This wasn't space where he had seen the stars blur by in white tracers and had passed through comets and planets. Space wasn't empty, neither was this place. There was a nothingness here that was not natural. Without thought, Gerald bared his teeth at the abyss, like an animal facing its enemy in the wild. Kerael's strong arm supported Gerald around his waist as he felt himself being pulled through the inky black. The angel's grip tightened and Gerald felt something in the void. He felt a chill as a terrible awakening was happening. The darkness had been alerted to their presence like blood in the water.

The hungry darkness came alive, he could feel them circling around him and Kerael. Whatever was out there seemed to detach from the darkness and were suddenly swirling around them. Bitter cold claws without a shred of mercy or pity grabbed at him from every direction, trying to pull him away from his angelic guardian. Gerald's fear took him and he imagined being pulled away from Kerael and then thrust into a ravenous maw that stretched out forever feeding a hunger that could never be sated.

Kerael tightened his grip around Gerald's waist again as the Void desperately tried to wrestle Gerald away. He felt the angel swing out in a punch and heard a scream without sound. A mental wail echoed through Gerald, and he knew with icy certainty that if Kerael let him go, something horrible beyond imagining would befall him.

With a screech and a hiss like rotten steam, whatever was out in the darkness redoubled its efforts to get at the young soul, a speck of light through the never-ending black. Gerald held on tight to Kerael as he made his way through, and Gerald didn't see what hunted them but in his mind's eye they were night-mares made real. He recalled George telling him of the Elder Gods and their minions from an H.P. Lovecraft book he was reading. Imagining snippets of these abominations frayed his sanity and he was glad he couldn't see them in the black. The light emanating from Kerael was a barrier but did not illumi-nate. Gerald could feel them out there on the edge of light exuding fear and terror, and Gerald was caught in their icy grip. He was a rabbit surrounded by jackals.

But the jackals feared the lion, and Kerael was a lion. He expanded his aura and where the light went the darkness retreated and kept them at bay. The horrors of old night cried, they roared, but most importantly, he was kept safe by their oldest enemy, a being who destroyed their beloved darkness.

After a few more moments the void seemed to retreat before them, beaten back by Kerael's aura and power. Kerael loosened his grip on Gerald who felt rather than saw the darkness giving way to something else. They entered into a world of gray where Gerald could not see anything but eventually, like fog clearing off the bay, something he had heard and spoken about since he was a boy emerged, a place he hoped to always go with his family and friends.

3

HEAVEN

Heaven. They had arrived. One second they were floating through the gray and the next, Gerald was there. The nightmare through the void receded away as he could only stand there and try and take it all in. Emotion built inside his chest as he surveyed paradise. He tried to hold it in but he broke down, dropped to his knees, and openly wept. He had never done that his whole life and he had suffered great loss, been through tragedy. Now, no more than a few hours into his afterlife he was openly weeping on soil so brown and rich with life that it absorbed his tears like a sponge. He could smell the earthy loam. Heaven was home.

He knew instinctively that this was where he was truly born; the pull on his being was unmistakable. Every person who ever was had come from this place. They were all tied together like the great swirls of color that flashed across his vision as he saw flowers in vivid hues of red, blue, purple, and gold. His eye was drawn to grass so green so deep and lush that it felt like a baby soft carpet and you could smell how vital it was.

The sky was blue so light and clear that the clouds seemed like floating bins of cotton. The breeze that was swept by smelled like cookies and pie mixed with that smell you get only after a summer rain.

"I never thought..." Gerald tried to verbalize what he was feeling to Kerael, who stood patiently to his side and smiled.

"There's more," the angel said.

Gerald nodded absently in Kerael's direction and walked into a field where he saw a large shape in the distance. He tried to place where he had seen it before and as he approached the massive shape, he began to notice people. They were of every creed and color. Some were walking and some, astonishingly enough, were floating by. They all nodded in greeting or a warm hello.

He noticed rabbits eating tomatoes growing wild. The tomato, after having been consumed, would grow back immediately and in reverse.

He smelled a strong, musky odor, and walking by him were horses, bison, and some large creature that looked like a cow but had only one emerald, green eye in the middle of its forehead. Gerald knew that this creature wasn't from Earth.

"It's a Gowan," Kerael explained from behind. Gerald had nearly forgotten that Kerael was still with him. "They don't exist on Earth but on the home planet of the Eloyie."

Gerald made a frown and shook his head. "So aliens exist," he deadpanned.

"The Eloyie are an alien race older than Man and they have been there with us almost since the beginning." Something brushed against him. The muscular frame of a lion walked by him. The bigger shock was that a lamb was walking with him and playfully bumping the lion. "Oh, come on!" Gerald shouted. "I get symbolism but that..."

He shook his head, and Kerael placed his hand on Gerald's shoulder and laughed with him. "Those two love to mess with the newbies," the angel said. "It never gets old."

Gerald's laughter faded as his attention was drawn back to the hulking shape coming into focus. As he got closer he could smell it, a very faint smell for something so large and reminded Gerald of cedar, but then he realized that the smell was coming from the leaves of the tree the creature was eating from. He continued moving closer.

Only a hundred feet from him it was pouring rain in an area maybe two hundred feet around and people were slip-sliding and diving onto the grass. He recalled as a boy doing that when it had rained. He loved to feel the way the warm rain fell on him and seemed to give him extra energy to keep on diving into that grass. His mother hated it, of course, because when he and his brother finally came home, they were covered head to toe in mud. He could play childish games if he wanted to, Gerald realized. He was in Heaven, after all.

His attention went back to the giant in front of him. Now that he was close enough, Gerald realized what it was. He could feel the breath of its exhale hit him from where he stood, and he had to crane his neck to see the very top of it. Its body must have been over two hundred feet long from head to tail. Its four massive legs were the size of ten telephone poles lashed together. The neck was very long and ended with a small head that seemed extremely content to munch away on the tree leaves.

"Why am I looking at a brontosaurus?" Gerald inquired of Kerael. "I mean, of all the things I thought I would see, this isn't anywhere on the list."

Kerael smiled and placed his hand on Gerald's shoulder. "All things that have been created are composed of energy. When that life form passes away, it returns here and if the form is needed again, then it is sent back to the planet it came from."

Gerald nodded. "So basically everything has a soul and

when it dies it comes back here to be reincarnated? I knew dogs have a soul. Too good not to."

Kerael smiled in reply. Gerald wiped off a large glob of brontosaurus drool that landed on his shoulder. "Ooh, that's gross!" Kerael exclaimed. He waved his hand and the drool on Gerald's shoulder disappeared.

"Can he talk like Mr. Ed?" Gerald asked.

Kerael laughed. "No, creatures who never spoke in life were missing the physical makeup and intelligence to speak." He paused. "But they are intelligent.They can understand you and will communicate with you but in their own way."

Gerald frowned and then his face lit up. "Hey, big guy!" Gerald yelled up to the brontosaurus.

The brontosaurus stopped chewing and looked down at him with expectation.

"You mind hoisting me up so I can get a better view?"

The brontosaurus snorted and then slowly started to lower his head. It wasn't able to lower it enough for Gerald, so it bent over far enough for him to climb onto its head. The brontosaurus stood back up and within a few moments, Gerald was standing on top of a brontosaurus and gazing out upon the heavenly horizon.

"Thank you. Mind if I call you Percy? You just seem like a Percy." Gerald smiled and rubbed its head fondly.

The newly named Percy snorted in response and held still to allow Gerald to see the breathtaking view of white-capped snowy mountains in the distance. He could smell the ice from where he was and see large birds and other winged creatures circling the mountain peaks.

"Those are the Choronus Peaks," Kerael said as he floated next to Gerald. "Those are the oldest mountains in creation. They were old even before the creation of Terra."

Gerald stared at them in wonder. Time passed for a while as

the three of them—Gerald, Kerael, and the newly named Percy enjoyed the scenery.

"This is unbelievable." Gerald barely choked out the words as emotion once again overwhelmed him. "Thank you," he said to the angel. "And thank you, big guy, for taking time out of your day to give me a boost."

Percy snorted and shook his head a bit as if to say no problem.

"I mean it, you guys have made this special for me, I won't forget it."

They stood and watched other creatures walk, fly, swim, or a combination of all three move about them for a while. Gerald tapped on Percy's head and slowly Percy lowered himself down so Gerald could climb off. Once he was down on the ground again, Percy snorted a goodbye and walked off to find some more tree leaves to chew on. "Thanks again!" Gerald waved as Percy departed.

Gerald looked around him and asked Kerael about the other creatures he saw, specifically the non-Earth creatures. "So that thing I saw before with the one green eye?" Gerald starts.

"Yes, the Gowan. What would you like to know?"

Gerald pondered this for a few moments. "Where are they from again? I was distracted but you said they were from EElack or something like that"

"Eloyie, pronounced El-ohh-ee. They are from the home planet of the Eloyie," Kerael explained. "They are one of the oldest races in the universe and they are a great ally."

Gerald frowned at the realization. "Aliens are real and if Heaven is real, then so is Hell. I figured that one out when we went through that place." Gerald shuddered thinking of the void.

"That was the place that was, we were created in the place that is. We have been at war with what dwells in the abyss since the beginning, it never relents" Kerael said with a weariness that illustrated this neverending grind. He then inhaled slowly and gave an equally tired smile.

"Let's not dwell on the negative today, shall we? Today is your day and I wanted to keep it that way." He beamed a smile at Gerald that sort of put his mind at ease and he nodded. He didn't want to dwell on the negative either. "There's plenty of other things that we can discuss, and I'm not the most qualified to do that for you."

"Not you then who?" Gerald asked, confused.

Kerael warmly smiled and approached him. He placed his hands on his shoulders and turned him around. "How about your parents?"

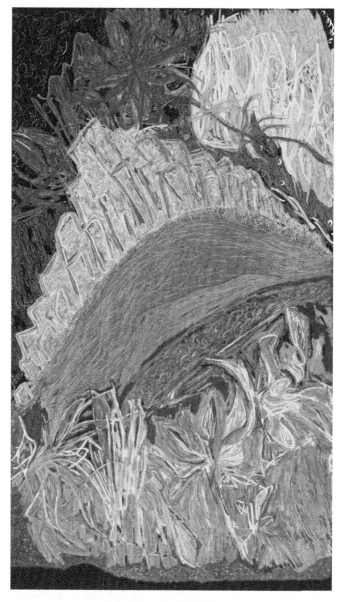

Heaven's Gate By Chad Maldonado

4

FAMILY

A cool wind blew across Gerald's face. He caught the smell of freshly baked cookies which captured the essence of who he was in life. It was the smell of long days at play as a child, afternoons spent fishing with his father, his brother, and his best friend, and visits as a man with his own family. It was a sweet reminder of home, family, and how coming home dirty and bleeding was a reward to little boys and a reminder to grown men who sometimes forget that simple things are always best.

As Gerald slowly turned around, his body trembling so badly that Kerael had to keep him upright, another soft scent suddenly replaced the cookies. It was the smell of lavender, his mother's smell. In that light smell was strength, an unbreakable force that never wavered or gave in when things were at their worst.

Everything around him was spinning even if he was only just turning around. The hair on the back of his neck was on end as if an electrical charge was running through him. His chest was so tight with emotion that he couldn't breathe. Once he had turned around, he realized he was looking down. He was almost afraid to look up and face his parents. The searing pain of loss came back all too fresh as he slowly moved his head up.

He recalled the emptiness he felt once both his parents had passed on. The tears he shed in life for them began to flow anew as he looked into the faces of his parents Ralph and Kathryn.

"Hey, son." That deep, soft tone in his voice conveyed so much with so little effort as his father greeted him. The face that greeted him was a face he hadn't seen in forty years. His father looked like he was back in his mid-forties again. To Gerald, that was the height of his father's power and strength physically. The deep blue eyes lined with crow's feet from too many smiles and intense thought, the patrician set to his features down to the aquiline nose inherited from his forefathers in the highlands of Scotland. The long graying hair that he always had to sweep out of his eyes. As in life, he had on his favorite Dungarees, flip flops, and his favorite t-shirt, an olive drab Army-issue shirt that he gave his father when he returned from the war.

A sharp ache hit him in the chest as he remembered the day he buried the old man with the t-shirt in one hand and his grandson George's football jersey in the other. "His two favorite things from his two favorite boys," he recalled his father always saying.

He failed to fight back tears and gave his father the hug he had been waiting to give him since he had passed. He felt hot tears fall on his father's chest and then he felt something wet on his forehead. He didn't look up, but he knew it was his father's own tears that fell as well. His father was a big man at a solid six foot three and a half and well-built from constant exercising, and he felt like a child again even though he himself was a solid six feet one inches or so.

"It's real good to see you," his father said as he continued to hug Gerald so hard he was having problems breathing.

"Ralphie." The warm tone of his mother's voice was followed

by her hand on Gerald's shoulder. His father stopped hugging him and he faced his mother again. This wasn't the face he last remembered that was ravaged by illness to a shade of what she was. Instead, she was the tiny five foot one fireball of her mid-thirties with the wavy red hair to match, the same red hair he himself possessed and luckily kept throughout his life.

Her face always reminded him of Lucille Ball with her dramatic cheekbones and small pointy chin. Her Irish heritage was there in the warm sea-green eyes that, just like an ocean, could go from bright and serene to stormy and dangerous if you crossed her.

His father was a great man who taught him to be courageous in the face of fear. His mother couldn't teach him that because she was fearless. Being in her embrace was something that now made him whole.

Gerald laughed out loud. She laughed in return and hugged him again. He and his father both laughed at that and they all hugged each other, cried then laughed again. For what seemed like an eternity they kept cycling back through all those emotions until finally, they had run their course.

"You hungry, son?" His father asked him.

"Can we still get hungry?" Gerald quizzically asked.

"Sure, if you want to be. We don't need food to live but it wouldn't be paradise now, would it, without your mom's cooking?"

They all laughed, and Gerald nodded. A polite cough to his right reminded Gerald that Kerael was still with him. "I totally forgot you were still with us," Gerald said apologetically.

"That's alright. Tends to happen but it's the best part of my job." Kerael beamed.

"Well, I'm sorry all the same." Gerald struggled to find a direction for their conversation.

"No need," Kerael said as if reading his thoughts. "I am done for now, but I'll be around, so settle in and enjoy yourself," he said. "God bless you, Gerald. You have earned it."

Gerald extended his arm and shook Kerael's hand. "Thanks for everything."

Kerael shakes Ralph and Kathryn's hands as well. "I don't have to tell you that your son is special." He gave them one last smile and with a deft move, the angel leaped into the air with his wings unfurled and was gone in the blink of an eye.

"He certainly knows how to make an impression," Kathryn said.

Gerald and his father grinned in agreement.

Ralph turned to his son. "You ready to go home?"

Gerald smiled at his father and put an arm around both parents as they led him home.

As they walked, the terrain slowly changed, almost too subtle for Gerald to notice, but every now and then he caught the shade of the grass change to a darker hue of green, and the trees slowly morph from pine, fern, willow, oak, and every other kind of tree you can imagine, including a tree that had red leaves and was shaped like an umbrella, into the pecan and maple trees he knew growing up back home. With a shock, he realized that he was walking down the same dusty road that led up to his house back in Georgia.

He stopped dead in his tracks and fully took in his surroundings for the first time. To his left was the stretch of old wire fence that Paul Miller the rancher had put up after the war. A quick glance to his right confirmed that the old pecan tree that had a piece of its trunk torn out when a truck hit it was also there. He stood as still as a statue watching the dust come off the road as the wind kicked it up.

"It's the damnedest thing, isn't it?" his father said to him. They all stood in silence in the middle of an old dirt road that existed in their hometown of Georgia, and to Gerald it made no sense but complete sense at the same time.

He looked expectantly at his parents for an answer. His mother was the first to speak.

"Sweetheart, from what the flyboys say, it's a physical manifestation of what we most desire to see or love the most."

Gerald thought about this for a moment. "That's irony for you. I lived my life and tried to be a good person, and when I reach eternal paradise what I most desire is to be back in Georgia." Gerald looked up into the sky and asked. "Why couldn't I have been born in Hawaii?!"

Everyone laughed and a peel of thunder rang out as if in answer. "Watch out there, son. They do listen to you up here," his father said.

Kathryn put her arm around Gerald and hugged him. "You disappointed?" she asked him very quietly.

Gerald looks at his mother, feeling that warmth come off her like a summer breeze. "No, to be with you guys again is..." His emotion swelled again and just shook his head. She took his hand and led him down the road to home.

Ralph slapped his son on the back just like when Gerald was young and had done something good. "Let's get you home. The barbecue's already started."

5

HOME

The concept of full circle wasn't something Gerald ever really thought about, at least not until today anyway. He walked off the dirt road and onto the paved road where his family's house resided and realized how unbelievably right everything felt. Except for the two years he and Lia spent in the north he had been born, lived, and died within a fifty-mile radius of his home outside Savannah, Georgia. He was sure those lucky souls who had lived in much more scenic areas probably had a nice mansion on the beach overlooking an eternally beautiful sunset sipping on margaritas as the gentle waves lapped against their eternally tanned and smooth skin.

As he made his final approach to his home, he realized that they could keep their version of paradise, here in front of his family home, built by his great-grandfather Angus, and yes, he was incredibly Scottish, as his father used to joke about him, subsequently added onto by his grandfather George, his father, and him when he added another two bedrooms and bath to accommodate his mother-in-law Lucy in her later years once John her husband had passed on.

Gerald passed a window. This entire time it never occurred

to him to see what he looked like, and the shock of it had him staring at himself in the reflection of the glass. He was back in his mid-thirties, it seemed, and the strong jawline and forehead he inherited from his father were offset by his mother's cheekbones.

"Never took you for the vain type. " Ralph said as he placed a hand on his shoulder.

"Sorry," Gerald said. "I am just getting adjusted, I guess. Been a while since I looked like this." He took one last look at his reflection and then turned to his parents. They all shared a knowing nod with each other and started for the heavenly version of his family's backyard.

As he walked to the backyard, he stepped right into the old groundhog hole that always seemed to reappear every spring for as long as he can remember. He was surprised at the burning pain he felt running through his ankle.

"You alright? We forgot to tell you that hole was still there," Kathryn said as she steadied Gerald.

"Ow!" Gerald exclaimed as he bent down and rubbed his aching ankle.

"Check this out." They both turn to Ralph as he flips open a buck knife and without saying anything, cuts deep into his arm with the knife.

"Hey!" Gerald exclaimed as his father mutilated himself. An instant later his breath caught in his throat as the wound started to heal itself. In moments, the cut was gone as if it were never there. "That's something," he said softly.

Ralph walked up to him., "You just think about it and it will heal itself."

Gerald looked down at his still throbbing ankle and then back at his parents.

"Go ahead," Kathryn said.

He thought about his ankle and thought about it but nothing happened.

"Stay relaxed," Kathryn said encouragingly.

"Make believe you're doing yoga." Ralph chuckled.

Gerald frowned at his father, exhaled, and thought about his ankle, focusing on it and trying to stay relaxed. He breathed in deeply, focusing his mind on his aching ankle. He started to feel an itchy kind of feeling and as he focused harder he felt a quick-burning flare of pain in his ankle and then the pain was gone. Gerald breathed rapidly, trying to overcome the shock of the pain he felt and weakly nodded, giving his parents the thumbs up before they followed him to the backyard.

6

BACK YARD BBQ

His parents were right behind Gerald when he turned the corner of his house and the ground beneath him changed from the soft lawn grass to the art deco brick patio area that branched out like a mushroom from the back door of the house to fifty feet out. There were so many people eating and drinking that at first, he couldn't differentiate any of the faces. The smell coming off the grill made his mouth water as he recognized the marinated steaks his father was famous for.

The chatter ceased immediately as everyone seemed to notice Gerald at the same time. No one said a word or moved for what seemed like an eternity but as one a cheer went up and Gerald was rushed from all sides by family and friends. His parents were right by his side as he saw long-missed friends and faces.

Grandpa George and Grandma Lisa were there to embrace their grandson. They had both passed away before Gerald was ten years old, but a little boy doesn't forget sitting with his grandfather on the front porch during a rainstorm and playing Monopoly or how his grandma's cookies started the lifelong addiction that had to be carried on by his mother and wife.

Both of his grandparents were recognizable, but they were both looking in their late twenties at most. *Grandpa was always young at heart,* he thought.

Grandma Lynn and Grandpa John both appeared as they did in their early fifties, each of them a half of the beautiful whole that made up his mother. Grandpa John lived to see his Great grandson George scrimmage as a Georgia Bulldog before he passed. Even now, the sting of that loss was gone like a tendril of smoke as he embraced both pairs of his grandparents.

The passing of years was as nothing as he was encircled by his family and friends. Memories and events from yesteryear came rushing back to him in a flood of emotion and pain as the memory of losing that person came back along with all the good memories. As he kissed hello to his third-grade teacher Mrs. Barnum, he thought about the loved ones still living their lives back on Earth. His wife and son were still there. Charlie, his best friend since they were boys, along with Max, his brother-in-law.

Gerald walked in from the front yard and saw his mother-in-law, Lucy, standing with her husband John. His breath caught in his throat as he saw her. She was the spitting image of his wife when he met her, with the same long dark glossy hair that showed her Creek and Yamasee heritage, and the bright blue eyes that showcased her high cheekbones and chin. The only difference was that where Lia was a tall woman, at five feet ten inches, Mama Lucy stood at five feet on a good day. She had the same fortitude that his mother had but it was contained in a stolid interior that never raised her voice in anger to anyone. She was a regal woman and even here in Heaven, you could see the goodness and strength of character that radiated like a haze around her. His father-in-law John stood right by her side as he always had in life, he gave a small smile and a nod and they shook hands.

"Hello Gerald," she said in that whispery tone that always

carried regardless of the distance or size of the room. "You been taken care of my daughter?" She smiled at the old joke they shared back in life.

"Trying to, but she can be a handful," he responded as they hugged for what seemed an eternity.

When finally they pulled apart, Lucy wiped the tears away. "Been dreaming about you. Been thinking and dreaming about you a lot lately." He felt her trembling as he placed his hand on her shoulder. "I knew you were coming even before the Angel came to tell us."

This didn't surprise Gerald because he knew in life Lucy had what she called the double seeing. That fear of the unknown and her ability was something that he couldn't touch or feel and that made it scary, "It's not any scarier than having faith in God. You never saw him but you know he's there, just feels right," Lucy would always say to him whenever she would have something to tell him or warn him about. For whatever reason, she would dream about him more than anyone else. He had gotten used to it long ago, but Charlie would never miss a chance to bust his chops about it.

"Better off with a voodoo doll, if you ask me," Charlie would say to Gerald.

"When you're ready you'll understand, sweetie." Lucy placed a hand on his cheek and kissed him on the opposite cheek like she had a thousand times before. This quelled the storm building in his mind, but only so much. He had no idea really what she was talking about, so he didn't want to dwell on it, Lucy smiled and with a nod said. "We got someone here that you got to see." Making their way through with pardons amidst the well-wishers, family, and friends.

As Gerald was pulled through the crowd he kept smelling the food, and it was driving him crazy so if they didn't introduce him soon, he was liable to get into fisticuffs. He pulled clear of the crowd and was led to the swings his father had put up when he was a boy.

They broke free from the crowd and on that swing that looked as fresh as the day his father set it up, with the eye-watering electric blue paint his cousin had asked for, was this woman in her late twenties. She was simply radiant wearing a white summer dress that hung past her knees. She had long brown hair that swayed along with her, and her brown eyes were...they were familiar to him, but he couldn't quite place the eyes with the delicately sculpted features.

Lucy smiled at her and with a nod, she left him alone with this strange woman.

"Hello, Gerald," she said with a roughly musical quality. He knew it but again couldn't place it.

"Hello," he greeted her stiltedly. She studied him with a smile on her face. Why couldn't he place that smile, he asked himself. And her perfume was so familiar.

"You don't recognize me, Gerald?" She smiled at him again and still the memory of a person eluded his grasp. It was there but he couldn't put it together.

"No, I'm sorry I don't, but I feel I do. That makes sense?" He hunched his shoulders nervously and smiled at her.

She laughed, clearly relishing the moment. After what seemed like an eternity came the reveal. "It's me, Melinda."

Like a thunderbolt, it struck him. Deep brown eyes and a smile that curved a little to the left. It was in her laugh and that rough musical tone of her voice. "Mel?" He was rooted to the spot as she got up and hugged him tightly like she used to, almost crushing his ribs with a strength that belied her size. "I don't understand," he managed to squeak out through shallow breaths. He had known Melinda all her life until she died from pneumonia at age thirty-eight, which was a miracle in itself due to her condition.

This was Melinda, but it wasn't; Melinda wasn't supposed to have lived even to thirty but when his mother's sister passed and his cousin Melinda came to live with them, his parents made sure she was afforded all the love, medical, and care you would give to your own child but still, this was and wasn't Melinda. She was special, she was different, and she was sick almost all her life.

Melinda was born with Down Syndrome and Melinda who would cry when she couldn't go outside because she was sick, and would follow Gerald and his brother Chance around or go with them into town. The Melinda he remembered could paint all these beautiful pictures free hand of whatever she saw. He recalled the way she was always humming a song to herself, especially when she would get tired. Seeing her in his mind's eye running around in a white dress. Yes, he remembered that now with her always wearing a white dress. She would even sleep with it on which caused some issues. Once you wear a dress for two weeks straight, white isn't so white anymore, so his mother wasn't having any of it. This little war between Melinda and his mother only came to an uneasy truce when his father came home one day with five identical white dresses. Melinda found this acceptable and would then change out of them. He saw Melinda in the eyes of this Melinda. He didn't know what to say or do as she released her hug.

"Want to sit down?" she asked. Melinda loved to sit on the swings all day and either swing around on them or play in the sand beneath the swing. He still remembered Chance bringing her a beach pail and shovel. No one had any idea what the heck he planned on doing with them, but once he got the hose and wet the sand, he and Melinda built a little castle that she then got to stomp on and then rebuild with him. The only way she would come off the swings was for dinner. She loved to eat just as much as she loved to play.

Gerald sat down with her and heard the familiar squeak of the swing as his weight settled on it and just kept looking at the ground, at her face, the ground, then the face, the ground, the face. "I knew I recognized that perfume," he muttered to himself. It was some kind of Elizabeth Taylor brand. Once Melinda saw *Cleopatra,* she couldn't wait to get that perfume so she could be just like Elizabeth Taylor. Charlie, God bless him, even bought her a plastic Cleopatra headdress that Melinda lost her mind for. She loved, loved Charlie and he was always so good with her. For all his jibing he was incredibly thoughtful and giving.

"Gerald, look at me." Melinda was smiling at him again and placed her hand on his. "You want to know how this is possible?" Melinda said this as she pointed at herself.

Gerald nodded.

Melinda scrunched her face like she had done so many times before. "From what the flyboys say—I picked that up from your mom, by the way—people like me, people with mental or physical handicaps, when we're alive, we have certain other abilities that normal folks don't usually see." Melinda paused, trying to frame it in words that Gerald's brain could understand. Melinda explained as she thought back through the years of her abbreviated life.

In some ways her thoughts were like the ocean in a storm, choppy and rough but every once in a while the storm would pass and her mind would be calm and still, and then she could see through it to something else...something bigger. "We have a more spiritual connection that most people don't have, we see things others don't see; the downside to that is that we usually have...other issues," she said.

Gerald nodded in understanding. "Mother said it all the time to us, I remember."

Melinda nodded. "She was right. Lucy saw it, too."

Gerald nodded, recalling the many times Lucy would take her for walks or tea and they would just chit-chat for hours. "When our souls pass on," Melinda continued, "we are freed. The flyboys call us ES' or Elevated Souls."

Gerald nodded and smiled. "That's very creative." It brought back some of the banter they had back in their old life. "You were beautiful in the old life and you're beautiful now, just different."

Melinda thought about that for a second and smiled. "Yep, well said cousin."

Gerald huffed a laugh and then got off the swing. "I've missed you." He gave her a hug of his own.

When they pulled apart again, she excitedly said, "I can do things." He looked at her quizzically. Melinda stood up, began to float up into the air, then disappeared in an eye blink.

Gerald just stood there stunned. "Huh" was all he could come out with. He felt a light shove from behind as she was now behind him. He turned and she was floating a foot or so off the ground. Light shone through her skin as she floated there before him that dimmed then disappeared once she touched the grass. "You can do these things, too,"" she said.

"I can?"

She answered with a wry smile. "In time. The longer a soul is in Heaven, they loosen their grip on the restrictions their mortal body placed on them." Melinda looked back towards the party. "Come on, let's get back to the others." She took his hand firmly and pulled him back towards the crowd waiting for him.

As he approached the crowd, the familiar smell of his dad's grilling wafted by, and he had a craving for a cheeseburger. Gerald considered how wonderfully ludicrous it was that he was here in Heaven with all his family and friends and all he wanted was a cheeseburger his daddy made, a Coke, and to sit next to his favorite cousin. As he waded through the crowd again, he was assailed from all sides with backslaps, hair tussles, and some jackass even tried to trip him.

They were making their way towards the grill when Melinda turned around and flashed him with that radiant smile. From the crinkle around her eyes, he could tell she was up to something. Before he could be nervous about it, he heard music playing and as he made it to the safe oasis of the grilling area where his parents could keep any hijinks to a minimum, he realized that there was a band playing on the side of the house from where he had originally entered the yard.

"How the heck did they set up so fast?" Gerald asked as he checked out the large stage area complete with lighting and sound that had suddenly appeared. This stage area was large enough for the drummer, bass player, keyboards, horn and trumpet player, and the four guitarists to move around comfortably in. The drummer was playing on an elevated platform so you could see him twirl his sticks. He pounded on the snare drum like it stole something. The band was playing Johnny Cash's "Ring of Fire."

The lights went down and suddenly an extremely bright spotlight was shining directly on Gerald. *Great,* he thought dryly. The singer on stage looked him directly in the eyes and smiled. He looked so familiar to Gerald. He wondered if he had seen him down at the café he took his parents to for Lia's birthday. His train of thought came to a halt though as the singer spoke.

"Hey, Gerald, how you doing?" the singer bellowed. The crowd exploded in a raucous cheer at this. "Get your ass up here, boy."

Gerald's eyes widened but before he could make his escape, his parents and surrounding kin grabbed him and threw him up into the air, and with that, he landed on a sea of hands that quickly shuttled him over the crowd and unceremoniously chucked him right onto the stage where he landed on his head.

It didn't hurt but seemed to bring out even more cheers and quite a few laughs.

The singer hauled Gerald to his feet. The singer smelled like a mix of patchouli, whiskey, Downy fabric softener, and chewing gum.

As Gerald's vision cleared and he got a better look at the singer, he still couldn't quite place where he had seen him before. The long, lanky dark hair that fell midway down his back, the long thin physique, and the old jeans and t-shirt seemed to enhance rather than detract from his looks.

"Being a southern boy myself from Jacksonville, I couldn't turn down a chance to welcome one of our own. " The crowd cheered at the singer's exclamation. "Even if you are from Georgia, I can't hold that against you," the singer chided Gerald.

"Gators eat Bulldogs!" The singer said into the mic which riled up the crowd.

The crowd good-naturedly booed the singer and Gerald joined in with them to boo him, which made the singer laugh.

"I guess I can't get another hot dog?" The singer looked over at Ralph who laughed, booed him, and then threw a Georgia Bulldog keychain on stage at the singer who stooped down, picked up the keychain, and raised it over his head to the cheering crowd, then placed it in his pocket.

"I'm keeping it!" he exclaimed, then placed his arm around Gerald and motioned with his hand for quiet.

Once the crowd settled down he spoke. "On a serious note before we return to the fun..." The crowd cheered again and quieted once he motioned with his hand again. "All your life you were told to keep the faith. That if you lived a good life and were good to your fellow man you would be rewarded."

Gerald looked into the crowd and saw them nodding, and the singer continued.

"Don't matter if you're a Jew or a Gentile either. Be a good person, do the right thing, try your best." The sporadic "Amen!" rippled through the crowd. "Amen is right," the singer continued. "There is a reward and from what I understand it, you deserve it more than most. You done right, now right's being done back."

The crowd cheered more forcefully and the singer raised a glass and everyone else followed and raised a glass of their own. "Enjoy! There ain't no hangovers in Heaven." He saluted Gerald with a swig of his beer and with a wave of his hand, the band started playing "Sweet Home Alabama."

It hit Gerald where he had seen this singer before. It was Ronnie Van Zant, the lead singer of Lynyrd Skynyrd who had died in a plane crash.

"Come on, let's get the family up here to help out our boy," Ronnie crowed.

Melinda floated up into the air and settled right next to Gerald. Lucy and John, his parents, jumped what must have been forty feet to land on stage. Both sets of grandparents floated next to him, both great-grandparents. Everyone in the crowd on stage and off was singing along to "Sweet Home Alabama."

For one sweet, crystal-clear moment, Gerald took it all in like a picture that you pick up after you haven't seen it in years: the family, the friends. Heaven, the absurdly cool appearance of Ronnie Van Zant, and even the changed youthful appearances of everyone.

It was all so clear to him that he had lived his life for this moment; This was his for eternity. What jolted him was that, along his life, there had been times when if he had made another choice, he maybe wouldn't be here right now. An icy shudder ran down his spine thinking about it but he also realized here, with all he ever knew and loved, were the reasons he did the right thing. They all contributed to him being the man he was, and he was grateful.

After what seemed like days of continuous partying and the singer repeatedly saying, "No 'Free Bird,'" he finally relented and began to croon out what may be the most perfect song ever written. All the couples instantly gathered with each other and began to slow dance. Gerald didn't have a partner and was about to walk off the dance floor/lawn when a hand gripped him and he saw the smiling Melinda.

"You know, this is my favorite song," she said quietly. As he turned and let her put her head on his chest like she had done so many times in life, he recalled just how special this song was to her. He remembered even till the day she died how much she loved "Free Bird." Sometimes when she would have one of her rare outbreaks of temper and even cookies wouldn't calm her down, the family knew to rush to the stereo and turn it on, and once the first few notes started up, that was all she would need and the temper was forgotten by the time the song ended.

Thinking back on it now, seeing her sitting on the floor, humming the words, and swaying to the music, he saw why deep down she loved it so much. She was that free bird. Her whole mortal life she was trapped in a prison of the flesh for which there was no escape, her mind and potent spirit a prisoner to one damn chromosome. *Would I have been as strong as she was?* Gerald thought as he looked into her eyes.

For an instant, it seemed like she knew what he was thinking, but then she just lowered her head against his chest again and left him to his thoughts. He looked around to see his parents kissing which of course shouldn't weird him out, but it did because no one really wants to see their parents do that stuff, no matter how old you get.

"He talks to me," Melinda interrupted. She was looking

intently at Gerald and for an instant, he saw light flashing in her eyes. "He talks to me in my dreams."

Gerald looked down and asked, "Who?"

Melinda looked up, suddenly somber. "You know who" was all she needed to say.

Gerald felt a shudder run through him because even though he was here in Heaven, he didn't think he could handle a meeting with the big guy. It just seemed like way too much to take in. "You can sleep here?" he lamely asked, trying to hopefully change the subject, but she wasn't to be deterred.

"If you want to, what you did in life, most people continue to do after," she said. "He speaks to Lucy, too."

Gerald nodded. That didn't surprise him; these two had God talking to them in dreams. "What does he talk to you about?"

Melinda slowly smiled. "You," she simply said. "He said you were coming. You are special."

Gerald was not sure how to take that. "I'm sure though that everyone is special up here, though, so it's not like I'm really that different."

Melinda stiffened and gripped Gerald's arms tightly. She stared right into his eyes. "You are different. Who you were in life carries on, and that's what makes you different." She said this so fiercely that he felt the psychic force of it push at him, and if it weren't for her holding onto him, he would have been blown back.

Everyone around them stopped dancing and Gerald's mother turned to them. "Everything alright?" she asked, concerned and even a little fearful of Melinda.

Gerald nodded and the intensity in Melinda subsided. "Sorry, I know you don't understand, but you will." He continued nodding, not understanding at all. Melinda could see the confusion in his eyes and smiled at him. That smile melted all of it away and replaced it with a warm glow that banished what they were even talking about. They danced for a bit and she looked back up at him, her face creased with concern. He raised his eyebrows to ask her if everything was alright. She smiled back, hugged him, and let the song carry her to better places.

7

PIECES

After the party when everyone had gone home by foot or flight, all that was left were his parents, Lucy, John, and Melinda. Dishes and any garbage instantly vanished as well as extra food and beer. With, one turn of his head the remnants of the entire party were gone like it never happened. The porch light was on and a breeze was slowly moving the weathervane on top of the house. "We're heading to bed now. If you don't mind we'll fix you breakfast in the morning?" his Father asked.

"That would be great. You got my footie pajamas ready for me, too?" Gerald replied.

His father snickered at him and both his parents kissed and hugged their son and went inside the house. Melinda and Lucy were holding hands and smiling at him.

"Ladies," Gerald said with a nod of his head. They both approached him and kissed him goodbye. John nodded and they shook hands. "Good to have you back." John said

"We love you, young man. We're happy you're home with us now. We'll talk soon." Lucy finished and with that, she and John just up and floated away.

Melinda smiled at him and started walking away. "Good-night, cousin," she chimed.

"Night," he replied. "You're not going to fly off or float away?"

Whimsically, Melinda turned and shot him another radiant smile. "No, I like walking home this time of night." With a wave, she walked away.

Gerald was tempted to bring up what they had spoken to him about earlier in the night because for the life of him. He looked down at a crack in the floor and when he looked back up, Melinda was a speck in the distance and then was gone. He also wanted to ask her where she lived since she always lived with his parents but that would be for another day he sighed.

He sighed deeply and took in the night sky filled with stars like he had never seen when he was alive. It was beautiful. A feeling of calm settled over him like a snug blanket and he basked in the simple comfort of it. His emotions were swelling up within him again as he realized that all that had been loved and lost were now found again and it would take him a long time for him to accept it. Not that this was a problem, he thought, but...

Gerald paused, seeing that he needed to ease off the deep thinking, especially since he was never really much of one. He chuckled to himself. Gerald left the deep thinking for his best friend Charlie. He smiled fondly at all the memories he shared with his best friend, *he is a great man.* He thought to himself. He wished he was here now to discuss all the deep boring stuff that his son George used to make fun of, yet if you gave George enough time, he would jump and put in his two cents.

Gerald stepped off the porch, looked to his right, and headed towards his house. The enormous Colonial home that his father, himself, Chance, and a slew of friends built with their own hands. He felt the grass underneath his feet and as he approached it, he could see the pale-yellow color of the shingles glowing off the porch light. It gave the house an almost eerie feel, but as he stepped onto the stairs and opened the front door, he realized that eerie wasn't right. Empty was the right word for what Gerald felt. Empty because his wife and their boy were still alive back on Earth. It didn't have the same vibrant hum of energy because it was just a shell now waiting for the family to fill it up with all the frenetic good things a family brought to a home.

As he walked through the foyer and living room, and into the kitchen, he smelled pecan cookies, the same pecan cookies his mom would make all the time for them. *God, I loved those cookies,* he thought as he stepped into the large open kitchen. Sitting on top of the kitchen island was a freshly baked batch.

Gerald looked around in a circle to see if anyone was there to surprise him, but no one jumped out. Satisfied that there wasn't anyone there, he opened the fridge to find it loaded with Sam Adams Cherry Wheat Beer which was both his and his brother's favorite.

Gerald looked around again just to be sure no one was there and grabbed a beer and some cookies. He turned on the kitchen light and sat down for his informal snack in his kitchen. With his eyes closed, the cold beer washed down the golden-crusted goodness of the cookies. This delicious combination was always an underrated treat as beer and cookies aren't a common mix, but you get the right beer and cookies, and it is out of sight, as his son George would say.

Gerald sat and leaned onto the edge of the kitchen table, sat in silence with his eyes closed for what seemed like an hour eating and drinking this way. *I hope there isn't diabetes in Heaven.* He said to himself with a wry smile.

8

THE RISING SON

Waking up to his first morning in Heaven was as good as a person would think it would be, absolutely perfect. Of course, it would have been better if he hadn't fallen asleep at his kitchen table or had smashed cookies stuck to the side of his face, yet no back pain from sleeping like a pretzel was pretty cool.

As he pulled the cookies off his face and dumped them in the garbage can, he looked outside into the face of a perfect sun rising in the distance. He had to stop saying perfect because it was getting annoying, even if it was true. He snorted. The sun seemed to fill his vision like a giant new penny while clouds floated above the sun as if it had a bad cloud toupee, which Gerald chuckled over. *I'm probably the only person that would think that was funny,* he thought.

The singer from Lynyrd Skynyrd was right; there are no hangovers in Heaven, he mused as he walked out of his kitchen out the front door and heard the squeak of his weight on the steps. He walked back towards his parent's house and was struck by how earthy and organic everything smelled. The morning dew clung like glossy film on everything, and the smell of that moisture was just as strong as the soil and foliage.

As Gerald walked up the stairs and opened the door to his parent's home, his mother called, "Honey, we're in the kitchen. Hurry up or you'll be late for church."

"Church?" Gerald was puzzled.

"You die and all of a sudden you can't go to church no more?" Kathryn asked as he came around the bend from the kitchen with a plate of eggs, bacon, chitlins, and hash.

His parents, Lucy, and Melinda were at the kitchen table eating. There was also a man sitting with Melinda. She was literally sitting on top of him. There was no personal space. That made Gerald feel weird thinking about Melinda being with someone, she never had any boyfriends when she was alive but *c'est la vie*, he mused.

He looked around the rustic Colonial kitchen he spent a large majority of his life in. The fans that spun even when it was cold out were there like always. "Keeps the hot air moving," his mom would say. He felt the dark oak wood flooring Chance and he had put down together when his dad threw out his back. It, looked just like it always did. He even saw the divots near the door when Chance had put a pitchfork into the wood chasing him around.

"Hey, cousin, come here," Melinda called, and the man she was with smiled and pulled a bar stool between himself and Melinda. He stood up and approached Gerald with his hand out. Shaking it, Gerald could see that this young man wasn't young at all. His face was no older than twenty-five or so and his black hair was so dark that if he wasn't so tan or olive-skinned, he would look like a movie Count Dracula with his features. No, it was in the eyes, dark, open, friendly eyes that spoke of age and something else Gerald thought as he tried to pin it down, and then it came to him because he had seen those same eyes in the mirror. Haunted. This man's eyes had seen and experienced a great deal of pain.

"A pleasure to meet you," the young-old man said.

"This is Marco." Melinda had risen and placed her arm around him. "This here is the boy I'm sweet on," she said, putting extra southern sass into it as she put her hand through Marco's hair.

Marco smiled and shook his head. "Your cousin has been telling me for the longest time about what a great guy you are."

Gerald smiled and shrugged. "I'm alright, I guess. Marco, that's not a name I heard a lot in Georgia. Were you from Italy or your family?"

Marco smiled. "I'm Roman, actually."

"Lucky you. You've been here a while then," Gerald said, smiling.

"I've been here and there." Marco glanced at Melinda and something passed between them.

"Come on, people, let's get a move on," Kathryn said. "Church starts soon so finish up. You hungry, honey?" she asked Gerald.

"No thanks, I'm good. Should I go upstairs and change?" Gerald asked as he looked around and everyone was in their Sunday best.

His father came up behind him and placed his hand on Gerald's shoulder. "Upstairs, son? No need. Watch." As Gerald turned and faced his father who was dressed in a tuxedo and black flip-flops, he noticed a ripple or a distortion in the fabric of the clothing like the wave on a pond, and then all of a sudden, the tuxedo was gone, and replaced by jeans and a t-shirt.

"How do I do it?" Gerald exclaimed.

"Just think about it, focus on it, and it'll happen."

"Just like you did with your ankle yesterday," Ralph added.

Gerald nodded. He was a little nervous trying to do it because the first thing that flashed through his mind was that he would try and change his clothes and end up buck naked in front of everybody. Mama Lucy suddenly chuckled as if she had heard him think it. Everyone turned and looked at her, but she just waved her hand for Gerald to continue.

"Ok," Gerald said aloud. He started to breathe in deeply and thought about a nice tan summer suit, the same suit he wore to church on many a Sunday. He focused harder and harder on it, and he could feel the fabric shifting around but then with no warning, it just stopped. He looked down and his clothes were the same. "Damn. Ok, one more time." He focused harder and harder and began to feel the clothes shifting and rippling. Right when he felt he was nearing the same point as before he gave a mental push fueled with a bit of annoyance, which seemed to really get the job done. His clothes began whipping all around him like they were a school of fish fighting for scraps, all churned up and thrashing movement.

With a final push, he closed his eyes and felt a surge of energy along with what sounded like a small sonic boom push out and the clothes changed. He could feel the fabric on his arms now and the dress shoes that replaced his flip-flops.

What he didn't count on as he opened his eyes was the three-foot radius around him that was blackened as if by fire and everyone around him was either on the floor or on top of a counter. The force that he expelled had blown out all the windows in his kitchen.

"What the hell!" Ralph screamed at him as he dislodged his head from the side cabinet. Amid the groans, everyone picked themselves up off the floor or dislodged themselves from various counters and cabinets.

Kathryn waved her hand and all the glass strewn about floated up and reversed itself back into the window panes where it melded back together. With a swell of energy and that knitting feeling he related to healing now, the rest of the kitchen repaired itself. He felt himself rising out of the crater he created, and it filled itself in as if its level was being replenished like pool water.

No one said a word as they mutely stared at him until Melinda couldn't take it anymore and softly said, "What the hell was that?"

Everyone in the room looked at Gerald, uncertain of what to say until his father came up to him, looked at him closely for a moment, then smiled. "That's something else," Ralph said, then slapped him on the back. "You need to learn to rein that in before you hurt somebody."

"Rein what in? I'd like to know what I just did," Gerald said with more than a hint of concern.

"We're going to be late for church. Mel, explain it to him on the way," Ralph said.

Melinda nodded, then smiled at Gerald. Marco, on the other hand, seemed to be studying him very intently until Gerald's mother interrupted.

"Let's get a move on, people," she finished. Everyone headed out of the house into the bright morning sunshine and onto the main road that led to church.

9

CHURCH

As the group headed over to church, you could hear their feet crunching on the gravel of the road, Marco and Melinda walked along with him and explained to him what the little episode in the kitchen meant.

"You see, that was your will manifesting itself into what you wanted," Marco explained as they walked along a road that had started to transform from a simple dirt road in Heaven's Georgia to a dark, solid dirt walkway, packed solid and with simple painted white lines along each side. "You just don't know how to control it yet, but the sheer force wasn't normal. That kind of force takes a long time if ever for some souls to be able to do."

"So what does that actually mean?" Gerald asked cautious curiosity showing on his face.

Melinda smiled at Gerald then at Marco and replied, "It means that you're...special." "Special, because of the force?" Gerald looked over at Marco who shrugged and answered.

"Not that force but yes, you have a very powerful spirit, your will as it were," Marco explained.

Gerald frowned, since he was so new to all this he didn't

have a scale to measure by so it was hard to see what the others saw. Marco nodded to him as if he heard what he was thinking.

Marco smiled in response. "*I did read your mind,*" he said without speaking. "*I am special, too.*" He tapped the side of his head he said to Gerald. He then spoke aloud so Melinda could hear. "The amount of power you can pull together is very rare for a young soul. You are like the young soccer player who can throw the ball very far down the field even though you have never played the game" Marco explained and then looked behind Gerald with raised eyebrows as if he was surprised.

"Come on, we're here. We'll talk later when there's time."

"Your analogy is all wrong but I get it," Gerald said to Marco as he turned around to find they were at church. How they had gotten there without him moving he didn't know but once he saw where he was, he decided now wasn't the time. Melinda took his hand as they entered CHURCH for the first time.

That this was a place of worship there was no doubt, but it wasn't a church in the conventional sense since it wasn't even in a building. They were on the edge of a hill. Each side had waterfalls that flowed down from such incredible heights you couldn't see the top of them. The water crashed down to the bottom of two seemingly endless pools filled with thousands of souls who were enjoying the waterfall and defying physics as the amount of water and the velocity of it should have been crushing them, yet it dropped a light rain on them at the bottom.

Some souls were swimming and darting in and out of the water while others hovered above it. Even from the distance they were at, he could feel the spray of the water on his face.

As he and his family made their way down the slope, Gerald could see balconies hanging in midair to allow families to sit comfortably wherever they felt like. Quite a few had made them from the waterfall itself, and the water still flowed even though it was held together as a rigid structure.

They had reached the bottom of the slope and were walking across a plain of grass that in some areas was emerald green, then gradually changed to light purple then pink, blue, red, and orange in a splash of seemingly endless color. It occurred to him that the grass areas were affected by the souls in that vicinity creating their own little reality. He caught so many different smells but he stopped and did a double take when he came upon a family who had an RV painted with NY JETS Green and white and had a grill out. An older gentleman wearing a Jet green chef hat and who was clearly the patriarch of the family was cooking up steaks, hot dogs, and burgers on the grill.

He made eye contact with the man and couldn't help himself by saying, "Go Falcons." The man just winked and smiled at Gerald then tossed him a beer and a hot dog that he caught. When Gerald looked at the beer, the lettering on it changed to GO, then when he looked at the hot dog, an indent appeared in it that said JETS then disappeared.

Gerald looked up and the man spoke to him with a heavy Long Island accent. "Trust me, the best dog you're ever going to eat, pal."

Gerald smiled and then nodded as he was pulled away by Melinda. "That was weird," he said more to himself.

Sure enough, that was the best dog I have ever eaten, he thought as he tried not to burn the roof of his mouth scarfing down the tasty dog. The odd thing was that when he reached that last mouthful, the hot dog regenerated so that he could continue to eat the eternal hot dog.

As Melinda led him through the gathered throng to their seating area, he glanced up at the main stage where he noticed a little bald, dark-skinned man with glasses sitting in a chair chatting with a long-haired man in a brown robe.

Gerald turned to Melinda. "That guy looks like Gandhi."

Melinda laughed. "It is." She grabbed his hand to lead him

to where they were seated. Family and friends were already in an area covered with blankets and picnic tables. Coffee and scones were laid out to pick from, and as Gerald sat down next to Melinda and his parents. He took a quick glance at Marco who nodded and smiled then reached his arm around Melinda and kissed her on the cheek as she whispered in his ear. Gerald was happy Melinda had someone, even if that someone could read your mind.

He turned back to Melinda and found Marco was gone. The almost-forgotten hot dog disappeared. *Clearly on a timer,* Gerald thought with a smirk.

A gong resounded before he could ask her where he went and all chatter stopped, a cheer slowly built up quickly into a tidal wave of sound that had the ground itself shaking in its intensity. Gerald was caught up in the wave screaming and hollering as the figure in the brown robe stood up and exchanged a hug with Gandhi. Gerald shook his head., It still freaked him out that it was actually Gandhi.

As the man in the brown robe stepped forward, one couldn't help but feel the sheer power that exuded from him. It made Gerald emotional because the power was of such well-being and goodness that it made you teary-eyed just being near him. At that moment, the man smiled, which brought even bigger cheers from the gathering. Everywhere he looked he could see the same emotions playing out on the faces of the people.

Gerald was awestruck as the man waved and raised his hands for silence and immediately the crowd ceased all noise. He turned to Melinda and whispered to her, "Is that Jesus?"

Melinda smiled at him and shook her head no, which disappointed him. "It's John the Baptist," she whispered.

The information shook him; here he was in the presence of two historical legends, completely different backgrounds and religious beliefs but there they were standing together for church.

Gerald looked past John the Baptist to Gandhi, who was standing along with everyone else now. He looked exactly as he did when he was alive: small and thin with a white robe on and round glasses.

Gandhi turned and looked directly at Gerald which felt like someone had turned up the temperature around him. Such was the heat and intensity in Gandhi's gaze. Then he winked at Gerald, which broke the spell, and he smiled back at him.

John the Baptist began to speak to the crowd which quieted. He spoke with a voice that went directly into the hearts of all who were there intimately. He spoke of self-sacrifice, brother-hood, and enduring faith, and that we are all here because during our lifetime we lived these things. We gave back to those around us and celebrated humanity by caring about them and the world we lived in. The details of the sermon were felt rather than heard, and it resonated within the hearts and minds of all who were present.

Gandhi stood up and he began to sing a devotional song, a Kirtan to Lord Krishna called Govind Jai Jai. He had a nice voice that carried through the assembly, and as he sang, the people sang with him. Joy, faith, hope, and belief were the theme of the hymn. People were standing on their feet clapping and dancing. It felt like a revival mixed with a Bollywood movie. No matter who you were or what you believed, the tenets stayed the same: be good to your fellow man, and take the time to understand them.

CHURCH continued with a song called Burdah, which is a Nadeem or religious song in Islam. They finished up with a Jewish devotional song called Siman Tov and Mazel Tov that was really upbeat, fun, and sung at weddings a lot.

Normally, Gerald had a hard time learning the lyrics to

songs, but once they started, he was able to sing along. Better still, he was able to sing along in Hebrew, Hindi, and Farsi.

While the people were still singing, Gerald glanced toward the audience and noticed that a group of men had begun to walk on stage. He sensed a wrongness about them that he couldn't put his finger on. Their stature, the way they walked. He could tell they were fighters. No, that wasn't right. They were warriors he realized. He wondered what warriors were doing in Heaven. They wore a strange sort of armor that had an odd texture to it. They each carried a set of armor as well.

Gerald's eye was drawn to one figure in particular as he made out Marco accompanying them. He was also carrying an empty set of armor that he placed down in a pile with two other sets.

The gathering sensed the presence of the men on stage and fell silent. The mood of the crowd changed as well, and Gerald realized what was wrong with the men. They were sad. Grief hung on them like a shroud you could almost see.

The crowd had begun to match the mood of the men on stage and Gerald made eye contact with Marco and nodded. He nodded back at him, and his eyes told a story that Gerald didn't want to hear. There was a sense of loss in his grief that Gerald found painful and achingly familiar.

Marcos broke eye contact with him and turned to John the Baptist who had come to the forefront of the stage and began to speak. This time he actually spoke verbally, and Gerald could see that the weight the men carried with them was magnified on John's shoulders. You could hear the pain as he spoke.

"Friends, sadly, that time has come again." He paused as he gathered himself. "Our brothers and sisters have been taken from us." He looked at the three piles of armor as he spoke. "We speak of sacrifice and hope. We hope that our children grow to be better than us and join us in the afterlife where they can share the joy and peace that we do." A murmur of agreement rippled through the crowd. "These three as well as countless others have given all they have and more. They were destroyed so that all we hold dear could live on and prosper."

With grief etched on his face, he looked back down at the armor again. "We must celebrate them if we are to honor them. Remember their sacrifice and, if called upon, carry on their battle to the very edge of time and space itself."

Without another word, he knelt down and with head bowed touched each suit of armor and gave a blessing. The warriors surrounded both the armor and John. They raised their hands and bowed their heads. Each suit began to float up and glow brighter and brighter until, with a pop of decompression, they were gone. John stood up and with a nod, CHURCH was over.

On the way home, there wasn't much chatter as each person was lost in introspection. Once the road began to change to the road home, Melinda approached Gerald. "Well?" She asked. Gerald kept thinking *Why were there warriors in heaven, who did those souls die fighting against?*

He looked into her eyes and shrugged. "It's a little overwhelming to be honest. It just blew my mind that Gandhi was up there with John the Baptist. It was the greatest thing I have ever seen."

"Wait, it'll get weirder," Marco added.

Gerald looked at Marco and smiled but Melinda answered. "What you saw up there today was the road, not the destination."

Gerald put his hand up to feign exasperation. "It's all so clear to me now," he said.

"Don't be so dense," she stated as she smacked his arm. She kicked some dust from the road onto his pants for good measure. "That's what you get" She threw in along with the dirt.

Gerald laughed, remembering her saying that whenever someone got punished when they were bad as kids.

"I'm serious," she said. Her features were set in such a way there was no room for argument. "What you saw up there was the path that each person takes in life. It's not about one or two things that you do, but the whole of your life. When you pass, it's the whole of your life that leads you here." Melinda shuddered suddenly and continued. "Or the other place."

Gerald shuddered. "I can't imagine," he said.

"You don't ever want to," Marco added with the grim finality of someone who's seen it firsthand. Gerald gave Marco a long look and was going to ask him about the end of the ceremony. "Come on, Gerald, today isn't the day to talk about these things," Marco said, reading his thoughts. He wanted to press the issue, but the look Melinda gave him brooked no argument.

"Come on you three, get it in gear!" Gerald's mother yelled to them as the tables in the backyard set themselves and with a gesture, plates of macaroni and potato salad sat themselves on the tables.

10

DREAMS AND IDLING

As Gerald lay down to sleep that night, he put aside the day's thoughts, plunked himself into bed, and was out like a light in no time flat. He dreamed that night for the first time in a long time. He couldn't remember the last time his sleep wasn't a black curtain that rose up with the morning. He dreamed of his life past, his beautiful wife, son, grandson, Charlie, his best friend in the whole world, the day he was married. He remembered in his dream how delicious the wedding cake was. It was a gift from his friend Maury who had lived near Little Italy in New York City and just loved the cannoli cake they had on Mulberry Street. He had to hand it to him, he knew his stuff because that cake was lights out.

A fight almost broke out when people thought there wasn't any left, but forward planning on his wife's part saved the day, and another full sheet of cannoli cake was brought out. In his dream, Gerald chuckled as he recalled Charlie and Chance protecting that damn cake until it was placed and the servers had cut it up.

He realized that in his dreams he could bring up different pieces of his life at will. He remembered fishing with his boy and Charlie down at the lake, how Charlie in his quiet, unassuming way was teaching George how to hook a worm the right way and ask it for forgiveness so it didn't hold it against him for using him as bait. It wasn't until years later when George saw The Godfather Part Two that he learned it wasn't an old family secret to get more fish. To this day so many years later he remembered thanking God for giving him such a fine friend who was as close as a brother. You can pick your friends but you can't pick your family, they always say, and he had as great a brother as you could ask for, but a friend who chose to be your brother is also a great thing, and it was right there as his friend and son made idle chatter in a creaky boat in the middle of a lake in Georgia.

As Gerald was idling his dream time away on his honeymoon, he felt something move into his consciousness. It was very subtle and he didn't even notice it at first, but he realized it was there when he tried to move into another dream. The presence stopped him from moving on and froze his dreams like a pause button on a DVD player. The presence suddenly began to expand itself into his consciousness and a million voices whispered the same thing to him over and over. "Watch," they said. "Learn." The presence wasn't threatening, and after the initial shock, curiosity won out and he gave a mental nod that he was ready.

Gerald was pulled up so fast that he thought his back would break. Faster he rose until he felt rather than knew he wasn't in Heaven anymore but in space. He saw the stars twinkling by as he zipped by at blurring speeds and then abruptly stopped in front of a gigantic gate that shimmered through every imaginable color. He watched as the ponderous gate slowly began to open and with it, a distant sigh could be heard coming from beyond the gate; Once the gate was opened, Gerald was pulled through by an unseen hand and he rocketed out of the gate which immediately began to close again behind him. The sighing grew louder and louder, and he could begin to make out voices in the sighing.

Gerald was being drawn to a planet. It wasn't Earth but it was a planet nonetheless, and as he entered the atmosphere, he noticed smoke in the distance. As he drew closer to the smoke, he realized it was from a burning building. No, not a building he realized, a city, an entire city was on fire. To his dread, he knew the sighing for what it was. Screaming, horrible screaming from a million throats as they died. Gerald found himself on a city street littered with the dead.

He bent down and looked at one of the bodies that covered the streets., It was the body of an alien being, as it wasn't humanoid at all. In fact, it wasn't even a mammal, as these unfortunates resembled a praying mantis. The blood pooling next to it was a light green and even in its dead state, he could see a certain bearing and beauty that remained even in death.

He heard more of the screaming which was more of a shrilling, and he ran across the street into an area where the smoke and fire seemed much thicker. He didn't feel the heat from the flames but he could smell the smoke and fire. As he followed the screaming, he caught glimpses of the buildings on fire and noticed they were see-through. They weren't glass but a sort of resin or wax like a beehive, and the buildings didn't so much as burn but melt. Occasionally something cooked off in a building which caused an explosion and rained down burning globs of the wax material. The screaming became much louder as he rounded a corner into a gigantic plaza. Rubble had been built up at the end of it, he could see it was to herd the creatures to this plaza.

Through the smoky haze, he got his first look at the enemy, and he shuddered in fear and almost ran away, not from the aliens who lived on this planet, for they were beautiful and oh so delicate in that beauty, but by the things that chased and herded them here. These were aliens, too, and were huge, humanoid beasts that towered at a height of at least seven feet on a frame packed grotesquely with muscle. Their coloring was hard to make out in the dim light but it appeared varied between, red, gray, green, and black as if they were a negative from a film cell, but it was their faces that were truly terrifying.

They were as unique as they were grotesque. One had two burning red eyes framed in a porcine face with tusks that jutted from their lower jaw like an evil boar. Another had the face of an insect with tentacles coming out of its mouth. Another had eyes in its belly. Another looked like a lizard with ridges up its back. He could feel the malice emanating from them in hot, stinking waves. There was a wrongness to them being here, *they didn't belong here*, he said to himself. They waved what looked like giant cleavers that they used to hack at the Mantis aliens. To his left, he saw two of the brutes laugh as they ripped a victim in two. They held one of the mantis down as they shot bullet holes into its torso and it screamed pitiably.

The screaming grew louder and threatened to overwhelm his senses. He staggered towards one of the abominations as it hacked at another poor creature but he passed through it. It didn't stop Gerald from trying and only incensed him into further action but to no avail. The more he grabbed and tried to get a hold of the monster, the more frustrated he became until he screamed his fury at the monstrosities in a burst of rage that pulsed out, for a second, the beasts seemed to feel. The monstrosities looked around and then became even more incensed, stopped torturing the mantises, and began a frenzy to kill the mantises outright as if to get back at Gerald for disturbing their perverse fun.

Gerald lost his mind at this last outrage and he unleashed his fury, but this time he didn't let go, instead built on it and continued to channel his anger until it wasn't just a blip in this reality anymore but a force. All around him, the energies were swirling in and around him. He had been clenching his hands into fists, and with a grim smile opened his hands. His rage blew out like an aftershock and the twisted faces showed fear for the first time, then pain as they began to catch fire and burn along with the buildings. The ground beneath him was gone and he was floating in the air. Seeing what he had done, Gerald focused again, feeling the energies quickly gathering to him, eager to unleash again, and with a scream he released a bomb burst of explosive energy that leveled the nearby buildings. He felt a pull and then he blacked out.

Gerald awoke with the sun shining down on him but not in his bed. He was in a hole. He feared maybe he had blown up his house in his sleep and quickly got up and came out of the crater he was lying in to find he was nowhere near home. He was in Heaven still thankfully, which was clear from the picture-perfect sky and loamy smells that permeated from the soil he was lying in. A shadow fell over his mind as he thought about the nightmare he had the previous night. His thoughts were racing as he tried to come to grips with what he dreamed and how real it was. He knew deep down there must have been some reality to it, but the bigger question was what was that thing or presence in his dreams, and why show him something so horrible? Even during the war he never saw anything so brutally violent. He shuddered thinking of what happened the previous night, and he could swear he smelled the faintest whiff of a burning building. *Aren't I in Heaven, though?* He whispered to himself. Nothing in the manual said anything about horrific nightmares after dreaming of your honeymoon unless you were in the other place. He didn't even want to spend a moment thinking about it. It didn't add up.

Another shadow fell over him, he thought it was one of

those monsters from the night before but when he looked up it was a brontosaurus calmly munching on some grass. It was his brontosaurus Percy.

"Hey," Gerald greeted him.

Percy gave a quick snort in response and then lowered himself down for Gerald.

"Get on?" When no response came, Gerald climbed aboard and sat down on Percy's head as he elevated back up and without a word between the two tromped back to Gerald's home. Along the way the sights, sounds, colors, and smells that would normally thrill any person to experience were muffled as he turned over what happened to him. He wasn't sure whether he should bring it up to anyone or just deal with it himself.

Once he was back in familiar surroundings, Percy stopped and lowered himself again and Gerald jumped off. "Thanks." Percy nodded, then turned to walk away, but before he could Gerald called out, "Hey wait!"

Percy stopped and turned to look at Gerald with a calm stare.

"You have any idea what the heck I was doing out there?" Percy snorted then walked away.

"Good talk!" Gerald yelled back as Percy disappeared. He turned to see his dad standing behind him, dressed for a morning run. He had his hands on his hips waiting for Gerald's response. "You Fred Flintstone now?"

Gerald laughed and hugged him. "I don't even know where to begin."

"Doesn't surprise me. Weird stuff always seems to follow you around." Ralph turned and looked back. "Come on, you hungry? Moms making breakfast."

Gerald gestured towards home. "After you."

He obliged and the two walked home, but inside his head, Gerald was thinking about the nightmare he had and whether to tell him.

"Dad?" Gerald said.

"Yes, son?" He replied.

Gerald struggled to find the words to explain what happened to him. Ralph cocked his eyebrows like he always did as he waited for a reply "I got all day," He jibed. "Everything alright?"

"Yeah, I'm fine," Gerald replied then began his approach. "Have you ever had any bad dreams or anything since coming to Heaven?" Gerald felt a lot better just getting it out there.

The look on his father's face, though, showed the opposite reaction.

"Are you serious?" He stopped in his tracks and stared at Gerald, then continued,

"Heaven, son. We're in Heaven. There are no bad dreams in Heaven. You have me....I have questions."

Gerald now knew it was a mistake to have said anything. "No, not necessarily a bad dream but something. I was able to control my dreams."

"And you happened to think of something bad and kept on that train of thought," He continued.

Though it was a lie, he didn't mind helping him out. "Yes exactly," Gerald added. "I was thinking of the war and got brought back to that time. It was crazy."

He laughed and patted Gerald on the back. "You had me freaked out. Nightmares in Heaven. Give me the heeby jeebies." They both laughed and continued home. Unbeknownst to Gerald, Ralph gave his son a sideways glance as if he was not sure whether he was holding out on him.

LATER THAT EVENING, as everyone was sitting around outside having a beer, Mama Lucy sat next to Gerald. "How you doing?" she asked as she patted his leg.

"Good, thanks. Just relaxing and taking it all in, you know?"

She smiled. "I do. Sometimes I wonder when the other shoe will drop."

They sat in silence for a while, then Lucy turned to Gerald. "How are you sleeping?"

His first thought was that his father gave him up, but then he remembered when he first came and what Lucy had said about the dreams. "Alright, I guess. Dreams here are very real."

Lucy's eyes were dark as pitch as she looked into Gerald's eyes "Nothing unusual?"

Gerald remembered his father's reaction to what he said. "They're dreams, so I guess, they will tend towards the unusual, but so far nothing too crazy." He smiled, feeling like an ass for lying to her about it.

"Let me know if anything happens. I've been dreaming but I can't tell why or what for yet." Before he could respond, Lucy stood and walked into the house.

11

THE CITY

Gerald woke up feeling refreshed after a dreamless sleep with the sun streaming through the bedroom window. He thought about just lying in bed all day, watching TV, and eating three hundred boneless wings...literally. Those pleasant and slothful thoughts went right out the window when he heard a knock on the door and then heard Melinda's sing-song voice call for him.

"You up, cousin?" she called from downstairs.

"I'm here, hang on a sec," he called.

Gerald got up out of bed, shook off dreaming of the three hundred wings, and willed himself into jeans, a Georgia Bulldogs t-shirt, and flip-flops and headed downstairs. Melinda and Marco were waiting for him in the foyer. Once he reached the bottom, he greeted them and hugged Melinda. He shook hands with Marco.

"What's going on, guys? I had planned to sit home and watch TV and have a couple of wings."

Marco raised his eyebrow and smiled at him.

"Sounds busy," he said in that tone which made him wonder if he had read Gerald's mind.

"Sounds wonderfully boring, but I wanted to take you into the city today," Melinda said.

"The city? Didn't know there would be one of those," Gerald replied.

"Of course, silly. Some people love cities, you know."

"Ok, let's go. This city have a name, and is there another one?"

"Nope, only The City, and here it's all you need," she finished.

"Only one? Must be big," Gerald added.

"You have no idea." Marco smiled.

They started walking on the road from home and within a few minutes, the road shimmered and changed into a highway that had walking lanes to both the right and left while every contraption known to man and beyond drove on the road itself going by. There were Model T Fords, Mustangs from every era, Corvettes, trolleys filled with people, an above-ground train, open-top buses, and a cowboy riding a horse who appeared to be speeding. *At least no unicorns,* Gerald thought to himself.

As they crested a hill Gerald got his first look at The City. It was almost too much to take in. The size of it boggles the mind as it stretches out as far as the eye can see. In places, sections of the city floated in the air which gave it a surreal look as one could imagine. Sections floated over a shoreline as well and in the distance, he could see tiny little speck people diving into the water from a height twice as high as the Empire State Building. It made him queasy just looking at them.

The fresco of colors that appeared to be painted on the sky couldn't be defined as the colors changed from a deep purple to a bright yellow. The color ranges within the same color from maroon to pink beggared description.

As they walked closer to the city, the city seemed to be coming to them. First, they were miles away from the city limits watching the city pull towards them like zoom on a camera lens. Before long they were walking through a massive gate made of gold and inlaid with ancient script.

As they walked through, Gerald tried to take it all in. Tall buildings that stretched beyond the eye could see were quickly replaced by onion-domed buildings more akin to buildings in a Russian or Turkish city. Brownstones lined up in a neat row took over the following block while a block of buildings no more than three stories high gave the appearance of a large township rather than a city. As cars, horses, and people zoomed by, Marco and Melinda took a step back to let Gerald take it all in. He could smell the familiar scents of a city, from the burnt pretzels to Chinese food, bus exhaust which wasn't very welcome because it smelled just as bad as it did on Earth, and then fresh coffee, that roasted smell that carries and cuts through anything and just pulls you in.

Melinda broke his reverie.

"You smell that?" she asked.

"Yep," he replied while lifting his nose like a bloodhound.

"I have to have a cup of that coffee," he exclaimed with a smile.

They both smiled at Gerald and led him to a small park area that had some small vintage shops and a couple of small restaurants. At one corner was a sign that read LANA'S CAFÉ, BEST COFFEE IN THE UNIVERSE." They headed towards the café and Gerald had to ask.

"This really the best coffee in the universe?"

"Hands down," Marco replied.

They walked into the café and the smell of the coffee was a lure that pulled you in. They got in line and within a few seconds the line had moved up to allow them their turn. The woman behind the counter, who must have been Lana, moved so fast she was literally a blur, along with the two other helpers who both appeared to be younger versions of her. The oldest version stopped moving and asked for his order. She was a tiny woman, maybe all of five feet tall and a little plump. She had her hair tied up in a ponytail and wore a visor.

"Hello, can I take your order, sir?" she asked Gerald with a warm smile.

Gerald acknowledged her and looked up at the menu list. There must have been hundreds of combos of lattes, coffee, espressos, and whatever you want a-cinnos.

She saw the bewildered look on his face and smiled. "Take your time, sir," she said warmly.

He smiled and looked over the massive menu and after a full minute or so still didn't have any clue.

"First time here, sir?" the woman asked.

"Yes ma'am," he replied.

"Great. I would recommend just our regular coffee with a dab of cream and sugar," she offered.

Gerald thought about it and turned to Melinda and Marco who both nodded approvingly.

"Ok let's get a regular coffee, and a t-shirt," he said, more relieved than anything. Trying to decide was giving him a headache.

She smiled and zipped off and back in an eye blink and handed a piping hot medium cup of coffee that smelled like Heaven, no pun intended. He also selected a raspberry and white chocolate scone to go with it, along with his new t-shirt, and when all three had their orders they went back outside and sat down on a park bench to enjoy the coffee and the day.

As he drank the coffee, he did have to admit it was awesome. The individual flavors just rolled off his tongue, from caramel, to chocolate, to a bit of citrus, to a nutty flavor. They sat in silence for a while until Marco broke the reverie.

"Great coffee, right?" he asked Gerald.

"Unbelievable," he concurred.

He smiled and they lapsed back into their own little coffee paradise. Gerald looked around the park and at the little boutique shops that surrounded the park. He noticed a large number of women going to a store with a sign reading MONA SWENSON over the door in flowery lettering. The women that went in all came out with handbags that ranged from basic black leather to an obsidian blue material that he couldn't identify.

"What kind of shop is that?" He pointed to Mona Swenson's.

"That's the Mona Swenson pocketbook boutique," she answered then added, "She was a world-famous pocketbook maker on Earth. You bought Lia one of her pocketbooks for her birthday one year."

"Did I?" he asked, not remembering at all.

Melinda sighed and smiled at him. "Men."

Gerald sheepishly smiled back at her, and Marco began to explain.

"It's very common, really," Marco began as Gerald turned to listen. "Whatever you did in life and what made you happiest continues on in the hereafter,"

Marco explained that Lana had a little café south of Allenhurst, New Jersey when she was alive and that the two girls were her daughters who loved the café as much as she did. Mona Swenson also carried on her life's passion here in Heaven. Most of the buildings were created by architects who had passed on and now didn't need to worry about budgets or even the laws of gravity to make their creations come to life. From bakers to candlestick makers, they were allowed to run free with their ideas and create works of art way ahead of what the living human mind could create. Monet had an art exhibit for his newest paintings, Van Gogh grew back his ear, and Little Willie Keenan was still making the best moonshine known to man.

Thousands upon thousands were still creating and evolving along with their creations.

Gerald listened in rapt attention at all the wonders still being created and conceived even now. He shook his head sadly though at one thought that crept in. "It's a shame none of these things will ever be seen on Earth," he said wryly.

Marco and Melinda both smiled at him, and Marco continued. "But they do, Gerald, they do. Heaven isn't just your reward after death."

Marco explained that besides Heaven being the paradise promised to those of good nature, it was also where the human soul was first created and molded before being sent on its way to Earth to live out its human life and fulfill its destiny. Creativity was first sparked there along with the souls and also sent down to Earth as inspiration to those special artists or creators who were deemed worthy and talented enough. He also explained how humanity was linked to one another like an orchestra, each part had its time and duty to perform within the context of the larger musical content.

"So one day we'll see these buildings on Earth, maybe some of this coffee?" Gerald smiled as he raised his cup.

"I hope so. I want everyone to be able to get a cup of coffee this good," Marco added.

"So that explains what you do," Gerald blurted without thinking as the scene at church came to mind.

They both became very still, and he saw fear and concern on Melinda's face for the first time, and that immediately made him regret bringing it up.

Marco put his hand in Melinda's and squeezed it before explaining. "You're very perceptive, to be clear, I don't love it." he said slowly grimacing. "It's my duty. That is a big reason why we do what we do. You went through that place before you came here. You're aware of what's out there and that we fight it."

Marco explained they could never lose or all would be lost. Gerald could see the determination of a man who fully believed in what he was doing behind the dark eyes. He could also see the pain and things best left unsaid because if someone ever thought war was fun, they had never been knee-deep in blood and shit.

Gerald didn't know what to say, so he just sat there and drank his coffee for a little while and stared at some pigeons that varied in color from yellow to green, and blue eating leftovers on the ground.

"When did you volunteer for this?" Gerald finally asked.

Marco just smiled at him and gently shook his head before he responded. "You don't volunteer; only a select few are asked."

Gerald nodded in understanding. "I am surprised. I am sure that you would have a line a mile long with volunteers."

"That line would stretch for a thousand miles, actually," Marco continued. "Heaven is too precious to have too many souls out fighting and bringing back that pain and suffering to those chosen to endure." Marco sighed heavily, then finished, "Heaven would be stained with too much pain. This is a place of healing and creation, not death and suffering."

Melinda kissed Marco on the cheek and put her head on his shoulder. The man stared at Gerald and then asked him the question he knew was sitting there waiting to come out. "How do they pick?" Marco asked grimly.

Gerald nodded for Marco to continue.

"Those souls who have been in battle during their lifetime are the first to be considered, seeing that they understand what it's like to end a life and hold up under that kind of trauma."

Marco also explained that not every person that had fought in a war was selected. Some had and couldn't take any more of that kind of pain, and there are others selected who had never had to bloody their hands in life but had the mental fortitude to do what was necessary. "Also," he added, "there is something else that goes into it."

Marco hesitated but Gerald nodded to him to continue. "The rush of being in battle," he stated, then continued after a deep breath. "Though you hate war and you know how ugly it can be, deep down you miss the rush...that heat." He paused and watched Gerald's reaction.

Gerald wanted to say he was wrong and that was crazy but deep down, he was right. Nightmares and pain still weren't enough to wash that little piece away from you that wanted to throw yourself back into the fire.

"It's eye-opening, isn't it?" Marco quietly said.

Gerald had no more questions for him and Marco didn't seem inclined to offer more info, so they left it at that.

12

MORE DREAMS LESS IDLING

Gerald went back home after being in the city and his thoughts kept going back and forth from what Marco had told him, to the disturbing dream he had recently. He had more than an idea they were connected.

As Gerald wished Marco and Melinda a good night and headed home, the sun was dropping in the sky, spreading low lit flames onto the horizon. The crickets welcomed him as he stepped into the house. Thinking about his past life, he knew he had fought in WWII but Marco said that didn't mean anything per se.

With ever-improving skill, he changed himself into pajamas sat down in front of the TV set, and started to idly flick through the channels. He caught an episode of HBO's *Carnivale* season five which didn't exist on Earth. Neither did a *Firefly* marathon of all twelve seasons, and a *Doctor Who* which he did remember watching before on Earth.

He put his feet up and smirked at the piggy slippers he had received from George for his birthday years before. He said they were Boss Hog slippers. Gerald hated how they looked but he had to admit they were super comfortable, and he didn't mind giving up some manliness in the comfort of his own home.

He wasn't sure how long it was before he had drowsed off, but he was startled to hear a silken soft whispering, the same whispering he had heard when he was in the living mist. The whispering began to grow louder which startled him, and he jumped to his feet. He realized he wasn't in his living room anymore. A feeling of dread lay in the pit of his stomach as he got a bearing of his surroundings.

The ground beneath his feet was sandy and the trees were very thick, and upon further inspection, he saw they were some type of palm tree. The heat was cloying and he felt the humidity cling to him like a coat. A wind was blowing and he caught the scent of barbecue or meat grilling. He also smelled a wood fire burning and cautiously started to follow the smell through the dense foliage. He didn't hear much of anything as the trees seemed to mask the noise.

As he pushed on through, he noticed the trees starting to thin. The smells were getting stronger, and the level of noise began to grow as well. If he had any qualms before, he knew that they were justified because he could hear the roars of some kind of animal, the same roars that the beasts from his other dream had.

Gerald's ire was up as he went into a full sprint. The trees thinned even more and the level of noise began to rise along with it. He crested a sand dune and like a hammer was struck down and fell to his knees by what he saw before him. There was a beachhead in front of him with the shoreline a half mile from where he was. There was a mass of wooden ships similar to old Spanish galleys in the water. More than two-thirds of them were sunk and destroyed while the remaining were trying to actually reach land rather than head out to sea.

He caught the heavy scent of diesel fumes and as the smoke

shifted, he could see makeshift ironside ships painted in mad dashes of red, blue, and green. The technology was more advanced than the old wooden galleys. The galleys that could were firing cannons at the Ironsides which had zero effect, as the cannonballs bounced off the metal hulls. The ironsides, on the other hand, were firing heavy caliber shells at the galleys that, upon impact, splintered the wooden hulls and caused horrific damage.

These monsters were systematically killing this race of beings occupying the wooden galleys. He could hear them laughing as they caused wanton slaughter. Gerald began to weep, and he felt himself heat up as he built up energy to strike out at these beasts.

The race under attack, from what he could tell, were humanoid in that they had two arms, two legs, and a head, but he could see a fin running along their back and the visible webbing between their fingers.

Gerald started sprinting towards the beach as fast as he could and when he hit the water, he could see the few remaining galleys being pushed under water and the monsters who engaged in wholesale slaughter were boarding the boats. They were physically superior in strength and size and were using that to deadly efficiency. To see these beings cause so much damage and pain built up the fire inside.

Gerald began to rise off the ground until he was level with the deck of a nearby galley. He began to harness that rage and anger into focus which he was going to unleash upon these abominations, as he was about to unleash a massive burst of energy upon these monstrosities he began to feel a pressure on him. He could feel it surrounding him and as he unleashed the blast he had readied, it never landed but just seemed to fizzle out and no one was the wiser he was there.

"No!" he screamed and tried to gather another blast, but

before he could, he was pulled up and away from the planet so fast that he blacked out for a moment, and when he came to he was back in his living room. The silence struck him harder than any blow and after a few moments where he tried to catch his breath, he did the only thing he could do. He screamed.

13

APPROACHED

The path Gerald walked was strewn with gravel which crunched underneath his feet as he walked. The part of Heaven he was exploring definitely wasn't in the tour guide because it was hotter than a southern summer with a whole lot of humidity and foliage thrown in. He could smell the bananas ripening in the tree in the breathtakingly beautiful jungle region he was trekking through a half mile before he came to it. The fauna was a vibrant mix of hues and colors that staggered the mind because they couldn't possibly exist anywhere on Earth. He heard things moving around in the underbrush but didn't check them out.

The jungle, for all its beauty, was a distraction from the night before. The events were as clear as day, and what made it even more frustrating was he wasn't able to do anything about it. Why show him these things if they weren't going to let him do anything about it? *Or maybe, was this the whole point?* he thought to himself. They wanted to frustrate and torture him by not being able to do anything about it. The whole thing just made him seethe with frustration, and he picked up his pace to match his anger.

Abruptly the jungle began to thin out and became a savannah with tall grasses and little rolling hills in the background. The sun here was just as hot, and he jumped right into a watering hole along with a hippo and a crocodile that both greeted him with snorts and then went about their business.

The water was only about five feet deep, so he splashed in the cool, fresh water for a while and just floated there., He let his mind relax, hoping it would help him let go of what had happened the night before, but instead, his mind drifted right toward the prior night's events. Over and over in his head like a broken record, he saw what was done to those poor creatures. The joy those monsters showed reveling in the violence and death, made him sick to his stomach. *Why couldn't he help? Why bring him and show him these things and then idly allow this kind of evil? Why, why, WHY?* He raged to himself.

Gerald's anger manifested with the water beginning to bubble around him. He kept replaying the injustice of it in his mind until he exploded, unleashing a blast of force that expelled the water out of the watering hole and left him lying on his back in the mud. The hippo and crocodile were both blown backward and lying on their backs, and neither could get up. Eyes widened at what he had just done.

"Oh boy!" he exclaimed and then ran up and out of the watering hole to the crocodile whom he helped turn back over.

"Sorry about that," he said to the crocodile, but the crocodile wasn't having it and hissed at Gerald in return.

"Sorry," Gerald repeated as he came upon the stricken hippo. He tried but couldn't get the hippo over. The damn thing was too heavy; It was braying and complaining up a storm when Gerald stopped, out of breath. He turned to see the crocodile watching him.

"A little help, please? I feel bad enough already," Gerald said, and the crocodile snorted and pushed him aside to place its head underneath the hippo. Gerald came over and they both pushed, and the hippo finally got back up on its feet. The hippo then turned to Gerald and brayed long and loud in his face then pushed him. The crocodile had its tail behind Gerald's knees and tripped him up. Then both the crocodile and the hippo left with one last derisive snort. Gerald stayed on the ground for a few moments.

"I deserved that," he said to himself and the offended twosome.

"You have an interesting habit of making big holes in the ground," said a voice from behind Gerald who turned to see Kerael standing there. With a wave of his hand, the angel returned the water to the watering hole, and the damage was gone like it had never been.

"There we go," Kerael said, then turned to Gerald.

"Think it's time we talked," he said. Gerald walked up to Kerael and shook his hand.

"Finally, I thought I was losing my marbles." Gerald said to Kerael as they both sat down next to the watering hole.

"It's time you know what's going on."

Gerald nodded.

"Those nightmares you have been having," Kerael said which immediately got Gerald's attention. "They aren't nightmares."

Gerald exhaled.

"They are real," Kerael added.

"Ah," Gerald said, instantly the anger rose. "Those things happening were real? Deep down I knew it. Why did you stop me from helping those creatures or aliens or whatever they were?" Gerald demanded.

"That wasn't me that stopped you, but yes, that was quite a shock when you actually altered reality in a dream state. Rarely see that." He looked troubled as he said it.

Gerald stood up and pointed his finger accusingly at Kerael. "So you admit, that I was stopped before I could help. How dare you show me these things then take away any ability I had to stop those goddamn monsters?"

Gerald was incensed. He grabbed Kerael by the front of his robe and pulled him off his feet. "How dare you! You're no better than those monsters."

Kerael's face darkened like a thunder cloud and he grabbed Gerald by the throat and quicker than thought, picked him up and slammed Gerald down onto the ground where his imprint showed from the impact.

Gerald blacked out, but not before he felt what seemed like every bone in his body break. He awoke to horrendous pain that quickly faded when he felt Kerael place his hand on his chest then picked him up and set him back down on a knoll. "I didn't mean to lose my temper. We are nothing like them." Kerael said this with a firmness that beggared no discussion. Gerald was taken aback by the quiet intensity in his voice.

"If you feel that way, then why wasn't I allowed to interfere and do something? I could have helped."

Kerael looked at Gerald, breathed out slowly, and then began, "What you experienced was called the Awakening. It's a test that's given to those souls we believe can handle those sorts of things."

Gerald looked horrified. "So if I fail, I don't stay in Heaven?" he said.

"No no no," Kerael cut in quickly. "You're good. This is for eternity; there's no probation."

Gerald audibly sighed. "Thank God. Man, you had me worried."

"The Awakening, as I have said before, is a test. Not every soul gets this test. Only those we feel can handle it." Kerael waited to make sure Gerald was up to speed then went on.

To Gerald, Kerael seemed to swell in size as he continued and as the angel's shadow grew he detailed what was happening. "There is a war going on, a war that has raged since the beginning of time between good and evil. There are races dedicated to the light that have been with us since the beginning, and there are races that want nothing more than carnage and death. One of those races you have seen. They are not monsters, they are worse, they are daemons. They came from the darkness that was before this universe. That place I brought you through to get to Heaven. When God spoke the words 'let there be light,' and there was light, they didn't tell you there were things in the darkness. Vermin, these filthy things are seemingly endless, and they serve the dark as its foot soldiers because of their savagery, strength, and uncountable numbers. Other races have pledged to Old Night, but the daemons are the most despised and pose the largest threat to the universe in general. You follow so far?" Kerael asked.

Gerald nodded.

"I'm sorry for the way we go about it, but it is Heaven. Paradise is eternal and is there for those who deserve it, and we don't want to expose too many souls to Service."

"Like the Army?" Gerald asked.

Kerael nodded. "Exactly like the Army. You're fighting to stop those daemons from doing those dreadful things. Also, we fight to protect Heaven."

That shocked Gerald and Kerael read his face. "Oh yes, they have been trying for billions of years to get through the gates of Heaven. The good news is that an evil soul or anything unclean is rejected by Heaven itself, and it would take a massive effort over a prolonged period to even crack the outer defenses, but it's still possible as unlikely as it is."

As Kerael explained all this to him, Gerald was able to comprehend it and in fact, it made a lot of sense to him on some level the need for a fighting force to try and stop evil. Heaven and Earth had that in common, and he knew firsthand about fighting a war against tyranny and evil. The problem was that to fight tyranny and evil, you had to sacrifice yourself, not just your life but your body, family, sometimes beliefs, mental health, and a litany of other things you didn't get back.

As if he was reading his mind, Kerael continued. "We know what we ask is a tremendous sacrifice. Souls that make it into Heaven have earned it and deserve paradise for all eternity but even paradise comes with a price." And there it was the cost of paradise.

"What price?" Gerald asked.

"Well, you have to leave Heaven. Not for good and not all the time but you will need to leave for training and then any missions or theaters you would be assigned to. Once the mission is over, you head straight back to Heaven." He finished with a wave of his finger to emphasize the point.

Gerald nodded and sat down. A hundred thousand things were racing through his mind. He kept seeing the atrocities these monsters did to the innocent creatures over and over in his mind.The very thought of Heaven being invaded made him sick to his stomach. He was able to fight all the perverse things he stood against in life and his afterlife. It held an appeal to combat the atrocities these creatures had done right in front of him, that came popping up and that he was stopped from helping.

"What if I refuse?" he asked.

Kerael stood right where he was and just smiled. "We would be disappointed, of course. You have great potential but it's your choice, We would never force anyone into it. The stakes are too high."

Gerald nodded. "Why wasn't I allowed to help those poor creatures when I was able to make something happen the first time?"

This time, Kerael frowned and shook his head. "We rarely see a soul affect reality before from the dream state. You literally forced your way through with sheer anger and willpower."

Gerald sat motionless, waiting for his answer.

"To answer your question, though, as painful and terrible as it was, the point of us showing you these things is so you can see firsthand what evil is capable of doing without placing you in harm's way. Also, this is the most important thing. There was nothing you could have done for them. The death of that world couldn't be prevented. Our forces were turned aside at the main battlefront of that world. We had to withdraw before we lost everyone. If it helps, we were able to get 70 percent of the planetary population off-world before the end."

Gerald's rational mind understood what he was saying, but his emotional side wouldn't accept that there was nothing that could have been done. "70 percent? That's, that's a lot." Gerald stood up and faced Kerael. "So 30 percent loss of life is acceptable?"

Kerael gave him a hard stare. "Now you're just being difficult. We did what we could."

Gerald's fear and anger surged forward. "You can always do more, something...Anything!" He sat back down and kicked at the dirt, and after a few moments he calmed down and his anger was spent. "I'm sorry. I didn't mean to snap at you, but I just couldn't take being helpless. I don't normally get so emotional."

Kerael sat down next to him and placed his hand on his shoulder. "It's because you care. That's why we need you. One soul can make a difference. Maybe if you were there more lives would have been saved. Maybe we could have saved that world, I don't know. The point is you can do something about it."

There were times in Gerald's life when he felt the weight of the world on his shoulders. Now he felt that weariness drape over him like an anchor.

Kerael sat up and reached down to help Gerald up. "Take your time. You don't need to give me an answer right now. Take as long as you need. Whatever you decide to do, you cannot speak of it to anyone. This decision must be solely yours."

He walked off without another word and disappeared.

Gerald stood and looked towards the sun as it went down. He felt a brush against his back and found the hippo was back. Its large round eyes were boring into him and it seemed it was feeling for him.

"Thanks," he said to the hippo as he gave it a pat on the head. He turned around and walked back home.

14

FOR YOUR CONSIDERATION

That night at dinner, Gerald could feel Melinda and Lucy watching him. He knew they were worried about him, and it bothered him that he couldn't share what he knew with them, or anybody, for that matter. His parents could see something was bothering him but left him alone. They knew their son well enough to know that he would tell them when he was ready.

As he sat drinking a beer, he looked at the world around him differently. He felt disjointed and out of place, like watching a movie in a movie theater where he was there but only watching the show, no longer part of it anymore. He knew he shouldn't be so morose, but he couldn't help it. He thought his days of shooting up bad guys were over when he was twenty-eight and went back home to work with his father.

He remembered those days like it was yesterday: the fear, the danger, the not knowing whether you were going to live through the day. Accepting that you were already dead so you could carry on day to day, otherwise, the fear would rot you out and eventually kill you for real. He shuddered thinking about it now and was thankful that Charlie was there with him, and all his brother-in-arms who watched each other's backs. He missed the camaraderie and the binding ties that endure till the day he died with those men. *The good and the bad,* he thought. Life is about balance, when it slips too far to the wrong side, men are responsible for correcting it. He remembered those words from a man long dead to this day. That was an honorable man he remembered but not with affection.

Melinda and Marco came by and sat next to him. "Hey sweetie," she said and hugged him.

"Hey guys." Marco nodded in greeting and sat down opposite them so he could see the both of them.

"How are you doing?" she asked him, concern etched on her face.

He glanced over at Marco, who was sitting there calmly, and smiled at him when they made eye contact. "Good," Gerald responded. "Just been doing a lot of roaming around lately and have been thinking about stuff I guess." He knew he was a terrible liar.

"That's it?" Melinda asks. She seemed torn between believing him and pressing him further.

"Yeah, and you know, thinking about Lia, George, Charlie..." Gerald mumbled.

A knowing smile came across Melinda's face as Gerald laid down the cover. She lay her hand on top of his and hugged him. "Oh sweetie, I never even thought about that, but that should have been the first thing I thought of. That's a natural response to start thinking of the loved ones still alive and to miss them. I feel like such a duh!" She smacked her forehead with her palm and laughed. Gerald joined her in laughing, though he felt giddy nervousness to it which to him made him sound like a crazy person rather than jovial.

Marco laughed along with them, but it seemed to Gerald that Marco was also watching him. Did Marco know Kerael spoke to him already? Was he waiting for him to crack and say something? Gerald had to calm down before he freaked himself out.

"Good to see you smile," Melinda said. "Let me know if you want to talk or anything, ok?"

He smiled and nodded. "I'll be fine, just adjusting, that's all." Gerald got up and started for the house. "I'll be back. Heading inside real quick. Thanks, cousin." Gerald gave her a peck on the cheek and said goodbye to Marco.

He went into the house and went up to his bedroom where he lay down in bed and, within a few moments, he was asleep. Oddly, he didn't remember feeling tired or even wanting to sleep. He just was asleep, and he was drifting. He was in a nowhere place, unsure where that thought came from, but it seemed fitting.

He felt himself floating around the nowhere place which was nothing but a vast gray emptiness. He could hear whispering coming from a million different voices but just one voice altogether. Gerald couldn't make out what they were saying but as he focused on the whispering, he was drawn to it. Eventually, he made out what they asked, "Why have you come?"

Gerald was taken aback by this question because he was brought there, not the other way around.

"No," they answered by plucking his thoughts from the ether. "You have come here. whether you know it or not. Whether you ask or not, you come."

Gerald thought about what he came for but was not sure what he needed.

"Clarity," they answered. "You wish to make the right decision and feel you need more."

"Yes, I need more information before I can decide."

"There is no more to give. If the adversary succeeds, then what is left of the universe will be returned to a living Hell for all time. That is enough."

Gerald understood that it really was that simple, but what about his family, he thought.

"It can be that they will not know you are gone," they said. "Time is your ally. Years away is but an hour in Heaven. They will not feel the pain of missing you. It is all we can give so they do not suffer." They seemed still for a moment. "You are needed more than you know. One soul can make a difference. Ponder and decide."

Gerald nodded his thanks and, before he could say another word, he was back in his bedroom, awake and looking up at his ceiling. His insides were in turmoil. He kept going back to his time in the war: the death, the pain, blood. He had enough of that. It took him years to be able to sleep at night without fear and guilt. He had killed more men than he cared to think about. He didn't care to add to the tally, even if he would be killing actual monsters.

"I can't do it," he said to no one. He wept for a while and wallowed in the pool of his memories. He screamed how unfair this was to ask more from him. More killing, more death.

He had made up his mind he was going to tell Kerael he couldn't do it. He felt ok with it. His family wouldn't know, and he believed Kerael when he said they would understand. It would be like it never happened.

His mind was made up, nothing was left to say. Except it did happen and he would know. He would be the one that knew he had a choice. He could choose to make a difference. He could sacrifice. He could protect his family and everyone's families.

Gerald exhaled slowly and sat up, then got scared half to death when he heard a voice behind him "So you've made your decision then?" Gerald turned and saw Kerael sitting in a chair beside him smiling.

15

LAST SUPPER...FOR A WHILE

Gerald slowly went over to his parents' house for dinner. He was kicking dust clouds up with his foot as he walked. The dust clouds had a mind of their own and would turn into mini tornadoes that would spin around him and collide back to dust after a few seconds of tomfoolery. The golden sun was floating down from the sky as he made his way up the driveway and found Mel waiting there for him.

"I am surprised your neck isn't broken," she said.

"Huh?" Gerald asked, clearly distracted.

"Whatever is on your mind looks like it'll tip you over and break your neck" she replied with that sweet smile.

He exhaled slowly. "That obvious?" He walked up the stairs.

"You would get like that whenever something was bothering you. I can't count how many times you walked into stuff." She laughed and hugged him.

"What better time to ponder one's place in the world than when you are in Heaven?" Gerald said. He didn't lie when he said it but it was clearly a deflection. Mel saw right through it but let it slide and motioned for him to follow her inside where his parents, both sets of grandparents, Mel, Lucy, John, and Marco were visiting.

Gerald made eye contact with Marco who just nodded and shook his hand. They all sat down at the dining room table. The food was already there: steaks, chops, chicken, mashed potatoes, collard greens, potato salad.

"You remember having to eat salads for dinner to get that cholesterol down, son?" Ralph said to his son as he put his hand through his thick black hair. "We learned all about them cheat days, didn't we?" Everyone laughed at his joke. Gerald still hadn't gotten used to seeing his dad young again, so it gave him pause as he laughed. Cheat days became their thing when they had to watch what they ate or keel over like a chubby cow, as his mother would say. Champagne problems, Lia would say. Too much eating, drinking, and fornicating his son George said. Mind you, he was eight when he said that. It caused some consternation, but that was because he heard his Grandpa say it so maybe not such an illuminated child.

Dinner was moving along just fine but in between talk of a new series called 24, which had everyone on the edge of their seats, he didn't really say much. His stomach was tied in a knot waiting for the perfect time to let everyone know he would be leaving. Mel, Marco, and Lucy were all glancing at him as if waiting for him to let everyone know.

"Are you...you know?" Gerald asked Marco as he waved his hand around his head to signify if he was reading his mind. Marco smiled, shook his head, and spoke directly into Gerald's mind so no one could hear but him. "Whatever it is, I am not allowed to know until you say. Also, it is rude to do that, so I apologize."

Gerald nodded at Marco in appreciation.

"Whatever it is, I would like to know if you don't mind," Lucy says.

"Damn straight. This nonsense is getting on my last two nerves," Gerald's mother added.

Everyone was focusing directly on Gerald, waiting for him to spill the beans.

He took a swig of his drink, coughed a bit, and then began.

"So, I was approached by an angel," his dad interjected.

"Same fella we met on your first day here?"

"Yes the very same, his name is Kerael." Gerald continued. "You know when we went to church and at the end of service they brought out the soldiers and they were carrying that armor? Marco, you were on stage."

Gerald felt foolish adding that. Of course, he was there. Marco just nodded and had a sad expression on his face. *He already knows,* Gerald thought. Marco put his arm around Mel and squeezed her.

"No," Gerald's dad stated "Tell them you changed your mind. I remember you and Charlie when you came back. You both came back haunted, skinny as a rail, cored out, and carrying too much weight. I won't go through that again. We prayed every day that..." He couldn't continue and the room fell silent. No one was sure what to say.

Mel broke the spell. "I see how Marco comes back. I ask him not to go, but he says it's his duty. Why, why is it his duty? Why is it yours?"

Marco was as still as a stone, his face grim set.

Gerald grimly explained, "Because I can do some good, I can help. They have shown me what's out there. It's terrible and if it has its way everything and everyone will be gone or worse." He doesn't know what else to say.

"Boy and you've the bollocks to get it done, is that it?" Grandpa Angus was furious. "You're a donkey-headed mule, boy, always have been. If a good whack would do any good, I'd whacked ya."

Mel pleaded with her eyes at Gerald, pleaded with Marco who looked defeated but spoke again. "He has to make his own choice. You know mine." She bolted straight up and walked out, avoiding eye contact with Marco and Gerald. She was so angry her footsteps were burned into the wood floor.

The dinner dispersed and after everyone but his parents left, Gerald headed into the living room with a piece of cherry pie that hadn't been touched. He could hear his mother in the kitchen whisper speaking with his father. She was trying to be quiet but was never any good at it. Gerald could hear her telling his father to try and talk him out of it.

Gerald poked at his pie, sat on the couch, and waited for his father to come in. After a few more minutes of not having any choice but to listen to his mother way too loudly whispering, his father came in and pointed outside.

As Gerald and his father walked down the porch steps they saw Mel sitting on the swing. She looked over at them and then looked away as if she didn't even see them. "That one is all you," Ralph said to his son. Gerald smiled and nodded.

They walked in silence for a few minutes. The only sound was the crunch of gravel as they walked. It was a beautiful night. The moon, our moon, was shining brightly in the sky and projected so much light that it cast a glow which gave everything a surreal feel to it as they slowly made their way down the dirt road.

"You know, you can jump on projects here if you want to."

They both stopped walking as Ralph continued. "What you did in life you can keep doing, or if you want to try something new, that's alright, too."

Gerald tilted his head and listened to his father.

"The city has all these architects, engineers, tradesmen, they all collaborate and build new things. Eventually, it comes to Earth."

Gerald nodded and asked, "You work on any of them?"

"Sure have. I jump on the agricultural stuff mostly since that's what I knew in the life before. I did try my hand at a building project." George was animated about the subject as he continued. "Never did anything like it, but they like to go old school like when they first made skyscrapers. All the manual labor then they will switch it up and make machines that do the work. It's pretty cool."

Gerald smiled. "That sounds fun, Dad. I am glad you're keeping busy. An idle mind is the devil's playground, didn't you always say that?"

Ralph huffed a laugh in response. "Paradise can get boring. Here you can try anything you want. You want to be a surgeon and attach a hand back on? You got it. Try to make scones, no problem." Ralph was genuinely excited by the unlimited options available to a person in Heaven. The pang of sorrow that struck Gerald came with the sudden realization that as long as the wolves were at the door, he felt obligated to be the sheepdog. It would be worth it if all of this could continue and grow and if mankind would flourish even with the trials and tribulations it continued to thrust on itself.

Ralph noticed the change in Gerald's expression and stopped speaking. They both stood there in the middle of a dusty road in Heaven's Georgia staring at each other. Tears welled up in Ralph's eyes. Gerald's throat felt tight looking at his father's pain, a pain he was causing. "I tried. I knew I wouldn't be able to talk you out of it. Your mother, deep down knows it too." Ralph placed a hand on his son's arm. "I always said, make the right choice, usually the hard choice, but you make it. In the end, it will go the way it is supposed to."

Gerald dropped his head for a second and then looked at his father again. "Is this the right choice, Dad?"

Ralph looked his son in the eye. "No, yes. I don't know." He looked exasperated. "I know what Mel goes through worrying about Marco. The thought that you could die for good." Ralph shook his head. "I'll be fine. I was fine before."

Ralph looked at his son with an intense glare. "No, you were not fine. You were alive!" He stomped his foot. "You and Charlie were a mess. Like ghosts walking and talking. It took a couple of years for you to shake out of it. Not until you met Lia is when you broke out." Ralph grabbed his son by both arms. "You want to be like that again? A ghost among the living?"

Gerald winced under his father's tight grip. "We're not alive anymore, Dad."

That brought out the temper of the old man. "Ack, fool boy. We see what Macro is like when he gets back. He gets sadder and sadder every time. One of these days he'll mope himself away. If he didn't have Mel, he would be gone already."

"But he has Mel, and I have all of you. That's what family is for. To get through the bad times and enjoy the good."

Ralph dropped his head. He knew Gerald was going to leave just like he had back in 1941. He raised his head, let out a breath, and hugged his son. "No matter what happens, do the right thing. If you lead men, be first. Don't ask them to do anything you wouldn't do."

Gerald squeezed his father and continued on with what he had been taught as a little boy. "Be a team player. Set aside ego. Set an example." He and his father hugged for a long time. Gerald never understood why his father had been so tough on him and Chance, but he understood when he went to war. Men can become monsters and commit atrocities. Other men have to hold them together. Gerald had asked his father about his time in the Legion but his father never said a word. The faded Legion tattoo on his arm said it all for him.

They walked back towards the house after a few minutes. Mel was still on the swing and this time she was staring right at

Gerald. "I'll see you inside Dad," Gerald told his father. Ralph patted Gerald on the shoulder, waved to Mel who waved back and headed up the stairs. Gerald walked up and sat in the swing next to Mel.

"Lovely night," she said.

Gerald nodded. "Yep."

"I'm not angry with you," Mel finally said, Gerald looked over at her with a quizzical look in his eye, and she smiled. "Well, I am a little, but I am just scared. You and Marco are my closest people."

Gerald nodded in reply and had nothing to say in response. He had quickly learned that even though Mel looked different from who she was but her mannerisms were the same. "I remember Simon Windicutt pushing me down the stairs when I was leaving the store that one day,"

Gerald remembered that day as well. They were all children of ten or eleven. Simon Windicutt was the son of a local businessman who was also the grand dragon of the local KKK. Later on in life, Simon Windicutt would end up being famous for being the most notorious serial killer in Georgia's history. He was an asshole when he was a child: spoiled, entitled, and mean.

Pushing a little girl with Down syndrome down the stairs was something that he would do. Simon had called her a retard and thought it was funny. She was crying because she had scraped up her knees on the stairs. Luckily, she wasn't hurt any worse. Simon's father Thurston Windicutt was there and was as shocked as everyone else, but Gerald didn't think, he just acted.

"I remember what you did," Mel said. Gerald had punched Simon right in the face so hard he had broken his nose which exploded with blood upon impact. The double crack was so loud everyone heard it. One crack was Simon's nose and the other crack was Gerald's hand. Simon was on the ground crying. Gerald felt the lightning bolt of pain where he broke it but was still furious and let him have it. "You ever touch my cousin again, I will kill you!" Gerald remembered how still everyone was and no one said a word.

His father had picked up Mel, and Chance had run out the door ready to rumble but their mother grabbed him.

A crowd had formed as Thurston made his way to his son. "Get up" he snarled at Simon.

"He hit me, Daddy!" Thurston's face turned bright red, and Simon knew better than to say another word, so he got up and headed off to their car.

Thurston looked around and made his way to Ralph who handed off Mel to Lisa and approached Thurston. The exchange didn't last for but a few seconds, but whatever was said satisfied them both. On that day at least Thurston showed some humanity. *Too bad he didn't show it later in life,* Gerald thought. *Maybe his son wouldn't have become a serial killer.*

"You always had my back," Mel said as she slowly swung. "I got yours." She reached out her hand and Gerald grabbed it "Just get back safe."

16

SHIPPING OUT

"So where are we going?" Gerald turned to Kerael as they were walking down a garden path. The scenery was exquisitely cut into the colorful foliage that surrounded them. They walked past a scene of a seashore made from tulips, roses, and other flowers that included actual movement.

"We're heading to a crystal transport center, or CTC for short. It's the means for traveling throughout the universe for souls."

"No spaceship or something like that?"

Kerael laughed. "There are spaceships used by the differing races but a soul doesn't need a ship. You could travel yourself from one planet to another if you wanted to, but it would take much longer and be pretty boring, to be honest."

As they continued to walk the garden began to morph into an urban environment with streets and a pretty center of town with little shops and a coffee shop on the corner. "Ah, here we are." Kerael opened the door to the coffee shop and let Gerald in. "I love the scones here, you want one?" Slightly baffled, Gerald shook his head " I'm good."

As he waited for Kerael to pick up his order, Gerald looked

around and admired the stylish colors on the walls and the cool art nouveau that hung from the walls. He saw the picture of the monkey drinking from a bottle which was always one of his favorites.

He looked around to see that each table was set up differently with some having comfy chairs, others a sofa, and one even had a mattress where a couple was lounging, sipping some tea, and making out. *Geez get a room you two,* he thought.

Each table had a tiny volcano mound with a glowing crystal on top giving off radiant light. *Was never a big fan of those things,* he thought to himself.

"Ok, you ready to roll?" Kerael asked pleasantly as he munched on his scone and coffee. Gerald headed to the door and was about to open it when Kerael stopped him. "Where are you going?" Confused, he turns around.

"I thought we were heading to the CTC."

Kerael motioned him over to an open table. "We're here already. Come on, sit down." Gerald motioned over and sat across from Kerael, waiting for something to happen. "Something supposed to happen now?" he asked Kerael as he finished off his scone.

"Not yet, I have to set the coordinates first."

Bewildered, he watched as Kerael placed his hand on the crystal on the table. It glowed brighter and he heard a whispering that went away once Kerael removed his hand from the crystal. "You're all set. You just have to touch it and off you go."

Gerald nodded. "So how does it work again?" he nervously asked.

"Well since a soul is made up of energy, these crystals act as a conductor for that energy and can transfer it around to anywhere you want to go."

Gerald nodded. "Cool, and only souls can use it?"

Kerael smiled. "You're stalling." Seeing the truth in Gerald's eyes, he smiled. "It's ok. The first time is always a little interesting but don't worry, it doesn't hurt and it's really quick. Don't mean to be pushy but I have other appointments to fill, so I'm going to need you to get going."

"Of course, sorry." Gerald placed his hand near the crystal, said a last farewell to Kerael, and placed his hand on the crystal. In a flash of light then dark, light again, he was there.

17

DEATH WORLD TRAINING CENTER

Once Gerald got his bearings he was assaulted by the sights, sounds, and smells of his new surroundings. He was in a large hangar with a couple of hundred souls milling around. There were other races of beings mixed in but mostly they were at tables and what appeared to be a docking area where a large spacecraft was being worked on.

On the other side of the hangar was a giant creature with an eagle's head and wings and a lion's body being pulled through an opening.

"Let's go, princess. We ain't got all day." A hand grabbed him and pushed him through into a line with other recruits. They were pushed and prodded by the handlers into an open clearing outside the hangar.

"Attention!" A large man in silver gold armor was suddenly standing in front of them. "Let's go, get your asses in line now!" All the souls start scrambling to form up in lines. "Eyes front!" the large man screamed. "I am Colonel Wilkes and I welcome you to Death World Training Center!" He paced up and down the ranks, as he spoke. "You have chosen to sacrifice yourselves and for that, you are to be commended." He acknowledged the group. "But now your pathetic asses belong to us. More specifically me! We will see who among you is good enough to be the elite. We are the greatest fighting force in all of existence and you must earn your way into our ranks the hard way."

He stopped pacing and stood up front as men and women in similar armor formed up behind him. "The training you are about to endure is the most grueling, painful, and debilitating process there is; you will be broken down again and again to test your resolve, if you fail you may die for good." He let those words sink into all the recruits. Some looked utterly horrified by this news. "Each one of you has been assigned to a company. Behind me are your sergeants. They will call your name and you will stand behind them, is that clear?!"

They were all smart enough to respond, "Yes, Colonel!" And with that, the mind-numbing process of waiting to be selected had begun.

The first sergeant stepped forward and called out her list. "I am Sergeant Fuentes," she said as her long legs snapped to attention right in front of them, and began calling the names for the team. Once all the names were called and the chosen stood behind Sergeant Fuentes, the next sergeant stepped forward. He was a burly giant of a man named Sergeant Klukos. After him was Sergeant Verenz and then Sergeant Kohl. The hardest part was standing there while everyone was getting picked.

The next sergeant to step forward was Sergeant Miller. He was a long switchblade of a man who had the eyes of a killer and looked like he was born for war. This man scared Gerald and he hoped that he wasn't going to be picked by him. Of course, he was wrong because the very first person Miller picked was him.

"I want Gerald Argyll up here now. Let's go, you puke!"

Gerald groaned inwardly as he ran as quickly as he could to

stand behind Sergeant Miller who was already calling out the rest of the company. "David Howell, Simon Bach, Lincoln Presting, Don Stokely, Gio Pannella, Sasha Perez, Chris Hamilton, Vora Ganz, Gordon Red Feather, Rob Shuler, Dean Micheals, Travis Gentler, and Tony Weiss." All the recruits scrambled to their places behind Sergeant Miller. Gerald gave quick smiles to those he made eye contact with but made sure he had eyes front when Sergeant Miller turned that flinty stare on them.

They waited while the last of the companies were assigned and Colonel Wilkes stepped forward for closing. "Now that you have been assigned, I wish you luck and God's blessing. You'll need it for what's to come. Dismissed!" With a curt salute, we were done.

None in the new group were dumb enough to move or do anything until Sergeant Miller turned to them and with a quick wave of his hand, he had them follow him. "Let's go, turds." They followed him out into the jungle that surrounded the staging area and down a well-worn road. "Move it!" he screamed and started running. They all immediately started to follow him. He had them all sprinting and after a few minutes when it didn't seem like he was going to stop Gerald settled in for the long haul.

He lost track of the time through the haze of pain but he knew enough to know that Sergeant Miller was running them in a giant circle after seeing the same markers over and over again. To the company's credit, no one had slowed down or fallen, but each one was waging their war of wills with themselves.

It had gotten dark and they ran using their familiarity with the course to guide them. Periodically Sergeant Miller appeared next to each of them like an angry ghost to spur them on with the sheer menace.

As they were running Gerald began to notice movement in the brush alongside the path. He knew that it wasn't part of their group, in fact with the way whatever it was seemed to sway it didn't appear that it was human either. As the group kept running he noticed that the movement in the underbrush was increasing and he felt a thrill of fear as his mind processed what was following them. Giant plants, mobile giant plants stepped onto the trail in front and behind them. Some looked like giant Venus fly traps, others seemed to be moving trees with tendrils, and others seemed to be mobile vine groupings that had spikes along the vines. The old instincts kicked in as Gerald screamed a halt and ordered the group to go back to back. "Back to back, keep them in front of you, we're surrounded" He yelled. A Giant Venus flytrap approached along with a group of others behind it. Gerald prepared himself and called the others to prepare for attack. The blond Vora bared her teeth and screamed as lightning began to coalesce around her. Others clenched their fists as the giant plants came closer; the group prepared to engage.

"Stop, don't attack, " David Howell, a tall, thin, and muscular black man said and waved his arms to the group. He got in between the giant Venus flytrap and Gerald.

"They mean no harm, they just want to say hello," David said as he approached them.

"You know this how?" Gerald asked warily

"They told me, I can understand them." David said. He raised his arms and motioned to stop as he turned to the Venus flytrap group. The creature in the lead made hooting tea kettle noises.

"Uh huh, yes me too, we mean you no harm as well," David said to the lead creature who hooted again and then made the effort to turn towards Gerald and waved. Gerald, unsure what else to do, waved back.

"Is weird but they sort of cute" The blond Vora said and waved as well. One of the walking trees shook and hummed in response. "Hello, we friends" She finished

"Can you tell them to give us some space?" Gerald asked David. He didn't have to translate as they understood Gerald and melted back into the underbrush.

"See you later, we'll chat!" David said as the creature melted back into the jungle. Miller appeared and looked at David.

"You can speak and understand them. That's useful" he said then turned to Gerald.

"Good job puke. They are man-eating plants for sure but they are allies as well. " Miller said to Gerald. Miller then ruined the moment.

"Alright you useless pieces of shit, get back to running, let's go!" Miller snarled at them.

The group took off again, the man eating plants leaving them to continue their run. When the sun began to rise again after what seemed an eternity, they were finally led to a different area on the base. As they ran, they saw that they were entering a barracks area and shockingly, it appeared that most were occupied as they saw recruits coming out practically naked except for loincloths for men and bottoms and tops for the women. They were the only company who hadn't come back to the barracks the previous night.

Sergeant Miller led them to an unassuming barracks made of what appeared to be the same material as the armor and had them file in. Once inside, they stood at attention and waited.

Sergeant Miller walked up and down the company line, scanning each one of the recruits. Their limbs were on fire and they all wanted nothing more than to drop in a heap into the beds they stood next to, but they dared not.

Sergeant Miller stopped in the middle of the room and addressed his company. "Hope you douchebags enjoyed our little run because that was just the beginning," he boomed. "You have the privilege of being asked to fight for the greatest cause ever, existence itself!" He turned to make sure that everyone was giving their full attention. "Let me tell you dipshits a little bit about myself so we can get all lovey-dovey," he barked then continued, "I was a Marine Sergeant for the United States of America. I am a veteran of the Korean and Vietnam wars having served a total of six tours of duty, two in Korea and four in Nam. I know war, people. From a young age, even before my beautiful balls dropped, I knew what God had planned for me. I knew deep in my bones that this was my calling. I went to church every Sunday and I never uttered a curse word. I served in war honorably and never killed a man who didn't need killing." He paused and made sure they were all eyes front.

"When I died and came to Heaven, I was given the honor of being asked to train you pussies and try to mold those who were worthy into a fighting force that would make Him above gaze down upon us for even a split second. I was also permitted to curse. I was a pious man but I asked the powers that be and they said, 'Miller you curse all you want boy, you earned it,' and by God, I am now a complete man!"

It came to Gerald that this man was completely insane.

"So you toe rags are now mine. Our morning jog was a warmup. Shit, I could run for two weeks without feeling so much as a cramp, and here is the great news!" No one expected the coming news to be great. "So will you. You will be able to endure pain and suffering like you never thought possible. You will need to if you're to serve and survive. Make no mistake, it's a cold, cruel universe out there and the enemy will not show mercy or compassion to you." He scowled. "Rest up for five, then I want you outside in the main training area. Welcome to the war. Dismissed!" Without a look back, Sergeant Miller exited the barracks.

All the recruits dropped like puppets with strings cut onto their beds. "That guy is a maniac," A dark-haired man said as he slumped into bed. "Gio Pannela, how are you doing?"

Gerald shook his hand. "Gerald Argyll, pleased to meet you." Gio was a handsome, olive-skinned man with Italian features. He reminded Gerald of Marco in that dark Mediterranean way. "I tell ya, I was in the Army during WWII and the drill instructors I had back then were rough, but this guy, he makes them seem like cream puffs."

Gerald nodded. "I served in Europe, first wave D-Day, and then Germany at the end of the war and this guy scares me more than any of that."

"If he doesn't kill us, I think we'll be ok, though," a voice said from behind them. A truly massive and muscular black man appeared. "Don Stokely, nice to meet you guys." They both greeted him with handshakes.

"You seem almost chipper about it my friend," Gio said.

Don shrugged his massive shoulders in a surprisingly disarming way for a man so physically intimidating. "It's all new to me, I suppose. Just trying to stay positive."

"Have you ever served when you were alive?" Gerald asked. By now everyone in the barracks was listening to them.

"No." Everyone could see him struggling with what to say.

Sasha placed her hand on his shoulder to comfort him. "It's ok, sweetie, you don't have to tell us."

He looked up at her and smiled with child-like innocence but continued, "It's just that I'm not used to all of it yet. You see, when I was alive, I was a mechanical engineer."

"So you were a big giant nerd," Gio said and everyone laughed, including Don.

"No, I never weighed more than 130 pounds my whole life. I was in a wheelchair for the last twenty years of my life and couldn't walk."

Everyone was stunned to think that this massive man in front of them could ever be anything but.

Gio voiced what they all were thinking. "So now the outside matches the inside. Glad you're with us, pal."

David spoke up. "We better get out there, it's almost time."

As one they all formed lines and ran out to the training area with nothing but the fear of what Sergeant Miller would do to them if they were late.

18

HATE FOREVER

It spends most of its time dreaming. It never sleeps; that is a mortal construct. Yet it slumbers just the same. It remembers bits and pieces of its past lives. The women stored in the butcher's room, the stink of the blood and bowels laced with fear like perfume, a musk he could wear even after his deeds were done.

The meat of his victims was laced with delicious fear. He recalled luring men in another life, his sexuality promising base pleasures in exchange for attention, money, gifts, whatever the victim wished. Sometimes the base pleasures were fulfilled, but the men gave much more than money or gifts. Their lives were the real currency.

Revenge for a life of abuse and pain given to these men, the hole in her soul never went away but grew bigger with each victim. She was never caught but, in the end, all debts are paid. The experiments on human beings in that dark forbidden place, a place where fairy tales had originated. They would never know it was due to the anti-matter that floated in that place, unseen but radiant. Haunting the trees and soil itself. All these beautiful dreams he revelled in playing over everyone. The truth was it was none of these memories or souls. It was something far worse; it was an eater of souls.

These souls could pull from the ether and devour to keep it sated while it bided its time in this blighted place. Too much light, too much life. It yearned to return to the darkness from whence it came. It remembered the wars before time, the billions of years of conflict where it rose in power and served the elder gods before they were called such.

He remembered the final war, the warlord who changed everything. He who had ascended and destroyed the darkness of that old universe and replaced it with life and the dreaded light. Its hate was boundless. It savored that fury and pain. The cold, painful darkness. It yearned for it all to return.

That was why it agreed to be captured, agreed to be chained so it could wait. The higher powers had ordered it to do it which failed. It was too powerful for orders, They could end its existence but it would cost them much, too much. It was a Duke in the infernal order It chose not to lead armies as it preferred to destroy on its own. Its love of violence refused to allow it to share so it required an offering, a bargain that would benefit it. For what they asked, he knew he would get what he wanted. They would not give it to him; more threats and promises of pain and violence. Nothing worked. It knew its worth, so it waited for when they were ready to give it what it wanted. The word was given, the bargain was made, and it was promised what it truly desired: freedom, freedom to choose its own path. Even to bring back the darkness it would not obey. They offered ultimate freedom. No one would ever ask for anything if it succeeded. Free for eternal slaughter and pain, *what could be better than that?* It thought to itself as a long line of acidic drool dropped to the floor in a hiss.

It had bided its time and now it felt the sands of it trickle to the last. In this enemy world, It had seen others who had potentially been the target, but none proved worthy.

Now, searing through its alien brain like a bolt of lightning, it felt the arrival of a soul that would end its time and usher in an age of pain. It was chosen for the task because it did not make mistakes. It would ensure that the target was in sight before rising up and striking down the key to its freedom. What none knew about it was that for all the pleasure derived from charnel slaughter, the stink of death, and the fear that rode with it, the creature cherished the pain above all. It wanted to inflict maximum pain so that the tender meat was ripe with fear. It would confirm and feast on its target and then it would feast on this world. It would leave and then feast on other worlds till they were a dry husk. No allies, no enemies, all would suffer.

Its name was Goorga and this was its pledge.

19

SWEET SWEET AGONY

The company stood at attention in complete silence as Sergeant Miller, or Miller as he preferred to be called, strode up to them. He stared at each of them and then approached Gio, nodded at him, raised his hand, and materialized a knife. Everyone stared in wonder at how quickly it appeared. Everyone then gasped in horror as he plunged the knife into Gio's stomach and opened him up like a catfish. Gerald could hear someone behind him retch as Gio screamed in agony and fell to the ground. Gerald didn't think he just reacted. He went right at Miller. He felt that build-up from his dreams and launched himself like a fiery missile. He should have known he was in for it since Miller saw Gerald coming and just waited for him to get within striking range. Miller was so fast Gerald never saw but rather felt the fire explode from his throat. His build-up of power was extinguished like the guttering flame of a match in the wind. Sergeant Miller had torn out half of Gerald's throat. Gerald fell to the ground in agonizing pain. All he could see were Sergeant Miller's boots as he tried to hold in what was left of his throat. The pain was excruciating and Gerald just lay there choking to death. Gio's screaming was all he heard besides Miller.

Miller directed his ire at Gio. "You're not dying, you dumb-ass, you're already dead. Heal yourself right now!"

Under Miller's uncompromising gaze, Gio quieted down and began to focus. At first, nothing seemed to happen but then slowly, very slowly the grievous wound began to seal back up.

"Good, hurry up we don't have all day" Miller reached down, pulled Gio back up, and patted him on the shoulder. "You will need to master your pain. You will be injured, mortally so, but what would have killed you is now an inconvenience. You are required to heal from your wounds and get back into the fight immediately. Now, who's next?"

It was rhetorical because everyone got it next. Miller didn't move but raised his arm and pointed it at Don and with a flash incinerated both his legs. "Just because you're dead doesn't mean you can't die." Miller turned in a circle so everyone could hear him. "You cut off someone's head and that's a wrap, people. Why? It's where your consciousness resides, so protect your head. I don't make the rules, so keep your head on a swivel."

Sergeant Miller turned back and Gerald knew he was being addressed. "Get up, focus, heal, and be quick."

"Urk." Was all Gerald could say but he fought through the molten pain. If he had been alive he would have choked to death painfully gasping for air. He used the anger he felt for Sergeant Miller to heal his throat strand by strand, itching replaced the burning and after a few moments, it was done. Gerald felt exhausted. He was roughly grabbed and pulled to his feet where he saw Don standing already as if nothing ever happened.

"Tough group, that's good you want to protect your people," Miller spoke just so Gerald could hear it but then screamed in his face. " Don't you ever break formation or go after a commanding officer again or you're dead for good, you got me, puke?"

Gerald straightened up and responded, "Sir, yes sir."

Sergeant Miller gave Gerald a slight nod, a smirk, and then wheeled around and with a twist of his wrist exploded Gordon Red Feather's arms and then pulled Vora Ganz in half. Gerald sighed, It was going to be a long day.

～

GOORGA FELT the surge in power. A splinter of Its essence was watching this group with interest as it knew its prey was among them, the signs and portents that came to it in its fevered half-sleep were now more insistent. The surge was quickly extinguished by the one it hated most of all, the one called Miller. When it had killed the chosen one it was here to destroy, Miller would be next. It would also kill the rest of the group. They were not chosen but blessed and deserve punishment and death for this abomination. The combined power of this group was pure and clean, and it whispered of destiny.

Goorga was able to delve into senses others of his kind could not. The gifts bestowed upon it were many. It should have been higher in the hierarchy but it cared nothing for this, only the pain and death it could inflict. It also knew it was chosen because its own kind feared it. *They should,* it sneered, they would suffer as well. This close to what it hoped would be the end game it would be certain, so it focused its will and sent out a sliver of its essence to watch the one who could be chosen.

It was careful as always; the servants of the enemy had constructed a well-built prison for his kind. The problem in its construction was that it had misled them from the start and it was of a far greater caliber than what the prison could hold. If they knew what it was they would not have captured it. They would have destroyed it or tried to anyway. It would have relished that fight, but the timing was poor.

Goorga mused over this as it sent a fraction of its essence out of the prison. It easily evaded the traps and bindings that would have worked if he were a lesser creature, but for it, this was as easy as a cat moving through a maze of light. Acidic saliva burned the floor of its cell as it thought of the day it would shatter this prison and wreak vengeance on all of them. It would take great pleasure in making Miller suffer most of all and then devour his spirit so it could keep Miller close for eternity. Miller had injured it and worse, trapped it when it had escaped to break the monotony of its time imprisoned. It hated weakness most of all, especially its own. It would give Miller conscious-ness from time to time so that he could see the destruction it wrought and feel hope abandon Miller over and over again.

The splinter floated up and away once it passed the last of the active defenses. The splinter knew there were still passive defenses in place, so it made even its minuscule essence as small as possible so that anyone coming near it would not feel its pres-ence. It floated up, high enough to survey the area. It needed to scan from a high enough vantage point so it could pinpoint the target's location; it had to be certain. When it reached high enough, it floated and scanned for anything that could sense its presence. Satisfied that it would not be discovered, it opened up its senses and began to scan the area. It was seeking the soul heat of the chosen. In this place, it would be a challenge to confirm.

As it searched it flitted across many powerful souls, beings that brimmed with power, capable of hurting it if discovered, so it kept out of reach it moved on past the beings others called angels. It knew what they were, whatever names were chosen for them. These angels were on the opposite side of the coin. It bris-tled at their self-righteousness, believing they were good, and were right to be allowed to destroy but not one such as it. Goorga and its kind were hunted and hated, and that made it want to destroy everything all the more.

A familiar signature shook it from its bloody revery and floated down to the cabin that contained the soul that pulled it to the outside where it lurked out of range. It watched as Miller sat and smoked a pipe. He had on what appeared to be furred creatures with overly large ears on his feet. It was not sure what they represented as they could not have been any possible threat, nor did they appear to be very reliable. It had no need for such constructs but they angered it in a way it did not understand.

It did not think it expanded any energy but Miller froze, stood up, and ran outside. It shrank itself down even more and floated away retreating as carefully as it could.

Miller walked outside with his bunny slippers on and sniffed the air searching for his prey. The man didn't know why he did it, but instinct told him something was off. Miller sent out his senses into the ether and reached out as far as he could looking for something, anything. The cool night air was the only thing Miller felt on his skin. The miasma of the otherworldly senses he was able to apply told him nothing, and after a few minutes, he went back inside.

Goorga had floated out of range of Miller's scan but it had known the sharp pang of fear for a fraction of a second. That was added to the butcher's bill planned for Miller. If the signs had not pointed otherwise, Goorga would have sworn Miller was the chosen one. Goorga did not have time to ponder further as it was now drawn to its target. It flitted through the trees as it descended like a diseased spoor.

The large building where the souls gathered shined so brightly that it caused pain to it. The signs and portents swirled and guided Goorga to the inside of that building. Death waited there for it. The combined might of these souls could destroy Goorga, and it hated them all the more. Domination and inflicting pain were its domain only. They would pay, they would all pay. Doubt became fear, fear ascended to rage, and rage was the holiest of all.

Goorga floated down until it was able to perch itself onto the window ledge and watch its prey. The swirls and eddies flowed over and around a human with red hair. It was almost certain this was the long-awaited target, but then the swirls would flit around and circle another human, a female whose very essence spoke of razored violence. She was dangerous, it assessed.

Another swirl and it flowed around a dark-skinned man with long dark shiny hair. An olive skinned human patted the shiny-haired one and the swirls flitted around this one as well. It was frustrating as the swirls kept bouncing around the others: two black-skinned men, one slim as a blade full of animal potency, and the other burned with radiance barely containing its bulk. It did not like uncertainty but it knew this: all in this building would die, just to be sure.

It had not been paying attention and its anger had made it careless, it had splintered the window frame. Instantly the shiny-haired one that they called Gordon, the target, and the thin black man turned their heads at the same time to where it was. It abandoned stealth for expediency and flew off.

Inside, they all had heard the splintering wood. Gordon ran outside and checked the ground. David was right behind him sniffing the air and floating around the area for a scent. Gerald ran behind and scanned the skies. The entire group was outside right after taking a perimeter around the barracks.

"What is it?" Gio asked. His eyes glowed red and he looked up to the sky.

"Gordon, you smell?" Vora asked. Gordon stood still as a stone and after a second shook his head.

Vora turned to David who, after sniffing the air, also shook his head

"Are we being paranoid?" Gerald asked more to himself than to anyone else.

"Instinct no lie. Something you three pick up, yes?" Vora was glowing icy blue and crackling with energy.

"Instinct no lie" Gerald nodded to Vora. Whether it was a threat or not, something had been there and was now gone. The cracked wood around the window frame attested to something being there.

BATMAN LOBSTER

EVEN THOUGH NONE of them needed to sleep, the few moments of rest they got they chose to. Gerald closed his eyes and let himself drift off. He dreamed about his family, his thoughts floated off to a time that, though never simple, was cherished.

Gerald pulled the 1955 Ford Country Squire Station Wagon into the parking spot. George was so antsy to get out he climbed over the seat so he could open up the trunk door. "Easy champ," Charlie said as he grabbed George by his calf and he fell over to the side and almost did a header into the cooler taking up that side of the trunk. The reverse seat had been taken out so they could pack up for their day at the beach.

"George, hold your horses. We don't want to take you to the hospital now that we're here, do we?" Gerald asked with a smirk.

"No Dad," George yelled back as Charlie grabbed George and helped him climb over the bucket seat and into the truck. "Thanks, Uncle Charlie," George said once he was in the back.

"You got it, kid," Charlie said as he and his wife Aubrey got out of the backseat and into the bright summer sun of a Tybee Island morning. Charlie breathed in the salt air.

"I love that smell." George smiled and stepped back as the boy opened the trunk door from the inside. He was clambering down and trying to pull the folding chairs out of the trunk.

"Take it, easy son, we're here all day," Gerald said as he helped George with the chairs. Lia came around and chatted with Aubrey as the boys got the folding chairs and cooler out of the trunk.

The wind carried that salt air smell and Gerald inhaled it. He used to love that smell, loved it until he had landed on the beach of Normandy during D-Day. Now that salt air smell would always have a tinge of blood and gunpowder mixed in.

Pushing the trunk door closed, Gerald carried folding chairs in one hand and held one side of the cooler with Charlie carrying on the other side.

Charlie would tell Gerald he was being melancholy, but Gerald had to look up that word first before he had a good comeback. The year was 1960 and things were beginning to change. Students from SCAD and Savannah State were protesting as part of the quickly growing civil rights movement. Violence was common, and the people protesting were willing to take it to bring a new world into being. Thankfully, a better way was being shown that brought progress through unity and fellowship but that is a story for another day about a better man. Gerald felt compelled to take part due to his wife and son. Also, he had to help those who didn't have the money and influence to help themselves out and survive what they had gone through.

The shops were just starting to open as they walked towards the beach. Everyone was taking their time to enjoy the rising sun. Even George, who had been chomping at the bit to get out of the car, was holding hands and walking with Lia. He had a funny smile on his face. It was the same face he made as a baby when he had just eaten and got changed. He was content. They all were.

Gerald looked over at his best friend and Charlie nodded back in that familiar way. He was family and he always felt so lucky to have a friend like Charlie. Before, during, and after the war, he was a constant. He had saved his life and trusted him with the lives of his family. That was more important than his own life, as far as Gerald was concerned.

George, in the way only an energetic boy can, crashes through the deep water and pulled Gerald back into the sunny shallows.

"Dad, let me help you." George grabbed hold of one of the chairs, and Gerald and Charlie stopped so he could grab one and then hoisted it above his head then tried to run with it.

"You'll tire yourself out....what in tarnation am I saying?" Gerald said then called back to George. "Good job son, you want to try carrying two?"

Charlie, Aubrey, and Lia laughed at Gerald's joke. Anything to wear that boy out was a good idea. Like a puppy, you had to run them ragged as much as possible.

"You are not right in the head," Charlie said.

Gerald laughed. "You know that better than anybody. I must be tired. Work has been crazy, especially this time of year" Gerald said, referring to late summer and farmers getting to harvest soon. New parts, equipment, and hiring extra help, was a lot and it had to be done within a certain timeframe.

They made it to the sand and began the final stretch to the beach. By this time, George had run all the way down to the beach and picked the spot for them.

"Not bad, kid," Charlie said as George looked around one last time and then planted the beach chair down like a flag. He sat down calmly for all of two seconds, then threw off his sandals, and ran towards the water screaming like he was charging the enemy line. The group made it to his chair he hit a wave and was flipped head over end.

Lia gasped and started to run towards the water, but George emerged laughing like a little crazy person. He ran toward them and told them how fun it was then before his mother could say anything ran back and hit another wave. "He is going to get hurt," Lia worried.

"Kids are made of rubber. Even if he takes a few knocks on the head, he'll be fine. He's hard-headed like his pa," Charlie said. Gerald nodded in agreement, but Lia shook her head.

"The boy has no fear," Charlie said as he watched George search out the latest waves to jump into.

"Like his daddy," Lia said and put her arm around Gerald's waist.

Gerald looked at his wife.

"Not true. I'm afraid of you, sweetie."

Lia cocked her eyebrow at him and smiled.

"Oh good, we're getting lovey-dovey," Aubrie said and grabbed Charlie who blushed. "Come on, give Mama some sugar," Aubrie said as Charlie smiled and kissed his wife.

George demanded his father come and play with him, so Gerald and Charlie spent the next three hours playing in the water, throwing a ball around, then a frisbee, and finally, they threw a beat-up tennis ball to a two-year-old yellow lab named Gus who a heavyset man named Louie owned. He was a Cajun from Lafayette, Louisiana, and was in town visiting family. His wife Floradel had very light-colored hair, almost white that their daughter Adelaide also had. George and Adelaide had a grand time playing with Gus and eventually, Gerald and Charlie made it back to their chairs.

"I'm bushed," Charlie said as he cracked open a beer and handed it to Gerald, who waited for Charlie to get his open before tapping them together, giving their customary French cheer, "cul sec!" and drink. They did not say a word as they watched George and Adelaide play with Gus with Lia and

Aubrey chatting with Floradel. Louie had gone back and was fast asleep on his blanket.

"He's got the right idea," Gerald said. "I'm just going to mosey on over" He lay down on the blanket under the umbrella.

"Better make room to cuddle soon 'cause I think I need a nap," Charlie said.

Gerald smiled as his eyes closed.

"Dad, wake up!" George was shaking Gerald awake. The sun was high in the sky at this point and for a few moments, he wasn't sure where he was. "You were out like a light."

Gerald shook out the cobwebs and slowly stood up. His left side was burning and when he turned around, everyone there including Louie, Floradel, and Adelaide, chuckled with wide eyes.

"Hate to be you tomorrow...well, half of you anyway," Charlie said and smiled. He grabbed the Solarcaine from a bag and tossed it to Gerald who looked himself over and noticed that his left hand was bright red but his right was still freckly white.

"Huh, not so bad," Gerald said.

Lia looked concerned as she dug into her purse, pulled out a makeup mirror, opened it, and handed it to Gerald, who took it. The reflection back at him was not good. The left side of his face was bright red and an almost perfect line in the middle separated the sunburned half from the non-sunburned side.

"No good," Louie said in his heavy Cajun accent. Gerald had to agree.

George walked up to his father, looked intently at him, and then said, "Batman Lobster."

"Oh yes, sweetie," Lia said and chuckled. Aubrey and Charlie also started chuckling. He had no idea what they were talking about. "What does Batman Lobster mean?"

Gerald asked George who just smiled and looked at Lia who

answered. "Hun, you know George loves to read those Batman comics, right?" Lia asked. Gerald nodded. He knew who Batman was. "Well since only half of you is sunburned, you look like one of the villains Batman faces."

George beamed at this and said, "Yes, Mommy."

Gerald still didn't make the connection "Who do I look like?" he asked.

"Two Face man. Half of you look like a lobster and the other is your normal white," Charlie said.

Gerald finally got it. "Huh, so Batman Lobster it is." Gerald tossed the Solarcaine back to Charlie and told him to hit his face with it before he started to really feel it. Gerald felt the cooling spray hit his face and when Charlie was done, he started on his back. Gerald watched his son put on a towel like a cape and run around him like Batman Lobster.

20

BARRACKS

Eight people left between the first session of getting mutilated and the tenth: Chris Hamilton, Rob Shuler, Lincoln Presting, Simon Bach, Sasha Perez, Travis Gentler, Tony Weiss, and Dean Micheals. It left Gerald, David Howell, Don Stokely, Gio Pannella, Vora Ganz, and Gordon Red Feather to drag themselves back to the barracks. It was exhausting healing yourself over and over, but it was all mental. Miller promised we weren't done yet trimming the fat, more would drop...or die, as per his usual positive motivation.

"So doc, why do you keep the scar?" Gio asked David. David had kept a long scar that ran down the length of his forearm. "You didn't need to keep it when you got here. Do you see this mug? I have had acne scars since I was twelve. Now go and look at this skin." Gio ran his hand down his very smooth unlined cheek. Everyone laughed.

"Perhaps he keep as memento of defeating great warrior. Very hot, yes?" Vora chimed in. She was the definition of a Valkyrie with her long blonde hair, Nordic features, and fiery temperament. The scar talk was right up her alley. "I bet you have many scars, Gordon. You show us?"

Gordon the very solid and stoic Native Indian had nothing to say to that, but apparently, you can still blush even after you die. "Nothing like that." Everyone waited for more but he didn't follow up on it.

Thankfully, Gio put Gordon out of his misery. "Dude, no sir. We're a team. Come on, tell. Do you want me to tell you the shame of when I put a smoke bomb in my old nemesis Ricky Portenzo's mailbox? I confess, not a good day for the kid here, especially after my dad found out." David just smiled.

"Not now. I'll tell you if I make it."

Vora stomped off. "Ack, you are buzzkill, of course, you make team, Vora knows who." She pointed her finger at Gerald. "You, tell him."

Everyone looked at him. "You're doing great, David I loved how you regrew all your limbs after Miller blew them off" At this, everyone laughed. Gerald sat down and thought about how important it was for the camaraderie they were building to happen organically. This was a good group, he could tell, resilient and strong. Strong in the right way and he was happy to just be here with them.

The group was on the training field standing at attention when Miller strolled up to them smiling. Instantly everyone was tense. It was like having a crocodile trying to give you flowers. "Hello everyone, I hope you are ready for a beautiful new day," Miller pronounced. Everyone tensed even more. Gerald swallowed, thinking that he was about to get his throat torn out again. Others in the group were thinking similar thoughts.

Miller seemed inclined to let them squirm for a minute before continuing. "Congratulations, we have weeded out most of the unworthy. We have worked on self-healing so that in battle you don't have to think about it and you can continue with the fight." Miller paused dramatically. *He would be a terrible actor,* thought Gerald, but he was waiting for what was next like the rest of them. "Today we start your training on the offensive side of the ball. Each soul is unique as are your talents. Hallelujah, I'm sick of blowing you people up!"

Don raised his hand and asked, "Was that a joke, sir?"

Miller walked right up to Don and screamed, "You bet your big ass it is!" Miller addressed the group. "Give yourselves some room and get creative."

Vora slowly raised her hand. "No one has to get the chopping?"

Miller cocked his head to the side like a deranged wolf. "Not unless you want to, now have at it!"

The group broke off individually and in short order, Don had expanded himself into a hundred-foot giant that could fire laser beams from his eyes. Vora materialized a silver frost sword that radiated a deep blue glow and sliced through boulders like they were butter, and also there was a lot of lightning. David transformed into a twelve-foot tall wolfman and disappeared into the woods. Gio started to glow and materialized two large caliber revolvers that didn't run out of ammo. He switched to a large automatic weapon, then a Roman gladius which shot fire. "This is fucking sick!" Gio screamed as he floated away to blow up some shit. Gordon looked at Gerald, smiled, and then disappeared. Gerald quickly scanned the area to find Gordon but he didn't see a thing. He *must have teleported.* Gerald thought to himself but then Gordon re-appeared in the same spot.

"Were you there the whole time?" Gerald asked. Gordon nodded.

"I couldn't see you at all," Gerald said as Gordon waved and then disappeared again.

Gerald started to experiment. He had fire shoot from his eyes and incinerated a large grouping of boulders. He then flew into the air and fired energy from his hands like a human fighter jet. After some time, he floated down and thought back to the dreams that were shown to him to recruit him. They still haunted him.

Gerald remembered how, in a fit of rage, he was able to interfere and almost broke through the dream state. Gerald focused on the area around him. He was working on his breathing, trying to narrow his vision so he could replicate what he had done before. He was smart enough to know that he couldn't rely on anger to trigger his abilities. He was looking to change the area he was standing in.

He pulled in a breath and took in the colors, seen and unseen, of the world around him. He narrowed his focus on the tides of energy swirling out and around him. Gerald pulled in deeper, and the energy flowed right into him, like a tsunami drawing back water from the shoreline before striking.

Gerald kept pulling in more and more energy, trying to replicate the moment he had been able to break through the dream barriers. He was struggling to contain the energy as pain built up within him. After a few more seconds, the pain was excruciating and his stomach burned so badly he vomited liquid plasma. It incinerated a path fifty yards long and as he tried to move to expel the fire, he spewed in another direction. The movement caused a sharp pain which caused him to lose focus and without warning, he self-ignited. The explosion was seen on a planetary scale. Every sentient being on the planet felt it even if they didn't see it. Such was the energy expended.

GERALD AWOKE WITH A START. His head was still throbbing and he was naked. He wobbled to his feet and gasped at the damage he had unleashed. The ground for miles ahead was nothing but smooth glass that still smoked with the heat of the blast.

"Puke, what the fuck are you playing at?!" Miller screamed from behind.

Gerald whipped around in surprise and found Miller, and the team staring at him. "I, uh," was all Gerald could muster.

"I said practice, not go nuclear, you imbecile. You better control your shit or you'll get us all killed!" Miller stomped towards Gerald with the crunching of broken glass from where his step broke the smooth ground. In a three-hundred-and-sixty-degree circle all around was nothing

"Oh my God," Gerald said. The devastation was incredible. It awed and scared him at the same time. That changed to awkwardness quickly when Vora was openly staring at his naked body.

"Put some pants on, you hippie!" Miller screamed.

Gerald complied and even though he was now dressed, Vora gave Gerald's nether regions one more look, made eye contact with Gordon, and proceeded to look down at his nether regions again while hungrily smiling at him.

"Can you not do whatever it is you're doing right now please?" Gerald asked.

Gio just laughed and slapped Gordon on the back. "She's going to eat you alive, my man." Vora's smile broadened. "Yes, all of it."

That even made Gio stop in his tracks.

"Enough bullshit! Disperse and back to training. Puke, a word." Miller dismissed them which left Gerald standing alone with him. He didn't say anything for a moment. "Do you under-stand what you have done?" Miller finally asked in a calm, rational tone that concerned Gerald.

"No sir, I don't."

Miller walked around Gerald without saying a word until he was facing him again. "That should have killed you or at the very least injured you so severely that you would have been sent back for good. Do you understand what I am saying?"

"So, that was a good thing?"

Miller narrowed his eyes. "Remains to be seen. That kind of output is for the big hitters. I can't do what you just did."

"I see," Gerald flatly said.

"No, but you will." Miller turned and looked out across the plain and raised his hand. The flattened landscape started to reverse in front of him and spread. "Come on, help me out. This shit ain't going to fix itself." Miller yelled.

Gerald walked and stood side by side with Miller and closed his eyes but was unsure of what to do.

"Think of reversing the damage. Feel the air and soil, the ecosystem, it's all connected.That will guide you."

Gerald nodded and let out long deep breaths. He took in the swirling energy. He searched for the link that tied in all of the different parts of this world. He didn't need to be told; he just knew how to do it. He found the threads and, with the help of sentience in the earth, a mother Earth not the Mother Earth he was able to reverse the damage he had created, and the foliage and landscape were restored.

Upon completion, Gerald felt fatigued hanging on him like a wet blanket. He sat down to collect himself when Miller walked up to him.

"On your feet," he said.

Gerald complied as best as his weary body could. Miller stared at him for a moment and was about to speak when he suddenly tilted his head as if he were listening to something. Miller turned back to Gerald. "Get back out there, we'll talk later," He floated up into the sky and was gone in a blink.

∾

GOORGA WAS SEETHING in pain and fury. The splinter that had followed the chosen had been utterly destroyed when the explosion went off in the field. Goorga had not experienced this type of pain since its formative years before the counting of time when it was vulnerable and where it learned the purity of turning pain into fury. It had used this to destroy all its enemies and vowed to destroy this soul. The raw power the chosen one was able to hold for one so young was very impressive. Given time this could, would be a creature of vast destruction.

Goorga would devour this soul and take its power carefully, very carefully. It did not want to be at the receiving end of the type of power it could release. Goorga would not give him the time he needed to build up to it but would also be careful and strike at the right time. That splinter it had lost was gone forever. Very few things could destroy a creature of the immaterial so completely. It would feel that loss like a pulled tooth; the cavity would remain to run your tongue over it as a reminder.

GERALD WAS FLOATING through the forest, working on his multitasking skills. He floated while scanning the area, selecting targets then changing speeds while firing. Without physical limitations, he was able to do incredible things, but the mind would take time to expand where those physical limitations could be worn away and he could use more of his power.

He thought back to so many preachers and motivational speakers he had seen on TV and in person. They all preached that you had to believe in yourself, believe in God, push through your limitations, and do what they told you wasn't possible. "Look at me now, Jesus," Gerald blurted out. He quickly stopped and scanned around to make sure no one was around. Wouldn't make them think he was crazy.

Lightning lit up the sky a few miles away from him. It was raining lightning. This in itself didn't concern him much, and neither did the massive explosions until he heard Vora scream so loudly the sonics pushed him back and then what appeared to be a white flash from the opposite side in response. Someone had just fired on a friendly, *his* friendly.

He saw the team heading over from different directions towards the explosions. Gerald flagged them down before they headed over. He didn't want to head into an unknown situation without a semblance of a plan. After a brief discussion, quick hand signals, and a couple of quick options they all flew off. Gerald with Don trailing him quickly locked on the position and flew so quickly into the position that he ended up in the no man's land between both Vora and the unknown opponent. He hoped it was just some sparring, but this didn't feel like that. Vora was all for the violence but she was very careful about the group. *She wouldn't unleash on one of us.* He knew this instinctively and when he got sideswiped by a snowstorm concentrated into a massive javelin, he had his answer. The ice and snow he collided with caused excruciating pain and knocked him into a group of trees that exploded on impact with him. That wasn't someone in his group.

Gerald got back up and flew back into the fight. He had been knocked a good mile or two away based on the path of destruction he left. It looked like a plane had crashed and left a furrow in the ground.

When Gerald got back, he spotted the source of the conflict. It was a tall grim-looking man with short, blond hair. A lean Ivan Drago would be the best way to explain this man. He had wind and snow whipping around him and he was confronted by Don.

Vora was furious and surrounding her was a lightning storm she was generating, she was a proper Valkyrie. Gerald surveyed the situation, and right before Don was about to spring at the Iceman, Gerald stopped him. "HOLD!" he bellowed. He yelled so loud that his sonic blast that carried the word disrupted both Vora's lightning field and the stranger's ice storm.

Don stood down and Gerald flew right in front of the stranger. He felt others come around to surround the stranger. To his credit, he didn't flinch as Gerald approached him. "Cease-fire," Gerald said, loud enough for all to hear without any sonic booming. "Who are you?" He knew if he started aggressively it would get violent, and he didn't want to start something with an unknown.

The stranger didn't respond but he did stop the ice storm. He seemed very intent on Gerald, though, which made him feel uncomfortable. "I'm not going to ask again, who are you?" Gerald held eye contact with the stranger. He felt Vora moving from behind him "Hold!" he snapped at her, and she stopped. He waited for the stranger to answer.

"You the one who let off that blast?" The stranger had a soft voice filled with the promise of violence. He didn't have to speak loudly; he was someone used to dominating. Gerald understood men like this. They respected strength first. Men like this were dangerous because if they weren't the strongest, they would either follow, try to dominate, or come behind you to cut you down. Gerald knew in his bones that this man wasn't a sneak, but he wasn't someone who would follow others easily.

"You always answer a question with a question?" Gerald replied. He took a step closer to the man as he said it. The man tilted his head like a dog would when it didn't understand what was happening. The silence lay heavy as Gerald waited for the man to respond. He understood the game and he would make the man reply before answering.

The stranger seemed to come to a decision and replied, "I'm

called The Penitent." Clearly, it was said to impress him. Gerald did think it was cool but he wouldn't let on.

"That a first name or a last name or some kind of Madonna or Bono thing?" Gerald replied back. This threw The Penitent off for a beat as confusion played over his face for a fraction of a second. You could have missed it but Gerald was waiting for it, so he pressed further. "Who are you? Why have you attacked my friend? I assume you are part of another group like ours, but I expected better behavior than this."

Vora responded first. "He feels like Jarl, like you, but not like you. He is cold on inside."

Gerald didn't so much as twitch but he piggybacked on Vora's statement. "This true, Iceman? You part of another group?"

The Penitent was staring at Vora with a hooded look that was hard to read. "Yes, I am the leader of another group. I was following her when she sensed me and just attacked me. By rights, I demand an apology and demand punishment for this transgression."

Gerald was surprised to hear Vora attacked first but he didn't let it show, also he didn't believe him for a second. This one was playing the game, looking for a crack where he could assert dominance. *He is good, this guy,* Gerald thought. "She is a Valkyrie," Gerald stated. He didn't mean to say that, but it felt true. "She is honor bound to only attack when threatened. She wouldn't be callous about attacking. Why were you following her?" The answer came in his silence. "ANSWER ME!" Gerald boomed. The blast he let off knocked The Penitent back a few steps and caused his ears to bleed but he still didn't reply.

Instead, Gerald felt rather than saw figures moving into an ambush position behind him and Don. More importantly, he felt rather than saw the rest of his team move up and take positions behind this other group. Gio flared up and grew into a giant with massive firearms in both hands. David was in the giant werewolf form and had what appeared to be the local flora and fauna moving into positions around the other group. That concerned Gerald. He didn't want animals, no matter how deadly, to be hurt, so he hoped things would go no further.

The promise of violence hung thick in the air. One wrong move and there could be deaths. After a few moments and an understanding of how his people were now the ambushed and not the ambushers, The Penitent smiled and with a nod, his people left. He was about to leave but Gerald wasn't ready for that. "HOLD," he barked at The Penitent. Gerald walked up to him until they were no more than a hand's width away. Gerald had followed the crumbs The Penitent had left for him. This Penitent had followed Vora once Gerald had let off the blast. He knew Vora was part of his group and didn't want an open conflict with Gerald. The blast must have spooked The Penitent, so he had decided to come at him from another angle. Luckily Gerald had made sure that the entire team was in the area before he had moved in. This was another power move by The Penitent. If he didn't think he could take Gerald, he would beat him with strategy. Too bad Gerald had dotted his Is and had them hold back out of range in case of something like this.

Gerald leaned in and whispered, "You want a shot at the title, you come to me. You don't go through my people again, you understand?"

The Penitent's eyes widened for a second then went back to that unreadable mask. He nodded at Gerald, then turned around and left.

Gio, who was back to normal size again, came up to Gerald. "Well, that was exciting. Who the fuck was that guy?"

21

JARL

Gerald landed at the front door of Sergeant Miller's cabin. He was apprehensive because Miller wasn't known to be the chatty type, and after the events that happened the day before, he accepted the fact that he may end up regenerating his arms and legs for a few days.

The front door opened on its own. "Enter," Miller commanded from inside.

Gerald didn't hesitate and walked through the door. He was surprised to find a cozy, lived-in cabin with modern art pieces highlighted by Van Gogh's *Starry Night* hanging over a fireplace that was burning a warm moderate flame.

Miller was sitting at a farmer's table with bench seating on both sides. On that table appeared to be a bottle of red wine. Miller nodded towards the bottle.

"Yes, please," Gerald replied. He sat down as Miller poured him a glass.

"Made here. The soil is good and not very humid in this region," he explained as they clinked glasses.

"Cheers," Gerald said, then sniffed it and took a sip. He took in the flavors of the wine which ranged from slightly dry to soothing sweetness. It was damn good. "Wow, that is good. Maybe if the war thing doesn't work out you can start your own winery."

For the first time, Miller smiled. A warm smile that friends shared over a glass of wine. "Don't tempt me."

They both sat there in comfortable silence. Gerald recognized that something was going on, but it seemed unlikely Miller would offer him wine and then pull his arms and legs off. "So." Gerald tried to get the conversation going.

"Hmm?" Miller didn't say anything else, but he didn't have to. "Am I here because of the bomb thing?"

Miller nodded "That and the other thing."

So he knows about the altercation, Gerald thought.

"What you did in the field yesterday was very impressive. We don't have many souls or beings who could have done that much damage. You need to harness it as soon as you can. That kind of heat is going to draw attention to you. You understand what I am telling you?"

Gerald thought back to yesterday. "The Penitent," Gerald stated and Miller nodded. "Did you send him?"

Miller raised an eyebrow then shook his head.

"You were aware of him, though. Who is he?"

From the thin smile on Miller's face, he wasn't a fan. "This goes no further, you understand?" Miller waited for Gerald to nod. "He is someone that some feel shouldn't be here. By here I don't mean in Service, I mean Heaven."

Gerald didn't know what to say to this so he poured them both more wine and sat and drank for a bit. "So this Penitent who should or should not be in Heaven started stalking me once he saw I could do some damage." Gerald corrected himself. "No, it was because I was a threat to him. I saw he was someone that always needs to be on top, no matter what."

Miller nodded "What else?"

Gerald thought back and focused on the details of The Penitent. "He tried to goad me into testing himself against me. He wouldn't make the first move, but he pushed Vora into it. He's smart and wiley, not sneaky perhaps but he has subtly." Miller had straightened up and was fixed on Gerald. "He won't stop trying until he finds a weakness. The good news is he's predictable now that I have picked up the pattern. Still dangerous. His team will be formidable, too."

Miller nodded and spoke. "And that's why you're here. Between the power potential you have and your leadership skills, I'm making you the leader. What does Vora call you?" He asked. Gerald replied, "Jarl." Gerald felt the weight of the responsibility upon him. Some men were born to lead. He understood he was one of those men, but the burden of leadership held a terrible cost. The lives of his people were in his hands. He hated it. He knew eventually some would fall. It was the way of war, the way of the universe. Blood would always be on your hands no matter how hard you washed.

Miller broke him out of his sullen thinking. "We will be starting the final phase of training camp. Your group will be competing against the other groups. This will provide you with going against an opponent and also work on honing your team into a lean clean fighting machine. Finally, get you clowns into some shit."

22

KHOSENRINN FDEAÐ

As the group stood at attention, Miller announced that the next step in their training would commence, but some important matters needed tending to.

"Alright, team, now we will be preparing for live fire drills and competing with the other groups. I know you have already met a group leader," he said, referring to the situation with The Penitent. "Two things need to be addressed a-fucking-sap! One, your leader has been chosen. Puke! Excuse me, Jarl Puke, get up here"

Gerald hurried up and stood at attention in front of Miller. "Turn around and face your team." Gerald complied. "Look upon the faces of your brothers and sisters. Pledge to them loyalty, faith, and sacrifice," Miller stated.

"I so pledge," Gerald stated. He waited for Miller to say more, but nothing came, the man was not forthcoming. "I also pledge I will do all I can to get you back home, no matter what."

Miller looked over at Gerald and nodded.

Vora was very excited. "Yes, Jarl, how do you say? it looks good on you. Hip people say this, yes?" She stated. Everyone looked at her for a second. "What, I read the Cosmo, very good tips, look nice, be cool."

No one openly laughed but there were some snickers. Miller rolled his eyes, and Gordon stayed stock still like a statue until Gio elbowed him. Gordon turned beet red but didn't say a word.

"Second issue!" Miller bellowed. "What in the fuck is your team name? We need one, so let's have it."

Gerald signaled for them to huddle up.

"What about The Fellas?" Gio asked.

"Terrible, I no fella," Vora said.

"Good point, how about the Wolf Pack?" David added. The group shook their heads.

"The Bashers?" Don added. Another no go.

"Bulldogs?" Gerald gave it a try. Pass on that one.

They were stumped Until Vora spoke up. "I am Valkyrie." She stated to Gordon. "You are man of medicine." She pointed to Don. "You have power of heart." To David, she said, "The great wolf howls within you." She clapped Gio on the back. "You talk much." They all laughed, and she turned to Gerald. "You are Jarl. You have great power." She stopped and addressed the team. "Why we here?"

"We were asked to be here," David answered.

"Ja, why?" She walked up to David. "Why you, son of Fenrir, why not your best friend or father, why you, why us all?"

Everyone went stock still.

"We not special. We know better people than us, except maybe you Don. You are very nice." Vora was so passionate that the group could feel it, feel what she was getting at. "We picked because we strong up here," Vora pointed at her head. "And here" Then she pointed at her heart. "Each of us, we fight the evil, in our way, ja?" Everyone just looked at each other and then back to her.

"Ack!" She turned in a circle. "I pick you, I pick you," she said and pointed at Gordon then Don, and so on.

"We're chosen," Gio said.

Vora froze, walked up, and smacked Gio in the arm. "Ja, chosen" Vora's wheels were turning and then it hit her. "Khosenrinn fdeað, it means Chosen Dead. We are Chosen Dead!" she exclaimed.

"I love it," Gio said and looked over at Gordon. "Chief, you got a keeper there."

"Ja, he knows." Vora proclaimed.

23

GETTING INTO SOME SHIT

Khosenrinn Fdeað lined up together as an official team for the first time. Gerald was their Jarl or Captain or Sergeant or whatever they wanted him to be called. He was their leader, and they were the Chosen Dead.

Miller approached and explained that for the next few weeks, they would be drilling as a team, and each person's strengths and weaknesses would be utilized to conform within the team and maximize what it could accomplish. Base tactics like the phalanx, wedge formation, pincer move, shield wall, and all the ancient tried-and-true formations-and-tactics were discussed. Guerilla tactics were also reviewed heavily as most teams were normally outnumbered twenty to one, so discretion had to be the better part of valor.

Additional trainers were brought in so that there was actual opposition to the drills and maneuvers they were running. The team was exposed to live fire and had to work through the pain, instantly healing on the move, and adjusting tactics on the fly.

A few things started to become very apparent. Vora and Don were lunatics. They would charge into the heaviest fire and just destroy whatever was in front of them. "This won't do," Gerald told the team while they were taking a break. He explained to both Don and Vora that a holding movement was meant to hold and attract fire from the enemy while it allowed time for the rest of the team to circle and capture the objective. "Why? We break wall, the objective is no more." Vora drove the point home by smashing her fist into her open palm.

"We're going to die," Gio said, exhaling.

Gerald glared at Gio to quiet down and continued. "We can't rely on sheer power to do the job every time. A smart adversary will pick up on it and use it against us."

Vora looked at Gerald like he was a simpleton. "We are strong."

Gerald inhaled and then exhaled slowly. "Yes, we are strong, but we need to be strong up here." He pointed at his head. "You understand?"

She nodded.

"You good?" Gerald asked Don who nodded in the affirmative, but Gerald wasn't convinced. Don was drunk on the power he had and was falling in love with it.

The rest of the training period went much the same way. The group was frustrated because their ability to work through training scenarios was being compromised by the two-man wrecking crew.

Gerald was so frustrated at the end of another misfire where Vora and Don ignored orders and wrecked a bunker he smashed the ground in front of them and told them to get their heads on straight. To her credit, Vora tried to hold Don back initially until Don shook her off, and once he smashed through the sandbags, she ran up and fired a lightning storm that not only destroyed the bunker, but also lit Don on fire. He seemed fine with it but the trainers in the bunker were furious but didn't dare say anything because they were afraid of both of them.

During the second break, as the team walked out of the

training area, Gerald saw Miller speaking in low tones to some of the trainers and from Miller's body language, it wasn't good. Gerald stopped and waited.

Gio came up last and patted Gerald on the arm, "How are you doing champ?"

Gerald saw Miller was done and looked directly at him. "Ok. I'll talk to you in a bit." Gio took one look at Miller and hurried off.

Miller walked up to Gerald. "A word?" Miller started walking and Gerald followed. "How do you think it went today?"

Gerald got an icy feeling in his gut but answered, "I thought it went ok. Some positives for sure on how powerful the team is, very flexible…"

"Horseshit! Your group of retards couldn't follow simple directions," Miller bellowed. "That crazy bitch and Godzilla couldn't keep it in their pants. What the fuck are you going to do about it?"

Gerald thought about it for a moment. "I think I have a plan to take care of it."

Miller glared at Gerald. "That plan better be stomping some asses and getting them in line. You may be the leader now but that can change, you got me?"

Gerald nodded. "Loud and clear sir."

"Those trainers were telling me that the group The Penitent is leading is shaping up to be the best one by far. We were supposed to challenge them, but not after today. Everyone will hear about this performance. Your team will be a joke." Miller shot up into the sky and disappeared before Gerald could react.

As he headed back to the team, he took his time. Miller knew that stomping asses didn't normally work when they were alive unless it was a last resort. This was a test, of course. Gerald had to lead his way. He wanted to develop trust within the group, and with all these new powers he knew the allure to use them as a crutch was strong. Discipline was the key. They had to follow orders or they would all end up dead, again.

When Gerald reached the group, the murmuring stopped. Everyone waited for him to speak. "We need to talk about what happened today. Anyone want to start?" Gerald stated.

Don raised his hand and stood. "Pretty well?"

Gerald shook his head. Don deflated and sat down. "Vora, how do you think we did?" He asked.

Vora stood up and did a double thumbs up. "Many asses were kicked, ja?!"

Gerald blew out some air. "Ja, many asses were kicked but the problem is it was mainly our asses. Miller chewed my ass out afterwards, so I got nothing left back there."

Vora looked perplexed. "We destroy objective every time. What can be wrong?"

Gio groaned and Vora turned to him.

"What is it?"

Gio looked over to Gerald. "You weren't being strong up here." Gio pointed at his head. "We need to work together, and between you and Don over there, we can't get anything done."

Vora looked perplexed.

"He means we need to work on being smarter, work on timing, and when to strike. Miller was embarrassed. He said we were supposed to compete for the top group against The Penitent but he doesn't think we are even close to that."

Upon saying his name, Vora's face darkened like a thundercloud. "Ack, he is asshole." She spat on the ground, where she spat the ground froze.

"We need to listen and follow orders. You understand?" She nodded then Gerald addressed the whole team. "You disobey orders you can get your teammates killed. Don, I know it feels good to be stronger than the Hulk, but I need you to control yourself. If not, I am benching you, and you could be sent home. I need you to follow orders"

Don nodded and deflated further. It was quite disarming as it looked like a giant toddler pouting. Gerald was tempted to put an arm around Don but he needed to think about what he was doing.

When the team assembled again for the next set of drills, Gerald approached Miller. "Sir, can we speak?" he asked. Miller nodded and they floated up out of earshot. "I have a plan," Gerald stated then continued. "Don is the bigger problem. He's drunk on his power. I think he will follow orders after we talk but I want to make sure. Vora will follow once we get this squared away."

Miller nodded and then snapped his fingers. "I got just the thing. This wasn't supposed to happen till tomorrow but we can do it now. You idiots would blow up half the planet if we let this continue" Miller explained what he was going to do.

Gerald saluted and went back to the group. Once he was among the Chosen Dead, Miller addressed them. "Listen up, we're going to start the drill shortly but we are going to introduce an equalizer." He produced a device that appeared to wrap around a person's neck. It had a wood mixed with metal appearance. "This is a dampener. Once it is attached to your neck, you will be unable to use your powers and will revert to being a mortal again."

Miller paused to allow them time to reflect. He wanted to clamp a dampener down on both Vora and Don but Gerald had an idea that he hoped would work. Otherwise, it could be his last day as Jarl of the Khosenrinn fdeað. "When the drills are run if you are captured or disabled you will be forced to wear the dampener. You will still run the drills but without the benefit of your powers. Also, you will not heal so the pain will be excruciating." Miller looked around. "Dismissed."

The team got together and Gerald could see the reality sink in for Don. He hoped that would do the trick, otherwise he would have to turn things up a notch. "OK, guys, let's be smart, concise, and effective. We're not the hammer, we're the blade." Gerald looked each of them in the eye "For the Khosenrinn fdeað!" he bellowed.

They responded with an "Ahh oo" and went about their business. The objective was a bunker on a hill. They were prevented from flying up the hill due to heavy storms floating around the bunker. Even Vora couldn't ride up using lightning; she tried and was forced back down.

Gerald decided on a stagger attack up the hill. He had them in groups of two: one fired up, the other provided a shield. They would move and rotate so the one firing would be the shield and vice versa. The firepower that crashed down upon them was incredible. Massive ice spears, and lightning in concentrated patterns. Huge shells better suited to a destroyer were raining down upon them.

It took all Gerald's concentration to maintain a shield while Gio fired back up and took out the gun placements to lessen some of the firepower. The armor was thick so a direct hit was required to destroy them before the trainers reversed the damage.

Gerald had separated Vora and Don. Don was with Dave and so far so good. Dave was shielding them while Don could unleash massive concussive blasts that were taking out two placements at a time. When they moved and the roles reversed Don did an excellent job of shielding David.

Vora was with Gordon who was throwing up his shields and deftly moving them because Vora was sending a blanket of lightning that served as a shield while also destroying everything that it came into contact with.

The team was doing swimmingly...until they neared the top.

Whatever was protecting the bunker was impressive, as the combined might of the team couldn't damage the bunker and gun placements. Gerald ordered the team to hold their positions and then had them focus their fire on the closest gun placement in all their relative positions. This way he could order David to get between them before they started firing again and go after the trainers who were repairing the placements, once they were distracted the rest of the team could close in on the position and nullify the Bunker.

Don transferred to shield duty quickly and once David started firing bolts of energy at the focus point, the rest of the team followed suit. Vora was able to deflect a lot of the firepower this close to the bunker due to the limited room available. Any living being caught in this firestorm would have been obliterated.

Once the targeted gun placement was destroyed, David didn't hesitate and ran right through the hole created for him. He disappeared in a haze of smoke and fire backlit with lightning.

Once he was out of sight, Don stepped up and tried to create a wedge between the two gun placements. Gerald placed his shields around Don while Gio switched to protecting Gerald. Gordon moved over so that he could protect Gio, and Vora was using her lightning storm to protect and destroy anything that came for Gordon. After a few moments, we could hear muffled explosions and screams. David had made contact.

"Move up!" Gerald ordered. This maneuver would never have worked in life as they were purposely moving into a kill zone so they could make it easier to force entry once David took out the trainers repairing the gun placements. A much louder blast ensued, and the guns went quiet. "Charge!" Gerald yelled immediately.

The whole team moved in with Don leading the way. He sent

such a blast of force that he blew a hole where the opening was so that more than two people could go through the space.

"Hold!" David screamed from inside the bunker. No one could see him but the team heard him. "There's more of them in here than we thought!" he added. "Don't enter until I can clear a path." They could hear more explosions and a large flash of light "Stay out!" He yelled and more explosions followed.

The gun placements started winding up and began firing on them as well. The fire began to intensify as additional trainers surrounded them and added to the onslaught. The first signs of concern began to show on the faces of the team members. Even Gio, who had fought in the war, showed concern.

Gerald scanned the area and realized he needed to make the hard choice. "Pull back!" he yelled over the din. "Pull back, we need to regroup!"

Don, who was taking and receiving heavy punishment, looked wild-eyed.

"Don, get back here now!" Gerald screamed.

Don looked spooked and his eyes kept darting towards the entrance.

"Pull back right now!" Gerald screamed again. "We have no idea what is in there. Get back, now!"

Don was torn but he started to inch back. Gerald threw up shields to cover Don's retreat. A massive explosion followed by David screaming changed the game. Don heard him scream and immediately headed for the door.

"Goddamn it!" Gerald screamed. He turned to the rest of the team. "Stay back!" he yelled as he moved forward. He would try and make cover for Don so that he wasn't torn apart from the back.

Before Don could make it fully through the entrance, he was blasted back right into Gerald who luckily was able to throw up a shield so he wasn't flattened by Don's bulk. They ended in a heap taking intense fire that riddled their bodies with flames, energy blasts, plasma, and shells until Vora sent a shield to cover them

Don got back up and began to inhale. As he did so, he grew larger and larger. The intense fire seemed to bounce off him and he charged straight into the opening. As he hit the group of trainers at the entrance, everyone expected him to slice through them like butter. The exact opposite happened as Don hit the entrance. He struck an invisible barrier that caused the very walls to crack and get pushed back. He tried to keep pushing through and when it seemed he would make it, there was a massive explosion, and everything went black.

24

REPERCUSSIONS

Gerald awoke with a start, face down in the dirt. He turned himself over and sat up. The entire bunker was gone. The explosion had obliterated it right at the base.

What was left of a labyrinth was a shattered collection of walls used as kill zones and the stubs of murder holes. Gerald could see why David didn't see the hidden trainers initially, as he was expertly drawn in. Thankfully, only David had gone in, otherwise, things could have been worse which was saying a lot.

The Chosen Dead approached and they pulled Gerald to his feet. "You alright?" Gio asked. Gerald nodded. He noticed that Don and David were missing, and he got an icy feeling in his guts. *Are they dead?* he thought.

He scanned the area and saw Miller standing with the very alive Don and David. Miller waved Gerald over. He arrived to find that both Don and David had dampeners attached to their necks. "That almost wasn't a shit show." Miller motioned to Don and Dave. "These two knuckleheads got their balls clipped. Lucky it was only these two."

Miller floated up so that the whole area could hear him. "Listen up," he bellowed to the team along with the trainers standing together away from the team. "We're going to run it back. Same scenario, same group. Any questions?"

"You said the same group, sir?" Gerald asked as he stepped forward.

"That is correct. This includes the two that have been neutralized. You must incorporate them into the plan as you see fit, but they will not stay on the sidelines. Dismissed!" Miller floated off, leaving the team to stare at them. The trainers started to leave. Some shook their heads at the team and a few snickered. This was a hole that without any hope left to climb out of.

Gerald called the team together. He saw fear, he saw worry, he saw shame in a few eyes. What he also saw was resolve. No one was giving up. They all looked to him and he would not let them down.

Don came up to Gerald and hugged him. "I'm sorry." Gerald didn't know what to think but then David hugged Gerald, then Vora. "I'm not hugging him," Gio said, Gordon gave a slight nod in agreement as he would not be part of the hugging either.

He then smirked. "Now you know what we have been trying to get through that head of yours. You lose control, it hurts the team."

Gerald separated and made direct eye contact with Vora. "If this was impossible, he wouldn't have us do this right?" They nodded. "We got too caught up in all the superpowers. We need to think of a plan and execute it. Measure twice, cut once, got it?" he bellowed.

"Sir yes sir" they yelled back.

"Let's get to work," Gerald said and motioned them over. "Here is the key to our victory." He extended his arm and a wristwatch materialized on his wrist.

"Is bomb?" Vora asked.

"Is it a laser beam like in the Bond movies?" Gio asked.

"No," Gerald said.

"It tells time?" Don asked.

"That is correct," Gerald said.

"Nothing else?" David added.

"No, it is a simple watch. I want you all to materialize one. Vora, add one for Don, Gio add one for David please." Once they all had a wristwatch, Gerald continued. "Ok, we need to coordinate an attack plan based on timing because David and Don are not going to be able to hear or see us and vice versa."

"Are you going to sneak attack them?" Gordon asked.

"In a manner of speaking, yes. We're going to need to create weapons, armor, and shielding for both David and Don so that they can survive what is going to be coming at them. I am assuming they won't pay much attention to them since they are very limited. If they do unload on them, then that will make things even more difficult."

Gerald then went on with what he had in mind. The team, upon hearing the plan, added their pieces to it so that by the time they were done they were 70 percent confident it would work.

The Chosen Dead walked back to the base of the hill. Everything was as it had been before Don had blown off the top of the hill.

Miller was there to greet them. "Are you ready to go?"

"Yes sir," Gerald replied. Miller looked over Don and David who both had their armor on, along with shield generators and multiple guns and knives, and nodded his approval "What's the gun shoot?" he asked David.

"Sir, this is a pulse rifle sir, uh, laser gun, sir."

Miller smirked, "I know what it is, puppy chow. How many rounds do you get per clip?"

Don responded, "Twenty thousand shots per clip sir. We have fifteen clips that any one of the team can recharge instantly."

Miller seemed impressed. "Who came up with it?" he asked the team.

Gio stepped forward. "That's me, sir. I was a gun nut in life and loved science fiction movies. I patterned the guns after a gaming system I used to like to read books on. They used this style rifle because it was easy to recreate and easy to charge up."

Miller nodded. "Very good. I see the shield generators as well. Those won't hold up long if they use the big guns."

Gerald stepped in. "We know, sir, but we have no other choice. We know we're in the hole, but we can make sure they are as ok as they can be."

Miller nodded. More importantly, the trainers listening heard everything they said.

The Chosen Dead got into position and as soon as Miller gave the signal, Vora and Gordon created a mound at the bottom of the hill that David and Don took cover behind, and they started firing up the hill. They would fire at predetermined gun placements and then the team would pour fire into those areas so they could advance.

The Chosen Dead moved methodically up the hill at a steady pace. The strain of having two fewer team members able to add fire and shields was a strain, but so far they were all handling it fairly well. The issue was time. The team was halfway up the hill, and as Gerald looked back down the hill, the cover built for Don and Dave was being chewed away. They hadn't been hit with many of the larger shells, but they hadn't been ignored either.

Don and David started with a cover fifteen feet high and twenty feet wide with holds so they could move around and fire from different angles.The cover was half that size and getting smaller at way too fast a rate. The plan required them to hold out for a few more minutes.

Gerald checked his watch, and there were still two minutes

till the first phase was completed. "Can anyone reinforce the cover?" he asked.

"I will." Vora waved her hand and a piece of the lightning storm she had attacking the nearest gun placement broke off and covered Don and David. Even with the extra cover, it only lasted another thirty seconds.

Gerald did the math and knew that their cover would be gone in the next minute, which meant a change in plans. "Anyone else give them cover? We won't make it to zero," Gerald yelled.

No one on the team could provide additional cover as they began taking more firepower from trainers as well on the ridge. That concerned but did not surprise Gerald. He would have provided the cover, but he was using his energy on something else.

Things went sideways when a volley of shells hit the cover mound and blasted it away. It left Don and David exposed, and they began taking heavy fire. They were moving pretty well back and forth but eventually, their shields blew out. David's shield blew in a shower of white lightning and static. This was followed by a hail of fire that was brought down on them.

They both continued to fire back but eventually, it became too much. David got knocked out while Don kept firing and tried to stay in front of David until his shield exploded. When the smoke cleared both David and Don were gone.

Gerald took advantage of the pause in the action. The trainers and gun placements tried to figure out what was going on. "Charge!" he ordered and the Chosen Dead followed. They made it up to the entrance which provided some cover as the gun placements couldn't fire on their own bunker entrance.

The team strengthened their shields and waited the last fifty-seven seconds before phase two would begin. He just hoped that Don and David would be where they were supposed to be.

The firepower, though lessened, was still considerable. Down below at the base of the hill, Gerald could see trainers moving through the wreckage of multiple gun placements lying behind where they had the coverage for Don and David. He saw them signal and a few shrugged their heads. Gerald smiled. The jig was up and hopefully, they were in position.

When the exercise was started and the cover was being built, Gio had added in multiple gun placements using the same laser fire that their firearms were using. As per the plan, Gerald had taken control of the gun placements. Gio had also created realistic illusions that Gerald reinforced so they looked solid, and it was Gio who had answered Miller's questions. Gio was given control of the illusions as well, so he moved them around to different areas. He used the closest gun placements to fire so it appeared to all watching David and Don were moving around their cover to not stay sitting ducks.

The firepower suddenly increased as trainers moved off the walls and positioned closer to the entrance. The team returned fire while holding shields in place.

Gio was the first to have his shields fail. He took direct fire which pinned him to the wall. Gerald moved over and stood next to him so he didn't have to expand his range too far while also returning fire.

Gordon was next and Vora covered him while recovering from his injuries. Both instances took no longer than four or five seconds but they felt like an eternity.

Gerald checked his watch, and they still had twenty-nine seconds before phase two. He was beginning to think his plan was complete shit but it was too late now. He had to execute the plan and rely on his teammates.

Vora started to falter but Gordon, who looked exhausted, placed his hand on her shoulder and bolstered her. Gio was back in the fight and had scooped out the wall he was up against so that from a side angle you couldn't see him. It was smart; it prevented anything from straight on fire from even coming close to hitting him.

The fire lessened for a second but then redoubled. It fired directly at and around Gio which caused large chunks to be blown away. The trainers decided weakening the wall was a small price to pay for what appeared to be a certain victory.

25

DON AND DAVE SNEAKING AROUND

Don and Dave had stayed completely still until they saw that their ploy with the fake versions of them had worked. They were both armored and armed with the energy weapons Gio had created along with the shield generators but there was something else that wasn't accounted for. Gordon had imbued them with some of his ability to cloak themselves so they were invisible in multiple spectrums, not just sight. The armor they wore had been enhanced as well. It had been energized so that it functioned like an exoskeleton and allowed Don and Dave to climb up sheer rock walls and move at great speed.

David had noticed that he couldn't even get Gordon's scent when he went dark. Don drew on all his reserves so that he could stay still. He admired the way David could stay stock still and didn't even flinch when a large shell blew right by them. Don felt that old fear from when he was alive creep up and try to send him into a panic, doubts born of the physical weakness he had endured. A life spent trying to just crawl let alone walk rose like a leviathan from the depths to drag him down.

Don flinched when the shooting began, and David looked over at him. They made eye contact with each other. David ignored the tears running down Don's face. He knew what he was dealing with. David loved Don for his strength along with his goodness. They all did. He didn't want to see Don in pain but he also needed Don to overcome yet again and get moving. Their team needed them. He knew what he had to do.

Don felt himself becoming dislodged from reality. He was shaking like a leaf and was on the verge of running until David looked over at him and nodded. David then took out the chalk-board Gerald had created so they could communicate without speaking. On the board was written Khosenrinn fdeað. Don inhaled once and then he stopped shaking. The words on that board were why he was here, standing on a hill with his friend, trying to save his friends from the hell that was pouring down on them. A hell he had helped inflict on them by not listening, by letting his emotions run away from him.

The fear turned to anger. What kind of person would he be, Don thought, if he allowed fear to take away what he had fought for his whole life? Gerald had given both he and David a task even after their failure. Don appreciated how smart Gerald was for coming up with a plan that gave both of them a chance to directly contribute to victory. Don would reward that confidence in him.

Don looked back into David's eyes and nodded. The grim, hard look on Don's face told David that he was ready to go. They had a deadline to meet, and they were down to three minutes and twenty seconds to get into position.

Don and Dave started moving up and away from the gun placements. The hill that the team had to take had elevated rock walls at both ends, so they were forced to run the gamut of the guns with almost zero cover. As per the plan, they got behind the nearest gun placement and climbed up and around the base of it as quickly as possible. The team had concentrated their fire-power on the opposite placement, but they needed to be quick because once the team destroyed that placement, they would focus on the one Don and David were.

A large explosion signaled that the opposite gun placement had been destroyed so they both knew that the team would begin firing on Don and David's position. They were both a hundred feet above the placement when they stopped moving. Their energy was limited regarding the cloaking factor Gordon had provided for them.

Gordon had warned them to hold still if they were near a large explosion because the shields that protected them could interfere with the cloaking. Gordon was incorrect; that wasn't the issue. The issue is that when you have a very large explosion that shoots fire and debris for hundreds of feet, it will hit your position. The shield bubble protecting Don and David would become pronounced when the wall of fire and burning metal suddenly bounced off of an invisible barrier on an otherwise flat cliff wall.

Don and David froze. They both could see how the shield unnaturally deflected the flaming wreckage. They watched as trainers appeared above at the top of the cliff wall. Don knew what needed to be done. He signaled for David to turn off the shields.

Don turned his shield off and then David nodded his acknowledgement and did the same. Don signaled for them to start moving. They split off and slowly went diagonally up the wall so they could continue to get away from the spot but also move up closer to the target. David had to move further away for the moment to ensure that if one got hit then the other was still available to complete the mission.

After the trainers surveyed the spot where the anomaly occurred, they opened fire on the area. It looked like a waterfall made of fire hit the area. Of course, no anomaly showed up, so they spread the fire out along the wall to sweep it clean. David was able to move up quickly enough so that he was almost at the lip of the cliff wall, so he was able to remove himself from getting fired upon. Don wasn't able to move as quickly, so as he was about to remove himself from the line of fire, he was hit in the right arm by an energy blast.

The armor took the worst of it and thankfully there was enough fire so that it just looked like another energy blast ricocheting off the cliff wall. The pain was excruciating, Don was almost blown off the wall, and from that height, he would have been disabled and unable to continue. Don held onto the wall and braced himself using the exoskeleton of the armor to support himself. If another shot hit him without the shield on that would be it, either they would see him and blow him off the wall or he would be knocked off because it was likely one arm wouldn't be enough even with the help of the armor.

He could see the trainer above scanning the area where they were, and Don followed his eyes as he scanned right over his spot.

The trainer was preparing to fire when a head trainer came up to them from behind.

"What the hell are you doing?" the Head Trainer bellowed.

"Sir, just scanning, I think..."

"We have the team accounted for. I need you to pour firepower where it's needed, with the bulk of the team moving their way up the hill." he said "Now!" the head Trainer screamed.

The trainer immediately moved off. Don stayed frozen in place as the head trainer moved closer to the wall, and his eyes changed colors as he scanned through multiple spectrums. Don had never been so afraid in his entire life. He knew that he would be blown right off the wall and worse yet, leave David alone to finish the job.

After what seemed an eternity the head trainer was satisfied and stopped scanning and disappeared. Don waited an extra moment to ensure the head trainer was gone and started to climb up the wall. His right arm was useless, but he was able to use the armor to allow it to help him to climb up the wall. The pain was still really bad, as he wasn't able to heal himself, but he gritted his teeth through it.

When he was at the top of the cliff he was startled when an arm grabbed him. He let out a short cry which he curbed when he saw it was David who had grabbed him to help him up. They both froze, as there were still trainers nearby, but thankfully a gun placement exploded right when he yelled which covered it.

Don waited for David and when David gave him the signal, he boosted himself up with his legs and David pulled. When they were both at the top of the cliff, David patted Don on the shoulder, smiled, and gave him a thumbs up. He showed the watch time which showed a minute and thirty-two seconds. The team was about to take their position up in front of the bunker entrance.

Don and David moved away and around the trainers and quickly got into position as the fake versions of themselves were discovered. They used the moment of indecision to get themselves over the top of the bunker. The team was in position at the entrance. More importantly, the bunker had a hole at the top which was out of sight from the front of the bunker. This top was used by the trainers to fly in and out of the bunker without being seen and allow for clear sight lines to direct the flow of fire.

Gauging the distance from the top of where they were jumping wouldn't be ideal, as there would be a good possibility of getting injured. They saw movement around them increase while additional trainers were moved up and around to scan the ledge of the hill, no doubt looking for Don and David.

Don pointed down and waved to David to follow him. David nodded and Don started down the face of the cliff headfirst.

They both felt a slight buzz from their armor when it notified them that the power cells for both suits were below twenty percent. This was going to be a problem. They needed the speed and the armor provided to get down the wall swiftly. Otherwise, they would need to drain the shields and weapons, but first things first: they had to get in position, and they only had another minute to do so.

Don gingerly started climbing down. His right arm wasn't any good, and he didn't want to drain the armor too much by using it to help himself.

David also began climbing down but he went headfirst like a giant spider and made good time. Don looked up and saw that trainers were searching for them from the cliff ledge. He tried to climb down as quickly as possible without causing too great a disturbance along the cliff wall. He looked down and David had already made it to the bottom. He had his firearm trained up top in case someone spotted Don.

Time slowed as Don made his way down. The explosions and ordinance going off provided cover as well. but Don didn't breathe until he made it to the bottom along with David. They both looked down and could see the labyrinth the team would have to go through. That was what presented the problem; from the entrance to twenty-five yards in, the labyrinth had a ceiling, so they couldn't fly up until it was too late because the trainers could easily corner them and take them out. David had first-hand experience of just that happening. It was why he now had the dampener on his neck.

Don pointed and David could see the objective at the center of the bunker. It was a glowing orb they had to grab, but there were at least five trainers surrounding the orb along with multiple gun placements. For the team outside this was doable, but for Don and David, there was no way they could take out the trainers and gun placements, more importantly, they didn't have much energy for cloaking left. They only had ten seconds to get into position and no way to get there in time.

David had an idea. He tapped Don on the arm and pointed to the other location they needed to get to. David took off, exerting the last of his armor's cell power. Once he was in position on the other side of the ledge, David gave Don the thumbs up and jumped. Don was stunned. The fall wouldn't kill him, but it would disable him. Don didn't do any more thinking, but instead took his leap of faith.

David hit the ground at high velocity, and he felt his leg buckle and then flare into white-hot pain. He didn't activate his shields because he still needed them for what would come next. David landed far enough away from the center so that he wasn't seen right away. He heard a series of loud explosions and didn't have to check to know that the team had started their final push into the bunker, so David had to get in position now.

As David tried to put enough pressure on his leg to limp into position, Don also landed. Seeing how badly David's leg was twisted, Don twisted and landed on his bad arm purposely. The pain was incredible. Don had to fight to stay conscious due to the agony he was enduring. It had the result he was hoping for. He was able to get up and move with two good legs.

Don had also heard the explosions and could hear Vora even now screaming like a banshee of old. Their time was up; it was now or never.

David was making his way to his position when the power cell for his stealth cloak died. He had hoped to sneak across to his position at the easternmost point of the center, but he was seen almost immediately without Gordon's stealth energy. The trainers didn't waste any time and they began firing on David. He had no choice but to turn on his shield which was at 3 percent. He wouldn't have enough in the shields to survive what came next, but he also wasn't going to be the reason they failed.

The firepower that hit him next was devastating, which David was counting on as he ran towards his spot. He was hit in the back at an angle which blasted him off his feet and knocked him into a pillar. His shield held 1 percent still as he lay motionless on the ground. A group of trainers surrounded him and David raised his hands.

Don had made it to his side. He saw what little was left of David's shield so he made a decision. Still cloaked, he sprinted over to where David was, laid himself on top of him, and expanded his shield which also made David Disappear.

"Where did he go?" a trainer demanded at zero. Don and David tensed. Don had 6 percent left on his shields. He prayed it would be enough as dual explosions went off.

The blasts were timed to go off on the opposite ends of the chamber to cause as much damage as possible and hopefully destroy some of the labyrinths the main team was slogging through. The trainer standing over Don and David was blown away by the sheer force of the explosion.

The Chosen Dead hit the entrance to the bunker-like a freight train. They blew out the front of the bunker entrance and pushed their way into the labyrinth. The laws of physics were twisted so that as they pushed through they would encounter sections where it was far wider than they should have been even though they entered from a narrow hallway so they had to burn through massive amounts of energy to keep the shields up while the rest of the team got through.

Gerald checked the watch, and they had fifteen seconds left. He had no idea if Don and David had gotten into position, but for all their sakes, he sure hoped so, otherwise they would all be wearing a collar.

Vora was so exhausted, she knelt down on the ground but kept one arm up. Gordon had come up to her and pulled her up without looking away from the barrage of fire that rained down on him. Gio was moving around and laying down fire, but he was taking a lot of punishment as well.

When the watch ticked down to three seconds, Gerald yelled over to Gio to close in. Gio immediately moved up to where Vora and Gordon were. Gerald stood in front and started to pull in energy from all around him. Ignoring the burning pain from the firepower that was supposed to be used against him. He was able to absorb it into his body. Gerald couldn't pull in as much as he had prior because he didn't want to kill anyone and it was painful allowing himself to be shot, but this was a big risk nonetheless. If it was too strong, it could kill his teammates. Too weak and they would fail.

On zero, Gerald released his energy and was thrown back with the double detonations happening at the center. Gordon caught him as Gio and Vora protected them. Gerald was groggy from the use of power and couldn't see very well initially, but he waved his hand forward or what he hoped was forward. Gordon kept him upright as they quickly moved through what was left of the bunker and tried to get to the target before the trainers regrouped.

Vora stepped up and pushed the lightning field ahead of the group. She looked terrible. Her armor was completely torn off on the right side of her body and seemed to be glued with blood and partly burned into her left side.

Gordon didn't look any better. He didn't wear his armor but from the number of wounds left without healing, he looked like a bloody puzzle missing pieces all over the place.

Gio kept moving left to right in a tight pattern and had lost his left arm. He didn't grow it back but had grown a short swivel cannon that he was using to fire on targets to his left. It seemed to be moving on its own accord as well.

Gerald urged the team to keep moving forward. The objective was near and if they could get there in time, they would win the day.

The smoke cleared and he could see it sitting in the remains of the bunker center. Gerald was a mess. His armor was hanging off him in pieces, and he had to rip off the breast plate due to an internal fire causing him pain. He pulled off the plate and was able to quell it so he could focus on laying down fire as the Chosen Dead kept moving. There was no sign of Don and David. Hopefully, they were alright. They had done their duty and gave them the opening they needed to win.

Gordon lifted his head, turned and his eyes widened. He shouted a warning and then leaped directly towards the glowing orb that was the objective. The rest of the team looked behind them to see new gun placements placed at impossible angles along with what appeared to be every trainer firing upon them.

Gerald split his shields to cover the front and back while Gio and Vora rushed forward to back up Gordon who was flying towards the orb at high velocity while taking incoming fire. Gordon was weaving in and around the fire as best he could while heading towards the orb. Something caught his eye. He was within feet of the orb, and that was when he was tackled in mid-air by a trainer who had been buried beneath the rubble near the orb. Gordon tried to twist around and make another pass at the orb, but the trainer sent a spear right through Gordon and proceeded to ignite the spear so that it was surrounded by flame. Gordon saw the look of disbelief on the trainer's face as he halted in mid-air and pushed back towards the orb.

He was closing on the orb when another spear went through him from the side, followed by another close to the same spot and angle. The trainers halted Gordon's momentum and then drove him away from the orb. Two more spears went through Gordon as they pinned him to the ground and set him on fire.

From afar, Gerald watched it happen and felt his heart sink. He was unable to pull in a sizable amount of energy after the major explosion he had let off. He felt hollowed out and worn to the nub, he gritted his teeth and kept pushing. *Come on guys.* He said to himself as he began firing away and was hopeful to try and still make it since there was no sign of Don and David. Vora had gone wild; Surrounded and cut off, she lost all coherent thought and was lashing around her with a storm of such fury that it was incredible anything could survive it. Gio had turned himself into a walking armored gun placement that was firing from all angles.

The trainers weathered the violence and while they fought off the Chosen Dead's firepower a wall jumped up between them and the orb. Now the Trainers were firing down at the Chosen Dead. Even for Souls with as much power as the Chosen Dead, they were at their end.They had pushed past their limits minutes ago, but they knew that to stop now would be a failure. No one was willing to accept it. They absorbed so much punishment that now they were limping and missing limbs.

The trainers used a massive combined push of firepower so that trainers from the side could start using spears on them. Gerald felt two spears go through him and he blasted both trainers off of him, but three more spears followed. In a few more seconds he was pinned to the ground. Vora and Gio were still struggling but it looked like the end for them.

Don had awakened buried under the rubble the double explosions had made. David wasn't conscious but besides the cuts on his face, he didn't look badly damaged. The armor on his back had been blown off, along with his clothes. Don could hear the fighting above him intensify which meant The Chosen Dead were still in the fight.

He started to move and felt immense pain in his back. Don grimaced and pulled David closer so he could get them out of where they were at. He went cold when he saw that David's legs were gone below the knees. "David," Don whispered and shook him gently. David stirred and then grimaced in pain as he came around. "Hold on," Don said and began to shove some of the rubble off them. Don was able to go another half a foot and see that there was now a massive wall where the trainers were firing down upon the Chosen Dead. He couldn't see anything but he could hear Vora screaming.

Don was able to turn his head around and saw on the opposite side of where they were that multiple trainers had pinned down Gordon and set him on fire. Gordon, to his credit, kept moving and wouldn't allow them to ease off for even a second. Don's eyes widened and when he shifted. he felt the heat of the orb near his face. The rate of firepower had drastically reduced so he knew he didn't have much time left.

David, through sheer force of will and with Don pulling, was able to get himself up to see what was going on. "Go ahead," he said

Don smiled, David smiled back, and then Don reached up and touched the orb.

Gerald was able to roll over and snap the spears that had impaled him. He blocked a spear that went through his forearm and then multiple spears impaled him again. He felt multiple minds telepathically pinning him down. As he raged against the mental pressure of multiple wills bearing down on him he slowly started to raise himself up. He gritted thinking that he had a chance but was then slammed into the earth as multiple new trainers floated down to reinforce the mental press onto Gerald. He knew he wasn't getting up, there were too many minds united against him, and for the first time he heard that whisper. It always starts with a whisper, *You did all you could,* he heard it sigh. That was surrender talking, he ignored it as it got louder with every spear punched through him, every fire that burned him. It screamed at him now but he pushed on, even as his vision turned from gray to black. A horn sounded and every weapon being used on both sides disappeared. The spears impaled the Chosen Dead, all the gun placements, and the wall that had sprung up. All gone. "Victory, Chosen Dead," Miller announced as he floated down from the sky. Gerald looked around and when he saw the center of the room he smiled.

26

POST OP

The Khosenrinn fdeað were seated together at the top of the hill. The dampeners had been removed from Don and David and both looked none the worse for wear.

Gerald walked over to them and patted each of them on the shoulder. "Great job guys, you did it," Gerald said.

"*We* did it," Don corrected him.

"Ya, we all do this." Vora came up from behind and hugged them both. "You have taken away shame that we share. Thank you."

They all looked at Vora. The group could see how responsible she had felt over Don and David being caught.

Gordon placed his hand on Vora's shoulder and when she looked over at him, she smiled. This wasn't her regular bright enthusiasm. "We kill, yes?" smile. No, this was demure and soft. Gerald seemed the only one to notice.

Gerald turned as a pat on the back interrupted him around and found the trainers walking up to them en masse. Gerald took a step back but stopped himself when he saw the angry, focused, very scary faces replaced with warm, welcoming, and genuinely happy smiles. At the head of the trainers was Miller. He actually cracked a smile.

"Well done," Miller said to the Chosen Dead. The trainers came up and introduced themselves. Gerald overheard two of the trainers apologize for the spears and fire thing. Gerald shrugged it off with a grin.

When Gerald had made it through the high fives and well-wishers Miller pulled him over to the side. Miller stared at Gerald for a moment. "I'm glad I was right about you," he said to Gerald. "Others have been successful but what your team did." Miller shook his head. "The power you all displayed was incredible, special" He looked off in the distance "The way you worked Don and David in was something else. You didn't sideline them like everyone expected." Miller huffed. "You dared to send two unpowered knuckleheads to win you a victory." He patted Gerald on the shoulder. "Rest up, you earned it." Miller nodded one more time and then walked off. Gerald turned and went back to the celebration.

"That was nice," Gerald said to no one. His heart was full. He had missed the camaraderie of the service, the brotherhood. He also thought about his Lia. He had been so busy he hadn't thought of her but now with a lull in the action, he felt her absence keenly. These were the moments when he needed her the most. The bad times were easy; you just had to be there to comfort or just...sit and hold hands. The good times were sometimes passed over, but that was the time to celebrate each other along with whatever good things were happening.

"Tomorrow isn't promised," Lia would say. "Neither is today," Gerald would reply and smile.

Gerald left the crowd behind and headed back towards the barracks, wistfully thinking of days gone past and missing his wife.

GOORGA WASN'T aware of what had happened prior, as there was no way for it to get close enough to watch the Chosen without being detected. It had felt the power unleashed and it trembled with what little fear it had. Not just the Chosen's power, but also sensing the power of so many souls was an education in what the enemy could bring to bear.

Goorga always felt victory was inevitable against the encroaching darkness and what lived within it but this could not be allowed to grow. Destroying the Chosen would be the first step but not the last. The sliver of its presence that followed the Chosen had waited for the proper time. After the victory, the Chosen was now in contemplation, a perfect time for an attack. Goorga would wait for his prey to enter the narrow path up ahead and then collapse one side, then use that distraction to attack by breaking its chains and annihilating the Chosen with its full power. Goorga was in a position to strike. It was expanding out to the limit of its so-called prison, but it would wait for the prey to be where he needed to be before it revealed itself.

As Gerald entered the narrow pass he stopped, he felt something stirring in the ether. Gerald backed out of the pass and began scanning the area. He felt something coming towards him at a high rate of speed.

With a whoosh, Gio flew overhead, followed by the rest of the Khosenrinn fdeað. "Hey, figured we would walk you home. Don't want a man-eating plant to choke to death on your skinny rear end," Gio proclaimed.

Gerald smiled and approached his team, no, his brothers and sister. He knew combat and the blood ties it created. You could hate a man with a passion but step in front of a bullet all the same for him.

Goorga froze when he felt the rest of the Khosenrinn fdeað approach. It quickly reduced its presence so none were the wiser. It retreated with as much haste as it could so as not to be detected either. Frustration and fury combined to almost throw caution to the wind. It felt like launching itself at them all, making sure to kill the Chosen, but it also knew that with so many of the other souls present it may not survive, especially if the other came, Miller. It hated and feared him even more than the Chosen.

Goorga slithered back to itself after controlling its base emotions and would wait. The pattern of the enemy was predictable. Soon the time would come when it could strike.

FOR THE FIRST time in actual months, the group lay on their cots and rested. They didn't need to sleep but sometimes it was best to relax and unwind, let the mind rest. They all heard Vora leave the barracks but didn't think much of it. She tended to fidget so they were all used to it. More time passed and the night became quiet and still. The occasional animal noise was the only thing to break up the quiet. That quiet was torn asunder by a sudden lightning storm and massive explosions. Every member of Khosenrinn fdeað jumped up and headed out the door in the direction of the lightning storm.

They all knew it was Vora. It was confirmed when they heard her scream, followed by another string of explosions.

Gerald floated up and got his bearings. Vora was a long way off, at least two hundred miles. He headed off without a thought with the rest of the team trailing. All Gerald could think was that The Penitent had finally decided to have another go.

Gio flew up and screamed, "Fuck this guy, he is going down!"

They all were on the same wavelength. The Penitent wouldn't be permitted to attack a member of their group again.

On final approach, they encircled where the storm was thickest. He could make out Vora and the Penitent wrestling in the whirlwind. Gerald gathered his energy to attack when the storm abruptly died. What Gerald saw next was so astonishing that he almost blasted Don with the energy release. Standing in the middle of a devastated field a mile wide stood Vora, but standing next to her wasn't the Penitent but Gordon. He was stark naked and had smoke coming off his head, and his hair was standing up from the static electricity. Vora, also naked, was as nonchalant as one would expect from the crazy Valkyrie.

"Hello."

No one knew what to say, not even Gio. Gordon was blushing and when Gerald made eye contact with him, Gordon smiled. No one knew what else to say until David burst out laughing. They all laughed at the absurd picture of their two teammates, literally smoking and stark naked in a field.

"You worried she's going to kill you, Chief?" Gio said to Gordon.

"I have no complaints," Gordon said.

That got everyone laughing again.

Miller floated down into the middle of everyone. "You two put some clothes on." Once they were dressed, Miller stood there looking at the two of them. Finally, he spoke. "Nothing says they can't." With that, he floated up and left.

They spent the night celebrating the Viking way with mead and meat. "You disturb me my fun, now you must pay," Vora said, and so they did.

27

MIXER-ISH

The Khosenrinn fdeað woke up with massive hangovers. *Whatever that mead was made of was clearly made to kill you,* Gerald thought as he rubbed his eyes and slowly sat up. The rest of the team was stirring as well. It would have been a pleasant morning where everyone took their time and relaxed. Miller made sure that was not to be as he stormed in yelling fresh and early in the morning. "Good morning, you pussy bitches!!"

Everyone jumped to and stood at attention. Vora had a boob popping out which she quickly tucked away.

Miller rolled his eyes, then continued. "We have a busy day today, people. I want you at the main grounds ready to go in five. Move out!" He stormed out and left the Khosenrinn fdeað to prepare.

"Some night, huh?" Don asked.

Gio smiled at him "You can drink, my dude. I expected her to be able to pound them but wow, well done" He gestured over at Vora, who saluted back. "And this one," Gio pointed at Gordon. "Where do you put it, man? You must have eaten a whole cow."

Gordon smiled and then responded. "Old habits die hard.

You grow up not knowing when you're going to eat, you stuff yourself."

That caused everyone to pause.

"Do not bring the party down, Chief," Gio said to Gordon who smiled and changed into his armor.

The Khosenrinn fdeað lined up along with seven other teams, including The Penitent and his group. Everyone was at attention, eyes forward as Miller approached the gathered teams with a small retinue of higher-ups and an angel. The angel had his wings tucked back with a pure white robe that slung over one shoulder and left his arms and chest mostly bare. He stood over nine feet tall as well and looked every inch the glorious warrior of God that he was.

Gerald could see that he had the eyes of a killer and seemed ready to give a good smiting. The entire field was silent as a man of middle years walked up to the gathered teams. He was tall, whip-thin, and severe-looking with a long thin nose and thin mouth set in a perpetual frown.

Once he stopped, he took a moment to survey the field and its occupants. Everyone on that field felt this man's gaze. It was a tangible feeling, and one wonders if he was looking into their souls.

"Greetings, I am Regent Porter, and congratulations on making it this far." Regent Porter spoke to them with a low voice that carried to everyone there. "It is my job to manage this training planet and ensure that everything that can be done to get you battle-ready is done. We have decided to have a banquet so that you can all mix and speak with someone outside your team."

Gerald groaned inwardly as he thought about the night his team tangled with The Penitent. Porter snapped Gerald out of his brooding with what he had to say next.

"Before we do that, we wanted to give you all a glimpse into what you will be fighting." Porter paused for effect. "We have a prisoner that you will be introduced to. It is of utmost importance that you understand the nature and power of the great enemy." Porter didn't say anything else. He just nodded to one side and the teams started moving in that direction.

Miller appeared and walked with them. "Be ready," he said to the Khosenrinn fdeað. "This is what you are fighting against. You may have seen them in dreams, but it's not the same."

Gio walked up to Gerald. "I can't imagine anything being scarier than Porter. That dude is intense." He shuddered.

"He is great warrior," Vora added "He has slain many of the enemy.

"How do you know that?" Don asked.

"Cousin on mother side, Ogvei, he in battle like us. He tell me."

"Miller is greater," Gordon stated

"Chief, who told you that, a cousin on your dad's side?" Gio chided.

Gordon smiled and his eyes moved over to Vora. "No, it was me. Ogvei say enemy hate Miller. They hunt him." No one seemed surprised by that in the least.

David sniffed the air and hissed a warning. Coming up on their six was The Penitent and his team. No one said a word as he walked past. He nodded to Gerald and ignored the rest. Vora kept a death stare fixed upon him until his back was to her. The warrior in her wanted to strike but she stayed her hand ...for now.

The rest of the team was an interesting mix of souls just like the Khosenrinn fdeað. Behind The Penitent was a large Asian man dressed in furs and a round fur hat to match. He looked like a Mongol or a Hun. Behind him were female twins. They looked exactly alike with short, dark bob haircuts. They wore their armor with one sleeve exposed, and the outside left and outside right arms were armored. They also had multiple throwing knives strapped to their armor and what could only be described as a blunderbuss strapped to their backs. They were speaking with a muscular white man with long blond hair who didn't wear any armor on his arms and a short overly muscular black man.

They stared down the Khosenrinn fdeað and the blondie whispered to the black man who laughed. Gerald didn't like their catty act one bit. Rounding out The Penitent's team was a very tall, thin African man dressed in Zulu attire along with an almond-shaped shield strapped to his back.

"Love the shield, buddy," Gio said to him.

The Zulu warrior looked over at Gio and smiled. "Thank you, my friend," he said and kept walking past.

"I like him." David said

"Me too," Gio added.

They were walking on a paved road now and, just like the moving floor at an airport, the ground moved them along so that within a few seconds they were in front of a nondescript building. It was only one floor, but long like a large rectangle. It looked nothing like any prison one could think of. There were wards and sigils that glowed even in the daylight. The power emanating from them could be felt by everyone there. Whatever was in there wasn't coming out. Two large doors slid inward, and they were all led through to a center room where the enemy was being kept.

Gerald looked up to scan his surroundings and he felt the suppressive force from additional wards and sigils that were engraved into the walls inside as well. He could feel the sigils pulling the strength right out of him like a giant siphon. He looked around and everyone except for Miller seemed to feel it.

They started to file in through an entrance that had additional wards on it. Before they even saw the enemy, they could smell it. Gerald heard people gag involuntarily from it. The creature stank like an abattoir. The smell of congealed blood and fluids hung over everything like a soupy fugue.

Entering the room, Gerald was surprised to find that the creature was below them. Gaolers had dug the prison down into the ground, which makes sense because the earth itself was a shield against the unnatural. The bottom of the pit was covered in what looked like a gray mist.

Once all the teams had filed into the viewing area above the pit, Porter who was standing at a dias above the viewing level spoke. "You have all had the dreams. You have seen what the enemy can do." He let this sink in before continuing. "The enemy is legion. They are vast and numberless, and they would drown the universe in blood." Porter finished. His demeanor didn't change but the intensity was prevalent.

Everyone present felt the fury of Porter's words. Gerald looked around to see more than half of the people present, including the angel, baring their teeth.

"Now, gaze upon the enemy. Look upon the agent of destruction. Promise it and all its kind the death it so richly deserves." Porter's voice had risen into a roar and with a sweep of his hand the gray mist dissipated.

Down below, the creature became visible. It had to be at least eight or nine feet tall, humanoid in appearance. Its musculature was so swollen with muscle over its red skin that it was a wonder the skin didn't burst. Jagged shards of bone poked out of various places on its body, and its head had a surprisingly human face that featured two massive horns protruding from its forehead on either side. The eyes that stared up at everyone were solid black. The black of the void, of anti-life, and despair.

Goorga gazed around at the crowd. It knew its prey was here but to act would mean destruction. It cast its baleful glare at a soul that had darkness in it, but it moved on until he found the

Chosen he was tasked to destroy. It relished the shock of connection, of the promise of the death it would give to this soul. The feeling of glee dissipated when the soul glared back at it. Worse, this mere human soul promised its own death to give to Goorga. The thrill of fear that came worked its self-control loose. It would accept the soul's challenge and destroy it before it was also destroyed.

Staring into the oblivion that awaited in the eyes of the creature shook Gerald. He had encountered evil before, but this was different. This was evil in substance down to its very molecules. Gerald felt the fear rise to overthrow him, but in that fear, he recalled the devastation wrought upon the innocents in his dreams. He was here to do something about creatures like this. He had given up paradise to destroy just such a being. The heat Gerald felt rise off him in waves was the fury he now knew could destroy it.

The eyes of the creature changed. Gerald saw the fear in its eyes replaced with a fury all its own. Gerald would bring doom upon this thing here and now. He started to absorb energy from the surrounding area to blast this thing to hell when a hand fell upon his shoulder. The hand belonged to Miller, who made eye contact with Gerald and he shook his head. Gerald froze, unsure of what to do for a split second, but then powered down. Miller stayed at Gerald's side and for a moment, he made eye contact with the creature.

The look on the creature's face was a mask of pure hate. Miller didn't flinch. He dared the thing in the pit to do something. It decided discretion was the better part of valor and sat itself down on its haunches like a blood-colored hound. No one but Miller seemed to notice, but once Porter dismissed everyone out of the viewing area, his gaze fell upon Gerald and held it. Gerald felt like he was being scanned right through to the very darkest hidden places.

After what seemed an age but was no more than a second, Porter nodded and began speaking with the angel. Miller was still there when they walked out but left once they were outside and away from the stink of the monster trapped inside.

Goorga was furious. The one known as Miller had directly challenged it....again! When the time came for the Chosen to be destroyed, Goorga would make sure that Miller was not there. It would not do for any complications. Miller was its reward for killing the Chosen. Miller would be next to die after the Chosen.

All the teams were led back to the road that moved like a floor escalator. When they arrived, they were not near the grounds but up near the northern pole of the planet. A snow-storm raged around them and when they looked up they saw a gigantic fortress castle. All were directed inside to a feast hall where the teams all sat down. Each table was laden with foods of all types. The table for the Khosenrinn fdeað was laden with large slabs of steaks from all types of animals along with large containers of beer, wine, and diet soda.

"What is wrong with you?" Gio asked David. "Diet soda? Come on, man."

David smiled and added, "I had diabetes so I got used to the taste."

Gio nodded. "I get it, I loved the sweets. News flash: we're dead, bro. Sugar it up! I'm going to eat twenty cannoli and then laugh at the diabetes." David laughed.

"Attention!" All eyes turned to the front where Porter was standing on a stage at the end of the hall where all the most honored guests were seated. "Thank you all for coming, and thank you for volunteering for this. None of this is forced. You do this because you want to do it, and we are forever grateful. We have an honored speaker tonight who wishes to address you. With great admiration and respect, I introduce you to Bariel, captain of the 53rd choir."

Porter nodded to the angel who was present on the main field before. Bariel nodded to Porter and also Miller who was on the other side of the stage. Being so close to the angel, his presence was palpable. Sheer power and light exuded from him along with an undercurrent of violence always promised. This was the doom of anything bold enough to stand against him.

Bariel gazed around the room and then began. "Greetings. Now that you are all close to completing your training, you will all be sent to your theaters to conduct live military missions. Even with millions of souls fighting alongside millions of my brethren..."

Bariel paused as he thought about what he would say next. Gerald saw that Bariel took this personally. "We are hard pressed; the enemy is numberless," Bariel continued. "The creature you saw has power, yes, but the majority are easy enough to kill as in nature, a mantis can be overrun by many ants and taken down. You must be smart, flexible, vicious, and above all, victorious. We cannot lose." Bariel paused before he stepped off the stage.

Porter came back up. "Thank you, Bariel. Before we end your training, we will have one last exercise. Each team will compete in a tournament against the other." With no fanfare, Porter announced the teams competing. "Team Vishna's Vengeance will face The Glorious Children." The teams in question roared and a few bread rolls were thrown from one side to the other. "The Farseekers will go against The Dread of Evil." Those teams cheered as well.

"Yeesh, Dread of evil. Come on, man," Gio said. The team snickered as well because it was a little over the top but if it made them feel good about it so be it.

"The Redeemers," Porter announced, "Will face off against the Night warriors". The Redeemers were The Penitent's team. They all cheered except for the Penitent who simply nodded.

The Chosen Dead already knew who they were facing. "The Victorians will face off against Khosenrinn fdeað."

Both teams cheered and Vora tossed up a slab of beef that the leader of the Victorians, a slim Englishman wearing khaki shorts and a shirt. He caught the beef with his mouth and then swallowed it without ever using his hands. This drove everyone crazy. "We must drink with them after, ja?" Vora laughed and saluted their opponent.

After dinner, everyone was allowed to mingle and speak. The Englishman came right up and introduced himself as Reginald Spalding and then his team. He was as British as you could get: casual with violence, serious about good manners. "Lovely to meet you all. I look forward to competing and doing a good bashing about," Reginald said as he shook hands with Gerald and the team. "I heard you chaps are quite challenging. Can't wait to test that, my boy."

Gerald smiled and thought he was a good egg, as Gio would say.

The rest of the team was composed of two Sikh men, Davinder and Akwal, who bowed and were as polite and friendly as Reginald was.

"Love these chaps, fought in Africa with the Sikhs, best warriors I ever had the honor of fighting with."

Gio shocked everyone by approaching the Sikhs and greeting them in their customary greeting, "Sat Skri Akal." They both smiled and nodded.

"You have fought with Sikh then?" Davinder asked.

Gio nodded and replied, "In Italy, my friend. The British commandos had Sikhs with them. You guys saved our bacon." Gio bowed "Also, you guys got me to like tea which I never thought would happen."

Akwal laughed. "What is better than a cuppa?"

Gio laughed. "Have you ever tried cannolis?"

They chatted with the Victorians for a while eating together and drinking. "Hey G," Gordon broke the reverie by nodding behind Gerald. Standing there watching the group was The Penitent. Vora didn't say a word, didn't snarl, she just sat there calmly staring at The Penitent. Gordon sitting right next to Vora leaned over and whispered something to her. She looked over at Gordon and nodded.

"May I speak with you?" The Penitent asked Gerald. He looked at the table with both teams staring at him.

"Heard about the dust-up, watch yourself chap," Reginald leaned in to whisper to Gerald.

Gerald nodded and stood up. The Penitent walked over to an open balcony and Gerald followed him out. The snowstorm had quieted to a steady stream now. The cold didn't bother either one of them as they walked out to the edge of the balcony.

Gerald wasn't sure what to expect. He was surprised that he was even out here at all. He wasn't going to start the conversation, so he waited for The Penitent to say something. Thankfully Gerald didn't have to wait long.

"I would like to apologize for what happened," The Penitent said. Gerald turned to face him as he spoke. "It was...uncalled for"

Gerald nodded but didn't reply right away. He wanted to make sure this wasn't a ploy or some other head game. "Ok," Gerald began "Apology accepted."

They both stared at each other for a moment. The Penitent looked ready to say more but then nodded and left without saying another word.

Gerald stood out there for a moment and breathed in the chilly night air. The Penitent had terrible people skills, but he was trying. Still, when the time came, Gerald would give no quarter. He would make sure that his team came out on top.

28

TOURNEY TIME

The tournament started with very little fanfare. All the teams were lined up on the main grounds and it was announced that Vishna's Vengeance would take on The Glorious Children. The rest of the teams were told to head back to their barracks and wait for them to be called. This was done so that no team would get an advantage with what the objective for the round was. No one would be allowed to speak with anyone from another team until the round was completed. They were all isolated at the barracks which wasn't a big deal since they hadn't spoken with another team except The Victorians.

Gio had started barbecuing so the team slowly made its way outside to enjoy some steaks when the explosions started. Things escalated when a full-on earthquake happened... multiple times. The explosions continued for hours and continued for another eight hours when the second set of teams was called, The Farseekers against The Dread of Evil. Nothing was mentioned on who won or lost. It became apparent that The Redeemers would be next if they kept the order from the previous day.

Vora was not taking the waiting well. She had been walking

nonstop around the barracks and at one point she was running so fast in a circle around the barracks that she started to cause a tornado which began pulling up planks. She apologized and began to randomly blast stuff.

Gerald didn't blame her; the waiting was the worst part whether it was sports or war. Get it over with, if it's my day to die so be it but don't punish me with boredom. "An idle mind is the devil's playground," Gerald murmured.

David and Gordon looked over at him and nodded.

The second contest was over in a relatively quick five hours. The next announcement of The Redeemers versus the Night Warriors came up along with the sun on a new day. The sounds of the contest could be heard reverberating in the barracks as they sat and waited. It took till midday for the last contest to end.

The Khosenrinn fdeað jumped to their feet and headed to the main grounds. No one waited for them to be called and when they arrived The Victorians were approaching as well.

Reginald came right up to Gerald with his hand extended. "Best of luck to you, chap. Whoever loses pays the tab."

Gerald smiled, "Best of luck, be safe."

Reginald laughed. "Safe? That is not on the menu today my friend. Today I choose violence."

Gio and Vora laughed. "Violence, ja!" Vora patted Reginald on the arm.

"Attention!" Miller barked and both teams immediately got into formation and waited. "You lot are the last in this round. Leaders, approach!" Reginald and Gerald moved into position in front of Miller. "Today's contest is to attack and defend. Victorians, you will defend this small fort." Miller pointed and a facsimile of a wooden fort made of armor appeared near both teams. "You will situate yourself and defend this structure." Miller spoke to Gerald. "You, Khosenrinn fdeað, will lay siege to the fort and take command."

Reginald raised his hand. "When will we know who has won, sir?"

Miller immediately looked annoyed at such a reasonable question. "When I fucking tell you, you limey dipshit."

Reginald stood up straight and smiled "Very good, sir."

Miller pinned Reginald in place for a few seconds with a glare. "Prepare yourselves, and signal when ready."

When Miller left, Gerald turned to Reginald. "I'm glad *you* asked him that."

Reginald laughed and saluted Gerald, who straightened up and returned the salute, and then they both went to prepare their teams for the contest.

Gerald watched as Reginald barked orders and his team responded. Davinder and Akwal stood on opposite ends of the fort. Larissa the Puritan was floating right above the fortress with her eyes closed. A violet shield expanded from her and spread out to envelop the fortress. The Spaniard Borrea was in front and center on the wall, and the final member Dat, the small Vietnamese man, was not in sight.

Gerald had already discussed the opening strategy, and the team was spread out with Gordon on the left flank and Gio on the right flank. David and Vora were nearest the flanks and Don and Gerald were closest to the center. They were given the signal to begin. Gerald gave a nod and the team jumped into action. They all opened fire and, as per orders, focused on a singular point on the shield.

Larissa immediately opened her eyes, fluttered in the air, and grimaced. Borrea poured more energy into the shield which buoyed Larissa. The onslaught continued and after a few more seconds, the area in the shield being fired upon changed to Davinder's side. He had to grab hold of the wall with one hand and grit his teeth. This cycle continued for a while hitting different points in the shield until a realization came to Gerald.

"Cease firing!" Gerald called, he then signaled Don over. When Don stood next to him, he asked, "You feeling your oats today?"

Don smiled. "Always."

Gerald smiled like the cat that stole the canary. "You know how important discipline is, right? Not flying off half-cocked and so on?"

Don, still smiling, seemed confused.

"Right now, go no nuts. I want you to hit that shield with everything you got, just you."

Don's eyes widened and a feral grin slowly spread across his face.

"This is going to be good!" Gio yelled from his side.

Everyone on The Chosen Dead pulled back. Silence fell across the field. The Victorians watched as Don walked to the edge of the shield. They were just as curious as his teammates as to what would happen next. Don began to glow. He then inhaled, and as he pulled in energy he began to grow. Don spread his arms out wide and continued to pull in energy. You could feel it through the swirling tides invisible to the human eye but not to a soul. The eddies of ethereal energy were being drawn into Don at an alarming rate.

Reginald saw the danger and jumped into action. "Fire on him!" He didn't wait but started firing beams of energy that struck the titan that was now Don. He was almost a hundred feet tall.

The energy beams hit him and instead of hurting him enraged him, and he glowed even brighter. The Victorians threw everything they had at Don.

The Chosen Dead were not idle. Gio threw up a shield wall to deflect the firepower and was reinforced by Gordon while the rest of the team fired back at The Victorians. Don stood now at the edge of the shield and, with a roar that shook the ground for miles around, started to strike the shield.

The first impact caused Don to stumble back due to the ricochet from the shield. The Victorians on the other side of the shield were wide-eyed at the force Don brought to bear.

"Shields, reinforce them now!" Reginald screamed.

Don approached the shield and began to pound on the wall with everything he had.

The assault lasted for a few minutes and The Victorians, who were strained, handled it.

Don stepped back and began glowing again. Instead of growing, the glow began to center itself in front of his chest. Before long he had a mini sun floating in front of his chest that pulsed to the beat of a nonexistent heart.

Gerald watched as Reginald had his entire team gather quickly together to reinforce the shield as well as minimize it. *Smart*, Gerald thought. He admired Reginald as a leader. He was protecting his people first and foremost.

With a roar, Don Titan fired the orb which exploded when it came into contact with the shield. The explosion was so powerful it blew Don backward and out of sight. The light was so intense that it blinded everyone, but the noise told you the story. The sound was deafening; a mini apocalypse had been unleashed. A cyclone of noise and wind roared its doom.

After the explosion, Gerald had his team on the move. The plain was wiped clean of life. It looked exactly like the ground after Gerald had caused his explosion, nuclear fire melted the ground smooth.

The fort was still standing...sort of. The Victorians had minimized the shield so that part of the fort was protected so it appeared like the fort was in a snow globe. The parts of the walls not protected were gone and burned away clean. Only the main front wall was still there, along with some of the sides.

As the Chosen Dead moved closer to what was left of the fort, they were surprised by the Victorians coming at them in a reverse V formation. At their head was Reginald. "Charge!!" he screamed as they bore down on Gerald who almost allowed the shock of Reginald leading a cavalry charge to get the better of him, and he flew up into the air while firing to avoid being run down. A ghost of a horse was beneath Reginald and the hooves that just missed Gerald who would have caused serious damage if they had connected.

Gerald ordered the team to line up and face off against the Victorians who wheeled around with great precision and paused. "I say, chap, are you ready to surrender?" Reginald asked from across the field.

He knew that his team had the power advantage. There was no way they could defeat The Chosen Dead using man-to-man combat. This was not a man who quit. He would find a victory even if there didn't appear to be one. *I like this guy.* Gerald thought and then replied. "Upon careful consideration of your offer, I graciously decline."

Gerald motioned with his hand and the Chosen Dead fired back at The Victorians while charging toward them. The Victorians expertly wheeled away from their much stronger opponent and continued to find a hole in their flank. Gerald realized that Reginald was using cavalry tactics to buy more time. He was probing for a weakness.

Vora fired her lightning field which disrupted their formation, but they wheeled away from it with quick instructions from Reginald. Their discipline and teamwork would drag this out indefinitely if Gerald couldn't find a way to break the stalemate.

As the Victorians were wheeling around for another run, Gerald signaled to Gordon who disappeared. They were two men down now with no sign of Don. He wasn't dead, but he could be incapacitated. Gerald remembered almost blowing his head off when he tried the same thing. Hopefully, he was ok but he could use him now.

Reginald noticed that Gordon had disappeared and called for a halt and withdrew from the charge. He had Davinder and Akwal close up the flanks so that their backs weren't exposed. They began firing out into the field and as they did that, they hit Gordon who had crept up to within ten feet of their line. Upon discovering him, they poured on the firepower and quickly surrounded him.

Gerald's instinct was to charge in to save him, which he did, but something seemed off. *Why would the Victorians encircle themselves to fire on Gordon who was holding up so far?* He thought.

Vora had flown up and unleashed a lightning storm that descended behind the Victorians so that it would block the rest of the Chosen Dead's approach. It also proved to save them.

When they approached the area where the Victorians had been, a series of explosions went off which sent the Chosen Dead flying in all directions. No one was hurt by it but when they realigned, they had moved off to the other side of the field. Reginald wasn't going to let his team get caught in hand-to-hand combat but also needed to slow the Chosen Dead down.

Gordon had rejoined the group. The Victorians were constantly moving now. They were firing at range to distract rather than to do any real damage. Gerald needed something to disrupt their flow so that they could get in close and finish them off. The Victorians were too smart to get caught in a grind and proved it again when out of nowhere, a maze grew up out of the ground. The walls were twelve feet high and when Gerald blasted through it, they mended back together. The team floated up above the maze and was met with a thick white fog that appeared out of nowhere. The fog wasn't natural as it limited their vision in all spectrums.

"Very clever," Gerald stated.

"What now?" Gio asked. That question was answered when they were attacked out of the fog by the Victorians.

David was run through by what appeared to be a lance. He broke it off and wheeled around. "I can't smell them in this fog!" David ignited the air around him to clear some space. "Better," he said.

"Can you track who it's coming from?" Gio asked.

"Let me help." Gerald expanded his senses and felt the fog all around him but not much else. "Fire in the hole!" he yelled and then ignited the fog around him. He was able to burn the fog, his teammates, and The Victorians who had crept up in the fog to attack.

Reginald was behind Gerald but with the fog clear, Gerald grabbed Reginald in an invisible vice and then blasted him back into the fog.

"Got him!" David yelled and took off as the fog returned. David disappeared into the fog to hunt down his prey.

"On me," Gerald commanded, and then when they were all together, he ordered them to burn the fog. "Now!" he ordered, and they expanded the field so they were able to burn it all. They could see David across the field and when the fog cleared, even in a fiery inferno that replaced the fog, he was able to zero in on the fog's creator. David made a beeline for Larissa who was defended by Borrea, but David was able to grab a hold of her before Borrea could close.

David transformed into a giant man-wolf and clamped down on her shoulder with his claws. Everyone heard Larissa scream and then she dropped to the ground with David still clamped down on her. Borrea struck but couldn't dislodge David.

Gerald didn't see Reginald, so he focused his energy on the maze below and blasted it completely flat. He saw Reginald's body fly off and Gerald flew like a bullet towards Reginald, who had hit the ground and was struggling to stand up. Right before the collision with Reginald, Gerald fired a blast of energy that hit Borrea in the back. Seemed fair play since he was stabbing David in his back.

Gerald hit Reginald so hard that they caused a crater at least twenty meters deep. Before Reginald could try anything, Gerald clamped down on Reginald's neck with his version of a dampener. He wasn't sure it was something he could do but once he had studied the device and the way it muted a soul's energy, he understood the concept. The only difference was that where the dampener could mute the energy Gerald needed to transfer it. He needed to transfer the energy, so he drew the energy into himself.

He discovered that if he wanted to, he could drain Reginald dry, suck out his energy and leave him used up. He could kill him if he wanted to. Gerald did not want that at all, so he willed the energy that he drew from Reginald into a battery he had stored in his armor and used that energy to reinforce the shackles he had placed on Reginald.

Gerald rose from the crater and saw that Vora was engaged with Dat in an aerial duel. David was savaging Larissa while Don had rejoined the fight and was battering Borrea who was circling Don like a bird of prey but in reality, was just trying to keep moving so Don wouldn't do any damage.

Gio and Gordon were fighting a moving duel with Davinder and Akwal. It appeared to be pretty even so far. Gerald reached out and redirected some of the energy being looped into shackling Reginald into Larissa.

"Release her!" Gerald commanded and as soon as David moved off her, he attacked Borrea from behind and pinned him to the ground along with Don.

Once Larissa was secure, Gerald moved on to Borrea and they went down the line until Dat was the last to be confined. Gerald waited for the exercise to be over but no signal was forthcoming. "I have them!" he bellowed. No response. Gerald waited. He was struggling with the power loops as the battery could no longer sustain such an immense power flow. He reinforced the batter but knew it wouldn't last so he looked at Reginald and spoke. "Do you yield?"

He looked up at Gerald and smiled. "Never, sir."

The battery burned itself out and Gerald took the brunt of all that power. He had to directly siphon it and then used that to reinforce his captives. The price of pain was excruciating. He couldn't even ask for help because if anyone tried to loop, it could cause a backwash of energy and an explosion, and the realization he could kill the entire Victoria's team. He could either drain them enough to then release them weakened, or they could all be killed by the energy backwash. He didn't have much time; the pain was blurring his vision.

Gerald could feel his teammates standing impotently, not sure of what to do. There was a third option. Gerald could release them unharmed, but the backwash could kill him. It was an easy decision.

Right as Gerald was about to release the Victorians, he heard a rustle of wings and two massive hands grabbed him on each side of his head. Immediately the pain vanished, and the angel Bariel spoke into his mind. "I have control of the power flow; I will be able to release them without anyone being harmed. Be still."

Gerald waited while the pressure was released. His vision slowly cleared, and he could see Reginald and the rest of his team being helped by the Chosen Dead. "Be at peace" was the last thing Gerald heard when he passed out.

HE AWOKE WITH A START. Gerald was lying on the ground with both teams along with Bariel, Miller, and Porter standing above him. "You alright?" Miller asked.

Gerald sat up and nodded. He felt no pain. He felt pretty damn good. Being touched by an angel had healed him from the damage he would have endured after what he had done to himself.

"Well, get your ass up!" Miller demanded. Gerald complied and stood at attention.

"Victory, Chosen Dead," Miller proclaimed. He then leaned in and said to Gerald, "We need to talk."

The Chosen Dead went from worried to jubilant and The Victorians didn't hold a grudge as Reginald gave a sharp salute to Gerald and then to the rest of the team.

"Well done" He leaned into Gerald. "You had me worried there for a minute, chap."

Gerald shook his head. "Me too, my friend. Just glad it worked out."

Reginald smiled and then he and his team lined up. Both teams shook hands and started chatting with each other.

Gerald walked over to Miller who was now with Porter and Bariel. He stood up straight and saluted them.

"At ease," Porter said.

Bariel walked up to Gerald and sniffed him before speaking. "You should be dead." He then pointed to the two teams intermingling. "They should all be dead as well. What you did is not normal. By manipulating the energy flow the way you did you could potentially twist reality. There are angels, very powerful angels who cannot do that."

Gerald didn't know what to say to that, so he said nothing.

"It was very impressive but you must learn to understand your limits, or you will die the true death. Do you understand me?" Bariel finished.

"Yes sir," Gerald replied. "Thank you, I..." Gerald tailed off for a moment trying to find the words. "I was afraid I would kill them"

Bariel nodded. "That is why I stepped in. I saw what you planned to do." He placed a hand on Gerald's shoulder. "I approve" With that Bariel flew up into the air and left.

Miller stepped up. "I don't fucking approve," he said to Gerald. "Your jackassery almost got yourself and others killed. You need to work harder to get your shit straight, you got me?!"

Gerald agreed with Miller. "Yes sir, no more jackassery."

The next round of the tournament had the Glorious Children go against the Chosen Dead. The Chosen Dead had to wait while the Redeemers and Farseekers began their tilt.

Goorga watched the first round of the fake combat with complete disgust. It had watched countless of these contests in its time in captivity and never understood why there were no intentional deaths. There had been a few it recalled, apparently done by accident. How they mourned those weak souls. He would have celebrated the thinning of the weakest from his force. The nature of war was death and destruction. These souls spent so much time practicing, making war without any deaths, and repairing the beautiful carnage they wrought. When it was a spawn in the time before time there was no make-believe, there was murder in the dark, hatred of the weak which drove it to kill and torture them.

Hatred of the strong for causing it fear. It cherished these more. It would lurk in wait until the time to strike came and it then fed on the corpse of these stronger beasts and made itself grow in strength and terror. Nothing changes.

Goorga had watched the Chosen vanquish his opponents, had seen the power the Chosen wielded, and knew the time to strike was close. This Chosen, Gerald, he called himself, was far too dangerous to be allowed to grow to his full potency, but when he did kill this soul it would absorb its power, and then it would have the power to challenge anything in this abomination of a universe.

The contest between The Redeemers and Farseekers went on for three days solid until finally, The Redeemers were named the winners.

The Chosen Dead started heading out to the main grounds to begin their round against The Glorious Children. It was very foggy as they made their way down to the grounds, a natural fog that smelled of moisture but did little else to confuse the senses of the souls on this planet. The smell of rain was in the air as well so potentially the weather could play a role in the day's events.

The Chosen Dead arrived with The Glorious Children waiting for them along with Miller, Porter, and Bariel. Once the two teams were at attention, the next contest was announced. Once all were in position, Porter stepped forward. "Greetings," he said in his least threatening yet welcoming tone. "Today's contest will be a little different. Today you are tasked with finding a copy of this relic." Porter held up what looks to be a medallion with a cross inside, similar to a ringed cross. "This is located somewhere on the planet. You must retrieve it and bring it back here. Good luck." He turned and walked away, leaving the teams to their own devices. Miller and Bariel followed Porter.

"I guess we can start?" Gio asked.

The Glorious Children walked up to The Chosen Dead. Their leader was a small man of native Indian descent. From his garb, it appeared to be the Aztec or Mayan era. "Hello," he said in a low soft voice.

Gerald walked up and shook hands with him. "Nice to meet you, good luck to you," he said.

"Thank you. I am Qulitan. This is my team." He waved his

hand, and the rest of the team came forward. Yuri was a bald Russian with pale features and the flat face you saw of people of Slavic descent. McConnell was a dark-haired Irishman who wore jeans with suspenders and the old white cotton shirts worn during the Industrial Age all over the world. Titus Andronicus was a Roman but he wore modern jeans and a t-shirt with a cloak That made him look like a large kid playing dress-up. Liang was a small slender Asian woman with long straight hair dyed purple, and the final member was Mu'uta, a Polynesian boulder of a man who stood around six feet and had to weigh at least four hundred pounds.

Mu'uta gave them the surfers hang loose sign. "What's up, bros?" he greeted.

Once the pleasantries were done, they said their farewells and moved on to the task at hand.

They went back to the barracks and Gerald circled them up to hatch a plan. "Ok, any ideas on how to...?"

"I know where it is," David said calmly. The team all just stared at him. "The animals and man-eating plants told me," he explained.

"Of course, they did," Gerald smiled.

"It's in a small cabin on the other side of the world. It's guarded on the outside, so if someone is spotted, then they can teleport it. We need to get in without being seen."

Gordon stepped in. "Done" he stated.

"So sneaky, my man, so very good," Vora said and started to get into it.

"Stop. Not the time or place please." Gerald put out the fire, and Vora sheepishly nodded her head. David and Gordon took off and within the next five minutes, they had brought it back along with the announcement that The Chosen Dead were the winners.

"Never seen anything like it," Miller said to the team as they stood at attention. "That artifact has no way to be traced. You telling me a man-eating plant told you where it is?" Miller directed this at David who had a sly smile on his face.

"Yes sir. Her name is Dora."

Miller shook his head. "For fuck's sake. Now you're naming them? If I haven't seen you turn into that giant poodle, I would boot all your asses for cheating."

"To be fair sir, it was very open-ended..." Gerald started, then stopped when Miller laid a stare that could melt metal.

"Fair has nothing to do with it. You used what you had and it worked, that's it. Good job. Now get ready because the final starts tomorrow. DO NOT EMBARRASS ME!!!" Miller waved his arm and dismissed the team.

"I thought it was pretty fucking awesome," Gio said, and they laughed on their way back to the barracks.

Upon arrival, Vora and Gordon took off to hopefully not cause another massive sex storm. David, Gio, and Don invited Gerald to play pinochle which he declined. Gerald wanted to unwind in seclusion and take the next steps. As nice as it would be to demolish The Redeemers and their leader The Penitent, that didn't mean much in the grand scheme of things.

They would be heading to a live combat theater after this, and he wanted to figure out what he could say to get the team ready for when it was for real. It would be hard to get killed but still possible. No telling what they would encounter out there, and they needed to be ready. As his son, George used to say during his football days and after "Be first." They needed to be first, always. Otherwise, they could die for good.

It was a burden of leadership that you knew not everyone would make it back. You just hoped it would just be you and not one of your people.

Gerald shook off those negative thoughts as well. Those could grow like a weed and become difficult to remove once they are rooted into your psyche. He went outside and started walking around towards the main grounds. The night was cool, and he could smell the dew on the ground. Animals rustled in the woods, and he caught something running in the distance but couldn't see what it was.

He floated up into the air and slowly rotated around to catch all the views this world had to offer. Thousands of miles away, a familiar-looking lightning storm was raging. Gerald quickly rotated away from that, thankfully he didn't catch a glimpse of either of the two naked. He had enough to worry about without seeing any of that business.

He closed his eyes and scanned the world in the other sight. He saw everything in flowing streams of color that moved through the material parts of the world like the trees and ground. The streams of energy that he then followed were casually listing about waiting to be plucked by a soul for use in whatever fashion they desired. He felt such feelings, emotional and intense, knowing that he was part of that same energy. That something created all this and that he was allowed to fight for it.

His emotions swelled thinking of his family. That was until he felt a tug on that energy. He rotated to see in his mind's eye a massive tide of energy coming right towards him fast and aggressive. It promised danger and violence.

Gerald opened his eyes, ready for combat, Bariel streaked up to him and stopped so suddenly in front of him that it defied the laws of physics. Gerald relaxed slightly and nodded in greeting.

"Hello, Gerald, how are you?" Bariel greeted him with a surprisingly warm tone, albeit still filled with a promise of violent death but it appeared he was trying to be nice.

"Hello Bariel, I am well, thank you. How are you?" Gerald replied, not sure what else to say, so they floated in the air like two socially awkward teenagers until Bariel broke the ice.

"I wished to speak with you," he said. Gerald inclined his

head for Bariel to continue. "You and your team, but specifically you, have been discussed in the circles of power. Your abilities are exceptional. This is a good thing but there is danger in this as well."

Gerald nodded. "Thank you again for saving me."

Bariel waved him off. "No, that is not what I mean. Your type of power is dangerous because it will attract the enemy to you. Do you understand what this means?"

Gerald knew attracting the enemy was bad, but beyond that, no.

It must have shown on his face so Bariel continued, "It means something more powerful than you will come for you to destroy you before you can destroy it. You will grow stronger and stronger over time and practice."

Gerald understood the implications of this. He could cause his teammates to be in even greater danger than they normally would have to deal with.

"Shield your power, work on hiding yourself, do you understand?" Bariel didn't wait for an answer but instead flew off. *Would help if you could maybe give me some tips on how to do that.* Gerald thought.

29

THE FINALS

The sun rose up slowly in the sky on the day of the finals. It cast its light out in shards of orange fire and cleansed the world of the darkness.

The Khosenrinn fdeað stood at attention opposite The Redeemers. All the teams were at the main grounds today in their parade best. Everyone's armor was polished and reflected the rising sun like millions of points of light.

Porter stood like the warrior of old that he was, grim and beautiful like a stone statue carved in days long gone. Only the hair on his helm moving proved otherwise.

Miller, even in his armor, still looked like the old Marine sergeant that he was and always would be, his features set and predator eyes scanning the teams for any sign of weakness.

Gerald caught a glance of him and understood that Miller was the anvil he and his team were forged from, and he was grateful for it. Miller was a true warrior. Honor, courage, and will were the greatest assets a soldier could have.

Bariel stood at ease with his hands behind his back. His arms were bare but he wore a chest plate that shone like the sun, not from the reflection of the star, but it had its own inner fire that glowed with power. God had created Bariel as an avatar of war and the power that emanated from him now was truly fearsome. The interesting thing was that Gerald didn't recall this feeling of power exuding from Bariel before.

He made eye contact with Bariel, who flashed a grim smile, and Gerald realized that he was showing only him how powerful he was, or not because this could very well be what Bariel wanted everyone to see. Gerald nodded back at the lesson. He would make sure to control his power and give nothing away.

"Welcome to you all!" Porter addressed the field. "The finals mark the exercise before we go to make war on the great enemy." He paused. "We celebrate you all for your courage and sacrifice. You don't have to be here, but you are anyway. Thank you." Porter scanned the field "The final two teams will face off with each other. The objective is to capture the opposing team's leader. We will utilize a hundred-mile radius from this point for the arena. You are not allowed outside the radius, or your team will be disqualified. The leader must be neutralized with a dampener to be considered captured." He scanned the field and then concluded, "Best of luck to both teams. You have thirty minutes to plan your strategy."

As the teams left the field after being dismissed, Gerald watched as The Redeemers left the field. He called the team to stay on the field so they could discuss their plan. "Alright folks, this is it," Gerald started and then detailed out his plan to beat The Redeemers. Gerald explained that due to The Redeemer's nature, The Penitent would look to take out Gerald on one if he could, but would have backup if needed.

After he was done explaining his plan he asked, "Questions?"

"So you are big fucking worm on little hook?" Vora asked, not quite getting the saying right, but everyone got the gist.

"Yes, exactly, big fucking worm." No one said anything for a moment.

"It's risky," Don said.

"What if he doesn't take the bait?" David asked.

"He will, he wants to be the best and prove it," Vora grunted. "He is arrogant, he think he is best." Vora spat on the ground.

"Exactly, you all have to play your parts, though. We need to reel him in and close the net." Gerald looked each member of the Khosenrinn fdeað in the eye. "Agreed?" They all nodded "OK, let's get this done."

Everyone headed off, and Gerald and Gordon made eye contact. Gordon nodded and then disappeared.

"I love when he does that," Gio said and patted Gerald on the shoulder "You ready for this?" he asked. Gerald nodded. "We'll get to you as soon as we can," Gio finished and flew off.

Gerald scanned the area to make sure he was alone, closed his eyes, and then slowly vanished. He was using the same energy that Gordon used to make himself disappear. Gerald had asked Gordon for a small bit of his energy so he could use that as his template. He was not able to duplicate it perfectly and he was glitching in and out of sight. He had to focus fully on gaining control of Gordon's energy. It was ephemeral, like trying to catch a moving strand of a spider web in the air. The energy would twist and turn and didn't want to be contained.

Gerald was getting nervous because he didn't have much time to nail it down before the opposition was on top of him. The harder he grasped for it, the more the energy bucked and pushed away. He was frustrated and was losing faith. The colors of the visible world energy spun around and swirled in a pattern when left alone, but when he reached out, they avoided him and refused to be harnessed.

Gerald stood there looking at the color patterns. The invisible color ranges were spinning the opposite way and clashed with the visible world colors. "How the heck do you do it, Gordon?" Gerald said aloud to no one. He tried again to harness the energy, but it wouldn't allow him to. The harder he tried, the more it pushed back.

Gerald almost blasted a hole in the ground in frustration. That wouldn't work, he knew, but probably would make him feel better. Time was short and he needed to get this figured out. After their hijinks with hiding Don and David, they were able to find a way to track the team even with Gordon's energy. The armor suit still leaked residual energy which would appear so that avenue was cut off from him.

Gerald took a deep breath and stilled himself. He focused on the energy swirling in front of him. He watched the visible energy moving in its now familiar pattern and exhaled. Instead of harnessing the energy, he slowed his breathing and focused on the pattern itself, the way it danced and swayed.

That was when it hit him. The energy, like everything else, was a living thing. He extended his hand and continued to exhale and breathe slowly. He invited the energy to him, asking for its permission.

The energy pulled closer, curious. It knew he wasn't Gordon, but it also knew he was a friend of his. Even so, it was hesitant to accept.

Without realizing it, Geald had started to move his hand in the same pattern of energy. He mimicked the movements exactly. The energy responded in kind and after a few minutes of this, he felt a connection building. He tested this and moved his hand to the left, which the energy mirrored. He moved it again to the right and it followed again. He used his other hand to move over himself, to map where to go.

At first, it was slow going because he wasn't used to the movements but once he was comfortable, the energy spread itself out like a thin film over his entire body. He knew then he was invisible.

He needed to exert some focus to keep the energy working around his body. He then repeated the process with the invisible energy. This was much harder. This energy was in a spectrum that wasn't fully in this world, so he had to mimic a much harder pattern that dipped in and out of reality. It was like trying to catch a greased pig; too soft and nothing, too hard and it would flip right out of your grip.

This energy didn't care he was a friend of Gordon's. It didn't seem to care at all. He had the gist of it now, though. He weaved the patterns and even changed the pattern subtly. The invisible energy approved since its very nature included the chaotic and allowed for him to spread itself out and interlay with the other energy across his body.

Once that had been completed the two energies did something that he didn't expect. In a flash of light, they intertwined and created a third type of energy that pulsed and then lay still on their own once they overlapped, Gerald tentatively removing some focus on maintaining the integrity of the cloaking field.

He waited a moment longer to ensure that everything was stable and then sped off and went to an area that Gordon had selected. It was a grotto with a small waterfall and a cave behind it that would be perfect for what they were trying to do. It had an entrance that only two at a time could fit through and led into a large rectangular cave with no exit. They would think they were trapping him, not realizing they were the hunted until it was too late.

For the next few hours, The Redeemers were led on a wild goose chase. David and Vora drew them into the jungle area and used guerilla tactics to hit and run them. Vora didn't use her lightning field at all but focused her energy into small blasts of energy that she used to great effect. David was running in and around them using the man-eating plants to lay traps for them. He didn't want to use too many animals as they could be killed, so he limited their use.

The Redeemers caught on to the fact that they were being misled, so they rose up above the jungle and moved away to meet back with The Penitent.

"Anything?" The Penitent asked. They shook their heads.

"They are toying within us," The Penitent said

"They are hunting us," Benga Din the African man said as he floated up to the group. "They are testing us, prodding for weaknesses."

The Penitent said nothing for a moment. Benga Din was a hunter so he knew to trust his advice. "Where are the other two?" The Penitent asked. No sooner had he mentioned to them that the large white man who was Sical and the short muscular black man Tyrus appeared looking grim. The group turned to them. "Anything?" The Penitent queried

"Not a damn thing. We got hit early on by the big guy and the guido but they disappeared into the jungle."

The Penitent was livid. He couldn't get a read on them or their tactics. He knew they were using feints and misdirection, but to what purpose? He knew they could win by capturing him and yet they hadn't made a move to even try and capture him.

Where was the Indian? He knew that he could make himself invisible and that was a concern, but he had masked himself as well. There was no way he could track him.

He floated around scanning the area, his team was waiting on orders as to what to do next. The Penitent knew he had to draw him out somehow but the problem was how. His reverie was broken when he noticed storm clouds right above them and immediately, they were enveloped in a lightning storm which was accompanied by a familiar screech which set his teeth on edge.

A bolt of lightning struck him from behind and rendered him blind for a few seconds and when his sight returned, he could see they were under attack.

Don had crashed into Sical and Tyrus and both tried to wrestle with him but were unable to do more than survive without being crushed by him. The twins were fighting with David who had shape-shifted into the giant werewolf creature, and Kubak and Benga Din were locked in combat with Gio and Vora.

The Penitent made a beeline at Vora while she was engaged with Kubak. He would blast right through her and put the screaming harlot in her place.

Right before he collided every one of the opposing team members turned towards The Penitent and blasted him with energy attacks. Worse yet, Vora didn't even turn around but after the initial volley of attacks, he was hit with a massive lightning storm that separated him from his team.

The lightning struck him from every direction and caused excruciating pain. For the first time in a long time, he felt the icy tendrils of fear creep up his spine. They had planned this all along and he had fallen for it. Like a specter, he saw Vora floating through the storm. She was coming for him.

Outside of the lightning storm, The Redeemers watched as the storm isolated The Penitent from them and then as Vora moved off and headed into the storm. "Form a line!" Benga Din ordered, and they complied. They battled their way to each other and created a line facing the storm with the Chosen Dead opposite them. "Vanguard!" he yelled and they formed up into a spear formation, with Sical in front. Without another word, they charged straight into the line of the Chosen Dead and prayed that they could get through the storm before The Valkyrie captured the Redeemer.

In the lightning storm, Vora battled The Penitent using every ounce of her power. *He is strong*, she said to herself as she sent waves of current at him, she used the lightning to pull at his arms and legs and throw him off balance. The Penitent fought with a desperation she hadn't seen prior. She just hoped the team could hold them off and she could end it right here and now.

The Penitent sensed it, too, and fought with everything he had. He knew his team would be fighting to break through and rescue him, but he needed to hold off the Valkyrie. The storm pulled on him, white-hot fire grabbing at his arms and legs. He needed to get out of this storm soon.

The Redeemers hit the Chosen Dead like a battering ram to mixed results. Sical was blasted back by Don immediately, but the rest were able to push their way through using their superior numbers. They left Sical and continued into the storm hoping that they had enough time to save The Penitent.

The Penitent was fighting with everything he had, lashing out with frigid energy blasts in every direction. He was trying to keep track of the Valkyrie and neutralize her. The force shields he was trying to maintain were battered down within seconds.

Vora was trying her best to distract The Penitent while moving closer to him so she could try to clamp down the dampener. She was flying from left to right so she could get behind him, but so far, he was proving more difficult than expected. Vora fired a blast of energy that blew out The Penitent's latest shield. More importantly, it caused him to glance behind him. That tiny distraction was enough.

Vora flew right at The Penitent and slammed into him like a bullet, and they both went cartwheeling hundreds of feet. The hand-to-hand combat that followed was savage and unrelenting. If they were mortal, then one of them would have been killed. Nothing was held back. Vora stabbed The Penitent in the face. In return, he caved in her chest with his bare hands and tore into her before she tore off one of his arms. The arm reattached and they continued to tumble through the air.

Slowly but surely, though, The Penitent was gaining the upper hand. He used his superior power to batter Vora into submission. The Penitent saw his opening and blasted Vora right in the throat. It should have killed her, but the armor absorbed enough of the concussive blast that it tore out the right side of her neck. If it had hit clean, she would have died for good.

His eyes were wide. Her mouth moved but nothing came out. Vora was clutching her throat and was healing the wound. They both paused at the enormity of what he had just done. They both just stared at each other, not sure what to do. That decision was soon made as Vora was hit so hard by a blast from Benga Din who had successfully come through the storm field. Thankfully she was almost healed up, but it was enough to dispel her lightning storm.

With visibility restored, it became clear that members of both teams were engaged in a scrum more than combat. Benga Din had been the first to break free but after blasting Vora, he was blasted in turn by Don. Both sides untangled and squared off with each other. The Chosen Dead glanced at each other and without a word, Vora created another lightning storm that separated the two teams.

The Redeemers closed ranks and waited for another attack but instead after a few seconds the storm slowly dispersed and they were all gone.

"Damn it!" The Penitent screamed. He was seething. He was angry that he felt like he was being made a fool of by the Chosen Dead. He hated how powerful they were. Worst of all, he hated himself. He had just made it into Heaven, to begin with, as much as he hated the harlot he didn't want to kill her. At least not where he could be caught. *No,* He said to himself. That thinking was what almost got him sent to hell.

He stopped himself, took a deep breath, and realized that his anger needed to be channeled away from that kind of thinking. He had to think clearly without anger. When Gerald popped up, he would be there. He would prove he was the better leader; his team would be number one.

The Chosen Dead had regrouped. They were waiting not for The Redeemers who could try to hunt them down and look for payback, but for the signal. Vora hadn't said much but she kept rubbing the side of her neck. Whatever had happened during her fight with the Redeemer, she wasn't going to talk about it.

The hardest part was doing your part. They had to be disciplined and follow the plan but Don was pushing to go back and take another crack at The Redeemers and end the contest without Gordon and Gerald, but the rest of the team didn't agree. Vora broke her silence long enough to tell Don that they needed to follow the plan.

Goorga lay in wait. The splinter of its essence that had been watching the Chosen had overheard enough of the Chosen's plan to appreciate it. It would lay in wait, showing weakness to its enemies, and then strike them down. It was exactly what Goorga had planned, and he would relish the moment when the Chosen's soul was sucked dry of its potency, and power Goorga to a level that could challenge Death itself.

The only issue was it had to be the first one to the Chosen. The one called Gordon would be there to strike from behind. That complicated things, but Goorga had a way to deal with him.

The largest issue was that when Gordon provided a transfer of his power to hide himself the chosen took that energy and was able to copy his stealth abilities. This was something that even after billions of years of understanding the fundamental molecular structure of living matter, and experience honing its energies, Goorga was not able to replicate what this pathetic soul had just done. This creature unchecked would grow beyond the scope of even the most fearsome of its kind.

Goorga tried to track the Chosen once he disappeared, but it couldn't get a trace of any type of energy. Instead, Goorga released additional splinters of itself around the designated area so that wherever the Chosen showed himself he would be able to attack. The only issue with this was that Goorga would take longer to amass enough power once it escaped so speed would be of the essence.

The Penitent had sent out his team to search for Gerald. He told them to focus on him rather than any of the other members of the Chosen Dead. There were no further attacks, so he knew that the end game was close. No more deceptions, misdirection, or feints. This would come down to who was best, and The Penitent would be the one who came out on top. He would prove worthy and make up for his sins.

The image of the harlot came unbidden to his mind. Seeing her with her throat torn troubled him that for a second he wanted to finish her off, see her die. He relished the thought and at the same time hated it. He was given the chance to serve to redeem himself. He could have gone below and been damned, but they saw enough to allow him to save himself. He knew that wanting her dead was wrong. What made it worse was the look on her face. As much as she hated him and vice versa, she still wasn't trying to kill him. He was never good at self-reflection. Strike first and ask questions later had been his style. He had let his emotions run wild and he had almost killed an ally. The Penitent would have sunk lower into a mire of regret and self-loathing if not for what happened next.

A flash, no more than a blip that no one else would have detected, went by. It wasn't Gerald but the Indian Gordon.

Neither Gordon nor Gerald had shown up until now, and it only made sense that wherever Gordon was, Gerald would be there as well. The Penitent sped off. He would investigate and if he found them, he would then notify his team. He wanted the first crack at Gerald.

The Chosen Dead were ready when the signal came, and they stayed right where they were. They needed to draw in The Penitent and provide him with a false sense of security. They were concerned for Gerald but between him and Gordon, they all felt that they would more than hold their own even against a full team, at least for a little while.

Gio was ready to go. He was waiting for the time when Gerald and Gordon both dropped their shields so they could make a beeline to the grotto when he spotted something odd. He moved closer to it. "Hey guys, come take a look at this. It looks like someone has got a leaky engine."

Elation! After all its time in confinement, Goorga could finally start the hunt that would set it loose upon the universe. It just needed enough time to make it happen. The splinter closest to the flash that revealed where Gordon was sped off in that direction. Some of the other splinters it recalled. Others had a job to do.

The splinter nearest The Redeemers extended its tiny jaws and bit down on its limb. Black, oily fluid dribbled out of the wound. The splinter waved its limb and spread the droplets all around until there was nothing left and what remained dropped where it was, now a husk of the essence it just held. The Redeemers were waiting for The Penitent to notify them. Behind them, the small black droplets began to bubble.

Miller was standing outside his cabin wearing boxers, a white tank top, wearing his bunny slippers, and sipping on a freshly brewed coffee. He had picked up the flash as well and identified Gordon's energy signature. *If that one didn't want to be found he wouldn't be,* Miller thought to himself. It was a smart move. No other clues to follow but give them something to grasp. It's way too obvious to have Gerald flash, but to have Gordon do it? The kid had a shot to be scary.

Behind Miller, a second splinter from Goorga had joined the first. They both started the same process of opening up a limb and splattering their black, oily vitae on the ground before they, too, collapsed into spent husks.

Miller sensed a shift and quickly wheeled around. Something familiar was close by, something dangerous. Miller crouched down and an energized sword appeared in his hand.

Goorga felt the last of its splinters absorb back into its body. It stood up. The chains that bound it allowed for it to stand but it had not moved since it had been interred in its prison. The creature's joints popped as its long-dormant ligaments screamed in agony at the sudden movement. Goorga drank in the pain, It fueled it. So close to its objective. Acidic drool hissed off the floor beneath it in anticipation. The final phase was about to begin.

Gerald prepared himself. He knew it was only a matter of time before The Penitent showed up. Gordon was hidden out front and wouldn't be seen until he was ready. Once both his and Gordon's cloaks were removed, the rest of the team would show up and then the fun would begin. In the next few moments, one of them would be the victor. Gerald wouldn't rub it in The Penitent's face but he wouldn't stop Gio and Vora from doing it either.

The sound of the waterfall drowned out any noise that could be heard in the normal spectrum so Gerald had opened himself up to his other senses to pick anything up. So far only small animals and a man-eating plant were moving out there. Nothing to worry about...yet.

Gordon was watching from his hiding point. He was using

all his senses but was as still as a stone. Nothing would know he was there until it was time to reveal himself. He worried about Vora which he knew she would complain about. "I am strong, I save you, my chief," she said with a smile. He appreciated their quiet time together. He was just a man, and she was just a woman. That she shared her softness with him and no other made him feel emotions he never thought he ever would, especially during the trials and pain of his life.

Gordon's reverie was cut short by a sudden movement out of the corner of his mind's eye. Whatever it is, it was being very careful not to be detected. Gordon initially thought that it was The Redeemers, specifically the African warrior Benga Din. He was a fine hunter, he thought. If anyone could escape detection it would be him.

Gordon was careful to cast the net a little further, careful to escape detection. Even cloaked, he could be discovered if he scanned too quickly. Whatever it was slowly crept over near the grotto pool. It did not touch the water but Gordon was able to catch a glimpse of something. This creature most definitely was not Benga Din. It had a cloak as well, not as good as Gordon's but good enough to hide its aura and shape. It was a grayish blur against the sandy edge of the water.

Gordon held himself still. His instinct was to strike at it. It screamed at him too, but he couldn't be sure this was something sent from The Redeemers, so he stayed where he was. He would watch and wait. When the time came, he would strike.

The creature scuttled away from the water's edge and thought to conceal itself as it moved back into the thick foliage opposite the water. It was on an elevated mound and appeared to be doing something as it seemed to shake back and forth briefly, then it moved on to the other side of where it was, which was another elevated mound. Then it seemed to lay still and nothing of its essence was left.

Gordon knew that those two points were ideal for an ambush. If it was somehow marking the locations for The Redeemers, then he and the rest of the team would be ready. Those were the ambush points they would use.

Gordon was alerted to a second larger creature hidden much further up that slowly made its way down. The cloaking on this creature was even better, no more than a wispy phantom that moved so quickly that you could mistake it for a rustle of the wind. Gordon knew it was no wind. It moved to the water's edge and seemed to cast its gaze over the area searching for something. It had to be either Gerald or Gordon.

Gordon watched as it descended into the pool of water. It barely moved the water as it made its way through and headed underneath the waterfall. Even with the turbulence of the water, the creature seemed to move without difficulty. It stood still, and Gordon then felt it scanning the area. It was searching for them. It had to know they were here.

He stayed as still as a statue. He knew deep down that if he was detected, something terrible would happen. Gordon struggled to push down the growing sense of fear and despair that emanated from this thing. He was on a knife's edge, waiting to see if his cloaking would hold up against whatever this was. Whatever happened next, Gordon knew this thing was wrong like the creature being held captive, and he would kill it.

The waves of fear and despair suddenly disappeared. Gordon picked up another approaching, and he didn't dare open himself up in fear of detection, but when he went back to where the creature was, it was gone.

Gordon scanned out. He picked up The Penitent. Gordon focused on the wildcard. This creature was not with The Redeemers, and Gordon recognized one of the enemy when he saw one. He slowly made his way out of his hiding spot and began moving. Gordon had hidden himself at the bottom of the water pool and he followed the path of the creature. Whatever this creature had planned, he would be there to meet it.

Goorga had found its prey. There were two splinters of itself floating unseen from the guards placed to watch over Goorga. They lay down on the floor and began the process of splattering the viscous contents that passed for their blood all over the floor. The spots of blood began to bubble and expand. Dozens of them all started growing into various forms of Goorga, all twisted abominations. The sensors and alarms went off and immediately the wardens of his prison were locked in combat with Goorga's blood spawn.

Goorga needed the spawn to complete the transfer. It was one thing to send out splinters of its essence and another to transfer completely from itself to the location where its prey was. Goorga couldn't fight its way from one end of the planet to another, not with the opposition he would face the entire way, but it could send itself via energy transfer. This would allow his enemies to focus on one point while it gathered its strength. When it had killed its prey and absorbed its power it could then destroy them all.

With a shower of multi-colored sparks, Goorga broke its chains. They had limited its power but nowhere near enough to keep it incarcerated. The five wardens were battling the blood spawn and so far, they were holding off the wardens, but Goorga needed to start the process before they brought in additional resources to deal with it. Goorga looked up and sensed the presence of one who could destroy it.

Gerald was sitting in the back of the cave cross-legged. His eyes were closed. The scent of the moisture clung to every surface. This far back into the cave, the sound of the waterfall was muted but still a constant drone of noise that could lull a person to sleep. The sound had no effect on covering if someone was coming. There were too many other senses being used for that to happen unless it was Gordon who wouldn't allow you to be seen unless he wanted him to.

"What do you fight for?" The words echoed through his head. His father always said that to him when times were tough. Gerald pondered those words as he scanned the area while sitting in the dark. After this was over, he and his team would be shipped off for live action. The fact that you could die...again troubled him. The old fears came back to him from his days of war.

Making the right decision was usually making the hard decision. You knew men would die; you just hoped it wasn't as many as expected and that you could sleep through the night without seeing them trouble your dreams. His scans picked up something faint coming through the waterfall. If it wasn't for being able to copy Gordon's ability, another person may not have picked up on it. It wasn't a physical thing. Whatever it was moved through the water as if it could pass through it like a thing of spirit, not flesh.

It was the haze. It tried to fit in with reality, but reality refused to accept it. It was not meant to be here. That thought came unbidden to his mind. It was more a subconscious warning. Whatever was coming through was wrong. It crept closer to Gerald, approached the narrow passage slowly, and then stopped.

It seemed to sniff the air around the entrance, then went still as a stone, just a haze spot near the top corner of the passage. Then quick as a thought, it launched tendrils of itself throughout the cave and one struck the invisible shield Gerald had erected like a battering ram. The shield splintered and broke, and the force of the impact sent Gerald crashing into the back wall of the cave with enough impact to cause cracks in the wall and shake the entire area.

The Chosen Dead had circled up. The bubbling black drops

had sprouted horrors beyond imagination. They had all seen these creatures in their dreams but to face off with them was something altogether different. The stink that poured off them wasn't just physical but spiritual. It was a repellant mix of bloated corpses and corruption, and it crashed over them like a stinking wave. A normal soul's natural reaction was always the same. They all took a step back. The feeling of wrongness was the next thing you felt from them, then despair, pain, and loneliness.

"They shouldn't be here," Don growled. The daemons, because that's what they were, numbered thirty. They surrounded the Chosen Dead who circled up to protect themselves. As they prepared to launch themselves at The Chosen Dead, the last reaction came to the fore. The evil and wrongness that exuded from them reminded you of what was at stake, at the horror that would be unleashed on the universe if they were allowed to win....that could never happen. The Blood spawn of Goorga attacked The Chosen Dead. Vora's scream of defiance filled the air.

The Redeemers were caught in a hectic scramble for survival. The twins were fighting for their lives. Six of the blood spawn had spat acid that slowly healed wherever it struck, and the twins had taken the brunt of it but they were able to get a breather when Tyrus came to their aid and was able to slice one of the creatures from the head to the groin in an almost straight line. That killed it permanently in a flash of putrid black smoke.

The twins were able to counter and grab the bare arm they had so their outer armored arms were free. They began to spin around and around until they were a blur. At that moment, the remaining creatures became the hunted. Two were immediately vaporized and the rest began to pull back.

Sical was tackled to the ground and the blood spawn moved into position to dismember him. To his credit, Sical was fighting like a madman as his life depended on it. They managed to pull off one of his arms before he was able to cause one of the monsters to catch fire. Sical blasted another sideways into the spawn on fire. He picked up his arm and reattached it. Benga Din, who had killed three of the creatures, threw an energy lance that consumed another creature that had gotten behind Kuback and would have taken his head off with extended claws.

Goorga had locked onto his prey. It paused because it could not pick up a trace of Gerald in the cave. It did not have the time to wait it out so Goorga would send out its tendrils. Goorga paused. If the other was with him, it could delay it from killing its prey. The decision was made when a rustle of wings precluded the roof of the structure from being destroyed when Bariel the angel arrived.

With a roar that shook the structure, Bariel brought a flaming sword into existence and within seconds had slaughtered Goorga's blood spawn. Bariel turned back towards Goorga, roared again, and charged towards Goorga. Bariel was met with a shield Goorga had erected. Goorga could not fight Bariel, at least not yet. It needed to transfer its essence to the blood spawn so it could kill Gerald. The problem was the more its essence was transferred, the weaker the shield would be. If Bariel got through too soon, it would not have been enough to destroy Gerald. Bariel began a barrage of sword strikes that boomed miles away. A sickly green shield light flashed against golden white light as Bariel continued his assault on Goorga's shield.

Miller did not wait for the Blood spawn to fully develop but used his sword to destroy the first growing mound closest to him. The other developing spawn retreated from Miller, stopped growing, and ran towards each other like a corrupt ant line to form three distinct bodies. Miller gave them no time and lashed out at the nearest creature in front of him. This time an arm lashed out to block his sword. Miller fired energy blasts which it dodged and avoided with blurring speed.

Without looking, Miller formed another sword to block claw strikes from one side and a stream of burning acid that he mostly evaded. However, some hit his side and he recoiled from the burning pain in his side where the acid struck. Miller set off an explosion that pushed back the three large and now-formed monstrosities that had fanned out before him. One of the spawn tried to creep behind Miller, but he caused the area behind him to catch fire which hit the creature, and it squealed in pain from the flame that it came in contact with.

The three creatures then spoke in one voice that sounded guttural, as if it was not used to speaking in this physical realm. "Your reckoning is here, Miller. Do you not know your enemy?"

Miller scanned all three creatures. They were all around ten feet in height, warped caricatures of a humanoid being. Twisted limbs where one leg was shorter than the other for one. Another had barely a limb on one side, and another that extended out grotesquely. The last had its head in the center of its body. Miller scanned through the realms, seen and unseen, and saw the truth of his foe.

"Yeeesssss, now you see," the blood spawn hissed.

Miller was shocked, it was the creature that was kept a prisoner and that he had captured those many years before. "How could you have escaped?"

The blood spawn gurgled as if it were drowning but was doing a parody of a laugh. "I allowed you to capture me little morsel I have been waiting. I wait no longer." The three spawns began to move in, but Miller put up a wall of flame to prevent them from coming closer. "Tell me why," Miller demanded.

The blood spawn paused and then tilted their heads in unison like a group of corrupted dogs when facing something they didn't understand.

"Why did you let me capture you?" Miller demanded.

The blood spawn stood still for a moment. When Miller thought they were going to attack they answered him. "One among you, you have the same prophecy, yes?"

Miller nodded.

"Then you know what he can become? You should have killed him when he first came here"

Miller knew exactly who the blood spawn meant. "There are many with his power."

Goorga replied "Many yes, but they do not manifest that power, they are limited in scope and not flexible enough."

Miller increased the flames.

The three blood spawn moved in unison and walked directly into the flames. They did not make a sound. The stink from their burning caused Miller to almost gag but he held firm as they made it through the flames.

"You shall suffer this day," the blood spawn said before leaping as one at Miller.

The Chosen Dead were unleashed and fought with abandon. Vora let all her rage out upon these creatures. Her fear had grown exponentially not for herself but for her team and Gordon. She had spent her human life proving her worth as a shield maiden. She had married but never had the chance to have a child. That chance was taken when her husband was slain in the lands of Rus. Vora had mourned for her husband Jurgen. She would have married again but she was slain two years later by raiders from Rus. That was the enemy then.

She thought she had known hate, but she was wrong. Her foe in front of her now was hate incarnate. They made it very easy to reciprocate that hate. Vora had burned three of them to ash and couldn't wait to burn more.

David was transformed into his man-wolf form and avoided the acid spit from multiple monsters. He had been burned before, and from the missing patches of fur he made sure to avoid it since the burns didn't heal quickly.

Don smashed two of them apart and threw another through one of its brood. He noticed that they were lined up blocking their way to where Gerald was. These creatures could die and would stay at a distance but then they would close in whenever any of them moved west. The realization hit him. "They are trying to kill Gerald!" Don roared. "They are keeping us here!"

The creatures understood and they began to fire volleys of acid into the Chosen Dead's ranks. The acid could do great damage, so they brought up shields that burned the shields themselves. They tried to get past the blood spawn, but they were able to keep them angled off from heading to him, and they wouldn't send anyone off because there was a real chance these creatures could kill one of the Chosen Dead for good.

Gerald hit the back wall of the cave hard enough to crack the wall and cause the ceiling and surrounding walls to shudder. Small pebbles and dust rained down as he fought through the pain that would have killed a living man. As the dust settled, Gerald was able to get a good look at what had attacked him. His heart sank as the stink of death and decay sallied forth from the nightmare that came through the mist. Gerald recognized it: the creature from the holding cell. It was larger than what he remembered, exuded more power, bloated with it. As it moved closer, it had no fear of Gerald, and it seemed to expand ever so slightly. A flow of corrupted energy flowed into it, changing it, expanding its power. That's all he saw as Goorga pushed a clawed hand forward and Gerald was instantly pushed back into the wall, unable to move.

Goorga moved so quickly that it appeared that one moment it was in the middle of the cave and the next was right in front of Gerald. The creature was drooling acid from a human face that smiled to expose a mass of fangs that should not have been able to fit into its mouth. "I have you now," the creature said, surprising Gerald when it spoke.

It looked up suddenly and seemed to be listening to something. Gerald could see that the flow of energy was still flowing into Goorga, and a ripple across the monster's face saw another subtle increase in its size. The stink was the worst part. but the acid that drooled onto Gerald's cheek and shoulder burned horrendously.

"If only we had more time." Goorga cocked its horned head again as if listening. "Goodbye, Chosen one. Just know I will devour you and use your power to destroy."

Gerald went ice cold. This was what Bariel was speaking of before to him.

Goorga opened its fanged maw, and it kept opening. Its jaw bones detached as it reared up like a snake to clamp down onto Gerald's head. Acid rained down on Gerald and he gritted his teeth while he struggled to fight the effects of the monster's hold on him. The pain made him buck like a wild man, and the rage that came with the pain fueled him. Slowly Gerald was slipping out of the creature's grasp, but his time was up as Goorga started his final strike. "Grk!" was all Goorga could get out. Gerald was fighting to free himself and suddenly there was a spear sticking out of the monster's chest and then the monster caught fire from within.

Gordon had a hell of a sense of timing. He had stalked up to the creature and waited for the perfect time to strike, for the time it would have its back turned and he could lay it low. The power the creature had over Gerald broke, and he slid down the cave wall. Gordon and Gerald nodded to each other as they approached with shields up, a sword for Gerald, and a spear for Gordon.

The now-prone body of the creature continued to burn, and the stink that emanated from it was terrible.

Another presence approached and both Gordon and Gerald turned to see The Penitent walking in. He ignored them and focused on the burning body. "Is that what I think it is?" The Penitent asked. The energy flow into the creature began moving quicker into the body of the monster. Before Gerald could shout a warning, the fire was out, and three black, viscous arms shot out to impale Gerald, Gordon, and The Penitent. All three were paralyzed as it injected acidic venom into them. Instantly they were all in agony and unable to move.

Goorga stood up and the burned parts of it fell away in a shower of stinking black dust. Goorga turned to The Penitent. "Why are you with them?"

The three blood spawn came for Miller who was now covered in acid burns. He was too battle-hardened to let the burns slow him down, but even he could only take so much damage before it would affect him. Miller fired with his left hand, and the earth grew up around the spawn, encasing it. He charged forward and fired energy blasts at the creature and then set it on fire.

While the spawn squealed in pain Miller pivoted and fired more energy blasts at the spawn on the right and then followed up with slicing off its right arm which was twice the length of the other arm. He charged it and set the arm that flopped on the ground on fire ensuring it wouldn't come back into play.

Behind Miller, the creature trapped in earth broke free and came for him. He turned in a circle and materialized a sword in his other hand which he used to slice the spawn missing an arm in half. The body instantly vaporized as Miller turned into the attack of the spawn previously trapped in rock and blocked both swipes of its acid-dripping claws. The spawn snapped at Miller's face but was met with a head butt that knocked out multiple fangs. Miller paid the price because the acid burned his eyes and face badly. The burning spawn latched its teeth into Miller's shoulder from behind, and he screamed in agony.

The Redeemers were struggling with the spawn. They weren't able to kill the remaining twenty or so creatures as they kept moving, and only limited telepathic control worked on pushing them around. They had placed shields up as well.

"We must get past these creatures!" Begna Din yelled as he fired volley after volley into the spawn's ranks.

Sical and Tyrus were severely injured from venom being injected into them. They fought on but were limited as the venom worked its way out of their bodies. The twins and Kubak continued to make frontal assaults. They were able to kill one of the spawn, but the other spawn closed ranks and wouldn't allow for that tactic to work again.

Benga Din knew that if they stayed any longer something terrible would happen, he could feel it. His teammates also felt it, their urgency showed in every action they took. "We must break the line!" He motioned and the team formed up behind him. "Charge!"

They took off at the speed of light at the spawn line. The sickly green glow of their shields flickered as the spawn waited to receive the attack. The Redeemers knew this was a last-gasp attempt. If they couldn't break the line, then whatever evil these spawn were doing would happen. They had tried to move in the direction of where The Penitent, their leader, and Gerald, the leader of the Chosen Dead, were located. Losing those two would be devastating and could not be allowed to happen.

For all his flaws, The Penitent was a good leader and had earned his place. None of the Redeemers would allow him to come to harm without a fight. Everyone by now had heard the stories about Gerald's power for a soul so young. He was also a good leader and along with respect, there was love for him among his team. *Good men died; it's what they do in war, but not today.* Benga Din swore to himself.

The Redeemers struck the front line like a lightning strike. The shields were blown out and the front five or six spawn were driven back. One was destroyed by the feedback of energy from the shield collapse, but that was it. The spawn had waited patiently for The Redeemers to make a mistake, and now they would pay with their lives.

The spawn encircled The Redeemers and struck at them from different angles and pushed their way in. The spawn pushed them into the ground and showered them with acid and claw attacks.

Benga Din gritted his teeth from the pain of the acid. One of his eyes was burned out. Kuback had been impaled multiple times and screamed when the venom was injected. The twins were separated and fought like alley cats, cornered, injured, and dangerous. Tyrus and Sical stood back to back. They both could barely move, and it appeared that the spawn was toying with them as they would slash them, laugh, and then retreat to do it again.

Sical had no right arm after it had melted off, and Tyrus was floating as he was missing both feet. To their credit, they refused to quit.

Die well, my friends, Benga Din thought as he was impaled from multiple angles and blacked out for a second as the venom pumped fire into him.

The twins were finally cornered and impaled. They screamed in agony as they dangled. Even then they tried to fight and were able to break off a poisoned limb.

An explosion near Benga Din threw him off his feet. At first, it seemed muffled and far away until he felt the limbs penetrating his torso were quickly pulled out. Immediately he had full control of his senses and took Gio's hand.

"You alright there pal?" Gio asked with a grim smile.

"Much better. Thank you, my friend." The tide had suddenly turned.

Don was the cause of the explosion. He had hit the line of spawn at their thickest and sent them flying. Vora sent lightning into a grotesque creature with three arms that ended in crab claws and burned it to nothing. David flashed across the field. His face where parts of the acid had burned it were smooth and healing, but he was still missing hair. He slashed the limbs holding up Tyrus and Sical. Another explosion pulled all eyes over to Reginald and the Victorians who took the rest of the spawn by surprise and cut them down in short order.

The Victorians moved to Sical and Tyrus who were the most injured and barely responsive. The group laid hands on the two of them and used healing energy to accelerate the wounds that had been inflicted on them by the spawn. Once the rest of The Redeemers had been healed up, everyone gathered together.

Reginald greeted Benga Din. "How are you feeling, old chap?" They shook hands.

"Much better, thank you, my friend. It was a close run."

Reginald nodded. "Too close. Lucky thing we happened to be close to these chaps so we could help them out. They had the same vermin problem you did."

Benga Din smiled. "No such thing as luck, but grateful all the same. We need to go, I can feel a fell hand closing upon us all."

Gio stepped forward. "Let's go, the bad guys are where our guys are." Without another word, they all grouped back up and took off.

The main piece of Goorga in what remained of the prison structure was exerting itself. The angel Bariel was striking the force shield Goorga had placed with such ferocity that the walls had been blown out. All that remained were the cornerstones.

Bariel had not relented, and the cost to power the shields was now taking its toll.

Goorga felt the presence of other souls and saw Porter and other powerful souls descend and bombard the shield with their power. Goorga had miscalculated as the shields buckled before being reinstated with its will. It realized that it would lose a portion of itself before it could complete the transfer of its essence and would have to kill the Chosen One quickly or else it would run out of time, and worse, be diminished permanently.

The Penitent's eyes widened as the Daemon addressed him. Even through the burning pain, the worst was being addressed by this creature of darkness. The shame that followed burned worse than the acid. The Penitent saw the look on both Gordon's and Gerald's faces. He thrashed and tried to sever the pulsing limb that had speared him. The venom was slowing The Penitent down. Gordon had cut half of the limb off and was fighting off smaller limbs that had protruded from the main body of the Daemon. The Penitent also saw the flow of energy and knew that if that thing got any stronger, they would all be dead.

Gerald had been able to cut through the limb. He had severed the limb internally using his will and closed the hole in his chest. He raised his arm to deflect another throbbing limb from decapitating him. Gerald fired a blast at the creature's face which had some effect, but it was washed away in another ripple across the creature's body that saw it grow even more. If that flow of energy wasn't stopped, they would all be dead.

Gerald looked over at Gordon who had been struck by additional limbs, so he sent multiple blasts into the limbs which allowed them to break off. Gordon dropped to the ground and disappeared. The limbs scrambled around the area but were unable to locate and grab onto him.

Goorga was frustrated. He was running out of time. What

was left of itself in the prison structure was quickly dwindling to nothing, so it needed to kill the Chosen now.

As if reading the monster's mind, Gerald put up a force shield ahead of an onslaught of limbs. Gerald gritted his teeth and exerted his will against that of the Daemon.

Gerald had bought time for Gordon to collect himself and hang upside down at the top of the roof. The Daemon had created a throbbing, veiny vine wall so that it could separate Gerald from them which confirmed that this creature was here to kill Gerald. That could not happen. His people were coming. He could sense it, but he sensed others as well, things made from the Daemon. As much as Gordon wanted to help them, Gerald needed him. First, he had to free The Penitent.

The Penitent was struggling with the limbs and the burning pain when the limbs retracted followed by a voice that hissed into his mind. "Be at peace. I do not wish to harm you, Penitent."

The Penitent felt icy tendrils of fear run down his spine. "What do you want, Daemon? Leave this place now." he demanded.

Goorga hissed and gurgled its laughter. "I cannot but I wish to bargain with you. I see a soul that is at odds with its nature. I sssseeee yyyyooouuuu." It slithered into his mind. " You have been misled. Why should you not lead all others? You have felt shame when you should have been exalted." Goorga purred its poison into the ear of the Penitent.

The Penitent was rigid with fear. What the creature spoke of were thoughts he had dwelt on many a time. "How can you know such things?" The Penitent demanded as the limbs quivered around him.

"I see the stain on your soul, the darkness. You were told it is wrong, evil. What is that but another way to control you? Help me kill this Chosen One. Do you want to be the apex leader? Not with this one present. He will always be your better."

The Penitent was stock still. Everything the abomination said was true. He was a natural leader, but Gerald was more so. He was a man who led other leaders. He had charisma, willing to sacrifice himself for his team.

The Penitent saw his failings magnified. The wars, the deaths of the men he ordered because of his orders. Each one he thought was necessary, victory above all.

"All the pain and suffering was not necessary, unless you wanted to inflict it upon those who deserve it, and they all deserve it, don't they?" Goorga hissed more bile into The Penitent's mind.

He recalled back to when his wife and children left him. He was too hard, too rigid. His wife had said, "Not everything is a war. Your family is what you fight for and you forgot that." Her tears fell to the floor before she left with Jacob and Lisa.

The anguish he felt remembering that day returned as fresh as the day it happened, the first time he had wept since he was a child. He didn't need anyone, he had thought, but he was wrong. He tried more drinking, but that just washed whatever was left of his life away in a flood of whiskey and regret.

The day things changed he remembered waking up sick to his stomach. He hadn't spoken to his family in months. He had lost his job weeks ago. He had the money to drink but not food, and even with nausea cramping his belly, the gnaw of hunger was finally winning out.

He shuffled down the street until he saw the "Jesus Saves" sign. The light that came from the neon sign was as tired and sick as everything else around it. He remembered the stink of cigarettes and bleach along with the smell of hash that caused his stomach to growl like a cornered animal. He walked up the stairs into the building. A man in a sharp new ice cream white suit that was the fashion at the time was shaking hands with Mother Claire, the nun who ran the shelter. She was old when he was a young man and just seemed to not have aged he remembered. "Thank you, John. I don't mind saying we needed this" Mother Claire said in the slight brogue she still carried from the old country. "God bless you, John."

John, in his ice cream white suit, The Penitent remembered thinking was just another bigwig looking to feel better about themselves while the rest of the schleps scraped by. John in his ice cream white suit leaned in and hugged her. "You were there when I needed you. I wouldn't be here if it wasn't for you and this place." *Do not judge a book by its cover.* Came unbidden to his mind

The Penitent remembered looking into an old smudged mirror and seeing the dried-up, grim scarecrow he had become. His lights were on, but nobody was home. He looked around and saw the same thing on the faces of each of the other lost souls looking for a bite to eat. To think that John with the ice cream white suit, and he forgot to mention the matching hat, had been a lost soul just him. He didn't want to believe him. *Who was he to have his life while he had nothing?* The Penitent raged, and if John with the ice cream white suit had been closer, he would have killed him.

"You gave me hope that I could fix myself, fix my family," John with the ice cream white suit had said.

The Penitent froze at that moment. Rage was gone. It was replaced with shame, sadness, and fear of never seeing his family, and the last emotion was hope. Hope that he can see his family again. He couldn't breathe, he couldn't move. The Penitent was nailed to the floor in a whirlwind of emotions. The room swayed sideways as he started to fall.

John in the ice cream white suit rushed forward and put his arm around The Penitent's waist. You carry enough drunks, you know best how to move them around. "You alright there, pal? I gotcha. Come on over here and take a load off." John helped The

Penitent over to a folding chair in the corner of the old bingo room.

Mother Clair was right behind him with some water and a bowl of hash. "You're going to be alright," she said to The Penitent.

For the first time in a long time, The Penitent believed that. He looked up at John and saw him for the first time. He had sandy-colored hair parted to the side and was about the same age as the Penitent but looked older due to the drinking and life living on the streets. What he said next changed his life. "I would like my family back."

John, the fellow lost soul and wanderer, looked him right in the eye and nodded.

The Daemon's limbs twitched waiting on The Penitent. The Penitent saw the truth in the trap the daemon had laid for him. It knew his ego which had destroyed his family once would be his undoing. He remembered judgment. He knew how close he had come to eternal damnation, the balance of the good and the bad. It was all about the choices he had made then, and the choices he would make now. The Penitent had made his decision.

The Daemon, who must have been able to see his thoughts, also knew his decision. "A pity, you would have died last." The limbs were quicker than the shield The Penitent tried to erect. They speared his body from multiple directions at once. Before they could pump venom into his body, the world caught fire.

The sudden presence of the Indian followed. The Penitent wasted no time and added his own fire to all the limbs, and between Gordon and The Penitent, they burned all of the limbs there. A wall of bloody vines that looked like veins blocked off where Gerald was. That was where they had to go.

Gordon turned to The Penitent "I knew you would make the right choice."

The Penitent did not know what to say but gave Gordon a thin smile, nodded, and changed the subject. "Let's save your friend." He finished before they both turned and began to batter the wall of vines.

Miller was on fire. The spawn had latched itself onto him and sunk its arms and legs into his body so it could not be dislodged and pumped venom into him. He could feel his body being consumed from the inside out. The other spawn swung down with a claw that Miller evaded. The second swipe caught his arm and ripped it to the bone. The third swipe caught him in the shoulder and part of its fellow spawn's arm. The blow caused him to fall to the ground which caused the spawn attached to him to grunt and shift its head slightly. Miller took advantage and was able to focus enough through the fiery pain to shoot the creature in the side of its head. It didn't die, but from the mewling, it was close.

Miller could feel the venom rapidly diminish in his system as he was able to start to heal himself. The third spawn grabbed Miller by the leg and picked him up, so he was in the air upside down with the second spawn still feebly clinging to him. The third spawn growled and when it increased its growl, Miller knew it would strike and where. He turned his torso in the air one hundred and eighty degrees. If he timed this wrong, he would die.

The spawn holding Miller struck, he twisted, and where Miller's throat would have been was now its fellow spawn. The claws struck the spawn attached to Miller and took off what was left of its head, neck, and upper back. All that remained before the attached spawn's body disappeared into black dust was part of a spine that stuck out. Miller fired energy blasts at both of the creature's legs. It crashed to the ground which left its arms which Miller had sliced off with a dagger he had materialized.

Miller floated over the body still upside down and stuck the dagger into the last spawn's throat and sliced its head off. Miller hit the ground as the last spawn's body exploded into black stinking dust. He lay there for a moment. He wanted to rest but he knew that there was work to be done. Miller focused on healing himself which took much longer than it should have due to the acid and floated up into the sky. He had a creeping sense of dread that he didn't have much time left to stop it.

The assault was relentless, and if Gerald didn't know any better, desperate. Goorga wouldn't let up. It was intent on killing him. Gerald had not stopped moving in minutes as the creature threw acid, fire, and sickly green energy blasts at it. The issue was that as long as that flow of energy kept adding to his strength, he wouldn't have a chance to stop it.

Goorga could not afford to let Gerald live and was frustrated with how resilient Gerald was being. It wouldn't matter soon. Goorga was nearing its full potency. What it would lose should not make any difference.

Gerald could hear behind the wall of flesh-like vines that Gordon and The Penitent were trying to break through. Goorga used its power again and was able to batter the shield Gerald had put up. It divided the blast so that when it struck the shield, it sent Gerald straight back into the cave wall again and this time, it left an outline of Gerald's body. The power that Goorga had to immobilize Gerald was being reinserted as it grew stronger. It needed to kill Gerald soon or it would be undone.

Gerald was pinned to the wall again. He had recognized the energy pattern of the mental hold that this monster was able to exert and had been weaving and ducking away from it, but now it had increased again in strength and he was unable to hold it off. He kept fighting even though he was pinned to the wall. He was able to have the earth climb up and drag at the Goorga's feet, but it just slowed it down for a few moments.

Gerald remembered manipulating the energy that trapped

the Victorians. He caused a cave-in that buried Goorga but it only delayed the creature for a few seconds. Gerald focused on the energy stream. He reached out with his senses and touched it. He recoiled instantly. In a brief moment, Gerald had caught a glimpse of what this creature was and what it would do if it managed to kill him. "Souleater" he whispered. It would devour him and then use his power to devastate anything it came into contact with.

As much as it repulsed him, Gerald stretched his senses back into the stream of black bile that made up Goorga's energy. The raging flood that he dipped himself in could not be contained or stopped. There was just too much power for that, but with the right angle and pressure, it could be deflected and redirected.

An explosion of earth let Gerald know he was out of time; Goorga was coming for him. Gerald focused on an area of the energy stream and visualized it as water. He cordoned off an area by using his will to create a separate rift. The energy was flowing the same way, but he had a semblance of control. Blinding pain in his chest brought him back to Goorga, who was standing in front of Gerald and had extended a tendril that had gone through his chest.

"You won't escape me now," Goorga hissed, enveloping him in a gag-inducing stink as it spoke. A blast of energy did not do much but cause a smudge on Goorga's face. "Weak." It hissed.

Gerald used that distraction to go back to the river of bile energy and willed it away to another smaller stream, still heading in the same direction. He quickly separated that smaller stream into even smaller streams. Once he was sure he could handle some of them, he exerted his will and directed the energy into two different locations. The first was the vine wall which caught fire immediately once that energy had struck it. The second was at the area of the floor behind where Goorga was.

Goorga felt something change, and not in a good way. Suddenly the energy transfer had been changed. It did not realize that it was Gerald until it was too late. The wall of vines was on fire, and then it was catapulted into the air with massive force as its own energy was used as a weapon against it. Goorga felt terrible pain spear through its back from the kinetic energy that had blasted the floor. It flew headfirst into the wall in front of it where it struck face first and felt the top row of its fangs snap off.

Once the energy was available, it needed to be arranged molecularly back to its standard state for Goorga's makeup. The energy transfer happened partly in this dimension but partly in the other place, unbeknownst to Gerald. This allowed it to flow faster but there was a process that needed to be done before it could be added back to fully rebuild Goorga.

The Penitent and Gordon had burned the last of the grotesque vine wall. They both charged in and saw that the Daemon was stuck headfirst in the back wall of the cave. Gerald was staggering towards them. His hands maneuvered what appeared to be black blood in the air. Gordon and The Penitent realized that somehow Gerald had tapped into the energy flow the Daemon was using and had used it against him.

Goorga pulled its head out of the wall. Its human-like face with too many fangs was splattered with black blood and broken pieces of fangs stuck in its face. Gerald extended his arm, and a flow of that tainted energy was blasted back into the creature and sent it back into the wall. Gerald saw Gordon and The Penitent. "We have to kill it now. If it gets all its energy, it will be too strong."

The world was on fire. The Chosen Dead, Victorians, and The Redeemers' battle with Goorga's blood spawn had set the area around the grotto on fire. The water in the grotto, usually twelve feet deep, had almost all been burned away so that you could now walk knee-deep in it. The creatures they were fighting were tougher to kill. The blood spawn had caved in the entrance to the cave in their effort to slow down any hope of rescue. The Daemons stunted the combined might of the three teams. They needed a new strategy fast if they had any hope of reaching Gerald, Gordon, and The Penitent before they were killed.

Goorga shuddered in ecstasy as it felt itself expanding again. The broken fangs in its mouth fell out and new ones grew in and then enlarged so that the laws of physics were pushed beyond their limits as its mouth opened wide in a horrific pantomime of a smile. It almost felt whole again. It had enough of its essence back to kill the chosen and as a bonus devour its allies.

Goorga extended its thick muscled arms and sent multiple viscous strand arms of itself to impale Gerald, Gordon, and The Penitent. They initially were able to hold the attack at bay, but the monster's sheer power was not to be denied.

Gordon's shield was the first to break. Any hope of retaliation was quickly turned into a fight for survival as a limb swooped in to take off Gordon's head, but he blocked it by allowing his arm to be impaled instead.

The Penitent sacrificed himself by weakening his shield so he could set fire to the limbs that had snared Gordon. The Penitent left himself open for attack and was first smashed into the far wall by a thick limb that swung at him and then battered him into the wall. Once The Penitent hit the wall, he didn't have a chance to slide down as Goorga sent a thick stream of acidic drool right into him. The screams from the Penitent were soon drowned out by the roar of a charging Goorga.

Gordon tried to stop him, but Goorga extended its claw and enveloped Gordon in fire, then with another wave sent Gordon crashing into The Penitent, who looked like a living skeleton.

Gerald was mortified and impressed that The Penitent was

still on his feet. All other thoughts were dashed as he raised the floor of the cave to block Goorga, but that did little as the Daemon just smashed through it like a freight train.

Goorga raised its clawed hand and sent a wave of force that went right through Gerald's shield like a cannonball through a glass pane window. Both of Gerald's legs were shattered and before he could fall to the ground in agonizing pain, Goorga tackled Gerald to the ground. Gerald roared in pain and desperation and fired concussive eye blasts into Goorga's face to little effect. Goorga picked him up by the throat and squeezed so hard that blood squirted out both of Gerald's eyes and ears. Gerald would have died if it weren't for both Gordon and the living skeleton that was The Penitent leaping on top of Goorga. The distraction was enough to loosen Goorga's grip and Gerald, who could barely see as he tried to heal as quickly as possible, focused on the monster's elbow and sent as much force as he could into it.

The elbow shattered and its arm from the elbow down went flying. The creature's roar was so loud it sent Gerald flying into the opposite wall of the cave where the narrow entrance was. The monster grabbed both Gordon and The Penitent and threw them both to the ground so hard you heard a sonic boom and then they both lay at the bottom of a crater not moving.

Gerald picked himself up and steadily rose to his feet. Goorga picked up its arm and reattached it. It then vomited a vile stream of acid that broke through the shield Gerald had erected bit right into his torso and burned down the right side of his face. Gerald was in so much pain he couldn't even scream. Goorga came for him, and Gerald was too weak to do anything about it.

At the prison structure, the shield wall that the main body of Goorga had erected finally came down. The combined might of Bariel and the souls who had added to the attack finally smashed through. What was left of Goorga there had shriveled up to a miniature version of the Daemon Goorga. Once the shield was down, the glamor that Goorga had erected was also gone, and everyone there could see the sickly green energy flowing up and out of the room.

"Transference!" Bariel boomed as he pointed at another team leader Thufir, a Persian, in his flowing robes. "Follow it," Bariel said no more as the Thufir streaked off followed by Porter.

Bariel aimed his sword at the husk that was left of Goorga. The husk looked at Bariel and smiled "You're too late," it said before Bariel burned the creature down to an atomic level. The holy fire destroyed it utterly.

Bariel looked around at the remaining personnel and at the signs and portents and saw how close they all were to catastrophe. The creature that had allowed itself to be captured was a soul eater. Possibly, The Souleater, a Daemon of great power that had survived the death of the old universe by draining souls.

Many of the creatures of that old horror of a universe consumed souls. Many still do to this day, but they consumed them like a person would eat a steak. It fueled and nourished you but that was only for a short time. The differing energies that made up a soul or one of the creatures from the dark universe could only devour the energy in much the same way a person ate, but this creature was able to transmute some of the energy. If the stories were true, it could keep a soul alive within itself for millennia while it fed off of it and also utilize that soul's power.

Once Bariel was certain he had destroyed what was left of this part of the Daemon so that it could not reunite with its main self, he flew off to kill the rest of the creature before it was too late.

Goorga looked down upon Gerald who had half of his body

burned so badly that his right arm was gone at the bicep and the right side of his face was an empty hollow. Surprisingly, Gerald's face was healing much faster than it should have as the acid slowed down any healing considerably. It wouldn't matter, Goorga thought, as it raised its arm to take Gerald's head before the flow of energy was halted.

There was an impact as the connection was severed and the last of the energy flew into Goorga, but that last piece of energy came with the memory of the remainder of Goorga's essence being destroyed. That came with fire and pain as Goorga saw that piece of itself destroyed forever. A part of it that had been there when the old, dark universe was young, trillions of years old, burned away by the angel.

Black, viscous blood poured out of Goorga's fanged maw and then he caught the ghost maelstrom of the fire that followed. Goorga's body started to burn from the inside out and it shrieked in pain and fury at the loss of a part of itself.

Gerald, who was just now regaining sight in his right eye, raised a shaky left hand and added more fire to the monster. He didn't have enough strength to re-route any of the creature's energy. Goorga shrieked even louder as Gerald sent additional fire into it, but it didn't last long. The fire that burned it and killed a part of itself, due to Bariel's holy flames cauterized the wound that was the missing piece and went out. The pain was excruciating, but it brought Goorga pleasure. Its lessening would be temporary, soon it would play at being a god.

Goorga closed its eyes that were now bubbling back into shape and sent two tendrils into Gerald and then sent another into the crater where Gordon and The Penitent were now stirring. Goorga would now devour all three of them and then destroy this world utterly. It would cause its core to explode and send this vile piece of dirt screaming in anguish into the cosmos.

It pulled the struggling prey into it so that it could devour them more quickly. At the same time, Goorga was slowly pulling in the wayward energy that Gerald had used to injure it back into itself. Even for one such as Goorga, there was a process to reabsorb its essence back into itself. Goorga could sense that the souls outside the cave were almost done with killing its blood spawn, and it knew that other souls and Bariel the angel were only a few moments away, but that was a lifetime compared to the time it would take to devour his prize and then kill them all.

Mouths grew out of the limbs that were attached to Gordon, The Penitent, and Gerald. These smaller mouths oozed more acid that they splattered on the three of them as they were pulled into the mutated mouths of Goorga.

The monster's teeth had closed in on all three of them when a thunderous impact hit the top of the cave and a body hit the bottom of the cave like a missile. When the dust settled, Miller stood in his boxers and bunny slippers streaked with blood and bile from the blood spawn and fired two extended lines of pure white energy into the body of Goorga. The effect was immediate as it squealed in pain as huge chunks were torn off of Goorga's torso. The creature dropped all three of its intended victims, and Gordon and The Penitent used the chance to shoot fire and energy into the Daemon's body.

Gerald fought to stay upright as he pulled a fang out of his head, this helped clear things up and he contributed his fire to the barrage on the monster. Its body was burning and the screeching intensified.

From above the cave a primal roar echoed as Bariel made his descent into the cavern. The cavalry had arrived. All in the cave felt not just Bariel, but the other souls hurtling towards the cave.

Goorga curled up into a ball like an oversized hedgehog. The burns and rents in its alligator-like hide began to heal as a shield was erected that surrounded Goorga and expanded upward at a frightening speed. Miller saw what was about to happen, but as he began to shout a warning, a primal roar that vibrated through the entire cave became a sonic boom that knocked everyone to the ground as Bariel ricocheted off Goorga's shield at such a high rate of speed that every bone in his reinforced body was broken.

Inside the shield dome, the noise from the outside was muted. Varying colors of the attacks being wrought upon the shield shone but to no effect. A simple pulse came out of Goorga that sent everyone else in the cave flying backwards and bounced off the shield wall. Miller rose back up, one of his bunny slippers was missing an ear and another an eye as they loudly scuffed the floor. The Penitent was healing but still looking skeletal with half of his head nothing but a skull with an eye attached. Gordon generated an energy spear and crouched down.

Gerald had still only healed his eye and left the rest as is. He didn't feel any pain. He had willed his system to not relay it to his mind. He looked around the cave and was picking up on the pattern of what made up Goorga. He was understanding the molecular makeup of the Daemon, the atoms that didn't come from this universe, the dark energy from an older, darker horror of a universe. It made Gerald nauseous seeing this but it helped him understand.

From the abomination of a smile on Goorga's face, Gerald wasn't sure he would have time to do anything about it. "None of you ever make it easy," Goorga hissed.

Gordon threw his spear which Goorga allowed to hit him. It just shifted its body and snapped the spear in half. It took the piece in front of it and shoved it down its throat. The shaft stuck into the inside of its skin like a snake that had swallowed its prey. It then disappeared as the spear was absorbed.

"Ahhhh yes, now that's what I shall do to the rest of you." Goorga closed its fist and Gordon crumpled like a tin can. Blood and bodily fluids went flying. It was a wonder he was still alive. The Penitent leaped in the air and seemed to avoid the initial assault by Goorga but when The Penitent ran along the cave wall sideways and made another leap, he was stilled in midair and pulled right into the claw grip of Goorga who took one of its claws, cut halfway through his neck, and added some acid to it so it wouldn't heal right away. Goorga tossed The Penitent away like an old doll.

"You cannot die too quickly," it hissed at Miller. "My prey must be alive while I consume." It ran an overly large tongue over its lips. It didn't seem bothered that the fangs were cutting the tongue as it went.

Miller wasn't having it. "Fuck that!" He went on the offensive and began moving and dashing around the interior of the shield bubble. Miller did not make himself an easy target while he fired energy blasts at Goorga. This frustrated the monster. Even when it tried to use the evil version of the force, that was the best comparison Gerald could make. Miller, though slowed, was able to break free of Goorga's force weapon. "We'll get through. You can't hold out forever," Miller roared as he attacked Goorga over and over again.

Goorga sent out multiple splinters of itself that Gerald and Miller were able to quickly destroy. Gerald noticed that as they were destroyed the wisp of smoke that made up its essence started to gravitate back towards Goorga where it was reabsorbed.

There was a loud boom coming from above. It appeared that Bariel had healed up enough to rejoin the fight.

"Your time is almost up," Miller said as he floated up to eye level and thrust a spear made of energy into Goorga. He tried to set Goorga on fire but the flames sputtered. Quick as a cat, multiple limbs shot out of Goorga. Miller burned the ones in front of him but missed the four coming from behind. They pierced Miller at multiple places and then they grew larger and longer and enveloped Miller so that all you could see was his head and bunny slippers.

Gerald went straight at Goorga and cut away the limbs surrounding Miller. Gerald felt the psychic pull of Goorga as it tried to slow him down. The limbs that had dissolved floated back to Goorga. Gerald focused his will and enveloped those wisps of Goorga in flame and burned them to nothing.

The effect was immediate. Goorga screeched and black, viscous blood ran down its eyes and nose holes. Gerald glanced over at Miller but he was out of commission. The barbs that lined Goorga's limbs had pierced all over his body.

Gordon and the Penitent were slowly healing and out of the picture, and the booming from the shield told Gerald that help wouldn't make it in time. He came up with a plan on the spot. It was a terrible plan, but if it worked the Daemon would die, along with the very high likelihood that Gerald would die along with it.

"Hard choices need to be made. You have to make the hardest for yourself," Gerald's father's voice echoed in his head.

Gerald didn't let Goorga catch a break but sliced off its leg at the knee and then set it on fire. Goorga shrieked so loud Gerald only heard a ringing for a few seconds before sound returned. Before Goorga could attack, he floated up towards the shield and began to pull at the structure of the shield. If he could pull enough to make a hole in the shield, then Bariel and the others could break through. That was the secondary intention.

Gerald was flattened into the shield wall as Goorga flew up and slammed into Gerald from behind. He had erected a shield of his own to prevent an attack. The power that Goorga wielded shattered his shield and flattened Gerald into the burning ozone of Goorga's shield wall. Gerald could slowly take small pieces from the shield, but it would not be enough, especially with a raging greater Daemon on top of you.

Goorga pulled Gerald back to the cave floor. Both hit like twin meteors and left another indent on the floor. The beast floated up with multiple tendrils wrapped around Gerald including across his face. The pain as the barbs pierced his face was excruciating. Gerald could feel his essence being sucked in by the barbs as they tightened. The revulsion he felt at this violation only strengthened him for what he had to do next.

It wasn't that Gerald couldn't absorb Goorga's essence, but it would be like consuming raw sewage. You could do it, but you would die from eating it. Gerald reached out to who was there with him.

Gordon felt the call, raised his eyebrows in shock, and then responded. He understood the assignment and with a heavy heart allowed his energy to be pulled in for what Gerald required. The pain and weakening of Goorga trying to suck Gerald dry complicated the process.

Goorga seemed unaware of what Gerald was doing. Its shield was strong and would get stronger as it devolved to its baser self. The predator now had the taste of blood, and it was ravenous for more and unaware of its surroundings.

The Penitent saw what was happening and also answered the call. He understood what was going to happen and was saddened he could not get to know this man.

Miller also understood and with grief as his main motivation, he gave of himself as well.

Gerald wondered if this was how the monster had grown to such power. It was clear it had the talent for absorbing others of its kind, and eventually others unlike itself. The vampiric nature of what it was scared Gerald. He could do what this creature could do. How long had it taken for it to succumb to that and be the monster that it was? Gerald didn't need to delve into that cesspool for answers. He had things to do, and killing this Daemon was tops on the list.

Gerald pulled the energy provided by the three other souls. By now he was feeling nauseous and disoriented but he was able to move that energy into a flow that he could control. The barbs on his face tightened, and Gerald almost blacked out and lost the connection to that energy, but he pushed through. When the flow was ready, he let it spread across his face. The relief was immediate. No more nausea as the barbs were shattered and the tendril around his face was burned away, completely down to nothing.

Goorga shrieked again as it felt the loss of itself once again. Gerald let that flow sweep across his body and removed any particle of Goorga's stinking matter from him. The energy whipped around him in a whirlwind.

Goorga roared in rage and fear. This was something it had not known could happen or even exist. Gerald felt the pressure of trying to control these varying flows of energy from three distinctly different people.

Gordon, The Penitent, and Miller in his now burned and soiled bunny slippers, which somehow still managed to stay intact surrounded the Daemon and Gerald. They gave all that they could.

Gerald was the one controlling the flow, and he wouldn't kill one of them to save himself. That's what would happen if he let go. They would all die, and he would live if he let that outlet feedback into them. Someone or something would die today, but not them.

Gerald controlled the bucking whirlwind of energy as best he could. The shield Goorga had erected was gone, and Bariel and the other souls had descended. Bariel saw it. Gerald would die, unless...

Bariel couldn't get through the maelstrom encircling both

the Souleater and Gerald, who now was solely focused on gathering as much energy as he could and had moved it like a bucking bronco to surround Goorga. Through gritted teeth, Gerald brought down the energy into a pincer that burned Goorga wherever it touched.

The Daemon tried to make itself small but it had nowhere to go. "How are you doing this?" it snarled through the pain it felt at being burned.

Gerald bred teeth at the daemon. "I won't survive this," Gerald said as he absorbed energy into himself. This energy allowed him to see more clearly the makeup of Goorga.

Gerald grabbed a horn on each side of Goorga's head. His hands burned as he came in contact with the daemon's horns. Gerald grimaced and then with a wail of purest pain from Goorga that came from every part of its filthy being, He pulled and twisted so that Goorga's head split in half. He placed his hands into the split and kept going.

Goorga bucked and tried all it could, but it was futile. Gerald tore the Daemon in half. His hands caught fire as his hand burned through the black viscous tar that made up Goorga's blood. The energy Gerald had used whipped around the remnants of the cave.

"Everyone out now!" Bariel roared, Gerald was moments from losing control, and the angel wasn't sure he could save him a second time.

Gerald spoke one last time to Goorga who, though in great pain, was still alive even with its body split in half down to the waist. "I'll never see her again." Gerald closed his eyes thinking of his wife, and the energy bucked and began to get wilder. It needed an outlet, and Gerald had just the one to provide it.

He breathed in and exhaled for perhaps the last time and forced all the energy at his disposal into burning Goorga down. Though the beast was huge at over twenty feet in height, its size in the other realm was far larger. Gerald chased and hunted every part of its being and brought judgment down upon every molecule of it. It answered for the trillions of years of crimes and depravity it had visited on the old universe and the current one.

Bariel watched as Gerald directed that energy to destroy the Souleater down to the last molecule. That had directed a massive amount of energy but the soul of a human even with very high limits, there was still too much power left that it was a certainty. Gerald would die once the last of the Demon was gone. If he did not internalize the overflow first so it could be weakened by him being burned to ash then releasing the energy outright would be worse than a hundred nuclear bombs.

There was no regret as the last of the being known as Goorga finally perished after trillions of years of destruction. Gerald wondered if at one time it was different, that years of vampiric living had changed it. No, he knew deep down that Goorga died as it had always lived, a creature of evil and chaos. There was nothing to save, so nothing would be saved.

Gordon, The Penitent, Miller, Porter, and Bariel's retinue joined the angel. They all surrounded Gerald and witnessed the death of a greater Daemon by a new soul. They all witnessed a power in Gerald that could destroy everything if he was allowed to grow. They witnessed his fears of becoming like Goorga and drain others to further his power. Each one thought the same thing, even with the certainty of the true death "Should he be allowed to live?"

Gerald was ready to die. He shouted a warning as the energy finally got the better of him. A last goodbye to his wife and family was the last thing he remembered. The explosion that resulted could have devastated the planet, even once it had burned through Gerald there was still too much energy but with Bariel guiding everyone, he had directed the seething mass of energy upwards so that it flew harmlessly into the atmosphere.

The energy that Gordon, The Penitent, and Miller had provided would return to each of them in time.

Porter, seeing that Gerald was losing his grasp on the energy, ordered Galves and Ro, his subordinates, to gather the rest of the people there. Porter grabbed Bariel who didn't even acknowledge him as he worked to save Gerald. Porter, Galves, and Ro fired down into the ground and sunk the rest of the team under the ground.

Bariel did all he could to try and save Gerald, but even he wasn't sure as with a final pulse, Bariel and everyone else in the cave were blown into darkness.

30

AFTERMATH

Teams Chosen Dead, The Redeemers, and The Victorians who had been furthest away had been blown back a few miles but quickly gathered back to ground zero.

The grotto was completely gone. All three teams had been ordered to guard the perimeter after they had dealt with the last of the blood spawn. The retinue that had descended into the cave when it was still there was not in good shape. Alive, but not in good shape.

Porter, along with his two subordinates that made up his retinue, Galves and Ro, had weathered the explosion best. The indent in the ground around the three of them had shielded them the best they could. They had pushed everyone down underground to further shield them from the blast. The energy was being directed upwards to begin with, and their shields would never have been able to withstand a full-on blast. They made sure to place themselves in a position that would deflect as much as possible.

Galves and Ro were regrowing their eyes and, once completed, they both vomited what appeared to be excess energy. Porter had to regrow the arm he had raised to direct the energy blast with his shield. He spit out a glowing glob of energy, scowled, and then went to work on Bariel.

The angel was in awful shape. Both of his wings had been burned off along with his hair, and his torso was burned black all the way around. Bariel's face seemed mostly free of burns.

Porter helped Bariel up "You two, let's go!" he barked at Galves and Ro. The two ran up, laid hands on Bariel, and closed their eyes. The angel began to glow and grimaced in pain as the combined energies of the three souls started to work on Bariel, to a point. The terrible burns on Bariel's torso began to heal but stayed black as all three of the souls had to stop from pain and exhaustion. The stress was evident on their faces.

"I'm sorry, sir," Ro whispered to Bariel.

Porter looked furious. "Again!" Porter yelled.

Galves and Ro looked at each other, sighed, and nodded. They went to lay hands on Bariel again, but he stopped them.

"It's alright. I will heal on my own." Bariel turned his back to walk away.

"Maybe we can help, pal," Gio said as all three teams floated down to them.

Porter looked them over and nodded. "This is different. This will drain you," he warned.

"Sounds like when I gave blood during the war. They always took too much but we got a lollipop. Let's do it."

Porter stared at Gio and smirked. He nodded toward Bariel, who had returned.

"I can help guide their energy so it is less draining on them," Bariel stated.

All three teams surrounded Bariel and laid hands on him. He immediately started to glow and this time the healing was much improved. All the burns on his chest flaked away and pink new skin came through. His hair regrew, and his wings started as a skeletal outline then fleshed out with new feathers sprouting into place. At the end of it, he looked good as new and floated up to break contact.

"Thank you all," Bariel said in his deep baritone.

All three teams looked fatigued but nothing they wouldn't quickly recover from. They began intermingling. Gordon and Vora quickly embraced. Gordon would have pulled away sooner, but Vora grabbed him by the face and kissed him. When they separated Gordon's face was a very deep pink. He was not one for public affection. Vora didn't get the memo.

Laughing, Reginald walked up to Gordon slapped him on the back, and added "My woman kisses me like that, I would have had my pants off already, chap."

Everyone was in good spirits, but Vora walked over to where Gerald was. "Where in fucking fuck is my Jarl?" The laughter stopped as everyone gathered where Gerald had been when the explosion happened. There was an imprint in the ground of his body, but the body itself there was no sign.

Gerald was back in the place he had visited before he got into Heaven. The same wooden post was next to him. He felt as terrible as he looked. He was missing both his arms from the bicep down, his legs were gone, and his torso was caved in. One side of his face was gone. Even the bone in the skull had been burned away. He noticed he was floating which isn't that big of a deal, but Gerald wasn't the one keeping himself afloat.

"That's me," Kerael said as he appeared in front of Gerald. "Hope you don't mind, You seemed like you could use a break."

"Thanks, I feel awful, look pretty bad, too, I imagine. Am I dead again?"

Kerael smiled. "No, still only dead the one time, though you do look awful. Here." The angel waved his hand and instantly the pain Gerald was feeling was gone. Kerael waved his hand again and Gerald floated down to the ground to stand on his newly healed legs.

"Thank you." Gerald moved his arms and legs and felt his face to confirm it was all back the way it should be. "You just wave your hand and poof, all done?"

"Poof, yes." Kerael's smile disappeared as he continued. "We need to talk." There was a pause as the angel seemed to think about what best to say.

"That I am the chosen one? That's what that Daemon said. It's why he tried to kill me. That what we need to talk about?"

Something twitched in Kerael's face at the mention of the Daemon and he nodded in acknowledgement. "I'm sorry." He extended his arms. "We're sorry. We had no idea what that thing was or how far the enemy would go to destroy you."

Gerald nodded. He was angry but he also knew that this monster could do exactly what it did from firsthand knowledge. "So how could it hide itself like that from you?"

Kerael thought about it. "It was exceptionally good at hiding its aura or power if you will. What it could do is unheard of though. You have been around Bariel. You see how large he is. He can contain his power to a point, but he couldn't do what this thing did."

"It was a creature of the physical world and partly the spiritual realm. It was hiding itself there, in that dark place."

Kerael cocked his head. "You know this how?"

Gerald nodded. "I hunted down the last of its essence there and burned it all."

Kerael went right up to Gerald and grabbed him by both arms. "Promise me you will never go there again. You have any idea how lucky you are." Gerald grimaced in pain which Kerael noticed and released him. "Sorry. You have no idea of the danger you placed yourself in. That isn't just a place or dimension, it's actual Hell." Kerael watched as Gerald processed what he had said with shock. "That was the old universe. Now it's where the souls of the damned go.

It's worse than what you read about hell being, much worse."

Gerald nodded. "You brought me through there when we went to heaven"

Kerael nodded. The angel approached Gerald again and this time gently placed a hand on his shoulder. "You should be dead after what you just did. I don't know about the chosen one. That is too simplistic for what you are but we would have addressed it after training camp and before we sent you out into combat so you had a better chance to protect yourself. The enemy only sees power and you are not the only person or creature that has immense power..."

Gerald cut him off. "How can I do that exactly?"

Kerael waved his hand and all around them, energy swirls and eddies were flowing up and around everywhere. "Watch me." He moved away from Gerald slowly. At first, the swirls and eddies were moving and swaying all around. As Kerael moved away from Gerald, the swirls and eddies began to noticeably calm down. He stopped moving when he was twenty feet away from Gerald and the air was very still. The energy flows were calm and smooth.

Gerald looked around where he was standing and noticed that the swirls and eddies were still moving and flowing all around him turbulently. Kerael walked back over to Gerald. "What you are seeing are called signs and portents. The more they move around like that, the more important the individual."

Gerald looked around and nodded. "Why is that, and how do I protect myself?"

Kerael made a table and chairs appear. On the table were what appeared to be coffee cups full to the brim with coffee that smelled amazing. "First things first, coffee." Gerald smiled and sat down across from Kerael. "Light and sweet?"

Gerald picked up the mug, took a sip, and marveled at the creamy, caramel flavor of the coffee. "Good stuff, thank you."

Kerael smiled. "You're welcome. I know you have had a rough day. So, souls and beings such as myself are like fish in a great ocean, an ocean of energy that we don't necessarily see but it's there. You follow?" Gerald nodded as he gulped down his coffee which began to fill itself back up. Kerael continued, "Within the great ocean the souls and beings move around. What has been known for an unknown period is that anyone who can cause change to the great ocean causes more turbulence as they move through it. The ability to change or who has a destiny the great ocean reacts to. As you can see from me, nice and calm, You, craziness."

Gerald pondered what he was told before answering "First off, you're not a nobody"

Kerael smiled. "You're too kind," he said to Gerald.

"You can do things easily that even Bariel can't do, so save the 'just a simple servant' act."

Kerael raised his hand. "You're very perceptive."

Gerald took another sip before continuing. "I get that the ocean of energy is reacting to me and, can I say potential?" Kerael nodded. "How can I conceal that if I am also energy?"

Kerael extended his arm and the signs and portents around Gerald disappeared.

"What did you do?" Gerald asked.

"I can manipulate the eddies and flows of energy by smoothing them out."

"So I will need to learn to do that?" Gerald asked.

"Correct, you will need to quell that energy by reducing your fingerprint. Work with Bariel on this and he can help you master it."

"Bariel mentioned that I could attract bigger fish. I can't imagine anything bigger than that monster I just killed."

Kerael shook his head. "Unfortunately there are much bigger fish out there. Learn to keep your head down."

"So as the Chosen One, what can I do that is so special?"

Kerael thought about it for a moment. "First of all, don't call yourself that but to start, you should be dead. You were badly injured but anyone else besides maybe Bariel would have died from what you did against Goorga."

"That was the monster's name, Goorga?"

"Yes, Goorga the Souleater. Many out there thought he was impossible to kill. An ancient being of great power, for one so young to have killed it is unthinkable let alone possible. What you can do for one so young is even hard to quantify"

Gerald sat there, unsure of what to say. "That doesn't clear anything up. Sounds like a bunch of words that sound very impressive but very little content."

Kerael smiled. "So you shall learn in time isn't going to cut it?"

Gerald smiled and shook his head.

"You have an insight into the universe that comes naturally. You can see the molecular design. You were able to copy Gordon's ability which by the way is very rare. He is the second person to manifest that ability. As you go along, you will be able to better manipulate the energy that is there, and when you pull stunts like you did today not have your arms and legs blown off."

Gerald raised his coffee mug. "Cheers to that. So, to confirm, I didn't die, I survived it on my own?"

Kerael smiled and made a face. "You did, but Bariel helped."

Gerald smiles back. "Good guy, Bariel."

Kerael nodded. "Yes indeed. Not much of a conversationalist but I am hoping working with you humans gets him to open up."

"Huh. Interesting. I think I should have him spend time with Gio. He'll either open up or kill him."

Kerael laughed and they sat in silence for a bit.

"Anything else I should know?" Gerald asked.

Kerael frowned, looked into his coffee mug, and seemed to be deciding on what best to say. "Things will not get easier. Goorga will be the first of many, and you will suffer."

Gerald's face held still. He didn't want to show Kerael how shaken he was at this moment. "That is by far the worst pep talk in the history of pep talks. Are you trying to get me to quit?"

Kerael wore a thin smile as he replied, "It's too late to quit. You know it, I know it. The choice is still yours but..."

"There is no choice, we both know I won't quit." They both sat in silence "I'm ready," Gerald said to Kerael, who nodded and waved his hand.

Gerald stood in the indent in the ground that his body created. All around him were the three teams: The Victorians, The Redeemers, and his own Chosen Dead. Miller, and Bariel along with Porter and his retinue were also there but they all had their backs turned to him, looking for something. "What are you guys doing?" he shouted.

Everyone there, including the angel, jumped in surprise and stared at him. "Where in fucking hell did you come from?" Miller demanded. They all approached Gerald, but Bariel got there first and seemed to sniff the air. "Remarkable, not a stirring in the ether whatsoever." Bariel finished his scan and then placed a massive hand on Gerald's shoulder "Happy to see you are still alive."

Porter came up next. "How are you alive is what I want to know," he added as he patted Gerald on the shoulder in a rare show of affection.

"I'll tell you how. it's because he's a tough motherfucker," Miller said as he stood behind Porter and nodded. Miller remained dressed in his boxers and bunny slippers. He had repaired the slippers so they were back to their fuzzy best.

"Ya, he is toughest motherfucker." Vora pushed her way through the growing crowd, ignoring Porter's death stare as she almost knocked him down and put Gerald in a bear hug that lifted him off his feet.

"Oof, ok, ok" Gerald huffed.

Vora let Gerald down but scrunched her nose "You smell like Daemon assholes" Vora grabbed Gerald's head and kissed the side of it.

"I'm sure hell is full of those," Gerald replied.

Bariel sniffed him. "She is correct, it is not an....asshole per se, probably worse."

"I don't even want to know what's worse than a bunch of Daemon assholes, but I'm glad to see you in one piece pal." Gio came through and hugged him. Gerald was soon enveloped by a large group happy to see him still alive and congratulating him on killing Goorga. He was preoccupied until he saw who he was looking for. Gordon was in the back of the crowd in deep conversation with The Penitent. Gerald made his way through and when The Penitent saw him, he nodded to Gordon and backed away to the side so they could speak.

Gerald walked right up to Gordon and hugged him. He had saved his life at the risk of his own. Even with the danger they were all in, this is what Gerald had missed: the bonds of brotherhood. It never failed to awaken that deep part of himself that seemed to seek out like-minded people. "Thank you, my friend," Gerald whispered to Gordon.

Gerald caught The Penitent moving away into the crowd, but Gerald came up and stopped him. "I see you," Gerald said to The Penitent. "We all do. I would be dead if it weren't for you."

There was nothing more to say. The Penitent was rigid. Emotions played across his face until he set on a thin smile and a nod.

"Wait!" Vora walked up to The Penitent and extended her

hand to him. "You saved them both. We have no quarrel, not anymore."

The Penitent looked to Gordon who gave The Penitent a thin smile and nodded. Slowly, as if she would shoot lightning out of her hand, he grasped her arm in the warrior's fashion and nodded.

Everyone cheered. It was best to bury old resentments, otherwise they fostered new animosity.

Everyone returned to their respective barracks, but Gerald was ordered to command. Miller walked with him. "Sir?" Miller turned to Gerald. "What happens next?"

Miller kept walking a bit before answering, his bunny slippers scuffing the ground as they walked. "They want to get you in the field." Miller stopped Gerald "First, we have to make sure you can conceal yourself. We can't have you attracting too much attention." They continued walking

"Working on it." Gerald had seen how Kerael had disguised his aura for him, but Gerald had other ideas on it but would speak with Gordon when he got back on it.

Upon arrival at command, which was just an open-sided building, Gerald was surprised to see Kerael speaking with Bariel. Porter, Galves, and Ro, along with additional personnel, were speaking as well. Everyone turned and greeted Miller and Gerald.

"Sit down," Porter ordered Gerald, who complied and sat down at a table that materialized along with PB and J sandwiches and bottles of cherry wheat beer. Gerald raised an eyebrow at Porter. Those were Gerald's favorites. "You earned it," Porter replied with a thin smile.

"Thank you, sir." Even though Gerald didn't need to eat, he wolfed down a bunch of sandwiches and had at least four beers as he detailed what had happened to him, how he had defeated Goorga, and what he was able to do...so far.

Everyone there except Kerael and Bariel seemed happy enough to drink some beers and grilled Gerald for hours to pull every detail they could. Once they had completed their questions, they discussed the next steps with Gerald and his team.

"As long as he can disguise himself, I see no reason he can't serve. He needs to practice and live combat to sharpen his skills. We can't afford to not have him in the field," Kerael replied to a question from Ro.

"Still, his youth is a liability. He is more powerful than anyone in this room except for you two angels," Ro pressed.

"This a problem?" Miller interjected "He killed a greater Daemon, The Souleater itself. He will be able to handle himself and he's not alone."

Bariel stepped in. "I wish to offer myself to assist him. He will need it, at least until he can better control his powers. I can teach him."

Porter frowned. "We'll acquiesce to what you proposed, but this is highly unusual."

Kerael smiled. "No more unusual than having a greater Daemon allowing itself to be captured so it could kill this one." He pointed at Gerald. "This just proves his importance. It was imprisoned way too long to have allowed itself to be captured for any other reason." Kerael looked around the room before continuing. "The great enemy will stop at nothing, do whatever is necessary to achieve their goals. It would be a disservice to us and to him if we do not allow him to fulfill his potential."

That ended the meeting, and when Kerael went to leave, Gerald stopped him "Who are you?" he asked the angel who didn't order anyone to do it, but they did it anyway.

Kerael looked at Gerald and smiled. "Just a traveler."

Gerald stood there, mouth open. "What the hell are you talking about, and is that from the Jim Morrison movie?" Gerald responded. "You have a lot of weight for a recruiter."

Kerael smiled again. "I do other stuff."

Gerald glared back, annoyance showing plainly on his face

"I'm one of the good guys, that's all you need to know for now." As Kerael said this, he seemed to grow in stature and all the light in the room seemed to be pulled into him. The next instant, it was as if nothing ever happened "Take care of yourself." Kerael patted Gerald on the back and left.

Gerald turned to Bariel who had approached. "He seems to be pretty high-ranking, right? He would have to be able to have you be my chaperone."

Bariel looked like he wanted to say something but then just nodded and walked away.

31

DOWNTIME

After the fracas that was the finals of the tournament, all parties agreed to call it a tie for first place. No one wanted to have to go through that again after battling Goorga.

Everyone had downtime until their orders came in and each team would be sent to their respective assignments. The Chosen Dead had meandered over to the Victorians, and Reginald surprised everyone by carrying a seventies-style boombox playing Van Morrison's "Into the Mystic." Reginald had set up a very safari-style lunch table loaded with food. "Really like this chap. After my time, but he's a Belfast boy just like me, so cheers," Gio chimed in. "You should have seen him when he was young. Handsome guy, Older, not so much."

Reginald laughed. "The damnable weather. We get a bit worn, chap."

Gio replied. "I hear that, time catches up to everyone. Have you listened to The Beatles yet?"

Reginald grabbed his chest in much exasperation. "How dare you, sir! Of course, I have. They are the greatest band ever."

Benga Din approached along with the Redeemers. "Lovely band, the Beatles."

Reginald jumped up to greet him and the rest of the Redeemers who came with various jugs of wine and beer. Sical was carrying literally half a cow.

"My friend, welcome! Be seated." Gordon came right up to the Penitent and shook hands with him. Vora oddly didn't seem to mind and greeted The Penitent in the warrior's fashion, hand to elbow.

A few hours into the festivities, everyone was having a good time. Miller and Porter were actually laughing at something that Bariel had said. "Never thought that one had a sense of humor," Gio said to Gerald. The twins giggled as they passed a ludicrously sized ale horn amongst them. They caught Gerald looking, offered the horn, and he shrugged and downed some of the smoothest, sweetest mead he had ever had.

"That's very good," Gerald said as he passed the horn around.

"The best part about it is no cooties," Gio said with a laugh "Being Catholic, I liked the whole wine thing but not after everybody in the church had a swig...the germs, yeesh."

Vora, who had drunk everything everyone had brought in mass quantities, chimed in. "Cooties sound fun."

Gordon loosened up after prodigious amounts of alcohol joined in laughed, and replied, "No, cooties are bad...sort of."

Everyone had a good laugh at that. Gerald noticed Benga Din and Reginald sitting together laughing like old friends and had to ask, "Did you two know each other? You know, when you were alive?"

Reginald laughed at that and Benga Din smiled. "No, chap. In fact, we were enemies." Both Reginald and Benga Din laughed and clicked their drinking glasses together. They both saw the confusion on Gerald and everyone else's faces "I loved Africa. I loved its people, the animals, the way the sky was so blue that it seemed to go on forever. I fought the Zulus, and then

I was allied with the Zulus when we fought the Dutch incursion," Reginald explained.

"Boers. We fought a whole war called the Boer War," Benga Din added.

"I stand corrected, the Boers. Appropriate, bloody boring lot if you ask me." Reginald extended the bore in boring to extenuate his feelings about the Dutch colonizers who eventually supplanted the British. "One thing I learned in a lifetime of war," Reginald's demeanor completely changed. He stated. "Sometimes you have to kill men of honor or they will kill you." Reginald raised his glass to Benga Din then everyone else. "I never hated them and I hope they never hated me, to be frank. I did my duty as best I could but I learned that when you were eye to eye with an honorable man, He looked over to acknowledge the women, "And women, of course, ladies." Vora shook her fist at Reginald in mock anger. "I knew that they were doing their duty as well. The hardest men to fight were the honorable men defending their land."

A dark cloud came over Reginald's face. The Sikh men and Benga Din all laid a hand on Reginald. "Cheers," is all Reginald said in response. Whatever burden Reginald carried, he wasn't ready to lay it down.

"Why you gotta bring the party down, my man?" Gio came up and slapped Reginald on the shoulder to shake him out of his sudden doldrums. "Let's party, for tomorrow we die!"

The crowd cheered and that also raised Reginald's spirits as well. "Well said chap, apologies," Reginald said and raised his glass for much more robust cheers.

"Why do you retain your scar, my friend?" Benga Din inquired of David who was speaking with Kubak and Tyrus.

David looked around and made eye contact with Gio who had been asking him since day one.

"Come on, spill it," Gio said and made it a point to sit cross-legged in front of David, then materialized a beach chair for him to sit on. "Best way to listen to stories around the campfire" David sat as still as a stone, didn't say a word, and waited. The crowd went silent. Miller had come down to join and materialized a beach chair of his own right next to Gio.

"David, spill beans. That does not work, drink milk," Vora shouted not realizing that she got one saying right and a general look of confusion on the other.

David, realizing that he wasn't going to be able to get out of it, stood up, cleared his throat, and began his tale. Even nervous he was cool and calm except for him clenching and unclenching his hands "So, not sure if you all know this but I was a veterinarian when I was alive" David began.

"You don't say? Chap, I saw you dancing a samba with one of those man-eating plants," Reginald yelled for the crowd.

David blushed and smiled. "It was a bachata." That drew some blank stares. "It's a Dominican dance similar to salsa and...."

"Dance lessons later," Miller interrupted. "Spill the beans and drink the milk, let's go!" Vora gave a thumbs up as if to say "See I told it right!"

David smiled, coughed into his hand, and continued. "Ok, so, there are no dancing plants in this story." Everyone got a good laugh out of that one. "Got back from Nam, I had been out of school, and practicing as a veterinarian for about five or six years by them. I always loved animals. Loved plants too, have a heck of a green thumb," David added by giving the thumbs-up sign and turning his thumb a bright neon green.

Miller was unimpressed and rolled his hand in the move-it-along gesture. "Tough crowd. Ok, here we go." David continued on with his story and how after five or six years doing his dream job he found he had a real gift with animals. All the animals loved him, whether it was a big St. Bernard or a tiny lap dog, a floof of a kitty, a bunny, or a hamster. Even the reptiles liked the good doctor. If there was a skittish or aggressive dog that no one else could handle, they would just call in Doctor Dave and he would calm the animal down mostly by just walking in. They knew and he knew that they would be alright. He was their friend and was there to help. Sure, he had some scratches from a nervous or scared cat, but that was indirect due to them holding on to him but never a swipe or an aggressive scratch. David felt that he was different. The animals in his care felt that he was different, and special.

This was proven when a sick boa constrictor had been brought in and tightened itself around the neck of a fellow veterinarian Lisa Owens, all five two and a hundred pounds of her, and was squeezing the life out of her. The assistants and other doctors on duty had tried to pull the animal off Doctor Owens, but nothing was working.

When David ran in, another doctor was pulling a tranquilizer into a syringe. David had ordered the doctor to stand down. The boa constrictor was sick and had already been administered tranquilizer, and he knew that any more would kill it. He was reminded that if nothing was done soon, Doctor Owens would be strangled to death, and, judging by her labored breath, she didn't have long.

David walked up to the boa constrictor. The assistants were holding on to each end, and two more were struggling to get a foothold to pry the snake off Doctor Owens. Time seemed to slow for David as he walked up. He was close to the head already and as he laid his hand on its neck, the boa constrictor responded almost immediately. "Hello Jean," David had said to the boa constrictor. He began to move his hands closer to Jean the boa constrictor's head and for the first time, it seemed to relax

The assistants took advantage and were able to move Doctor

Owens out of danger by freeing her from the stranglehold Jean had on her. That wasn't what made it different, though. It was when Jean crawled around David's neck and nestled there and seemed to fall asleep. David credited the tranquilizer administered before, but everyone knew it was David and his gift with calming animals.

No more than a week after that Happy was brought in. Happy was a one hundred-and fifty-pound Rottweiler mixed with lab, and God only knew he was about thirty pounds overweight. Happy had been in before and was always a well-behaved boy. He was in today because he was in obvious discomfort. Happy wasn't eating or drinking water and had a general malaise. He had eaten a towel and now couldn't get it out. Worse, he couldn't get anything in.

An assistant had placed Happy on the table and prepped him for surgery. Happy, knowing in that way animals do that something was going to happen, became agitated and had to be held down as David was administering the needle. David leaned over to place the needle into Happy's leg and Happy jerked. The assistant didn't have a good hold of Happy and Happy bit David. The dog's fang caught David in the forearm and then when David pulled away, the fang caused a rent down David's forearm. The room was still. David, the assistant, and even Happy were in shock that an animal actually bit him, especially Happy.

Happy started to cry and gave David the sad puppy eyes. David stroked Happy's head let him know it was alright and gave Happy his injection. David got stitches done by Doctor Owens, and he then completed Happy's procedure. Happy continued to come in for another six years. He gained another twenty pounds and at the end couldn't walk without pain anymore so was put to sleep.

David finished the story, and no one said a word, everyone was trying to take it in. "That, I do not get. Why you not tell us?

Happy was a good boy who had a bad day is all," Vora slurred as she held on to Gordon for dear life. It is possible to get stinking drunk even after you die.

"He let his guard down. He took his gift for granted," a new voice chimed in. The Penitent was sitting opposite David, and everyone turned to him. Vora looked to The Penitent and then to David who nodded. The Penitent continued. "We've all seen what he can do with animals, the plants, everything. Not surprised he was good at being a veterinarian in the world past. What he learned, what we all learn one way or the other, is that when you take what you have for granted, it can be taken away from you."

Gordon and Gerald were intently staring at The Penitent. They both had seen what he had gone through, how close he had come to damnation, and they both nodded when he made eye contact. Everyone else understood now why David didn't want to share how he got the scar because he was ashamed that he took his gift for granted. That he could have let those around him down, most of all himself.

"Question." Gio, who was so drunk that Sical and Tyrus had to help him up after he failed to get up on his own, said. He pointed right at The Penitent "What the hell is your name? You know how annoying it is to have to call you the Pemberton-man?" Gio realized he had not even come close to getting the Penitent's name right and waved his hand. "He knows it, but he won't say." Gio pointed at Gordon and almost fell over before Sical, who was giggling, grabbed him and got him upright again.

Gordon smiled and put his hands up to say "Not for me to say."

Gio swayed in the nonexistent breeze waiting for an answer. They all were.

The Penitent looked around at everyone. His jaw muscles were clenched. He looked as tight as a piano wire. The Penitent looked back over at the Redeemers who decided the matter each with a slight nod. The Penitent exhaled. "My actual name is Eugene Thomas Cardinal," The Penitent, or Eugene, stated.

Gio stopped swaying. His mouth was wide open, and then he burst out laughing. "Eugene!" he bellowed and fell on the floor laughing. Everyone else burst out laughing as well.

Eugene did not expect that reaction. The baffled look on his face slowly was replaced with the spread of a smile.

"I am not calling you that," Gio told The Penitent.

"And here I thought two of the most interesting people here are boring as fuck," Miller managed to get out between gales of laughter.

32

HEADING OUT

After the festivities, which lasted another two days all the teams returned to the barracks and were allowed to move around and socialize with the other teams. The Chosen Dead were watching David teaching a man-eating plant how to cha cha. Gio cautiously walked up to David and his man-eating plant. "I don't get it. Why are you teaching this....plant, how to cha cha?"

David turned his head, being mindful of the many root legs that he was helping his man-eating plant Mervin with aligning. "He wanted to learn. He likes Latin music."

Gio cocked his head to the side in mild confusion. "Let me know when he wants to start square dancing."

Mervin made a hissing noise like a tea kettle going off. David, who appeared to be listening to him, started smiling and nodded. "He prefers Latin music; country is nice but not enough zazz to the dancing"

Gio pointed both finger guns in Mervin's direction. "Latin it is."

Miller floated in from above and immediately stood at attention. "At ease," Miller said, and everyone relaxed. He turned to Gerald. "A word?" Miller floated away, and Gerald followed him to the command center. Miller didn't say a word or even look at Gerald as they headed for an open space command room Porter and Bariel occupied.

Porter nodded to both Gerald and Miller. "Be seated," he ordered, and everyone in the room sat in old-fashioned leather chairs with thick padding that felt like you were sitting on a cloud. The lights dimmed in the room and Porter began dressing Gerald. "We had a hard time trying to find a first post for you and your team. Eventually, we settled on the planet Carsadax." He waved his hand and a planet appeared on the screen. Even miniaturized it looked huge, with large areas of green that stood out along with areas of brown and blue where the oceans were. "This planet is ten times the size of Earth. It has a varied terrain. Massive jungles along with giant mega deserts." Porter pointed to the green and brown areas that stood out. "The oceans are so large that we believe the lowest point is thirty times lower than the Marianas trench on Earth. This place is gigantic."

He leaned on the wooden table that the hologram of Carsadax floated above. "You and your team will be sent here for your first assignment. This planet is in the ass end of nowhere but within the last year we have seen movement by the enemy." Porter waved his hand and a few small red spots that represented the enemy appeared in the desert regions. "We noticed them moving in small detachments of no more than ten thousand or so in these desert regions." He waved again and the red spots were magnified so you could see enemy encampments. "Lately there has been more activity and an increased presence. We need to know why. Could be nothing, could be something, but from experience, it's always something."

Bariel stepped up. "Bariel will accompany your team," Porter said. Bariel nodded to Gerald. "We already have boots on the ground." Porter waved his hand and blue spots appeared in the deeper desert away from the red spots "The enemy knows we're there and has started to amp up their numbers. Even with the increase in numbers, it's a good place to get your feet wet."

Gerald raised his hand and Porter nodded. "What kind of numbers are you talking about, sir?"

Porter thought for a moment before answering. "I would say two to three million. That's a good first fight, not a major encounter." Gerald was stunned at the numbers and Porter smirked. "The majority of the enemy are nowhere near as tough as that monster you killed. These are low-level Daemons that you will be able to go through like tissue paper." Porter waved his hand and the hologram of Carsadax faded away.

He turned to speak to the rest. "Keep your eyes open. From all indications, this looks like a small incursion, but we need to find out why they are there. The enemy will conceal what their real motivations are so keep your head on a swivel. You leave in two days. Dismissed."

Gerald and Miller stood up at attention and saluted. Porter exited the meeting room.

"Are you coming as well?" Gerald asked Miller.

"No, I have more recruits to get ready. Don't get yourself killed." Miller didn't give Gerald a chance to respond as he flew off, leaving Gerald to find his way back.

Upon Gerald's return to the team barracks, he discussed the assignment with the team. He fielded all their questions and joined in the excitement. The sense of excitement was palpable when the other teams came by to discuss their assignments, it seemed to turn everyone into an excitable child. Forget the fact that they were all being sent to an active war zone where they could die. The feeling of finally doing something was prevalent.

The following day, Miller came by the barracks. He floated down and once everyone was at attention, he addressed the team. "Tomorrow you will leave for your assignment. I wanted to let you all know that you will all be fine. The way you handled yourselves in the battles with the blood spawn proved that." He paused and softened when he spoke again "Each soul is different, unique. What makes humanity special is that uniqueness combined with free will that makes us special. We have all heard about working for the greater good. Well, let me tell you, when individuals choose to come together of their own free will to work towards something, we make it fucking happen!"

Miller clenched his jawline. Everyone there could feel the passion in his voice, the emotion pouring off of him. "We can do anything. Don't you forget it. I'm proud of you all, you're all special. Succeed and do not die!" He finished with a salute so crisp you heard the wind tear as he snapped his arm up for the salute. The Chosen Dead returned the salute just as fervently. "God bless you," he said as he turned from them and floated away. The Chosen Dead needed a few moments. So did Miller, who took off as quickly as he could so they wouldn't see how emotional he was.

Later that night, The Redeemers and the Victorians came by bearing food and much drink. Everyone sat down around a large bonfire and drank a combination of ale, mead, scotch, and whiskey with beer thrown in. The Redeemers were heading out to an outpost situated on a moon called Arvour. It was a mid-sized engagement, so they were being attached to a much larger battle company. The Victorians were heading to defend an alien planet called Ixna that had been under siege for the last three years. This was a large-scale engagement where they said the enemy was so numerous, that they showed up on scanners as a red spot that was hundreds of miles long.

"Your assignment seems...underwhelming, chap." Reginald was trying to be polite but he was saying what everyone else was thinking. The Chosen Dead had gotten a boring assignment at the ass end of the universe.

"No disrespect to anyone here but I believe slaying a greater Daemon would allow for an engagement far larger than what you have been given," Benga Din said as he sipped ale from a Viking horn Vora had provided.

"It is peculiar, but it also makes sense," The Penitent said. Everyone looked at him.

"Do tell Eugene" Gio quipped.

The Penitent smirked before continuing and pointing at Gerald. "That monster was waiting for him, or someone like him," The Penitent started. "What's to say, what else will be out there looking for him? We already know there's worse out there. It's smart; don't invite trouble, it's easy enough to find on its own," The Penitent finished.

"Too right, chap. Cheers," Reginald raised his glass. The Penitent refrained from drinking but raised his hand anyway.

"Cheers to you, Jarl Reginald! May you find victory and feast while your foes choke upon the bones!!" Vora yelled. Everyone there loved it and cheered.

"I'm using that!" Gio yelled.

The rest of the night devolved into eating, drinking, and dancing with man-eating plants. Mervin made an appearance and humored Gio by doing some square dancing.

33

CARSADAX

All the teams stood at attention on the parade grounds. The sun was rising and as its red orb covered the field in golden light, Porter stepped up to the dais and saluted the field. The field saluted back. "You have all been given your orders. Now you will be sent out into the universe to do battle against the great enemy." Porter paused. "That's the easy part. You are all good people. You choose to be here, to risk your lives a second time. That is not so easy." Porter nodded at the field. "I salute you. Sacrifice, that is what separates you from the great foe. You are willing to leave your well-deserved paradise, your family, friends, and loved ones to jump into a bloody war with no end." It seemed to every person there that Porter stared down every one of them. "It has been my privilege to have you here and see you grow into an elite fighting force."

Porter's intensity increased. "I ask you for one thing, one thing only," Porter growled. "I ask for victory. We can never lose. The cost is too high, only victory" Porter roared.

"Only victory!" the field responded.

"Dismissed!"

The team broke up and headed to where their sergeants directed.

"Let's go, time to head out!" Miller yelled to the Chosen Dead who followed Miller as he flew off to the CTC.

Once the Chosen Dead landed, they smelled the ozone burn of souls using the CTC. A rustle of wind behind the team signified the arrival of Bariel.

Miller stepped back and saluted one last time. The Chosen Dead returned his salute. As each member of the team walked into the warehouse building that housed the CTC, Miller nodded and gave a word of encouragement to each member.

Gerald was last. Miller extended his arm which Gerald took in the warrior's fashion. "Keep your head on a swivel."

"Yes sir." Gerald released his grip and watched Miller pat Bariel on the arm.

Gerald and Bariel walked into the warehouse and approached the CTC. The crew that was working the CTC was waiting for them.

A tall slender man approached the Chosen Dead and Bariel once they were all together. "Welcome, my name is Carson, and I manage the CTC. Please circle the transference crystal please" The Chosen Dead complied and Bariel moved into position as well. "Chosen Dead we salute you!" Carson stated. The rest of the crew who were standing at attention also saluted. "Place your hand upon the crystal please." The Chosen Dead did as they were asked.

Bariel was the last to place his hand on the crystal. He turned to Carson and nodded. Carson acknowledged him and waved his arm. The crystal began glowing and then as before there was light, turned black, and then light again.

You could feel the difference immediately between the training world and Carsadax. They were now in a large white tent similar to what you would use in the circus. The ground was covered with a blue carpet that seemed uneven and appeared to be covering sand as the heat blew in through the tent flap. The gravity was different, lighter. The air smelled differently as well, much drier.

An alien, one of the Eloyie, approached them limping. He was tall, thin, and wiry with long white hair in a ponytail and silver armor. The difference in the way the Eloyie moved compared to a human was noticeable. There was a fluidity that humans just didn't possess. The limp came from a wound bound around his right thigh.

Bariel smiled, approached the Eloyie, and greeted him, eying his wound. "Good to see you again, Oriel. I hope you are well."

Oriel flashed a very white smile in return. "I will be fine in a few days. Spear caught me is all."

Bariel patted Oriel on the back. "I am glad, my friend. Come, let me introduce you." Bariel turned to The Chosen Dead and introduced the team to Oriel, who bowed and placed his hand over his heart.

"Greetings, Chosen Dead. Welcome to the Carsadax Theater." The Chosen Dead greeted Oriel in return.

Oriel turned to Gerald. "You are the one who destroyed The Souleater?"

Gerald nodded, unsure of what else to say.

"You need to work on calming the signs and portents better, you are inconsistent. I can assist if you wish?" Oriel asked. He cocked his head as a dog would when you ask them something they don't understand. It was slightly off-putting.

"Yes, thank you, I appreciate it," Gerald said as he looked around him and concentrated, mostly on calming the aether that surrounded him.

"Excellent, follow me please." Oriel turned around, and the Chosen Dead and Bariel followed him out of the CTC Tent and out into the new world where a large red sun cast a slightly red tinge on the bleached sand that sank as they walked. They began to float above the sand so they didn't sink into it. They were at the heart of a large encampment.

As they followed Oriel, they flew above the throng of soldiers and were given a view of a vast desert without end. The sun's reddish tinge covered everything as far as the eye could see. At certain angles, it looked like they were flying over lava and not sand. It was breathtaking.

They flew hundreds of miles, and all they saw was a molten sea. After a few hundred more miles, they began to hear a noise that would drift in and out of their hearing but after a few hundred more miles, it became unmistakable. It sounded like a low hiss, and as they continued following Oriel, the hiss began to grow louder.

In the distance, a spot appeared, at first it looked like a black spot. As they flew closer, they began to make out that it wasn't black but green, the deep green of a jungle. The jungle was still hundreds of miles away but it was growing. The hissing grew louder as they flew closer and they started to differentiate the sound. It wasn't just hissing; there was what sounded like roaring, screams, and an undulating sound that seemed to shrink and grow.

They crested a hill and the source of the noise was revealed. Below them miles away but covering the land like oversized locusts was the great enemy. The stink that exuded from them could be smelled from where they were. Opposite, a host of easily two million daemons for the enemy stood the front lines for the forces of Heaven. The contrast was shocking. Different flags were fluttering in the hot sun that signified the Eloyie contingent which numbered two thousand strong along with another three thousand souls. That was it. Over two million stinking, screeching monsters against five thousand souls and allied aliens.

The enemy had staked their lines and appeared to be waiting to attack.A few hundred miles away behind the enemy lines was the beginnings of the jungle region.

The Chosen Dead followed Oriel down, and they were greeted by the commander of the Eloyie Shilo and Commander Ho, a seven-foot-tall Asian man who bowed to the team in greeting. "You are most welcome," Commander Ho said. Shilo just nodded in greeting and then went back into the command tent. Commander Ho and everyone else followed him in.

The Chosen Dead entered the room and were introduced to Commander Ho's personal guard. Spurs jangled. "Howdy" A tall, thickly mustachioed man dressed in a long coat, black vest, and cowboy hat greeted them. "Name's Wyatt."

Gio, Dave, Don, and Gerald all looked at each other, then back at Wyatt who just smiled. "Nope, ain't him. Lots of fellers around that time had that name." Gio cocked an eyebrow and didn't appear to believe him.

Next was Krakov, a tall Russian dressed in the same armor as the rest but he had colored most of it black and added bat wings as the pauldrons. Bleda, a Hun, was next. A long top knot spilled down his shoulders and back, and he nodded to The Chosen Dead.

Amunet, who appeared to be Middle Eastern, looked up from the opposite side of the table and greeted them. "Welcome," she said. The last was Orsulix, a Gaul of medium height who had fashioned his armor in the gladiator fashion with one arm exposed. Orsulix lowered his head and crossed his right arm across his chest in salute.

Ho signaled for everyone to approach the table. "You have been brought here for your first assignment," Ho began. "Normally the enemy would increase its presence slowly, but there has been an upsurge from their CTC that we have been able to pick up on. This world has no significance. Besides large predators of mammalian origin and reptiles, there are no higher forms of life on this world, so there are no souls for them to reap and destroy. The army outside is not considered a major threat either." Ho, let the team think about what he had just said. Why would the great enemy expend any resources here at all? Something wasn't right but no one had a clue as to what...yet.

"What about the jungles?" Gerald asked, "Has there been a presence there?" He recalled that Carsadax's hologram seemed to have a blip of red that showed up and quickly disappeared.

"Yes, we have sent scouts into the jungles and have not discovered anything. It appears that any enemy presence is merely transitional," Ho explained. "We still send out scouts to cover the jungles just to make sure they are not hiding anything, it will be almost impossible to find them due to the sheer size of this jungle. It is three times the size of Eurasia."

"I would like to assist your scouts if I may," Gordon offered.

Commander Ho looked at Gordon. "You are the one who can disappear, yes?"

Gordon nodded.

"Good, you may begin as soon as possible. Our scryers have not found anything. It makes me nervous. I do not like to be nervous."

Krakov growled, "No, he does not."

Commander Ho nodded at Krakov and then turned back to the team. Nervous for Commander Ho seemed very different for him than for normal people. He did not seem to express any emotion except held back aggression. He turned to Gerald "You, we also know about." Everyone in the room turned to Gerald. "You are a risk to all around you but the personal risk for you is much greater. We will work with you to make sure that you can cloak yourself properly and assist you when possible."

Commander Ho then nodded his head and the table blinked to life. An exact miniaturized depiction of the enemy on one side and our forces showing on the other appeared. The contrast in size was comical with a four hundred to one ratio. No one in the room seemed the slightest bit phased by the odds, though. "If they hold to their previous attacks they will attack again tomorrow. The upsurge in CTC activity correlates with this as they are bringing in additional reinforcements for the losses they have suffered."

"Is the leadership still the same?" Amunet asked.

"As far as we know, the leadership is still two mid-level Daemons. They direct the attacks and so far, nothing bigger has come to the table."

Gerald raised his hand. "Sir, where do you want us tomorrow?"

Commander Ho smiled. "The tip of the spear." With that, he dismissed them.

The Chosen Dead made their way through the camp to a tent at the back and noticed the Eloyie were able to manipulate their environment the way souls could. A tent peg that had come undone was repaired and battened down with a hand wave. The smell of fresh hay heralded their approach to a tent stable that housed horses. One was sea green, another pastel pink, while a third showed mottled shades of deep purple. They were taller and more slender than a horse from Earth and far more elegant and ethereal to look upon. The horses matched the Eloyie.

They passed the stables and said hello to the Eloyie who greeted them either with a hello or a simple nod. The flag had The Chosen Dead sigil, a blue flag with the tree of life in the middle, erected. Once The Chosen Dead were settled into their tent, Bariel bid them farewell. "I will leave you now," he said. "I have other arrangements. I will you see tomorrow"

Inside the tent were sleeping cots arranged three to each side with the middle open along with a table and chairs at the far end.

"This is still better than sleeping on the ground in Sicily," Gio said. Everyone sat down on their cots.

"Isn't it warm in Sicily?" Don asked Gio.

"Not in the wintertime. We were in a coastal town called Gela. At night the temperature would drop to the thirties and the wind would whip off the water. Didn't help we had to sleep on the street for a few weeks"

Vora came up to Gio and pinched his cheeks. "You are poor baby, so cold."

Gio grinned "I was, I was very cold. I didn't have our boy over there to keep me warm." Gio winked over at Gordon who shook his head.

"And you will not," Vora said matter of fact, and then changed the subject. "Commander Ho, he is very serious, like Porter and Miller."

They all understood what Vora meant. These were men who have been through war, many wars. Their faces reflected that fact. None of those men and women in that tent would ever know peace again. Even in Heaven, peace would evade them. It was a sobering thought and from the sudden change in atmosphere in the tent, they all felt it.

Gerald went outside and began to walk the perimeter. The sun had begun to descend and the sand across from him had reddened so it looked like a fire that swirled and moved with the wind. The dry air that gusted over everything also brought a dusting of sand that settled everywhere. Gerald willed his armor off and floated over the sand in a pair of jeans, a white t-shirt, and tennis sneakers. He floated up higher to get a better look at the enemy and the jungle beyond when he was stopped.

"I would not go any higher," Bariel warned. Gerald stopped and turned to Bariel who just seemed to appear. "If you rise above a certain level you will draw fire from them. Very inconvenient."

"Thanks for the heads up," Gerald replied.

Bariel was looking around Gerald and noticed the signs and portents swirling in and out of visibility. "You are inconsistent. Oriel will be able to help you with this."

Gerald pondered for a moment before replying. "How is it that again? You are an angel; I would think you would be better with that sort of thing."

Bariel flicked his wings out in response. "The Eloyie are a race created for what you call magic. They see more clearly the skein of creation. Very similar to how you see it, why you are unique."

Gerald took that in and nodded in response.

As if on cue, Oriel flew up to greet Gerald and Bariel. "Greetings to you both," Oriel hailed. "I wished to work with you before the battle tomorrow. I would have come to your tent but this is better. It also allows me to catch up with an old friend."

Bariel smiled in response. Gerald was glad to see Bariel loosen up and was struck by the similarities between the angel and the Eloyie. They were very similar in appearance to human beings but not human. Their movements, though similar, were not the same. Oriel moved with a fluid grace that humans did not possess, and Bariel, with his size and the sheer power that exuded from him, was most definitely not human.

"I understand you have been able to mimic the ability of the one called Gordon?" Oriel asked as the three of them hung suspended over their camp.

"You are very well informed," Gerald said.

"Knowledge is power." Oriel thinly smiled. "His ability alone is remarkable. He can render himself invisible in multiple planes of reality. He, you, and one other are the only beings that can do this. Humans are full of surprises. None of my kind can replicate that. It's incredible. For you to be able to do the same just based on his energy."

"So can you help me?" Gerald asked Oriel who inclined his head.

"I can. You recall how you mastered the ability to cloak yourself?"

Gerald thought back to how he had to take the two very different energies and work with them, not force, but coax them to work together for him. "Yes, it was tough to get them to work together," he said.

Oriel looked over at Bariel and they shared a look. "Care to share or would you like to get a room?" Gerald quipped.

Bariel looked surprised then shook his head and sighed. "Humans and their humor. I am still not sure if it is a blessing or a curse."

Gerald shrugged

"Apologies, but we were both realizing that the way you see the energy is how we as angels and Eloyie see it. It is all a living thing. Mostly it is latent energy and is malleable just by reaching out to touch it." Bariel extended his arms and created a fire in both of his hands, then closed them to create his sword which winked out of existence with a flourish. "Humans, it takes many years to be able to see the energy this way. They feel it, yes, but they do not understand it."

Gerald nodded half understanding it. Oriel interjected. "It is understandable that you do not fully understand this as for you it is instinct. You do not need to understand how to breathe but you just do it. That more digestible to you?" Oriel asked,

Gerald nodded.

"Good, so the same way you were able to replicate Gordon's cloaking is the same way you will calm the signs and portents... but different."

Gerald rolled his eyes.

Oriel moved closer to Gerald. "Cloak yourself," he commanded.

Gerald complied, and he asked for the energies that allowed him to cloak himself to work with him. In a few seconds, he had disappeared.

"Remarkable. I do not see you at all in any spectrum." Oriel exclaimed. "Show yourself." Gerald complied. "Very good. Now do you see the signs and portents?" Gerald focused and was able to see the swirls and eddies that surrounded him. "They are not visible to most beings, so the beasts down there do not see any of this. They are not powerful enough to. Neither are the two mid-level daemons that lead them. It is beings like the Souleater, and others who can," Oriel explained.

"The signs and portents are another form of energy, similar to what you have worked with to cloak yourself" Oriel explained as he raised his hand to make his point. "But there is a difference. These energies that make up the signs and portents are reactionary energies, not latent." Oriel looked to see if Gerald was following.

"Like a ship moving through the water. It cuts through and causes a ripple effect," Gerald added.

Oriel's face lit up. "Very appropriate, yes. You are the ship, the universe is the water. When the ship goes faster it creates a greater wake." He moved his hand across his chest and caused ripples to appear in the air. "What do you do if you are swimming and don't want to splash?" Oriel asked, altering the analogy.

"Dive under the water?" Gerald stated.

Oriel nodded. "Yes, very good, you need to dive under the water. There are underlying layers to this energy. You need to learn to navigate below the level where the universe reacts to you"

"Great, and how do I do that?"

Oriel waved his arm and the signs and portents illuminated brightly so each swirl of energy was lit brightly against the lowering sun. "Look deeper into the energy. Tell me, what do you see?" Oriel illuminated the signs and portents even more.

Gerald focused intently on the too-bright energy all around him. He was worried that the enemy would see it

"Focus on this, do not worry about them," Oriel said, reading his mind.

Gerald focused and initially, all he could see were the colors. He moved around it and watched how the energy around him would swirl as he moved. He zipped around in a circle and noticed the energy move more quickly. Soon he realized that the analogy to diving beneath the surface was partially incorrect. There was no linear plane to dive down to. "Move slowly," Oriel offered. Gerald did as he was asked and moved very slowly away from Bariel and Oriel. As he moved, the signs and portents also slowed. This wasn't helpful unless he planned to move very slowly in the middle of a battle. Gerald held still. The energy swirling around him calmed even more.

"Look closer," Oriel said from within his mind. Gerald did as he was asked and closed his eyes to concentrate. Around him, he saw that there was a small field of energy, his aura. He focused on that aura field. This was calm. In that space, there was no turbulence.

Gerald took his focus and cast it into that aura field, in here he found the answer. Like everything else, he was connected to the universe. This field was no different, but this was where his energy and the energy of the universe combined. Here was where he dived. He was able to work with the energy here and extend this field out further so that it calmed all it touched.

"Very good!" Gerald heard Oriel say. "You have stilled the turbulence. If you are seen by a being of great power, you would show as someone of no significance."

34

THE TIP OF THE SPEAR

The following day, as the red sun rose above the horizon, the enemy began to prepare for the attack. Roars screams, and a variety of screeching cut through the air as the enemy began to ramp up. The much smaller force opposing them was already lined up and in formation. The Chosen Dead were indeed the tip of the spear. Gerald, Vora, Gio, Don, and David were aligned ahead of the rest of the force. Commander Ho and his contingent, which included Bariel, were lined up behind The Chosen Dead with the rest of the force.

Most of the Eloyie were on horseback with a thousand-foot soldiers lined up with bows and arrows that glowed behind them. It had been explained to The Chosen Dead that the enemy would begin each attack with a show of strength, they would screech, yell, and roar at them for a bit. Soon they would attack.

The front line of the enemy forces stretched horizontally in front of them and barely held in place by the captains who led various groupings of daemons, they were roaring orders to direct and hold them. There was a level of organization to the enemy army even if they were barely constrained.

Commander Ho had utter disdain for what he termed "a childish primitive display of stupidity." Gerald agreed with Commander Ho, but he also knew no one did anything without a reason. He learned painfully through experience why he had Gordon scouting the enemy encampment instead of standing with the rest of the Chosen Dead.

Vora wasn't happy with this at all. She was furious as if it was a slight against Gordon and indirectly her. "Is first, he should stand with us!" Vora yelled at Gerald in the tent the night before. Gordon had to calm her down and explain that what he was doing was more important. She eventually calmed down and she said she understood but was still agitated. Vora was standing at attention facing the Daemon horde and didn't move a muscle. A muscle twitch from her jawline every once and a while was the only thing that showed she wasn't a statue.

Gordon had taken the long way around and made his way to the rear of the stinking host spread out to his side. He floated above the ground to ensure he did not leave any marks or tracks.

He paused to look at the tiny opposition that opposed the vast army. In front were his people, the Chosen Dead. His heart filled with pride and a pang of regret. He wanted to stand there with them, side by side with his brothers and Vora. She had changed him. He never thought that he would ever be truly happy, not after living, not after all the pain and suffering. It was enough to do what he could for his people, which at times seemed like nothing. Once and a while, though, someone would come back to the reservation and show him that his efforts were not in vain.

That wasn't happiness, though. Being with her, that was happiness. She was full of life, so loving and giving, and she had her pain. The pain she tried to hide, but he found it like everything else he chose to seek out. He wanted to remove that pain for her.

Sometimes, she would tell him about her past, little by little, following her path with her dropping little breadcrumbs. He always wished she would say more but knew enough to stay silent and let him get to it in her way, not his.

An increase in the horrendous volume of noise took Gordon out of his reverie. He watched as the daemons began their attack. The heavenly force was situated in front of a high cliff wall which forced the Daemons to attack from straight on and ensured that flanking maneuvers would be extremely difficult at best.

The familiar sign of a lightning storm began to swirl above his people. Gordon wished he could stay and watch, better yet join, but his task lay ahead. Gordon had to wait while the vast body of the corrupt host had engaged in battle before he could move. The press of bodies would have made it impossible for him to move through and not be detected. Not true; he could move through them if he wanted to, but his old instincts and what he had learned when alive kicked in. Fewer enemies meant easier movement whether you could ghost through them or not.

Gordon waited patiently and when the massive throng of monsters finally passed, he went into the camp. There was a massive amount of dust in the air from the charge so even if he wasn't cloaked he would have been able to move through it with ease. The smell of the encampment was atrocious. The stench the monsters gave off was appalling but it was magnified with excrement all over the ground. Gnawed and broken bones from their meals were scattered all over the ground. From the way they created their resting places, they would eat and defecate in the same place.

Gordon almost gagged from the various stinks that arose. His worst fear wasn't detection; it was touching anything in this disgusting place. If anything got on him, he feared it would stick to him forever.

Gordon floated through the camp until he was able to locate the two leaders of the daemons. One of the leaders was thin to the point of emaciation with its rib bones showing through the pale mottled skin of its torso. The head was reptilian and had one horn sticking out of the right side of its head, and its clawed hands had three fingers.

The other leader was grotesquely fat and its skin was a dark red. The face seemed almost human, save for the one eye it had in the center of its head. It had greasy, slicked-back black hair and as he watched, it shit right on the ground where it added to an existing pile of feces. He found them easily enough, but what he didn't expect was for them to be speaking to what looked like a human soul with a drab, dirty black cloak on.

Gordon moved closer so that he could listen to what they were discussing. From his intel, none of them were told of there being any souls among the enemy, only Daemons. This changed things. The niggling feeling the enemy was here for something increased. Souls, whether they were good or bad, were powerful; they were a resource not to be wasted.

Gordon moved closer to where the soul was speaking with the two Daemons. He gritted his teeth as he floated down to the ground and lay next to a giant pile of bones covered in all matter of bodily fluids.

"...How long?" the cloaked soul asked. Gordon was able to get a better look at the soul. It was a man with short hair and thin sallow features. He noticed some sort of necklace or collar around his neck. It looked similar to a dampener but Gordon saw that there was some sort of sickly green energy emitting from the collar.

"As long as is required. We have reinforcements moving in for a larger attack after this one" the fat Daemon gurgled.

"We could destroy them if we were allowed"

"You have orders," the soul said in a raspy voice. "Follow them"

The Daemons hissed at the soul who, to his credit, didn't flinch.

"Do you want to discuss it with him? I can ask him to come and you can give your grievance to him directly." The soul didn't budge but the two demons seemed to shrink at the thought of speaking to *him*. " I do not want to have this discussion again. Follow your orders until you have new ones."

The fat Daemon shit in response and used his tail to whip some of that fresh shit in the soul's direction. This got a reaction from the soul. "You disrespect me?" The soul backed up and seemed to expand. He began to glow and when he clenched his fists, fire erupted from them. The two Daemons responded in kind. The skinny one opened its hands, and the claws on each digit expanded out to the size of daggers. The fat Daemon reached behind it and pulled a rusty, feces-covered sword from its rectum. The two daemons spread out and were prepared to attack the soul who glowed with deep red energy.

A massive explosion lit up the entire sky behind them from where the battle was occurring. All three of them froze, unsure of what to do until the soul put out the flames in both hands "See to your duties." Neither Daemon wanted to stop their attack but the wailing grew louder from behind them signifying that something was wrong.

Familiar lightning in the distance grew closer. After a few tense moments, the two Daemons snarled at the soul and turned to the returning horde. Apparently, not in very good shape. The soul stood stock still for a moment longer, then turned and made his way out of the camp towards the jungle a few hundred miles away.

As Gordon followed the soul, he heard the hum of a CTC and turned to see more Daemons joining their brethren. Gordon made sure to get the position of the CTC. It wasn't very big and could easily be carried away, but he made sure to get its energy signature so he could track it and when the need arose, destroy it. He followed the soul as it moved with great speed across the desert towards the jungle. Within a few minutes, they had traveled a few hundred miles and the edge of the jungles quickly approached. Gordon expected the soul to slow down but instead, he sped up and hit the edge of jungles so fast that the trees and vines he swept past were blown back by the velocity. Birds were sent skyward and small animals went scurrying as the soul zoomed past.

Gordon did not want to lose the damned soul, so he matched the speed and plunged into the jungle and immediately had to swerve to avoid hitting a group of trees in his path. If Gordon had hit them, he would have alerted the soul that he was being followed. It took Gordon a few moments to get used to avoiding the trees and still following the damned soul. It became easier when he got closer to the soul so that he could follow in the wake created. Like a wave created by a passing boat, Gordon was able to follow behind and avoid the obstacles the soul was avoiding.

After a few moments, it became obvious the soul had passed this way before and the number of times he had to swerve was minimal. The damned soul was smart and was using minimal effort to move through the jungle but still moving fast enough to avoid detection from above. Gordon was following the damned soul for over an hour when the soul dipped down into a valley, took a hard right turn, and disappeared.

Gordon pulled up short after the turn and went up higher to see if he could spot the damned soul but found nothing. He went down the trail to where the soul was and still nothing. Gordon was cloaked and knew that he had not been found out, but he was cautious as he moved around the area to ensure he wasn't going to be ambushed. He pushed his senses out through the multiple layers of reality, but nothing. The damned soul had vanished.

Gordon couldn't be sure that maybe this damned soul could do what he did but if he could, he scanned the area for the same energy he used and found nothing.

He spent some time searching, he was torn on whether to try and move forward or go back. Finally, he turned around and headed back to camp, eager to inform his people of what he found and even more eager to see how they had done in their first official conflict. He was fairly confident he could find the enemy again as well.

Back at the battlefield right when the Daemons made their initial charge, The Chosen Dead were ready and waiting for the first of the grotesque monstrosities to hit them. Though they were sentient beings, they were anti-life. The air around them seemed to protest their existence in this universe.

"Chosen Dead!" Commander Ho called "Let us know when you want us to engage, if things get too difficult, we will assist."

They all turned to Commander Ho who smiled in return. "Let us see what you have to offer." He raised his arm and roared. The Chosen Dead roared back.

"Ok, you heard him!" Gerald yelled over the din, increasing in intensity with each passing second. The horde would be upon them in moments. "I do not want to have to ask them for help. Do any of you want to call for help?" Gerald added. He got his response as the Daemons closed in. They saw how few a number there were and expected easy prey. The Daemons hit their line like a tsunami and instead of washing The Chosen Dead away, it was the Daemons who were broken apart.

All five members of The Chosen Dead had combined their shields and as one pushed the shield wall from one end of the attacking line to the other. The initial charge cost the enemies thousands as they were smashed to a pulp on those shields. Thousands more followed as their momentum ran them right into their brethren. The shrieks of the dead and dying were deafening.

Gerald raised his right arm and flashed two fingers. The Chosen Dead dropped their shields and the horde fell over themselves to get going again, and then Don ran from the line towards the Daemons and expanded himself out to a sixty-foot giant ebony avatar of war. Don's footprints thundered and he spread his arms wide and slammed his hands together. The shockwave blew apart all that stood before him for a hundred yards. In a matter of moments, the enemy lost another twenty thousand of their number.

The Daemons closest to him tried to overwhelm Don, but he moved so quickly for his size that they flew off him as he blasted them with kinetic energy that he fired from his hands.

Gerald raised his left arm and displayed all five fingers. Vora leaped into the air and screamed her war cry. Lightning clouds formed imminently and she began to cover the field in a lightning storm that destroyed thousands more. She descended with her frost blade glowing and swept it back and forth in front of her. Nothing survived in the path of her blade.

Commander Ho, his contingency, and Eloyie all stood shocked at the amount of damage that only two of these souls had unleashed.

Oriel approached Commander Ho. "Should we engage?"

Commander Ho shook his head in disbelief. "I had told them to ask for help once they felt it was required but I do not see that happening, do you?"

A howl so loud that shook the ground brought everyone's attention back to the battle as David, who had transformed into a twenty-foot-tall werewolf, leaped into the middle of the Daemons and began to slash his arms left and right. Dozens died. More died when David slammed his fists into the ground and the ground rose and swallowed thousands more. The cracks in the earth spit Daemon ichor all around. Daemons halted their attack and began to run back toward their lines.

Gerald called over to Commander Ho, "Should we press them, sir?" Commander Ho ordered the Chosen Dead to stand down. "We have them on the run, sir," Gerald pushed. This was the perfect time to wipe an enemy out with their back to you.

"Fall back. If we press the attack, they will disappear into the jungles and then force us to root them out or destroy the jungle to get to them," Commander Ho explained.

Gerald fired three pulses of energy into the air and all the members of The Chosen Dead returned. None of the Daemons tried to engage them.

"Shit, I didn't even get to show my stuff," Gio griped.

Gerald smiled and patted Gio on the back, then turned to the returning team members. "Great job, guys." He first bumped Don and David and high-fived Vora who loved to high-five.

"Was easy, not like blood spawn of Souleater," Vora said.

"These are low-level Daemons. They do not possess the power the Souleater had," Commander Ho said. "The blood spawn was an extension of the Souleater, thus the increased durability." The Chosen Dead stood at attention and saluted Commander Ho who returned the salute. "That was...unexpected," Commander Ho said to them as he came closer to them. "For such a young team, you are all very powerful."

Oriel came up with his helm under his arm and bowed to Commander Ho "I see we are done for today," he said with the driest of humor.

Another Eloyie approached on a beautiful seafoam green horse and moved with such grace that it appeared to barely touch the ground with its slim hooves. He jumped to the ground and saluted Oriel first then Commander Ho. "Permission to secure the field."

Oriel and Commander Ho saluted back "Reloa, greetings. You have not met The Chosen Dead," Commander Ho said.

As Reloa came closer, you could see he was much bigger than Oriel, in height and weight. He was broad for an Eloyie, a physical specimen. He had a long scar down the left side of his face that seemed to enhance his ethereal looks. "I have heard much. Now I have seen more. Greetings to you Chosen Dead" Reloa bowed to them, and The Chosen Dead bowed in return. He turned to Gerald. "You have ruined our fun, and the horses needed the exercise." A hint of a smile flashed across his face as he said this.

A quick nod and Reloa took a step and leaped onto the back of his horse. He drew his sword and bid them farewell. Reloa made a signal to the cavalry, and they joined him as they galloped at speed to the near-empty battlefield.

35

POST OP AND THEN SOME

Later on, Gordon returned and, after relaying what he found to Gerald, a post-op meeting was called. The Chosen Dead, Commander Ho's team, Bariel, Oriel, and Reloa met in the command tent. Gordon detailed the small bit of conversation that the two leader Daemons had with the damned soul. Once the soul was mentioned, everyone perked up. A human soul, good or evil, had power. Some could potentially destroy a planet themselves. Something was going on.

Once Gordon detailed losing the aforementioned soul, things became even more interesting. Souls, besides Gordon and Gerald, did not just disappear.

Bariel had an odd look on his face when Gordon finished. "So, you are sure this damned soul was not there anymore?" he asked Gordon, who nodded in the affirmative. "Did the air seem any different, perhaps a cloaking such as your own?"

Gordon shook his head. "No, I searched for the same energy that I use to cloak. Nothing seemed out of the ordinary. One second he was there, the next, gone."

Bariel didn't say a word, but all in the room could tell he was thinking. "You can take me there, yes?" Gordon acknowledged that he could. "I will lead a scouting party compromised of The Chosen Dead to where Gordon lost this damned soul and discover what they are trying to hide." Bariel looked at Commander Ho, who acquiesced to Bariel, who then turned to Oriel and Reloa. "I leave it to you to repel the next attack but be ready to assist once we find them." They both bowed their heads and pounded their fists on their chests in unison.

Gerald approached Bariel. "When do we leave?"

The Chosen Dead and Bariel went back to their tent and practiced cloaking the entire team. Gerald was able to assist Gordon with creating enough energy to store in their armor. They knew that the enemy wouldn't know to look for this, so they were pretty sure they were ok.

In his armor, Bariel looked like a walking tank with long, flowing locks. They provided his armor with triple the energy to account for his aura, which radiated so much power even with him controlling it and dimming it the cloaking energy was used up at triple the rate.

They flew out and around the edge of the army and then headed out into the open desert towards the point in the jungle where Gordon entered following the damned soul. The red rays of the sun-splashed everything with swirling fire as they traveled. Nothing was out here, save an occasional small scurrying mammal.

Soon they came upon the edge of the jungle and followed Gordon in. They were able to keep up with the pattern he led them which was the exact path Gordon had followed the damned soul. He did this hoping someone else following would catch something that he missed.

The Chosen Dead swept out so that they could extend the range they followed, but so far, no one caught anything out of the ordinary in the lush, green jungle. When they arrived at the bend where Gordon lost the damned soul, they spread out and spent hours searching the local area.

Bariel swooped above the tree line and flew through the local area in a radius of no more than a few miles but nothing was found.

The rays of red sun which barely seeped through to the ground lost what little hold they had on illuminating the area as the sun went down for the day. Gordon was frustrated. They all were. He looked around him and all that looked back was a small mammal that looked like a cross between a squirrel and a rabbit. It sat contently munching on acorns it had snatched from the tree limb above it. Gordon nodded to the animal and looked above it to where the top of the tree limbs they had passed were leaning in the direction they had traveled. He looked back down to the ground and then whipped his head around so quickly he startled his furry new friend who jumped up higher and chittered at him. "The trees," he whispered.

Instantly Bariel appeared next to him. Gordon pointed to the trees they had flown past. Even at a reduced speed, they moved at over a hundred miles an hour and the trees, more specifically the branches, showed the path where one of them had passed and broken a twig on a branch.

Gordon motioned for Bariel to stay where he was and slowly went over to the bend where the damned soul disappeared. He slowly floated through the area and the path he would have continued to take. After the bend, the area opened up, making it more difficult to track.

Gordon went to the end of the small opening and began searching for something, anything that gave away where the damned soul had passed through. He was about to give up and bring David to see if he could try and communicate with the trees when he caught it, a little nothing that only a seasoned tracker could find. A twig on a large tree bent back as if something large had flown by and brushed against it.

Gordon got closer and was exhilarated to find a piece had peeled off as if it had snagged on something and been pulled off at high speed. Gordon went further afield and found what he was looking for, a trail. Even Bariel, who was a great and powerful warrior, was not a tracker, not like Gordon and his people. They were born to it; if you were a bad tracker, you were a dead tracker.

The Chosen Dead gathered around Gordon upon his return and pointed out where the tree branches and small twigs off the branches were bent and occasionally snapped. Gordon explained to them that the damned soul didn't just disappear and was gone but was somehow cloaked and kept going but hidden.

A grim smile played across Bariel's face as he extended his arm to motion Gordon to lead the way. Gordon nodded and the team, including Bariel, slowly floated and followed Gordon as he made his way deeper into the jungle.

Night had fallen. Hours had passed but for them, the night was no hindrance in sight. Pitch black was as clear as a sunny day. Slowly, they made their way through the thick night. The buzzing of insects and the occasional screech of animals were the only company for The Chosen Dead and their angelic comrade.

Gordon had to double back quite a few times as he lost the trail but was able to find it again in short order. A few more hours passed, and it was now in the middle of the night. Gordon was so engrossed in tracking that he didn't notice that something was wrong. He raised his fist to halt and everyone tensed. He listened and heard nothing. The normal background of nature was silenced. No animals made a noise or even moved in the underbrush, no insect noise either. It was as if every living thing had left.

Gordon had seen that before when there had been a fire. The animals went scurrying and flying away. This also happened when a large predator was tracking its prey. It had been what saved his life when he had been stalked by a massive timber wolf while out hunting as a young brave on his first hunt. If he had not listened to the children of the forest, he would have not been ready when the wolf pounced on him and almost killed him. Even now Gerald recalled the hot breath of the beast as it snapped its massive jaws an inch from his face. His spear had been the only thing that saved him. Now, in this alien jungle, Gordon felt the same thing. There was a large predator somewhere near.

Gerald signaled Gordon and he floated over to explain. Gerald ordered the team to spread out and follow Gordon slowly. After another hour of moving through the blanket of the jungle, they came upon a rise. At the top of the rise, in the distance, they gazed upon a massive valley covered in clouds. None of them had realized they had ascended high enough to an elevation that high till now. In the middle of the valley stood what appeared to be a large structure covered in moss and vines. The top of it appeared to stand above the clouds.

Gerald looked at the structure and noticed how the clouds seemed to thicken up around the structure as if the clouds were being emitted from the structure. He pointed this out to Bariel who seemed perplexed. He seemed about to say more but withheld it. "We need to get closer" Was all Bariel said.

They moved out and down the side of the valley. The team was slowly floating down and, upon hitting the cloud layer, started to have issues with staying afloat. Bariel was not affected but the look on his face was very troubled.

After a few moments, Don fell to the ground and had to grab

a tree branch to avoid rolling down the hill. They all quickly descended as their powers began to falter and they got back on solid ground. Bariel stayed afloat but landed along with the rest.

"Something in this fog, it acts like a dampener," Don said as he dusted himself off.

"Not only that, we're visible again," Gordon said as he waved his arm. "I can't pull the cloaking up in here."

They all looked around and suddenly everything became more sinister. What a moment before had been them descending through a cloud layer now gave them the eerie feeling of being watched. That something could attack them at any moment through the thick cloying mist.

Gerald moved close to Bariel and whispered, "Can you sense anything?"

Bariel raised his hand for silence and slowly lifted himself back up and moved around with his eyes closed as he did so. The angel disappeared in the mist.

The Chosen Dead took up positions on the incline they stood on and waited. Even sound was stifled in the cloud cover, but no one dared speak any louder than a whisper for fear of something hearing them.

A twig snapped as loud as a shotgun blast. Everyone turned to see Don with his muscular arm raised. He had moved and stepped on it. They all visibly relaxed.

A swooping movement put them back on the defensive and ready to strike, but it was only Bariel returning. He pulled them in close so they could hear what he had to say. "While we are in the cloud cover we are blind. Nothing can be transmitted either. Once we clear the clouds, you will be able to use your powers again," Bariel explained.

"Stay calm, stay quiet," Gerald added to the team.

"Is spooky," Vora, who had been very quiet the last few hours, chimed in.

It took them almost thirty minutes to clear the cloud layer and then another hour to reach the bottom of the valley floor. The cloud cover seemed to cling to them even after they had cleared it. The cloaking for the Chosen Dead, except for Gordon and Gerald, was not working properly. It kept short-circuiting and the power level reader showed near empty. Gerald and Gordon tried to recharge them but were unsuccessful. The armor and battery seemed to have been affected by the cloud cover. They were all able to use their powers, though, so that was a blessing. However, the jungle was so thick down on the valley floor that floating or flying was near impossible due to the number of vines and foliage.

Gordon led the way and for the next few hours, they did not see a thing, only the living green blanket of the jungle. Every noise was amplified. The animals and insects were here but they wouldn't tell their secrets. Gordon was completely in his element. David was right behind him trying to gather scents and reach out to the animals around them, but either they weren't intelligent enough to speak with him or they were unwilling to.

Occasionally, through a break in the trees, they would get a peek at the monolithic structure at the center of the valley. The structure was still obscured and almost completely covered in moss and vines but, here and there a small patch of bone white would poke through the wall of greenery. It was still a very long way away but the way the clouds seemed to swirl around the giant structure, it almost seemed as if the clouds were reacting to it or even coming out of it, but it was hard to tell from their vantage point.

Darkness fell across the valley but it made little difference to The Chosen Dead. They continued to move through the dense jungle towards the structure. Whatever was happening in this world had to do with that and the clouds that nullified soul powers. That alone would be enough to draw the forces of the great enemy here. So far, though, nothing but the thick jungle was there to meet them. No other living thing for miles around.

Bariel walked with the rest, and Gerald approached him and whispered, "Have you ever seen anything like this before?"

Bariel kept his gaze moving around to secure the area and answered, "Nothing like this. I could not pick up anything once we entered the cloud cover. Everything gives off energy but this...." He was quiet for a moment before continuing, "The structure itself gives off nothing. If it were not so large and visible, I would not be able to see it otherwise. It is there but doesn't exist at any other level or frequency."

Gio approached. "It looks like the clouds are coming out of it, too, right?"

Bariel stopped and looked at Gio, then called a halt. The angel closed his eyes and was as still as a statue for a few minutes. Gerald was about to tap Bariel on the shoulder when he opened his eyes. "I'm not sure," Bariel said before continuing "Whatever that structure consists of, defies any type of scanning or being read. Rest a minute. I want each of you to try as well."

Don sat down cross-legged and tried but at the end, he slumped forward and shook his head. Vora tried next, then David, Gio, Gordon, and finally Gerald. They all failed to read anything off of the monolithic structure. Gerald tried to read the energy signatures of the jungle around him to ensure he still could and was able to, but when he tried to scan the cloud cover and the structure itself, he got back nothing. It read as Bariel stated. You could see it and it looked solid but didn't seem to exist otherwise.

Once everyone had a chance at failure, they moved on. It was disquieting that an angel didn't seem to know any more than the rest of them. They continued their trek. The red rays of the sun crept through the canopy of trees and poked through here and there.

They traveled like this for another few days. Nothing but the jungle was there to accompany them. The worst part was the stillness and unnatural quiet which seemed to weigh them down with unknown dread, a dread that seemed to push down harder than gravity as they got closer to the massive structure still days away from them.

As the team pushed on through the jungle at twilight on the eighth day of their search, Gordon suddenly raised his hand in a fist to call a halt. He signaled for everyone to stay put, then moved into the jungle and within moments had disappeared.

The team dropped down to stay out of sight and waited. If they were alive they would all have been drenched in sweat from the heat, humidity, and stress.

Gordon reappeared behind them and they all almost gave away their position from the surprise. The old skills he had learned on Earth allowed him to move through dense foliage without making a sound.

Gordon gathered the team and detailed what he had found. He had noticed broken branches and tracks, human tracks ahead of them. Gordon stalked ahead and found a path cut into the jungle. He had turned on his cloaking and followed the path for a few hundred yards. He did not encounter another soul on the path but it was clear that this path was used frequently. There were multiple footprints and it appeared the ground had either been burned or poisoned so that it would slow the under-growth. In a jungle like this, even setting fire to a large swath of it wouldn't mean much; it would regrow again quickly. It made sense to see a trail now. They were so deep into the valley and so close to the nulling effect of the monolith that discovery was all but impossible. He checked ahead but did not see another soul.

Now they had to make a decision. They could follow the trail and stay in the jungle for cover, or they could cloak themselves by having Gordon on one end and Gerald on the other. They could make great progress walking the path but the chance for discovery was greater even if they were cloaked. They could follow the path from the jungle which was slower but less likely to be walked into on the path.

In the end, expediency was decided. The cloaking between Gordon and Gerald was solid and they were both able to overlap the team as long as they stayed closer together. The team stepped in the path which was wide enough to have four people walking side by side. If anyone came, they would stay silent and move off the road back into the jungle. They moved cautiously but that was still faster than the progress they would have made maneuvering through the dense jungle. They moved swiftly and silently for another few hours.

As the sun began to rise again and flood the path with bloody light, they finally encountered the enemy. Gordon held up a fist and shook it left and right quickly. The Chosen Dead quickly moved over to the left side of the path which included Bariel, Gordon, Vora, and Don on one side and Gerald, David, and Gio on the right side of the path as they had discussed. Gerald could mimic the cloaking but it was deemed smarter to give Gordon the extra person in Bariel to cloak as he had better control of it.

After a few tense moments as they sat quietly at the edge of the path, they smelled the enemy before they saw them. The familiar stench of corruption and rot assaulted them along with the smell of burning foliage. They came into view a few minutes later. Daemons, at least twenty of them, trod the path as they went by. The lead Daemons were vomiting fire onto the pathway to clear it. Once the front four had exhausted their supply of fire vomit, then four more took their place to spew even more onto the path.

The Chosen Dead tensed. Bariel slowly crouched down even lower. If he had to attack he would leverage himself to destroy them as quickly as possible. They could wipe them all out in moments but if this group did not return, then eventually that would be noticed and someone would come looking for them.

When the Daemons came upon their position, the various stenches were enough to make you gag. Four new Daemons had come to the front to begin vomiting fire anew, and the splash of the initial discharge ricocheted off the ground so hard that a stinking glob of fire went right into the jungle and landed right onto Don's arm. The noise of the fire vomiting suppressed Don's grunt of pain but if you were looking into the woods you would see the fire glob suspended in the air before sliding down to the ground.

A Daemon at the rear snapped its head over to where the glob had fallen to the ground. Every person on the team watched as the Daemon looked right at where they were. Even crouched down you would have had an easy time spotting them, not to mention the giant angel who stood out like a sore thumb from everything around it. Thankfully the cloaking held up. They watched as the Daemon sniffed the air and after a few more seconds turned its attention back to the task at hand.

They stayed hidden for a few more minutes before moving back out. The fire burned quickly and as they began walking back on the path, they could barely feel the heat anymore. The ground was burned clean of any growth and was baked hard enough for them to walk on it without making any noise. They were on the move for another day of walking the path, avoiding other Daemons that walked past from the direction of the monolith as well as the return of the fire vomit daemons heading back in the same direction as the team.

As traffic on the path increased, the team made sure to stay cautious and slow down. After another day and a half, they came upon a crossroads. The team kept going straight, though. Whatever was happening here was happening at the monolith which now took up their view. They could see the thick foliage covering it and now closer through the small pockets, some kind of writing etched into it showed the bone-white stone of the monolith. They didn't have the time to try and read it, of course, because the pathway had consistent foot traffic.

After a few more minutes of walking suddenly the path gave way to a much larger road. They could smell the stink of the Daemons and burning foliage. This much larger road had just been burned clean. It was the equivalent of a six-lane highway. The ground sloped down from this point as well.

Gerald instantly started thinking that if they needed a large roadway like this, it was to support heavier troop movement. He called for the team to stop and signaled for everyone to move over to the same side of the road. Gerald pointed for everyone to follow him into the jungle.

As they began to move into the jungle, they heard a rumbling coming up the road. They moved deeper into the jungle as a behemoth approached. It looked like a massive version of a dump truck put together by a lunatic. The truck had seven massive wheels twenty feet high, three on each side and one on the back that allowed for the vehicle to spin around if needed. The slabs that made up the walls of the truck were thick and rusted in certain areas. Occasional scorch marks were strewn across its sides. A Daemon who appeared to be fused into the cabin drove it. Only its head was present, and thick wires were drilled into its skull so it could control the truck. A plow in the front looked like the prongs of a giant fork. Thick front nozzles dripped fire vomit all over the plow and front of the truck. It was as wide as the new six-lane highway road and was an ingenious way to plow a new road. The creature that controlled the monstrosity let loose a plume of fire and then cackled and cried at the same time. Either seemed acceptable for that sad, evil thing.

They left the awful machine behind and followed Gerald into the jungle to an outcrop that allowed them to view the base of the monolith below. Once they had positioned themselves on the outcrop, what they saw below chilled them all to their very core. The ground surrounding the monolith had been scoured of all growth along with the base for half a mile around it. An army of Daemons was crawling all over the area like ants. The monolith had a large open doorway which the Daemons were driving various vehicles into and out of.

All eyes turned to the real source of concern. There were three full teams of damned souls doing multiple tasks, They all wore long black robes with hoods on them. Some had the collars that Gordon had described, while others did not. These were resources that could turn the tide in a battle.

Suddenly the daemons squawked and ran for cover, and the damned souls looked up, immediately bowed their heads, and kneeled. With a rustle and gust of wind, two fallen angels landed near the open doorway.

Bariel stiffened and bared his teeth. He didn't even realize he was doing it but the animosity ran so deep within him that the reaction was automatic. The fallen angels below were not much different in appearance from Bariel. Both were as large as Bariel with similar aquiline features to his. There were differences. One, the armor they wore was a matte black and appeared to be carved from onyx or cooled lava rock. The wind carried the stink of sulfur that seemed to emanate from the armor as well. The second difference was the anger and hate that poured off of them. They radiated great power that reeked of hate and fury. These two could destroy worlds and if they still knew how to laugh when they did it, they would.

The two fallen angels stood and one of them, with a wave of his hand, allowed the souls to rise. Most of the souls stood and left the immediate area. Three remained, apparently the leaders of the teams. They bowed again to the fallen angels and began a discussion. From this distance, they were unable to hear, and none of them wanted to try anything that may alert the enemy to their existence. The team watched and when the two fallen angels entered the monolith the team pulled back to the jungle area so they could discuss.

"Whatever is here we stop them from acquiring it," Bariel said as he gritted his teeth. He was using self-restraint to stay calm.

"Agreed, are you alright to continue, Bariel?," Gerald said

The angel slowly turned to Gerald, and he looked furious. Bariel was clenching and unclenching his fists. No one was sure what to do because it appeared that Bariel was about to strike Gerald.

Gerald stood still and calm. He didn't move at all and maintained eye contact with Bariel. He made a slight head nod towards where the fallen angels were.

Bariel regained control of himself and let out a long, slow breath. "Apologies. My kind do not forget. You are never betrayed by your enemy." Bariel stopped himself and then continued again. "I am ready. I will not let my emotions get the better of me again. If I have a chance to kill them, I will take it."

Gerald nodded and sighed with relief. "Fair enough, I will hold you to that. We are in agreement that whatever is down there is important. We need to know what it is so we can stop them from getting it." They were all in agreement. "Are you sure you have never seen anything like that thing?" Gerald asked Bariel, who shook his head.

"I have not. I have seen structures similar to this monolith before, but they were much smaller pylons that were at best twenty feet high. and they are placed around planets at important junctures."

"What is the function of these pylons, may I ask?" Gio inquired.

"These pylons are set up by the hundreds around a planet to...." Bariel stopped what he was saying. "That doesn't make sense," he said.

"What, what doesn't make sense?" Gerald prodded Bariel.

"The pylons are set up around a barrier planet. These are planets at the edge of the human known universe. Even with the improved technology, humans have only been allowed to see only a piece of the universe. More importantly, it prevents most major incursions into the known universe so we can keep Earth away from the war as much as possible. This was agreed upon after the war in Heaven when Lucifer was cast down."

"Why does this pylon not make sense?"

"The substance of these pylons emits a null field but it is very limited, just a few miles so that is why there are hundreds of them on the barrier worlds, sometimes thousands. They are placed where they can be amplified by ley lines to boost their signal" Bariel started to space back and forth. "This structure seems to be made of the same or similar material as the pylons but it emits a very powerful signal on its own, most likely due to its size which explains how no one has been able to discover it."

"That's not true," Gio pointed out. "We got a bunch of bad guys down there who seemed to find it no problem."

"You are correct. They acquired the information on its existence. This thing has covered their movements and they have been able to amass a sizable force here. There is a great prize here. We must alert our forces."

Gerald stepped in. "One problem at a time. We need intel first. We need to head down there and find out what it is they are looking for."

Bariel nodded. "What do you propose?"

"I head down there cloaked and find out as much as I can. Gordon will back me up and come with me."

"One of you, not both. We cannot risk you both being captured or killed. We need one of you to be able to escape and contact our forces if things go bad. Gordon is the best; he should be sent back now so that we can rally our forces and also call in for more to deal with the damned souls and...the fallen ones." The last came out as a snarl as Bariel calmed himself.

What he said made sense. Gerald was able to cloak but Gordon could hide even without the cloaking. He could make it through the cloud cover and use his skills while Gerald would not and get caught even if the souls were limited as he was.

"Do the fallen ones have the same limitations as you did in the cloud cover?" Gordon asked Bariel, who nodded.

"They will not be able to scan for you. They would need to hunt you the old ways. Be wary, they can still fly, and their power is not limited in the mist," he finished.

"What about us?" Vora asked, "We will not sit on ass cheeks."

Bariel raised an eyebrow at her but replied, "I would not dream of excluding you, shield maiden. You shall stay with your Jarl and cover him as well as the rest of you."

Gerald pointed at David. "He goes with Gordon as well. He's the most mobile and has a better chance at getting back then the rest of us except Gordon."

David nodded and turned himself into the hybrid wolf man.

Bariel nodded. "You will leave yourself vulnerable, even with you and your teams' considerable powers. Those opposing us down there are formidable."

"Them's the breaks, my man," Gio said. "If the bad guys are bringing heavy hitters to the party, then we gotta do what we gotta do. We can't worry about anything else. Hopefully, we get back up in time."

Bariel gave Gio a grim smile. "We are in agreement. The risks are acceptable."

Gordon went over to Vora. They both touched each other's foreheads, aware that everyone was right there. "Be careful," she whispered.

"I will see you upon my return" Gordon whispered, and they pulled away from each other.

David nodded to the team and Bariel. Don had gotten up and taken a few steps towards David when suddenly as if there was a short circuit and feedback, their cloaking shorted out. Gerald and Gordon shook their heads and started looking around for the source.

"Ow, what is that?" Don said as he grabbed his foot. "I just got zapped by this, it looks like..." He bent down to pick up what appeared to be an old silver coin lying on the ground. "Is that Latin?"

"Stop!" Bariel warned.

"What is it?" Gerald asked.

Before Bariel could answer, a lance pierced right through him. Another appeared soon after, next to his shoulder. Faster than any could have thought possible, the two fallen angels had impaled Bariel with black lances made of the same sulfuric rock as their armor. Coming out of the foliage around them were teams of damned souls with weapons drawn. They were dressed in long overcoats made of some kind of green fabric or leather, and a mist came out of a pouch that clung to them. What appeared to be a rock was rolled into the middle of the Chosen Dead. It looked to be a large green egg that opened an eye to look around at them. It then exploded and everything went black.

36

THE BETRAYER

There was darkness, then pain, and after an unknown amount of time, The Chosen Dead began to stir. The air was dry and smelled of Daemons, stone, sulfur, and blood.

Gerald began to regain consciousness. His head hurt so bad that it felt like someone had hit him with a hatchet. For all he knew, maybe they had. A wave of nausea hit when he tried to stand up. He gritted his teeth and found there was a chain attached to a dampener around his neck. He was able to get on his knees and looked around. It took a few minutes to readjust between the explosion and the dampener. It felt like he had the mother of all hangovers.

He found himself in a large room with a vaulted ceiling. In the center of the room was a CTC. It appeared to be old and chipped. *That explained how they were able to conceal their numbers and bring in all these resources.* Gerald deduced. A section of the room was curtained off. A large fire was going, and what looked like strips of meat on a large skillet were being placed onto the fire. Daemons stood guard throughout the room, as well as a team of hooded damned souls keeping watch on the Chosen Dead. From their body language, they didn't seem too concerned seeing as the team was chained to the floor with dampeners on.

The rest of the Chosen Dead began to get their bearings. No one said a thing. They were waiting to see why they were still alive. Don tried to break free but to no avail. David sat down cross-legged. Gio muttered some curses and started to look around, nodding to each of them in turn. Vora tried to pull the chain free, looked around, and then sat cross-legged as well. Gordon was missing.

Gerald looked everywhere but he wasn't there. He made eye contact with Vora who gave him a thin smile. They also didn't see Bariel. A feeling of dread pervaded. The last time they saw him, he had been pierced twice with black stone lances by two fallen angels. Bariel could very well be dead.

Emotion began to well up: anger, fear, hatred, each one vied for his attention. To think that one of their number could be dead was too much. They were imprisoned and helpless, they...

"Stop!" Gerald slammed the door on all of that. He took a slow, deep breath. He had to keep it together. He had been in worse situations in life and needed to focus on what he could at this moment to work out a plan. If Bariel was dead, they would deal with it later but for now, priorities needed to be adjusted.

Gerald scanned the room again and saw that it was huge. Even with a portion of it curtained off, it appeared to stretch for at least another three hundred yards into the darkness. Without his abilities, Gerald couldn't tell how much larger the chamber was but he had a feeling that it was much larger still.

The CTC started to glow, and a platoon of Daemons appeared. The leader of this platoon was much larger than the rest of them. Gerald was taken aback because this Daemon looked like a smaller copy of the Souleater. It had the same red skin and two large horns on either side of its head, an extremely muscular body with hooved feet, and large claws.

What reminded Gerald the most of The Souleater was the human-like face and black, malevolent eyes that shined with dark intellect. This beast wore black leather pants and a leather jacket with a fur collar and carried a massive mace strung to its back. It nodded to the damned souls and growled a command to move out to its underlings and they left the chamber.

"Quite the specimen isn't he?" a soft voice with a French or Israeli accent asked from behind Gerald, who jumped in surprise. No one was there a moment ago but the person who spoke walked into his view so Gerald didn't have to turn around. He was tall and thin and had the hood of his cloak down so you could see his face. He had bright penny-red hair and a short beard to match. His eyes were a dark green that seemed to change colors, from a lighter green back to dark green a moment later. He had what appeared to be a fresh rope burn around his neck. The damned soul saw him looking at his neck and smiled. He had a scent to him. He stank of musk and rotten flowers. There was no warmth in the smile, but he seemed to find some humor in it.

"Nice to see a fellow ginger," he casually said to Gerald. "In my day there were a decent amount of them. Imagine my surprise when I found out only three percent of all humans are redheads. Isn't that interesting?" The damned soul walked around each of the Chosen Dead, inspecting them. He didn't say another word as he stopped and winked at Vora who didn't even acknowledge his presence. The damned soul sniffed at that and walked back up front to address them. "I'm sure you have questions," he said. No one responded.

Amused, the damned soul looked over at another damned soul, who shrugged. "So you're playing hard to get. I respect that. May I have your names at least?" The Chosen Dead did not reply. "Come on, it's not like you are Daemons where if you know their full name, you'll be in my thrall. I'm trying to be courteous, that's all."

The damned soul looked over at Gerald who decided it wouldn't hurt to answer, especially if this guy seemed to want to be so "courteous." Gerald went to stand and his chain rattled which brought the damned soul's attention to him "Gerald," is all he said. The rest of the Chosen Dead followed up with their names.

When Vora told him hers, the damned soul brightened up. "Vora, I like that. An honest-to-goodness shield maiden. Don't see many of those. Contrary to what they say, shield maidens are mostly a myth. You have to be exceptional to be a shield maiden." The damned soul started pacing before he began speaking. "You must all be exceptional." He was thinking and pacing and then he stopped. "Where is he?"

They all looked at each other. The enemy hadn't missed Gordon after all. He didn't say anything and let the tension build for a few moments. From the look on Vora's face, her sole focus was on trying to kill this damned soul with her mind. The damned soul smiled, feeling like he had hit a nerve. "Where is he, you must be wondering." This caused an icy spear of fear to lance them through their guts. He was toying with them now; he had Gordon. "Fear not, your leader is still alive. Not in great shape but he'll live...for a little while anyway." The confusion was misread by the damned soul who continued, "I know he took a lot of punishment. Two lance strikes, pretty tough."

They all breathed a sigh of relief. Bariel was alive and they didn't know about Gordon. The damned soul misread them again. "I'm sure you are relieved but now I have to get down to business. First, how come I didn't read you in the jungle?" They all looked at him but didn't say a word. "It's weird, I can pick up movement hundreds of yards away and the only time I picked you up was when big boy over there stepped on it."

Gio spoke up "The coin?" he asked.

"Yes, my friend, the coin, this coin." The damned soul raised his hand, and in between his pointer and index fingers was the coin Don stepped on. David came to the realization and asked, "That is one of thirty isn't it?"

The damned soul slowly turned to David, touched his nose with his finger, and smiled. "Very good, I am Judas Iscariot." The red burn mark on his neck began to glow and he gritted his teeth from the pain that it caused him. "Now that we are properly introduced, I am going to need some answers."

The Chosen Dead were silent. Someone like Judas Iscariot was a name known throughout history, known to all even non-Christians. He was the epitome of betrayal; he was known as The Great Betrayer. This cemented the fact that whatever was going on, they needed to stop him.

Behind Judas, one of the fallen angels put his hand into the fire and pulled a trip of meat off the skillet. It didn't seem to bother him that his massive hand was burning as he stuffed a piece of the cooked meat into his mouth.

Judas noticed them staring at the angel. "Looks like meat's back on the menu, boys!"

With a wave of his hand, the large curtain was moved aside and the horror behind it was revealed. Bariel was lying face down chained onto a stone slab. His wings were staked to the ground as well, but the atrocity was that sections of his back had been carved out like a butcher, and the meat that was being cooked on the skillet was Bariel's. He was still alive.

37

FACE DOWN

Gordon woke up face down in the jungle. His body was covered with thick vines and branches from the explosion caused by the egg bomb. He was achy from the blast but worked to heal himself. The effects were slow to leave him but he felt good enough to slowly move and after a minute or so was crouched down with large leaves and branches tied to his back as a make-shift camouflage.

He tried to activate his cloaking but the effects of the blast lingered still. Gordon was as tense as a bowstring slowly headed back to where the team had been when the bomb went off. His main fear was that they were all dead. He was almost certain that Bariel was, but he pushed that and those other thoughts aside, even as they pounded like an off-beat drum.

He used skills learned in the old world and slowly watched the skies and the surrounding area for any signs of the enemy. He was fairly sure they were all gone, Their stink lingered but was no longer strong. The damned souls stunk almost as bad as the Daemons.

When he finally reached the location where The Chosen Dead were, his main fear that they were dead, even Bariel, subsided for the moment. He saw where Bariel had been impaled, saw that they dragged his body, and from the blood on the upper branches and the side of a large tree, it was clear the fallen angels had carried him away. That didn't mean Bariel wasn't dead, but it was a good sign nonetheless.

The rest of the team had also been carried away by the damned souls, as the footprints that sunk into the dark soil indicated. The thought of those creatures wearing the heavy, long coats had Gordon thinking back and discovering how the damned soul he lost had been able to do it. The pouches they had carried had the smoke coming out of...

No, mist. It was from the cloud cover, he surmised. *That was how they managed to hide. They sacrificed the loss of their powers to be able to approach the Chosen Dead without being detected. The long coats must have been used as blast protection otherwise who would carry the prisoners away,* Gordon thought.

When he had cloaked himself, he had seen the damned souls coming in and positioned himself behind one to kill him when the bomb went off. The blast was so strong that even with the damned soul in front of him acting as a shield, the blast had knocked him backward, and fizzled his powers temporarily. What saved Gordon from discovery was the blast itself. The sound was deafening, and the shockwave was large enough for the enemy to ignore the movement behind them.

As Gordon lay crouched down, using branches and leaves as camouflage, he began to work through the beginnings of a plan. He first needed to find out where the team was, collect any pertinent info, and come back with a force large enough to destroy these monsters. The first step showed promise. The trail the damned souls took was very easy to follow.

Gordon added more leaves and branches to his camouflage and slowly made his way down, following the trail of breadcrumbs left for him. As he slowly made his way down the slope, the trail turned as the enemy headed towards the roadway. Once the trail hit the roadway, Gordon could easily discern from the still fresh heavy tracks of a vehicle that they were loaded up and driven towards the monolith.

Gordon tried to cloak himself again but was partly successful. The cloak held for a few moments but it took too much mental energy to keep it stable, similar to a person having an asthma attack working harder than they should to breathe. Gordon focused on his old tracking and hunting skills. He receded into the jungle where the foliage would hide him from the souls and Daemons. The mist combined with the bomb had short-circuited his abilities but it should hopefully help him hide until he could cloak himself again.

Gordon used all his senses. He stayed low to the ground, moving slow and steady. No sudden movements. That was what brought attention. That was what required the most discipline, fighting your instincts and being still. He wouldn't know he was being hunted until it was too late, so every advantage he had he would use.

Gordon stopped so that he could close his eyes and carefully scan the area. That ability performed worse than his ability to cloak as the further he tried to go the worse the reception seemed to be. He wasn't sure if it was the bomb preventing him from scanning or the proximity to the monolith above them. Gordon had better luck scanning the old-fashioned way with his sight and then when he closed his eyes, and stayed very still, he could hear his surroundings better. The process was slow and tedious, but he knew this was the only way for him to move through the jungle and avoid detection.

Gordon also rubbed mud he found onto his face, torso, and legs. This helped to conceal him visually, cover his scent, and also his energy signature. If he was discovered before he could cloak, then they would be on top of him in no time.

Gordon made his way down towards the edge of the mono-lith. He felt better so he tried again to cloak himself and this time it was much better. He was able to hold it for a few minutes before fatiguing. Gordon made good use of his time and made it to within a hundred yards of the road that connected to the monolith. He looked up and saw how massive and old the struc-ture was. The number of vines and growth that covered it must have taken thousands of years to grow and thicken up like a blanket over it. This close there was nothing scan-wise, so there was no way he could send a message out or even try and detect his team.

Gordon also realized the monolith did inhibit his abilities due to the sheer strength of its emanating signal. He tried to cloak again and was able to, but it took effort. He would need to get into the monolith without being seen and without his cloaking so he could conserve his energy once he was inside.

A twig snapped twenty feet to his left. Gordon crouched down further when the stink assaulted his nostrils. Soon after, two Daemons tromped their way through the jungle. They made no move to hide their presence whatsoever. They looked very similar: gaunt, emaciated with gray, leathery skin with boils and small horns protruding everywhere. The main difference was one had a single yellow eye while the other had three yellow eyes fixed above long hooked noses.

They stopped walking and sniffed the air as if trying to track something. Gordon stayed calm. He didn't move a muscle as he watched them sniffing the air. His concern wasn't killing them but not killing them quickly and quietly enough.

They split off, with One Eye heading right towards him while Three Eyes moved around to Gordon's rear. The only reason Gordon didn't kill them was that they were now too far away from each other to kill cleanly. He considered pulling them towards him or crushing them, but with the monolith so close, he didn't trust that he could do it without something going wrong.

One Eye stopped a few feet in front of Gordon who got a good look at the creature's three long toes with claws that dug deep into the earth. Three Eyes moved closer as well. It took all his willpower to hold still while expecting a clawed hand to strike him in the back. They did not see or sense him, that was obvious, but all it would take was moving a few more feet in his direction for them to stumble on top of him.

One Eye began growling and crouched down in an attack position and Three Eyes crouched to attack as well. Gordon stayed still even as they readied for the attack. Hot saliva dropped onto his leg from Three Eyes. Even then, Gordon stayed still. He would have one chance to strike.

Drool from One Eye fell to the ground, and they both were growling so loudly that the ground began to tremble which spooked what appeared to be a small porcine creature the size of a medium-sized dog. Where a normal pig had relatively short legs, this creature had a pig's face with a round body but evolved to have longer legs so it could evade predators. As soon as the pig creature made its move, the Daemons bounded off to take it down. Three Eyes was so close to Gordon that when he jumped his three-toe-clawed feet stomped down on Gordon's arm and pushed it down into the earth.

Gordon clenched his teeth as Three Eyes rushed by and disappeared into the jungle after its prey. He stayed still for another minute to ensure that they weren't coming back and that another Daemon wasn't trailing them. Once he felt certain no one else was coming, Gordon gritted his teeth and wrenched his arm out of the ground. Three Eyes had stomped down so hard that Gordon's shoulder was dislocated.

He squeezed his eyes shut as he pulled the shoulder back in while healing himself. The ability was there just slower. If it was slow for him, then it would be slow for the enemy as well, Gordon mused, as the last bit of stinging pain drifted away.

Gordon moved his shoulder around to check it was fine and slowly moved back towards the edge of the road as he melted into the jungle and away from the Daemons. Gordon made it to the edge of the jungle and right across from the monolith. Next to the road, Gordon saw that the enemy was moving in and out of the entrance in increasing numbers.

Gordon looked down at the road and noticed that this close to the monolith there was an ancient roadway that had been built along with the giant structure. The stone seemed almost white and porous. This should have been worn away a millennia ago, but this was no ordinary stone. It had withstood an untold number of years in the middle of the jungle with negligible wear and tear. Gordon could feel the interference from the monolith this close and knew he had to get inside without wearing himself out.

He backed into the jungle, scanned the area, and found what he was looking for. A few hundred yards away from him parked on the road was a large vehicle that resembled a deuce and a half from the Vietnam era, except that it was three times the size with gigantic wheels that were unnecessary and appeared to have been slapped on for the sheer fuck all of it because a Daemon or damned soul thought it looked cool.

Gordon moved quickly and when he was within twenty yards of the vehicle, it began to move. He cursed under his breath, cloaked himself, and ran towards the monster vehicle. It was a strain to cloak himself, but he was able to grab hold of a handle and crawl like a spider underneath the vehicle until he found an area where he could hang from the bottom without being seen and, more importantly, didn't have to use his cloaking. Gordon choked on diesel fumes and stone dust from the road as he entered the belly of the beast.

38

FACE THE PAIN

The torture began in earnest with David being punched and beaten for a solid two hours straight by a variety of damned souls and Daemons. Both had bitten chunks out of his torso. One had bitten David's nose off so he sat exhausted at the end with a hole in his face and multiple pieces of his torso missing.

The Chosen Dead had raged against their chains and tried to force themselves free until they saw that the enemy relished the pain they were causing and almost in unison, they all sat down and waited their turn. The enemy hadn't killed them...yet. They would work on escaping, and then they would do the killing work on everything in the room.

Judas found it amusing. He seemed to find everything amusing as The Chosen Dead sat silent watching their brother being tortured so terribly. "Repent, sinner!" Judas yelled then waved his hand for his lackeys to stop working over David.

No one liked the way Judas was looking at Vora. To her credit, she didn't flinch and spat at him when he winked at her. Judas walked up to her and they all tensed but he turned around and spoke to the Daemons near Bariel. "Looks like your brethren have had their fill of your angel...for now." Judas looked down at Vora and smiled. It filled them all with a deep unease. Judas's every intention was there without him saying a word. They needed to escape before that came to pass.

"You know Angels can see in many different ranges? Their eyes are merely decorative." Judas lifted a finger and a bloated daemon with too small bat wings picked up an old, rust-encrusted knife and stuck the corroded blade into Bariel's right eye. After the various horrors inflicted on him, all Bariel could do was moan as his eyeball popped. The bloated Daemon extended an overly large tongue that stretched out three feet from its mouth and licked up the blood and burst eyeball. The Daemon shuddered and stuck its tongue into Bariel's eye hole which caused Bariel to scream.

"Enough!" Judas commanded. The Daemon ignored Judas and plunged its tongue deeper into Bariel's head. Judas moved so quickly that it seemed as if he just appeared next to the Daemon. Judas grabbed the knife out of the bloated daemon's clawed hand and then cut its throat with it. Judas then grabbed it and threw it down the long hallway at least four hundred yards where it impacted with a splat, and the remains of the Daemon slid down the wall in a black, leathery glob.

Judas turned to Bariel, who looked up at Judas with a burning hatred in his remaining blue eye. "Cheer up. This is a good news, bad news thing," Judas said with that false charm smile. "Good news is we'll heal up your back. Maybe your eye, too. The bad news is we're going to do it all again because you're too delicious to kill." Bariel just kept glaring murder at Judas who was walking back towards the Chosen Dead.

"What do you want?" Gerald demanded.

Judas stared right at Gerald and walked straight up to him. "I like you. I'm partial to gingers anyway but you, I like. You're a solid guy, am I right? Make friends wherever you go. A natural leader." Judas tapped the side of his head. "I always had a good eye for talent. I have a question for you, hero." Judas crouched down and faced Gerald. "You want to save your team?" Gerald didn't answer. He just stared right into his ever-changing eyes.

"You want to save them from the torture and abuse? Let's make a deal. We don't have to do it this way. It's more fun, sure but we're not animals..."

Gerald interrupted Judas. "No."

Judas just smiled and stood up. "Can't say I didn't try. Of course, I didn't want to try anyway, I prefer the torture." Judas pointed to Don. "You see that tall, dark, handsome guy over there? I'm going to beat him over the head with a stick I found in the jungle out there. I won't kill him but when I'm done I'll make sure I pop out both of his eyes." He then pointed at Gio. "The good fella over there? I'm going to slice him up real good. Been a while since I had Italian." Judas crouched back down. "You'll be last. I want you to see what we're going to do to the Valkyrie. I have a thing for blondes and, let me tell you, whatever I do to her will be nothing compared to what I'll let the Daemons do to her. She'll beg to die; you will beg me to kill her."

Judas got up and a thick stick appeared in his hands as he walked over to Don. Vora's eyes were as round as saucers, but she said nothing and then closed her eyes when the first impact struck Don.

THE MASSIVE VEHICLE was reduced to the size of an ant as it passed into the underbelly of the monolith. Gordon found some rungs that he could hold on to better and stay flat against the vehicle, as it was so high that if he hung down too low someone could spot him. The horrendous noise the vehicle made also helped, as anything near its path avoided the obnoxious-looking super truck and didn't want to get run over by the huge wheels.

The ground slowly went by as the vehicle continued inside the monolith. Besides the diesel fumes, Gordon smelled the stink of Daemons all around him thickening in the air like a fugue from the increased numbers. The vehicle descended into the earth for at least a mile before the rumble of the engine changed, signaling a speed reduction, followed by the vehicle stopping. Once the vehicle was turned off, Gordon cloaked himself and dropped down to the ground. He felt the crushing strain the monolith's effects had on him. He quickly moved away from the truck which was parked along with others in a ramshackle motor area with some hastily painted, questionably straight parking lines and got his bearings.

He was in a large chamber that looked to be over a hundred yards wide and another two hundred yards in length. Daemons were coming and going throughout, and Gordon had to evade and keep an eye out so he wouldn't collide with one by mistake. Gordon kept his breathing slow and steady so that he didn't expend any more energy than he needed to. He heard steps behind him and moved out of the way as a group of Daemons rushed by. Gordon evaded them and tried to slowly breathe through their stink, which proved difficult to do, but he moved away from them and backed himself against another overly large, parked vehicle.

They unloaded his vehicle of its cargo which looked to be machine parts and two large drill heads. Gordon knew he had to follow where those drill heads were going. Now the question he had was, what were they drilling for?

Gordon set out to find out when a pebble landed on his head. He looked up and was so shocked at what he saw he was almost run over by the truck he was next to. The Daemon driving didn't even bother to look behind him and left a line of cursing Daemons in its wake as it screeched the tires in reverse, then sped off back up top. One Daemon threw a spear at the truck that stuck to the softer top of it. Gordon couldn't blame them. Even Daemons had some etiquette when it came to driving.

Gordon made sure no one was around before he looked back up. The ceiling of the roof had to be the reason for the drilling. The team had been prepped before they stepped on the world of the geography of the planet. Above Gordon was a map of the continent they were on, including a picture of the monolith he was now under. There was a picture of what appeared to be the sun and the local constellations in the sky.

Below the monolith engraving was a smaller L-shaped object that stood out. It was darker than the monolith and everything else around it. The eye was drawn to it. It had glyphs sketched onto it as well that he couldn't decipher, but he deduced it was this object that they were here to find.

Before he started the next step in his plan, Gerald needed to see where they were digging. If they had found it, they wouldn't still be working. The strain of cloaking was starting to make his limbs feel like lead. Gordon needed to conserve himself because he had much to do still. He couldn't burn himself out now. None of the trucks were heading down to where he assumed the dig site was so he couldn't stow away again.

Gordon looked up again and stared at the ceiling. *It would hurt but it would work,* he thought. A few moments later, Gordon stood standing and stared at the wall. He took a deep breath and then in exorcist fashion, spun his head in a 180 so that he was now looking out onto the floor while the rest of his body was still facing the wall. The grinding of his bones hurt like hell and didn't get a lot better once he was done. Gordon, still cloaked, placed his hands and feet, which now had tiny hairs coming out of them, on the wall. He recalled how David said that spiders climbed up a wall using tiny hairs like these. It took about twenty feet up the wall before he got used to using the little hairs to attach to the wall and the surreal feeling of having his head twisted around so he could see below him.

When Gordon reached the top of the wall, he dropped the cloaking. He stayed steady and was able to move quickly along the ceiling. No one below thought to look up, but it felt like at any second he would be discovered. Within four hundred yards, Gordon saw why they didn't drive the monster trucks further. The ceiling sloped down maybe twenty yards so plenty high enough still but the road narrowed immediately so that it wasn't wide enough to drive one of the trucks through.

Gordon paused and waited while a pair of Daemons, who looked like plucked chickens, walked back towards the vehicle area, and then he sped along the ceiling to make his way to where the road ended. Makeshift lights had been added that all pointed down towards the hole being drilled. That worked to Gordon's advantage, as it made him easier to disappear into the darkness. The effect of the monolith worked to his advantage now as he was all but invisible.

Down below, the hole was completely illuminated. It was relatively large and the dirt that was drilled up contrasted with the walls and floor of the monolith. Gordon thought it odd that they were so carelessly drilling into the ground looking for an artifact. If it was so important, then this seemed careless in the extreme.

A damned soul walked over to the hole. He had his hood up like the rest he had seen so far and was carrying something that looked like a divining rod in his hands. He passed the rod over the hole and held it still for almost a minute before giving up and shaking his head. The damned soul disappeared and then returned with another who was holding a rolled-up scroll. They unfurled the scroll onto a small table with clips and used them to pin it in place.

Slowly, Gordon moved so that he was right over the scroll

and cloaked himself. He wanted to make sure he was able to absorb every detail without worrying about being seen even with his limited senses. Gordon felt the stress of cloaking like breathing through a straw underwater, but it was tolerable.

One of the damned souls had removed his cloak and even from where Gordon was perched, he could see a scar on the left side of the scalp cutting through dark, short-cropped hair like a lightning bolt. He also had one of those collars around his neck that looked part machine and part organic. This was the damned soul who had brought the scroll, and when he had finished clipping the scroll down, it revealed itself to be a map with a silver border.

The damned soul looked up right at Gordon. For a split second that seemed to linger for eternity. Gordon thought he had been discovered and would have to drop down and escape if he could. This damned soul seemed very capable.

"What are you doing?" the other damned soul asked. The damned soul ignored him and stayed glued on Gordon's location. The other damned soul was going to ask again when the unhooded damned soul turned to look upon the other who shrunk under the unyielding gaze of the unhooded one. Gordon paid attention to their conversation which revolved around the dig site, where they could be wrong on location, and so on. The map was the prize. If he was fully powered, Gordon would have been able to take a picture of it using his powers, but even that small expenditure would give away his location. The next best option would be to steal the map, but he would still be able to redraw the map accurately. The enemy could as well, but Gordon saw no reason to make things easy on them.

Besides the details on the chamber's ceiling, there were additional stars displayed around the sun. Also, there was a better view from where the monolith was to where the artifact was located. The artifact on this map appeared to be placed in a larger container that resembled a wooden chest with iron bands surrounding it. The same glyphs appeared on the chest. Gordon took in the details of the map which included the cloud surrounding the monolith and strange animals that had to be local. He could identify a serpent with four legs, a creature that looked like a hippopotamus, and one he could not identify that appeared to have a lion's upper body and a much smaller lower half with too small legs.

Once he had absorbed as much as he could, Gordon slowly retreated down the wall concealed in darkness. He took a risk and removed the cloaking so he could take a breather. He was located behind one of the lights so if the damned soul looked his way he would be looking right into the harsh lighting. If the soul tried to scan, he would cloak himself again. Gordon didn't want to take that risk, but he needed to take a break before he cloaked himself again.

Gordon went back to the chamber where the vehicles were with the picture on the ceiling. He would need to go back to his old skills.

Gordon scanned the ceiling and found the ideal spot right in the middle of the floor in between both entrances so he was not in anyone's sight lines. He waited until no one was facing his way and cloaked himself, then used his abilities to make himself the same color as the stone ceiling. Gordon then dug hand and foot holds into the ceiling so he was able to hold on without using any of his abilities. Even if someone looked up, they would look right over him. Stillness was the one requirement. The energy expended to change his coloring was minute but even with that, he felt it.

After waiting perched on the ceiling, the two damned souls returned with the scroll once again tucked under the scarred soul's arm. They headed for one of the oversized vehicles, jumped in, started the engine, and reversed.

A pack of Daemons placed itself in front of the vehicle. The scarred soul told them to move. The Daemons said they needed it. The scarred soul told them he wasn't going to tell them again. When one of the Daemons threw a spear at them the scarred soul caught it, threw it back, and impaled the daemon who initially threw it. He then revved the engine and ran the majority of them down. He didn't bother looking back to see if they would follow. Gordon cloaked himself and followed them.

SAVANNAH STATE SPRING DANCE

GERALD KNEW HE WAS DREAMING. He had blacked out from the beatings and his mind took refuge back to before he started dating Lia, back to the beginning, to the moment when he knew he wouldn't stop no matter what to be with her.

Gerald had driven out to Lia's family farm and visited the store they had where they sold produce directly to the local community. People from all over Savannah would come to the Barneaux farm because of the quality of their produce. This was the third time that Gerald had driven to the Barneaux Farm to purchase peaches. Gerald was sweating and nervous as he dropped peaches into a bag and once it was full, he wandered around the store casually looking at beef jerky and carrots. Every time he looked at Lia, he would get this jolt of electricity. When she made eye contact, his world would stop.

"Excuse me!" Gerald looked down to see the very tiny and very old Mrs. Culligan placing her tiny little hand on Gerald's stomach because that was as high as she could go. "Young man, you need to pay attention, You're too big to be lollygagging around," she said. Gerald quickly apologized to her and offered to carry her bag, but she declined. "I may be old but I am not feeble...thank you very much," she huffed, and as Gerald nodded again and wished her a good day.

He felt her tiny hand grab him and when he turned around she motioned for him to lean closer to her. When he did, she whispered, "Just ask her out already, boy. It's painful seeing you in here. You're not built for subtlety." Her deep brown eyes smiled warmly and winked. "Life is long, but opportunities are in short supply." Mrs. Culligan tapped him on the cheek and departed.

"Huh," Gerald said to himself. Even Gerald, as dense as he could be, could tell that was a sign. When he looked around, he saw how much he stood out like a sore thumb. Mrs. Culligan was right, Gerald thought, he wasn't very subtle.

Lia watched him, too. She had a smirk on her face and then went back to assisting the customer she was checking out. Mr. Barneaux who before was unseen, had appeared on the produce floor. He approached Gerald and greeted him. "Hello Gerald, how is your father doing?"

Gerald shook Mr. Barneaux's hand. "Hello sir, he's doing well. Thank you. Your family doing well I hope?" Gerald noticed Mr. Barneaux's blue eyes tighten a little bit but he replied, "Everyone is fine. You find what you are looking for?" The way he said it made it clear Gerald's time browsing the store was over. "Nice to see you again sir, I'll be on my way."

Mr. Barneaux nodded, they shook hands, and as Gerald waited in line, Mrs. Barneaux appeared and greeted him. "Hello young man, you looking both ways before crossing the street?" She looked so much like Lia it was unsettling, but where Lia had warm beautiful eyes, Mrs. Barneaux's eyes were hidden and mysterious like a bird of prey. Quick to notice every detail.

"Hello ma'am, nice to see you again. Yes, took a while but

now I make sure not to get run over." Gerald said and extended his hand which Lucy took and lightly shook it.

"You find what you need young, man?" Lucy asked. Now both parents were asking the same thing. Gerald was not subtle at all. He made eye contact with Lia who was watching the interaction with interest as she checked out the next customer. "We didn't see you much when you came back from the war, you or your friend."

Lucy threw Gerald for a loop. No one ever mentioned the war, but Gerald could see she was asking for a reason. What it was, he couldn't fathom. "I...needed time, ma'am. It wasn't a pleasant experience."

Lucy nodded. "I'm glad you're back." She nodded her head and left to go in the back.

Gerald was up next, and he stepped up to the counter and placed the peaches on a weight scale. "Hello, nice to see you," Gerald was able to get that out. He looked into Lia's eyes. For a moment he felt that electricity. The same feeling he had when he first saw her at ten. Lia, normally so sure of herself, looked away.

"Are you having a party?" Lia asked. Gerald was confused by her question, but Lia answered for him. "You have bought so many peaches that I thought your mother must be making pies for a party."

Gerald didn't know what to say to that except "Umm no, I like peaches." What a terrible liar he was. He was embarrassed that he could think of nothing else.

Lia's eyes twinkled in amusement. "That's all you like?" Lia asked. The air came right out of him and he opened his mouth and then closed it. A polite cough from behind had them both turn and see Lia's father motioning with his hand to move it along. Lia quickly gave Gerald his change, and he quickly said his goodbyes.

Right before he reached the door, Gerald turned around. He couldn't leave without asking her out, and he didn't want to buy any more peaches. He pivoted and, between the line and Mr. Barneaux watching him, Gerald spun back around again and headed out the door. Gerald cursed himself as he got into his car, cursed himself as he drove home, and when he got home. He barely slept that night. He had fought on the beaches of Normandy, running into machine gun fire. He could talk to a beautiful woman. That was easy, he lied to himself.

Gerald sighed as he lay in bed that night. No, it wasn't easy. He was petrified talking to her, but if he didn't ask her out, he would regret it for the rest of his life. "I can do it," Gerald said to himself. "I have to do this," the sad sack part of him quietly echoed.

THE FOLLOWING WEEK, Gerald and Charlie were working at the Savannah office. Charlie knew right away something was up. Gerald was antsy and kept getting up to look out through the window blinds covering the main window up front. After the tenth or eleventh time doing this, Charlie stepped in front of Gerald who tried to walk around him, but Charlie blocked him. "What're you doing?" Charlie asked Gerald, who kept making glances out of the window.

"What do you mean?" Gerald said as he tried again to walk around Charlie but was once again blocked. Charlie snapped his fingers to shake Gerald out of it, and Gerald got the message and sighed. Gerald told Charlie that he was hoping to see Lia who would be in town today. She was bringing in paperwork for her father's business.

"Yeah, not surprising," Charlie said with a smirk.

"What do you mean?" Gerald asked with real surprise.

"You almost got yourself run over the first time you laid eyes on her. Remember before the war when you saw her right outside?" Charlie said then continued. "I knew we would come to this. Here's what you're going to do." Charlie laid a hand on his best friend's shoulder. "You are going to ask her out. Be pleasant, polite, and to the point." Charlie made it simple for him which he appreciated. "Just stop getting up and looking out the window. You're wearing a hole in the floor and making me crazy." He grabbed Gerald by his arm and walked him back to his seat.

"I'm a grown man, you know." Gerald said to Charlie as he allowed Charlie to sit him down. "Stormed the beach of Normandy," Gerald stated with bravado.

"Yes, I was there. This should be easy," Charlie said with a smile.

For the next two hours, Gerald fought the urge to get up and when Lia appeared in the window, Gerald shot up, calmed himself, and then sat back down.

"Good job, breathe easy," Charlie said as Lia walked in and greeted them both.

Gerald quickly got up and walked to the counter. "Hello Lia, how are you?"

Lia smiled at him and that electricity again as they made eye contact burned through Gerald. Lia, who had much more composure, smiled and replied, "Very well thank you. I have the paperwork from my father."

Gerald grabbed the paperwork and dropped it into a bin next to him. "Looks good."

Lia smiled. "Sure you don't want to check it and make sure it's all there?"

He smiled and said, "It's always in good order, I'm sure that it will be fine." Gerald and Lia stared at each other for a few moments, and then she broke contact.

"I have to go. Have a nice day." Lia nodded to Charlie, who waved, and then looked at Gerald, who had a frozen smile on his face. He grimaced with a smile as Lia headed to the door. Gerald felt crushing pressure against his chest. He could not allow her to leave without saying something, anything.

As Lia opened the door to leave, Gerald blurted out, "I don't like peaches that much." Lia stopped and turned around.

Charlie rolled his eyes and smiled. "If you'll excuse me," he said and then headed out the door.

"I don't like peaches that much," Gerald said again but this time he went around the counter and walked right up to her so that he was less than an arm's length away. Her scent drew him in. She smelled like honey and wildflowers. Gerald swallowed and said, "I had to see you. I wanted to ask you out to dinner or something, maybe lunch if you prefer." Gerald exhaled as he finally got it out.

Lia's eyes grew big, and she went quiet for a moment. She was so still, she could have passed for a statue. "No," she replied and stormed out of the door.

Gerald stood there, not moving, not thinking, not sure what to do. He wasn't sure how long he stood there. A pain in his chest was constant, but it wasn't until Charlie came back with a smile on his face that then changed to a surprised frown once he had read the situation that it set in what happened.

"How are you doing?" Charlie asked with concern. He had seen Gerald fight for his life at war. Lead men under his command and make snap decisions in the heat of battle. What Charlie saw on his best friend's face was bleak. It looked to be the onset of despair. "Maybe it is for the best." Charlie tried to soothe his friend's pain.

Gerald looked at Charlie, nodded, and then sat on his chair.

"You would have obstacles that would have been tough to overcome," Charlie stated the obvious but he could see how much it hurt his friend. He was as surprised by this outcome as Gerald. He saw how they looked at each other. He would have bet his life on them at least trying to get to know each other.

Charlie went and sat down at his desk. Gerald turned and asked him, "Did you like her?"

Charlie pursed his lips and thought about what he was going to say before responding but he knew Gerald needed the truth even if it hurt. "She sure is easy on the eyes. She's sharp, too. Got some fire in her belly, and way too good for you," Charlie said with a sad smile. "I like her."

Gerald nodded and went back to work, his mind clouded and oddly blank. He couldn't focus on anything and when he did, it was the echo of "No!" running through his head like a herd of buffalo. Normally time flying by is a good thing when you are at work but for Gerald, he could have sat in that chair forever.

He did his work using muscle memory as his thoughts were now filled with Lia. He should have been relieved by her getting it out of the way. Gerald wasn't an idiot; he knew they would have had a lot of difficulties. The color barrier, even in Savannah, was real. He maybe would have gone to jail if someone said something inappropriate to her in front of him, but he would have been fine with that. He should be unburdened now about Lia, but he wasn't, it just deepened the ache. She had given him her answer, and he could now live with it. He would be able to eventually not feel a burning pain every time he thought about her. Maybe it would only last a few years to get over it, he morosely thought.

At the end of the day, Charlie glanced over for maybe the hundredth time. Gerald had not looked up from his work the entire day. He just grabbed a folder of papers and started going through them. Charlie stood up, put on his jacket, and walked over to Gerald's desk. Charlie stood there for a few seconds and when he saw that Gerald didn't even notice him, Charlie rapped on the desk to get his attention. "Hmm?" Gerald looked up at Charlie.

"Time to go.Come on, let's get a drink."

Gerald just shook his head and put his head back down. Charlie stood there a second and then leaned over and took the pen out of Gerald's hand. It took a second for him to realize that he had no pen, and he looked up at Charlie with a blank look on his face. *Not even anger,* Charlie thought with concern. "Come on, you need a drink. The heat of your despair is going to start a fire with all this paper."

For the first time since she left, Gerald smiled, though it didn't last long. "I'm good. I just want to finish up with all this paperwork." Charlie cocked his head expecting more. Gerald sighed and leaned back in his chair. "I'm...fine," Gerald said as Charlie cocked his eyebrow at him. "I'm a big boy," Gerald looked down glumly. "I just didn't think it would end like that." Gerald shook his head but then looked up at Charlie. "Go ahead, I'll close up, it is what it is."

Charlie nodded and turned around to leave. Both of them were shocked when Lia burst through the door. She took one look at Charlie and simply said, "Leave." Charlie was so shocked he just nodded over to Gerald and ran out as fast as he could. He didn't put on his hat or jacket and just ran out the door.

Lia walked up to the counter and rapidly began tapping her fingers on the old wood. She huffed as if she was furious and wasn't sure what to say. Gerald slowly stood up and walked around the counter. Lia increased the tempo of the tapping as Gerald got closer to her, and then stopped when he was within an arm's length of her. Lia huffed again, folded her arms, then unfolded them. Gerald noticed both her hands were clenching and unclenching as if she was deciding on whether to punch him or not. "If you're going to take a swipe at me, just don't hit me in the nose, it smarts," Gerald said, trying to break the tension.

That seemed to only make her angrier. Lia raised her eyebrows and folded and unfolded her arms again. Gerald took a step closer and was about to speak but she raised her hand to stop him. Her breathing was fast, almost like she was on the verge of hyperventilating. Finally, she broke the tension which had built up to an almost unbearable point. Lia didn't speak to him, she didn't yell, she whispered, "How dare you." She took a step towards Gerald who took a step back as she was very angry.

"Excuse me?" Gerald asked.

"You heard me," Lia said in response as she raised a clenched fist at Gerald and then opened it to mimic strangling him.

"I did, I just don't understand," Gerald said.

"How dare you," Lia said again with a decent amount of vitriol.

Gerald was still confused but replied, "You said that already."

That was the wrong thing to say her eyes widened and she stepped towards him as if she was going to try and choke him. "You are infuriating."

Gerald nodded and smiled. "On that, we can agree on"

Lia exhaled and placed one hand on the counter. "We both know it won't work." The color barrier rose between them. Neither spoke for a moment. Gerald had thought about all the issues and obstacles he would be inviting into both their lives. He knew there were many mixed couples but they were forced to live in the shadows and on the fringe. All the reasons flew up in front of him like a flock of startled pigeons but the one thing he did know was that he had to try. This woman in front of him was all he could think about. He had to at least try. He knew she felt the same way. Albeit she seemed angry about it, but he understood.

"We need to know," Gerald said to her. Lia looked him in the eyes and that jolt went through them both.

"What do you mean?" she asked but she knew the answer. They both needed to know if what they felt for each other was real if they could and would move ahead with it, if they both decided it was worth the trials and tribulations that would come with it.

"Let me take you out, wherever you want, and spend time together," Gerald said.

"Have you spent more than an hour with colored folk?" Lia asked the anger back in her voice.

"Two, actually."

Lia's eyes widened. She wanted to smile but it also seemed to make her angry at the same time. "Don't sass me right now. This is serious," Lia said, exasperated. "Colored folk are different. We will judge you, same as white folk. We have our own culture, our own way."

Gerald nodded. "I understand but we aren't that different, isn't that the point? We both grew up in the same town, we know the same people, speak the same language. Try being an American in Paris and not knowing a lick of French. They are snooty, too, if you don't know the language. We have a leg up," Gerald said with a smile and lifted his leg.

Lia snorted a laugh.

"I am willing to learn, willing to take whatever it is I have to. Your daddy will disapprove. I'll show him but I need to show you first. Who knows, maybe we won't get along. You already seem angry with me. I'm behind the eight ball already."

Lia smiled and shook her head at him. "You are a fool. What if I say no?"

Gerald's smile vanished then reappeared as what she said

sunk in. "You already said no. I figure the second no won't hurt quite as bad." He looked away at the admission that her no earlier hurt him. He didn't look at her for a few moments. He needed to gather himself. He felt that growing pressure in his chest again. When he looked at her again, she had moved a step closer and the look on her face was full of emotion. She stood there clenching and unclenching her fists.

Without thinking, Gerald stepped closer to Lia and gently touched the side of her face. Lia felt Gerald's touch and, without thinking, she leaned into his hand for a moment then pulled away.

She tried to catch her breath, thought about all the wrong ways this could go, and made her decision. "You want to see me?"

Gerald nodded and gave her space by backing up a step. He didn't trust himself to try and wrap his arms around her. If he did, he was sure she would sock him. "I am going to be performing at the Savannah State Spring Dance Concert. It's in three weeks." Gerald nodded. "You want to see me, then you can see me there." Lia finished what she had to say in one breath and promptly left.

Gerald watched her half walk, half jog past the office window. He stood by himself and inhaled the trail of her honey and wildflower scent and said to no one, "I'll be there."

From the corner of Gerald's eye, he saw Charlie's head looking at him from the side of the window. Charlie raised his eyebrows and then gave him the thumbs up as if to ask if all was well.

THE ONLY PEOPLE that knew Gerald was going to Savannah State for the dance concert were Chance and Charlie, who both insisted they go with him. With the civil rights movement starting to happen, the atmosphere could be dangerous for a tall white redhead walking into an all-black university. Gerald declined and told them that this was a test, a test he agreed to. Lia was right; outside the army he had never spent more than an hour with colored folk, and if he wanted to spend time with her, then he would be spending time with her family, her friends, and her community.

Gerald got along fine with everyone for the most part, but this was different. Mr. Barneaux was always pleasant and friendly with Gerald, but this was different. This was him pursuing his daughter. This could also complicate the business relationship that Gerald's father had with Mr. Barneaux.

Gerald put on his Sunday best, bought some flowers, and headed out in his car. Gerald's parents noticed a change in him over the past few weeks. They tried to get it out of both Chance and Charlie, but they held strong through both bribes and not-so-veiled threats. Ralph had questioned why Gerald was in such a good mood. "It's unnatural," Ralph said to Kathryn. Gerald smiled as he heard his mother chuckle at what his father said.

When he walked downstairs all dressed in his Sunday best, they tried to find out who he was going to meet up with. Gerald just told them that it was a first-time meeting and that she was involved in the arts.

"Ruthie played the violin, didn't she?" Kathryn asked Gerald, who had to suppress a laugh.

"She did but she isn't who I am going to see. I watched that movie already, Mama."

Kathryn pursed her lips. She liked Ruthie and she never understood why it didn't work out between them. "You were such a beautiful couple and you get along."

Gerald kissed his mother goodbye and ran out the door before he was caught up in the how and why of his failed relationship with Ruthie. Gerald knew why it didn't work out with Ruthie, and he was on his way to see her right now.

Gerald left the window open to bring in the warm night breeze as he drove down Route five sixteen. The twenty-minute drive seemed to fly by in a blink and before he knew it, he was pulling onto La Roche Avenue from DeLesseps Avenue. The parking lot was already full as he searched for a place to park and was forced to park at the very edge where he was able to squeeze into a spot.

Gerald was finally able to maneuver himself out of the car without damaging the flowers. The warm night air carried a hint of the magnolias that grew everywhere in the area and thankfully not the sulfur smell from the marshes or the paper mill. Gerald's shoes crunched on the gravel of the parking lot as he made his way toward the theater. He heard voices coming from ahead and to the side but he paid little mind to them as all his thoughts were focused on seeing her. The smell of her, those eyes. Gerald had that growing pressure in his chest again and had subconsciously picked up his pace as well.

He wasn't aware of his surroundings until a flash of movement caught his eye and he stopped and quickly assessed what was happening. "You deaf, white bread?" a large black man about the same age as Gerald had come around and blocked his path. "Don't tell me you were going to ignore me and just walk on by?" Gerald noticed there were three of them, one on each side. He watched to make sure none of them started to walk around behind him.

"Pardon me but I am just trying to get to the dance on time. I don't want any trouble." Gerald's tone threw them off. They either expected him to be intimidated or become aggressive. This option wasn't on the menu for them.

"Well, you found trouble by thinking you can just come here like you own the place," said the man in front of Gerald. He wasn't as tall as Gerald, but he could see that he weighed a solid twenty pounds more than he did. The other two were also not small but if he had to he could hurt them, which would be the worst thing he could do at this moment.

"I'm just here to see a friend perform."

That wasn't the right answer as the man facing Gerald visibly got angry. "Typical white man won't allow a black man to go where he doesn't want him to but turn the tables and the white man thinks he can go anywhere he wants. Things are changing white bread. This is our place. We don't want your kind here." That seemed to embolden the three of them. Gerald understood their anger and agreed that things needed to change. He felt for them but not at the expense of his safety. If they attacked him, he would take them out as quickly as possible. He wouldn't like it, but he would do it.

Gerald placed the flowers into his left hand and raised his right. Violence was the last option. He slowly shifted over to keep the man on the right from getting around him as he slowly started to move. "I was invited. I understand why you are so angry, and I agree with you, things have to change. I try to live right and do right by people. The worst people I ever met were white and a few black people, too. I like good people." Gerald stopped to see if what he was saying made a difference. "My daddy taught me that we help where we can. All I ask you now is you leave me be."

He didn't think he made much of an impact. The black man who had tried to come around behind him had now come up and was scrunching his eyes as if he couldn't see well.

"I know you, I couldn't see it at night but you got that red hair." Gerald leaned closer and realized he knew him as well.

"Thomas, Thomas Renton," Gerald said as he placed the face to a name. Thomas's father Steven was also a client of Gerald's father. Steven was a machinist who worked on farming equipment for the colored community in and around the Savannah area. Ralph never overcharged any of his colored customers, which was common practice with many of the white business owners. "My father said you were good people, never tried to charge more than you should." Gerald nodded to Thomas who had approached Gerald.

"What are you doing here?" Thomas asked, this time genuinely curious.

"I was invited. A friend is part of the spring dance."

Thomas turned around and spoke to the other two men he was with. "Leave him be, Bennie." The man Bennie who was the one facing off on Gerald went to open his mouth to say something, but Thomas cut him off. "He good people."

Bennie seemed surprised, but Thomas turned around, nodded, and moved aside. Gerald nodded to Thomas and before he continued on, he bid them farewell. "Gentlemen." Gerald then turned to Thomas. "Thank you and give your father my best." He waved farewell and headed back towards the theater.

By the time Gerald made his way to the entrance, the show had begun. The live band played as the opening act played out. The music had a lot of drums and bass to it and what sounded like Cuban bongos. Gerald walked up to the will call and gave her his name. She looked Gerald over and humphed but looked through her list. He understood now how a Black person felt walking down the wrong street in Savannah. Every eye was on him. No one seemed concerned about hiding it either.

"Hello," Gerald said to the students who walked by and were working the venue. Most had hooded eyes. Some were friendly, some not.

"Here you go, Red," the girl working will call said with the driest of wit as she handed Gerald his ticket. Gerald thanked her and headed toward his section. He saw a large poster with Obsidian Dance Repertory posted above the door for his section. He opened the door and was immediately hit with a wave of sound from the band hitting its crescendo. Gerald quickly closed the door so as not to be distracted by the light coming from the hallway. He turned around as the drums timed together with the horns and organ continued to build. On stage, The dancers swirled and moved with fluid grace and an increasing pace to match the music.

Gerald had never seen this kind of dancing before. The dancers' dress was based on Afrocentric clothes. The men didn't have shirts on but had on baggy three-quarter length tan pants and provided movement over a white grass dress. They wore different headdresses with varying animals, from an impala to a monkey and then a lion flashed by. They also had matching white grass decorations on their wrists. The women wore similar white grass dresses but with skin-tight shorts underneath. There were what appeared to be bikini tops with white grass covering all around from the chest to almost their waists. They also had grass ornaments on their wrists. The women wore headdresses as well: a hyena, and a bear. A swirling woman with a snake headdress floated across the stage.

Gerald stayed where he was, enamored by the dancers and the music. He was familiar with dancing and dance halls, but not this. This was like nothing he had ever seen before. The music and dancing brought out emotions in him that felt almost suffocating in their intensity. It was primal and well-orchestrated, each part moving in precision with the other like the mechanisms of a clock. If one was even slightly off then it would ruin the dance.

Gerald's breath caught in his throat when he saw Lia. She had been in the back line of dancers so he couldn't get a good look at any of them until now when the backline came up to take center stage. The music was at a frenetic pace. Lia was wearing a fox headdress, and she flowed across the stage, she was incredible. The increased pace of the music didn't seem to affect her at all. She floated over the stage like smoke, her beautiful face calm and focused as she twirled and spun and jumped.

The pace increased and the entire dance troupe moved and spun and danced along with it. It was an incredible display of artistry. Gerald thought to himself that even trying to do any of that stuff would send him to the hospital. When the music hit the apex, Lia took center stage with her group of girls and they all jumped up into the air while doing a spin and with perfect synchronicity, they all landed down into a split at exactly the same time.

"Amazing" Gerald said to himself as the audience broke out into applause. Without thinking, he joined them and screamed and hollered with everyone else. Caught up in the moment, Gerald walked down the aisle clapping.

Lia, who had jumped up and waved to the crowd, saw movement down the aisle and made eye contact with Gerald. He stopped as if he had hit a wall and just stared at her. He was looking at her like there was no one else in the room. Lia froze and stared back. She wasn't sure if he would have the nerve to show up, but she should have known. Jackass or not, when he looked at her, she felt it slash through her like lightning.

Reality kicked back in and Lia's fellow dancer in a leopard headdress tapped her on the arm and she ran off stage with the rest.

Gerald stood in the middle of the aisle and watched her as she headed off stage. He never took his eyes off her. Lia turned and gave him one last look and a brief smile before she disappeared.

Gerald came back to reality and as the band started back up, he looked over to his left and saw the Barneaux' watching him. Mr. Barneaux just watched him intently with his pale blue eyes.

Mrs. Barneaux nodded to Gerald and smiled. She then motioned her head for him to sit down.

On his way to his seat, Gerald felt like every eye in the building was watching him. Maybe they were since he stood out like a sore thumb. Before he sat down, he saw Thomas sitting with his family. Thomas smiled and nodded. The disapproval from a large portion of the crowd was palpable. Gerald sat down and a tiny hand tapped him on his shoulder. Gerald turned around to see Mrs. Culligan. "Hello ma'am, nice to see you again. Sir, how are you?" Gerald said to the Culligans. Mr. Culligan nodded and said hello. Mrs. Culligan motioned her tiny hand so Gerald could lean in closer. She squeezed his shoulder and said, "About time you asked her out. I may be old, but these eyes can still see." She laughed and Gerald smiled.

"Not sure everyone here shares your enthusiasm, ma'am," Gerald said.

Mrs. Culligan waved her hand dismissively "Times are changing, boy. Hear me, I see how you two look at each other. The person who should matter what they think is you to her, and her to you. They may not like it, but you have something. Don't be a fool, boy." She tapped his cheek and sat back.

Mrs. Barneaux watched Gerald the whole time and nodded. *She couldn't have possibly heard that* Gerald thought as he sat back. He looked over and she cocked her head in a little smile and then sat back as well. Gerald knew Mrs. Culligan was right. Right there and then he knew It wouldn't be easy, but he would fight for her. Whatever it took.

39

FACE THE HORROR

Gerald awoke with a start, the dream about the dance so long ago evaporating away the more conscious he became. The burning pain he felt where Judas had sliced off his ears was gone. The moaning and gasps of pain from his teammates had him bolt upright, but he forgot he was chained around the neck and he ended up jerking himself backward off balance and fell onto his back.

"You're awake." Judas was suddenly standing over Gerald. He leaned down and pulled Gerald up so he was sitting on his knees. "I know I said you would be last but...I lied." Judas beamed that insincere smile at Gerald, who tried to spit at Judas but the missing teeth and swollen tongue interfered. "You're tough, you're all tough. I salute you." Judas slow clapped as he pulled back.

Gerald glanced around and interestingly found Don's head slowly starting to heal up from the pulp it had been when Judas had battered him with a stick. David had regrown his nose and some of his skin, and Gio, whose torso had been flayed, was now starting to regrow his skin. The worst was yet to come, he knew. Vora had been beaten badly, but they all knew that Judas was taking it easy on her. Judas had beaten almost every inch of her body black and blue and torn her clothing to shreds while he did it. Her face wasn't touched, nor was she cut at all. Daemons would occasionally come by and giggle to themselves while they pointed at her. One of them had an enormous erection and it would move back and forth in front of Vora, never coming within reach but slowly circling like a shark closing on its prey.

Gerald saw through what Judas was doing. He was going to milk the terror from them, knowing that if he slowed it down, he could keep the team terrified of what was going to happen and not on trying to get a bearing on their surroundings or trying to escape. Gerald tried for the hundredth time to pry the dampener off but even after being beaten and abused, it stayed locked in with barely a scratch. One of them had to break free of the dampener if they were going to have a chance.

Judas had left Bariel alone for a while. He hadn't healed but was thankfully still alive. Gerald recalled his father telling him, "Keep your head when all others are losing theirs and you can overcome." At this moment Gerald felt helpless. His team was beaten, and he had no idea where Gordon was and if he could get to them in time before the inevitable happened. Gerald had no concerns for himself but was genuinely terrified for Vora and what would eventually happen to her. Judas was playing his game and he was winning.

Despair was clawing at him, pulling at him, trying to drag him down so that he would just give up and accept what was to come. That's what Judas was trying to do, what the enemy always tried to do. It was never a fair fight, always dirty pool.

"Two can play that game," Gerald said aloud, which brought Judas's attention right to him.

"Hmm, you have something to say?" Judas said as he walked over to Vora and tried to stroke her cheek. Vora bit his hand so hard he had to smack her. Her head hit the floor with a loud crack and split open, and she splashed the area with a gout of blood. "Look what you made me do!" Judas raged as his finger slowly healed itself. The monolith affected his powers. It made sense with having the vehicles they saw go by in the distance and the need for utensils and tools by the Daemons and the damned souls. If they had been able to use their powers, there would be no need to have any of this.

"I broke my own rules. Not the face, that's the money maker, baby." Judas, quick as a snake, grabbed Vora who groaned from the vice-like grip he had around her throat. He moved his hand over her face. She initially tried to fight him but stopped when she felt her injury healing. When she was fully healed, Judas released her moved away, and crouched down in front of Gerald. "You were saying?" Judas asked.

Gerald's mind raced, trying to grab onto anything that he could use to buy some time. He tried to use what little he knew about the damned soul in front of him, one of the most famous villains in history. Judas was smart, he was a manipulator, and he was powerful. He was in control, which seemed to be what he enjoyed the most.

"You said you have a nose for talent," Gerald said.

Judas cocked an eyebrow, then stood up. "I like to think so. You always want to work with good people," Judas said as the Daemon with the large private parts laughed. Judas looked over to the Daemon and waved him away.

"So you're recruiting us?" Gerald asked before continuing "Not sure why you think torturing us is going to sway us to work with you."

Judas gave Gerald the fake smile. "You are missing perspective."

Gerald looked around at Gio and Vora, who just shrugged. David cocked his head to the side, and Don didn't respond as he was listening intently.

"You are not mortal anymore. You have been to Heaven, you 'earned it.'" Judas used air quotes to accentuate the earned it part. "Who is to judge what is worthy of salvation? Why can't I say I don't want it?" he asked the group.

"Congrats, you got what you wanted then asshole" Gio replied dryly.

Judas turned to Gio, touched his finger to his nose, and flung a knife that materialized right into Gio's chest. Gio gasped in pain and when he tried to pull the knife out, it kept cutting his hands, as the handle was also a blade.

After a few moments, Judas smiled again and flicked his wrist and the knife disappeared. "The truth hurts," he said. "Plus, you didn't need to call me an asshole." Judas walked over to Vora and stood behind her. When Vora went to turn, he froze her so that she couldn't move. As soon as he started to move closer Don yelled, "Hey!" followed by the rest of the team futilely trying to distract Judas from doing anything terrible to Vora.

Judas raised his hand, and The Chosen Dead levitated as high as their collars would allow. He closed his fist which squeezed each of the members in an invisible vice and then dropped his arm. They all slammed down so hard that the ground shook. None of them were able to move or even think for a few seconds as their insides were smashed down as if they had fallen from a high-rise building.

Judas grimaced, grabbed his hand, and began to rub it. He was powerful, but the monolith still affected his abilities. The one positive of the dampener was that though it prevented the Chosen Dead from using their powers, they still could heal themselves to a point. The conscious part of who they were was the source of their identity, so it allowed for subconscious healing that worked the same way as if they had a body again.

Vora thankfully was also for the moment flattened to the

ground. Gerald tried to pick his head up to speak but was unable to due to his broken neck

Judas held his right hand tightly and clenched his teeth as he went over to Gerald to repair his head so he could speak. He left Gerald's body broken and in agonizing pain. "You were saying?"

Gerald took a deep breath as he rode out a wave of pain. "I don't believe you," he groaned out.

Judas cocked his head and waited for Gerald to explain. "You did want to be saved but....but you messed up"

Judas sat down next to Gerald and crossed his legs.

"No one wants to be the bad guy. Everyone thinks they are doing the right thing. The hard thing." Gerald was able to say before he was hit with a fresh wave of pain. His chest felt like it was on fire. He blacked out for a moment and when he awoke, Judas was over him

"I was a little overzealous." Judas raised his right hand which looked as if a few of his fingers were broken and with a soft glow, he repaired Gerald's rib cage and the rest of him. Judas sat back down in front of Gerald but grimaced. "Fucking thing is fucking me up," Judas grumbled as he referred to the monolith and its effects on the souls present. "Now, let's talk," he said to Gerald.

"You messed up, we all mess up," Gerald began. "You try to do the right thing with the information you are given. If you think that will help the best way, then you go with it but then if it doesn't work, you make amends for it, you keep trying." Gerald saw Judas waiting for him to say more. "When I was alive I killed men. I didn't know most of them but I killed them anyway. In a war that's just the way it is. I lied to people; I treated people who didn't deserve it poorly."

Gerald recalled all the things he regretted in life. Most of them were wrongs he had committed and even he wondered at times how he had gotten into heaven.

Judas didn't move, he just stared at Gerald. "Are you trying to save me?" Judas stood up and laughed. He laughed so hard that he had tears streaming down his face. "Oh shit," He started laughing some more, and the Daemons in the area who had no idea what he was laughing at began to nervously laugh along with him. "Praise be to He and all that, right?" The fake smile dropped from his face and was replaced by real emotion, the real Judas. Raging anger, and resentment highlighted on his face.

Judas grabbed his cloak and pulled it down so everyone could see the hanging rope scar that burned bright red around his neck. The pain as it brightened pushed him to get angrier and angrier. "Look at it!" he screamed at Gerald. "Look at it! You killed people and you still got into Heaven! I never killed anybody when I was alive. I made one mistake. One!"

The Daemons in the room moved as far away from him as possible. Bariel watched him in the distance, his one blue eye fixed on him. "You are right, though," Judas said to Gerald. "I do want to go to Heaven." He looked around the room, "That's why I am here. I am going to help these guys so that they can help me get to Heaven. And when I get there, I am going to burn it all down." Judas roared at them. "As for you guys, it has been fun, but we just kept you here in case there were more of you coming. Eventually, there will be, but you'll be long gone."

"Just kill us and be on way," Vora said. She spat as far as she could at Judas who looked at her and gave her that smile again.

"Kill you? No, we're going to take you away from here so we can torture you. We'll start with a hundred years or so. Do terrible things to you, all of you. There will be no salvation for any of you." He finished with dreadful glee.

Judas saw grim set features and unblinking eyes staring back at him. Internally they were all terrified of what he planned to do to them. Whatever Judas and his cronies were doing here, they thought so little of being found out that they had not even asked any questions about why they were there or how they had been discovered. They didn't care. The endgame was close, and The Chosen Dead needed to escape somehow.

Don slumped down. His head was slowly healing from the beating he had taken. After the beating, he passed out for a while but when he was awake, he was still not able to think clearly for an indeterminate time. He became aware of a chink in the chain that held him prisoner when the constant rubbing opened a cut on his thumb. He began to work at it and continued even when his nail had come off along with most of the skin and muscle had worn away. Don was down to the thumb bone, and that proved effective at slowly chipping away at the chink in the chain. Don began to go even faster. If he could break this side of the chain, he could free himself and get the dampener off.

The CTC began glowing and more Daemons came forth. This time eight, large and heavily muscled Daemons appeared. They had thick, yellow hair like a lion's mane with horns sticking out of the hair and carried heavy melee weapons like battle axes made with red metal, massive maces, and one had a whip with thorns set along the length of it. They all saw Judas and immediately started moving as far away from him as they could. The CTC which began to dim, glowed brightly again for a second, then went out.

40

SUBTERFUGE

Gordon followed behind the two damned souls as they made their way through the monolith. The monster vehicle wound its way through additional tunnels and began to climb up a spiraling roadway inside the monolith. Gordon used a combination of cloaking when he had to and jumping on vehicles heading in the same direction as the two damned souls who had the map scroll. He had made better use of his limited abilities by camouflaging himself as the same color as the vehicles. It was far less taxing on him and as long as he stayed still no one saw him. It helped that the sight lines were much higher than where he was holding on. The monolith was so well constructed that no light was coming in from the outside; it was well-lit with a glow emanating from the stone itself.

As they rose, they would reach a higher floor with roadways that went off into ante chambers. The vehicle Gordon was following had to slow to allow a larger vehicle past it from the next floor. It was moving so fast that if that vehicle wasn't there, He was sure it would have careened off the floor and plummeted down. Gordon jumped onto the vehicle and hitched a ride the rest of the way to their destination. He was laying on the massive bumper for another twenty minutes before the vehicle arrived at the very top of the monolith.

The air pressure this high up was noticeably thinner. The vehicle stopped moving and parked in an alcove. Gordon cloaked himself and slowly descended from the rear bumper. The two damned souls had jumped down already and headed into the only chamber on the top floor of the monolith. Gordon slowly made his way through the large doorway and followed the two damned souls through a chamber filled with urns, scrolls, and what appeared to be handles from old weapons that had rusted away from extreme old age. He navigated through the stacked Ailes loaded with their various dusty contents.

The two damned souls didn't say a word as they made their way. Here in this top chamber, you could see the surrounding area. The walls were not windows but see-through all the same. What made them more remarkable was that even with all the sun shining through, the room stayed well-lit but not too bright and temperate.

The footsteps of the two damned souls echoed throughout the chamber. Gordon made sure his steps were as silent as shadow as he trailed them. This top chamber appeared to be a hundred yards wide and another hundred yards long, in essence, a big square. The smell of the ancient scrolls and corroded weapons hung in the air so thickly that you could taste it on your tongue. Once Gordon walked past a large painting with a rotting canvas barely covering it. The painting showed some kind of an outline in faded green on a black field, and the bottom part of the painting had a hole in it.

It was easy to discern where the two damned souls were heading once they passed the painting. Hanging down at the end of the room was an old carving of a world tree made in a similar substance his armor was made out of, except it was almost black and not the silver of his armor. Below the large carving was a massive altar with scrolls being held in ornate holders. The rest of the scrolls were all tattered and broken down. One holder was empty, and around it the thick dust had been wiped away.

The two damned souls headed right towards the altar and once they walked up its steps, they placed the scroll on the placeholder, turned around, and left. On the way out the damned soul without the scar grabbed an old sword handle and pulled out a sword so old that the blade fell right off the handle

"Leave it!" the damned soul with the scar yelled to the other. The other soul dropped the sword handle in feigned fear and saluted the scarred soul. The scarred soul stopped walking and stared at the other for a few seconds before the other soul put his hands up and began walking towards the entrance. "Geez, no fun." The scarred soul clenched his fists and shook his head as he kept walking.

Gordon waited until they left the chamber and he heard the vehicle parked outside start back up and drive off. He quickly made his way to the altar and made sure no one else was in the chamber. Gordon moved to where the scroll had been placed and before he picked it up felt a surge of energy coming from it. He stopped and examined the scroll in his other sight. As Gordon focused more intently, he realized the top of it didn't radiate anything but the bottom was brightly illuminated. The stand itself was the source of the energy field.

He scanned around and found that none of the other stands had any energy readings at all. Maybe at one time, he mused, but perhaps they had fallen into disrepair. Testing a theory Gordon found a relatively intact scroll, removed the map's scroll from its holder, and switched it with the tattered one. At first, nothing seemed to happen but then the energy in the holder moved up and enveloped the old scroll. Within a few seconds, the old scroll was made new again.

Gordon went searching for a scroll that looked similar to the map scroll. Luckily multiple scrolls looked the same. The issue was finding one relatively whole one. Eventually, he settled on two scrolls that he combined and held while the holder melded them together.

At first glance, the replacement looked the same as the map scroll. Gordon had no idea how long it would take for the map scroll to deteriorate, so he needed to move quickly. He ran out of the chamber, caught up to the vehicle with the two damned souls, jumped back on the bumper, camouflaged himself, and allowed himself to be taken back down so that he could find his teammates.

Back where the journey started splotches of Daemon ichor remained on the floor where the scarred soul had run the Daemons down. Gordon had to cloak himself before they parked because the rear of the vehicle was exposed to the main roadway. He moved in the shadows as he made his way closer to the entranceway of the monolith. Once he was within sight of the entranceway, he pulled back, listening and looking for any sign of his people. The foot traffic along with the comings and goings of the vehicles made it difficult to hear anything worthwhile or provide any lead as to where The Chosen Dead were.

A familiar scent came to him in a wisp. Gordon lifted his head like a hunting hound trying to catch it again. He didn't have to try very hard to seek it again. The ozone stink of travel by CTC came in stronger. The source of the smell came from a contingent of Daemons walking towards the entranceway of the monolith. Eight tall, muscular brutes with thick yellow manes like lions and brandishing heavy weapons appeared. They had the scent of the CTC battling with the stink of brimstone and corruption as they moved past Gordon's position.

Relying on instinct, Gordon followed the smell of ozone. If there indeed was a CTC in the monolith, then he needed to see where it was and, if possible, escape back to his encampment so he could bring back reinforcements and save his team. The strain on Gordon grew as he moved along the corridor while cloaked. There was too much traffic to not cloak himself, and he moved through the corridor on foot so he could avoid colliding with anyone that he passed by.

The stink of Daemons, damned souls, and ozone grew stronger. The closer he came to his destination, the more thoughts that his people were gone for good encroached like unwanted guests in his mind. The real possibility that they were shipped off somewhere was playing over and over like a broken record. He gritted his teeth, *If they were gone, he would find them if it was the last thing he did.* He thought.

Up ahead, Gordon approached a much larger chamber than the one where the painting on the ceiling was. A hundred yards ahead he saw the familiar outline of a CTC on a stand made of the same material as the monolith. Gordon quickly moved into the chamber but stayed close to the wall so that no one could accidentally walk into him from behind if things got too crowded. Daemons were crawling all over the place here. There were hundreds of them, all shapes and sizes going to and fro.

Gordon was scanning the massive chamber looking for a break so that he could make a beeline for the CTC and go in once a chance presented itself. He felt it activate and, with a pulse of light, a group of Daemons similar to the muscular horned group he had passed before appeared. These had a row of metal spikes running down the middle of their horned heads, similar to a mohawk, and ridiculously oversized, rusty swords that for as decrepit as they looked, still appeared sharp.

Gordon made to leap over the Daemons and make his escape when he heard someone screaming. He looked over and saw Gio with a dampener around his neck, chained to the floor with his skin partially gone. Gordon's heart leaped in his chest and almost ran right into a Daemon that looked like a giant ladybug with a goat head. Gordon angled himself and saw a damned soul with bright penny-red hair, a beard, and an ugly red rope burn around his neck screaming at Gerald who looked terrible. They all looked terrible except for her.

Vora was bruised but had not taken as much punishment as the rest of the team. Slowly, so slowly Gordon maneuvered over to her. He heard the damned soul telling them that they would be taken away from here and tortured. Gordon saw the lascivious way that this red-haired beast looked and spoke to his woman, his light, and it filled him with rage. Then a Daemon with overly large private parts approached Vora in an overtly sexual way. He would have struck this daemon and the damned soul down in fury right then and there if the damned soul had not mentioned that whatever he was here for was close to ruinous fruition. The scroll held snugly across his back was also a big reminder that he needed to make sure that not only did they escape but also that they could stop whatever this vile thing was up to.

Thankfully his anger froze him fast and allowed him to gather his thoughts, and his gaze fell upon another silver coin a few feet in front of him. This was not the same silver coin that Don had stepped on, but similar enough for Gordon to know that to step on it would alert the enemy to his presence.

The damned soul left, informing them that there would be no salvation for The Chosen Dead. Gordon would prove that creature wrong or it would be the last thing he would do. He would strike him down and take his head for even thinking about touching her. Gordon's only concern was whether he would have the time to do it before Vora burned that creature down to his atoms. Champagne problems, Gordon had heard Gio say once or twice. He didn't know how much time he had, but he had a plan.

Gordon scanned the rest of the room and, once satisfied with what he learned, left. He noticed Don fidgeting constantly with his thumb and noticed that he had worn his thumb down to the bone and that bone was rubbing against a chink in the chain link he was attached to. Gordon went to approach Don and help him but thought better of it. There were too many Daemons in the vicinity, and even a small expenditure of power could signal them. He would return with help.

41

HEADLIGHT AT THE END OF THE TUNNEL

Gerald kept working on the chain attaching him to the ground. It was old and had rust but was deceivingly stout. Too stout, he thought. Doubt had taken up residence in the back of his mind and was now looking for more room up in front.

His team looked resolute but so far, none of them seemed to have anything close to an escape. Don, who had been unconscious, had been doing something with his right arm that Gerald couldn't see. It was small and subtle but he hoped it was something, anything that would make a difference.

Gerald was thinking of the few options available to them. When they were moved they would have to make their move. They could not let themselves be sent through the CTC to whatever hell was waiting for them. Gerald was thinking that if he was moving them, he would definitely leave the dampeners on and would just have the Daemons remove the chain in the ground to lead them to whatever fresh horror awaited them at the end of the CTC.

With Judas gone for the moment, the Daemons in the area all but ignore them, all but the creepy Daemon with the oversized sex parts who was moving back and forth towards Vora, each time edging a little closer. Vora did her best to ignore the daemon, and Gerald was hoping the Daemon would get close enough to Vora so she could do something terrible to that creep.

Something caught Gerald's eye by Don. It was...something. It appeared to be a heat haze that was there so briefly, he may have imagined it. Gerald wondered if maybe it was Gordon, but if it was, why wouldn't he have tried to free them? If he were Gordon, he would have had to search for them so he wouldn't go off halfcocked. He would have to have faith. Also, Gordon could not even be anywhere near their location, so he would hope but he would also work on freeing his team and not rely on Gordon.

Once one of them was freed, they would need to try and free the one closest to them. All it would take would be to break one of the dampeners. The dampeners were sturdy and resilient. They had taken as much abuse as each of the Chosen Dead had and, though scuffed and a few dents, held up. The dampeners had a keyhole in the back and so far, he had not seen anyone with a key, either hanging around their neck nor an evil key holder lurking somewhere. Gerald wished that some of the bad guy tropes would hold up but so far, they seemed intent on being real-life difficult. Once they disconnected Gerald, he would try and slip the chain under the dampener and see if he could pry it open that way. If it didn't work then he would either take his own head off or injure himself severely.

He looked around and tried to communicate with his people. "Guys," Gerald whispered. They all looked his way. "We get a chance, put the chain up and.."

A spear burst right through Gerald's chest. Out of nowhere, a group of Daemons kicked and punched him until he was lying on the ground motionless. One of the Daemons that looked like a rat with overly large ears and a very long nose spoke to all of them. "No talk!" it chittered. It then started laughing like a lunatic and faked that it was going to hit Gio, who was glaring at the rat daemon. Gio gave the creature the finger which the rat Daemon thought was hilarious. "You wish die soon," it continued to chitter, then walked off.

Gerald lay in a puddle of blood and turned his body to show the team who were all staring at him that he was alright. He used the blood as a lubricant under the dampener and he pulled it out to show them how to try and leverage the dampener open. They all nodded and each one did as he showed but that also didn't work. It kept them busy, though, while the CTC continued to glow and more Daemon squads came through to add to the roiling tide of vermin already crawling around the monolith.

As long as they didn't speak the Daemons left them alone. Even the overly large sex parts daemon got bored and went off to the other side of the chamber to do God knows what. The increase in troops coming in was another signal that whatever the enemy was planning, they were going to move into the next phase soon.

Don continued to work on the chink in the chain. The pain didn't get any better, but it didn't get any worse. Plus, it was nothing compared to the torture he had endured already. Don's thumb was half gone. The bone had been worn away but was slowly bearing fruit as the chink grew larger. One of them needed to break free. None of them wanted to go through that CTC. The unsaid was the bigger concern. They knew that when Judas came back that would be the last time they would see him. They needed to be able to stop him from doing whatever he had planned to do to them and, more so, Vora.

Gerald continued to try to pry open the dampener but that failed. It didn't matter as footsteps lumbered over to their location. The stench of Daemon was followed by the group of muscular daemons with lion's mane hair. Behind them was Judas. He was speaking with two damned souls wearing the black cloaks with hoods covering their faces. Judas raised his head and shushed the damned souls he was speaking with. He nodded to the Daemons who proceeded to spread out around The Chosen Dead and began to beat them into unconsciousness.

≈

THEY BEGAN TO STIR AND, one by one, they regained consciousness and sat up. Two of the muscular Daemons stood on either side of Vora, holding onto her arms. They had gagged her and held her firm. The anxiety they all felt was palpable. Fear hung in the air thicker than the mist outside.

Bariel was awake and staring at Judas with his one good eye. The two damned souls were dismissed. "I can smell your fear. That fear of the unknown is so savory," Judas said as he produced a large flaying knife. He approached Vora and stood in front of her. Judas flicked the knife and made a shallow cut on Vora's face. He placed the knife up to his nose to smell the scent of her blood. His eyes rolled back in his head and a tongue that was much too large flicked out of his mouth and licked the blood off the knife. "None of you are afraid to be tortured or even die. You're old school like me. I appreciate that. Gentlemen, and lady."

Judas walked behind Vora and made a longer cut on her back. She struggled but the Daemons held her tight. That too-large tongue came out and slid across the cut on her back. Judas was panting now and it took him a few moments to gather himself. He smiled watching The Chosen Dead and Bariel's futile struggle to free themselves. Now his smile wasn't fake; it was the smile of a predator, all flashing teeth and blood.

"Gentlemen, I admire that. Interesting fact why women are rarely used in war. Unsaid but well-known. That fear of them being violated." Judas still had that shark-toothed smile now. "Yes, it's real, you are hopeless, you will blame yourselves." Judas walked back to face Vora and the knife flashed again and Judas sliced off her left ear. The ear flipped up into the air and Judas grabbed it. "And it is your fault. You strong, righteous men couldn't save her. You can't even save yourselves. You allowed an angel of the Lord to be tortured and partially eaten."

Gerald felt physically ill. He tried everything he could to free himself, they all did but it was useless.

"Sometimes bad things happen to good people, and they deserve it." Judas went in and started to slice the skin on Vora's shoulder and peel it back. "Your sin is weakness"

Don had given up any pretense of hiding what he was doing. His thumb and pointer fingers were both gone, and half of his middle finger bone remained but he had made progress. He just needed a little more time. There was only a little bit left on the chain link. Don had slid the chain under the dampener as well and had been pulling on the chain link so that he could try and pull it apart. The chain was long enough that he could keep it close at hand while he pulled.

"You're going to watch me ruin her. It will happen in every way. Then you will be shipped out." Judas slashed out and the remains of Vora's armor came off as it was slashed apart.

Don pulled with all his might. He was using his ring finger as well and had also included his other hand to chip away. Slowly, painfully, the link stretched. Don pulled harder, and the link stretched a little further. Don's blood was making it slippery, and he had a hard time keeping his grip with the missing fingers. Don pulled even harder and with a snap, the link finally gave way and broke. None of the Daemons or Judas notice.

Don wrapped some of the chain around his arm and flicked the rest of the chain length right at Judas who was caught unawares as he was focused on slicing up Vora. The chain wrapped around his neck and Don yanked as hard as he could and pulled Judas down. Don ran up to one of the Daemons that held Vora, punched it right on its snout, and kicked its leg joint, and the beast went down.

He went after the other Daemon but before he was able to land a blow, Don was yanked back off his feet at high speed where he flew through the air Judas caught Don and slammed him into the ground so hard that he didn't move. No one said a word; the silence was deafening. There was a click, and then all hell broke loose.

42

PLANS AND PLANS

Gordon was all over the place emotionally. He didn't have much time to save them, save her. Worst case scenario he would destroy the CTC free his people and take their chances. The issue was the large number of upper-level Daemons, at least three groups of damned souls, and two fallen angels to contend with. Gordon didn't have much time either for what he had to do next.

He found a smaller chamber in a quiet area off the main avenue in the monolith. It appeared to be a room piled high with various broken tools and equipment. Gordon slowed his breathing and readied himself as the use of his cloaking had put a severe strain on him due to the interference caused by the monolith. Using offensive power took a toll but the steady grind to keep the cloaking up inside this structure had pushed him to his limits. It was as if he had gone nonstop for weeks rather than just a day or so.

Once he felt focused enough, Gordon camouflaged himself to match the walls and moved cautiously out of the room. The stench gave him time to hide before the scuffling footsteps and the squeaking of wheels badly in need of oiling grew louder and a large group of lower-level Daemons entered, one daemon on each handle, and began unloading new scrap from an old rusted wheelbarrow three times the normal size as the ones you would see back in the old world. Once emptied, they quickly left.

Gordon waited a few seconds before coming out of his hiding spot and moving swiftly towards the front entrance. Gordon's plan was to move along the wall and hitch a ride on the back of a vehicle heading back towards the CTC.

As Gordon neared the entrance and was going to turn the corner, a familiar stink engulfed his nostrils, and he came face to face with one of the lower-level Daemons who had just been in the junk room. They both froze, Gordon and a daemon that was an odd amalgam of a giant plucked baby chick with pincers for hands. Up close the creature's fetid stink almost made Gordon gag.

Not sure what to do, Gordon smiled and raised his hand in greeting. The creature, clearly not very smart, slowly raised his pincer in greeting as well. Gordon took a step back into the junk room, but the creature did not. Gordon wasn't sure if the Daemon was alone or not but if he stayed like this, then he was done for. Quick as a cat, he launched himself at the plucked chick Daemon who gave a quick squawk, and he pulled it into the room before anyone could see them, and broke its neck, killing it quickly and quietly.

Gordon picked up the now-dead Daemon and carried its stinking corpse behind a pile of scrap metal and broken drill parts. The feel of its skin was repulsive and oddly warm but slick with a mucus like substance. Gordon looked around, grabbed a flat piece of metal, and drove it into the chest of the now-dead Daemon. With a glance up to make sure no one was there, he quickly etched into the metal. Once he was done, he made sure the metal was firmly in place and then hoisted the creature over his shoulder, cloaked himself, the dead Daemon, and quickly moved out. Between carrying the stinking bulk of the Daemon and cloaking, Gordon was wheezing due to the effects of the monolith.

When one of the oversized vehicles came down the road where he was hiding, Gordon quickly ran after it and expended more energy than he wanted to so he could get a grip on a vehicle handle. Once he was hanging on to the back of the vehicle, Gordon gritted his teeth and swung the Daemon's body onto the bumper where it clanged louder than he wanted it to off of it but lay in the space there safely. Gordon waited to see if anyone onboard had heard it but thankfully nothing could be heard over the diesel-guzzling engine. He climbed up onto the bumper area and camouflaged himself and the dead Daemon's body. They swiftly moved through the monolith and had to jump off when the vehicle they were on made a right into a sub-avenue.

Gordon and the dead Daemon he was carrying made their way back to the main avenue and kept moving towards the CTC. The third and last time that Gordon had to jump off the vehicle he was on, he tossed the dead daemon's body off to the side but didn't get enough distance as a vehicle following them ran right over the lower half of the dead Daemon. Once all the vehicles passed and he was certain no one saw him, he pulled the dead Daemon back onto the side of the avenue and found that only its skinny chicken legs had been run over and crushed, and what was left was stinking blood and pieces of meat. If possible, the smell was even worse.

Gordon quickly cauterized the ends of the skinny chicken legs so they wouldn't drip their fluids on him or he was sure he would vomit if that was possible. He hoisted the creature up on unsteady feet. Thankfully losing the Daemon legs made it lighter to carry but cloaking this long was draining him faster now. Gordon dropped the carcass, leaned against the wall, and took several slow, deep breaths. He picked up the Daemon body, foisted it onto his shoulders, and moved out.

He entered the CTC and saw his people, The Chosen Dead, still chained to the floor. Gordon headed to the CTC itself and moved over to the empty side where he saw the new Daemons would appear when coming through the CTC and waited. He saw Bariel awake and watching as well. He wanted to free him. Even with the grievous wounds Bariel had taken Gordon knew the angel was still dangerous. Gordon hoped that the CTC would start up again soon. His plan needed for that to happen, and then he could work on freeing his friends and Vora.

Gordon's attention was brought to the approaching sound of a large group of muscular Daemons that he had passed back at the entranceway. They had provided him with the ozone trail of the CTC to follow. With them were two damned souls and the penny redhead who were in deep discussion. The muscular Daemons with the lion's manes approached and surrounded The Chosen Dead, and two held Vora tight while the penny redhead began to talk a bunch of bullshit. He held a flaying knife in his hand and gloated at the fact that they were too weak to save her, and then he cut into her.

Gordon's fury swamped him like a tidal wave and all reason threatened to fly right out the window. The Chosen Dead his people were all futilely trying to free themselves. They all felt it, the despair, and helplessness. Gordon didn't feel despair or helpless; he would cut this creature's ginger head from his body and kill everything in here for her.

Gordon stood up and balled his fists. He was in the process of pulling energy to him so he could fire an energy blast strong enough to vaporize the red head and possibly himself. The monolith caused everything to be harder. Pulling the energy felt like waiting for syrup to come out of a new bottle.

Some of the Daemons on the other side of the CTC began to

look his way. Gordon didn't care. He would blast this creature and then deal with the repercussions.

A sudden bright light distracted Gordon and when he turned, the CTC glowed brightly. Gordon had to decide, follow his plan or blast the red head. Every fiber of his being wanted to destroy him, screamed for him to fling all he had at the red head who defiled his woman. New Daemons appeared, similar to the muscular daemons but with metal spikes in their scalp rather than hair.

Gordon made his decision and moved over to the CTC with the legless, dead Daemon in tow. When he was certain no more Daemons would appear, Gordon moved closer to the CTC. The Daemons standing close by had already gone back to watching the red head torture Vora. The CTC began to dim. Gordon touched it and it brightened up again. A few daemons glanced over but didn't see anything and quickly lost interest. Gordon was about to grab the dead Daemon and throw it in when he realized it was still cloaked. Gordon wasn't sure how long it would last, but he couldn't send it through cloaked. It would take precious time away from what he was planning.

Gordon glanced around, dragging his view away from what was happening to his people and also making sure none of the enemy were nearby. He focused and expanded the cloaking to form a semi-curved cloaking wall around him and used the dias the CTC was on to cover behind him. Gordon felt a burning pressure in his chest as he finished creating the shield wall. It was as high as the rock dias that the CTC laid on but used less energy from the little Gordon had left to keep the cloaking going.

He grabbed the dead chick Daemon and removed the cloaking from it. That relieved the burning pressure he felt in his chest somewhat. He quickly glazed over to the surrounding Daemons who were focused on what was going on with The

Chosen Dead to notice anything. Gordon refused to look else he lose focus. He had positioned the dead Daemon and was going to have it touch the CTC when suddenly, all the daemons near the CTC rushed off toward The Chosen Dead. Gordon looked to see Don had broken the chain and flung it so it wrapped around the redhead and yanked him back. Don moved as quickly as he could and badly injured one of the muscular Daemons before the redhead had yanked Don back and slammed him into the ground so hard he left a crater.

Gordon used that distraction to hoist the dead Daemon into contact with the CTC. Instantly it disappeared and then began to dim again. Gordon was exhausted, he had nothing left. His vision blurred, he was barely able to keep himself upright, but he had enough left to focus on the locking mechanism on Gerald's collar.

Gordon passed out but before he did, he and every other being in the chamber heard the click. Gordon had freed Gerald from the dampener. All hell broke loose.

43

PAYBACK

Gerald struggled as hard as he could to try and break free. He was suffocating himself trying to pry open the dampener collar, and the collar, his hands, and the floor around him were wet with new blood stains. He needed to try and help Don who had somehow freed himself and had been able to disorient Judas and disable one of the muscular Daemons that had held Vora's arms.

Gerald was suddenly knocked forward as he was struck from behind by what felt like a surge of energy. He felt a burning in the back of his neck as something overloaded inside the dampener. Everyone was in stunned silence as Judas had recovered and struck down Don who lay motionless on the ground. The click was audible. Everyone including the enemy was looking around to see what the cause of it was.

Gerald knew. He felt it as soon as the dampener shorted out and the lock blew. The energy surge flowing into him was slow, and he needed to focus intently to pull energy to him. It felt like sipping a thick milkshake; it took forever initially to get some all the way through the straw but even at this slow pace, Gerald instantly felt and looked better as his injuries healed up, and as he stood he melted away the chain and dampener.

Gerald roared his fury into the face of the enemy and unleashed a blast of power that threw Judas Iscariot into the far wall. Gerald ran forward and fired energy blasts that ripped apart the muscular Daemons and turned them into bloody goo. He pulled more power in and focused on the dampeners that held the rest of The Chosen Dead prisoner, clenched his fists, and the dampeners on each of them were immolated.

They all jumped up and healed instantly except for Don who thankfully picked up his head and looked around. "What's going on?" he asked drowsily.

Gio ran up to Don and pulled him up while he fired multiple blasts of energy at the other Daemons who were blown apart. "It's a prison break, buddy, come on!" Gio pulled on Don and healed some of his injuries, but the strain of pulling energy and healing Don caused him to stumble.

"I got you," Don said, stabilizing Gio when he was almost healed.

"Gerald, Gordon is here behind the CTC!" Bariel yelled. As he strained with all his might and freed his wings, a wet tear splattered bright red blood all around him. Bariel tried to walk but with his grievous injuries and his using whatever he had left in the tank was unable to move much further as he gritted his teeth.

Vora screamed so loudly it created a small thunderstorm inside the chamber. The rest of the Daemons were vaporized by the storm, but after that, she dropped to the floor in exhaustion.

David caught her and ran with her over to Gordon, who was still unconscious. Gerald looked around for Judas but didn't see or sense him. He knew that didn't mean anything and that reinforcements were soon to come. "Circle up!" he called and went over to where Gordon was located, partially hidden by the base of the CTC. Gordon was out cold and had what appeared to be an old map scroll underneath him. "Get hands on him," Gerald ordered, and they all contributed to healing him. Gordon woke up with a start and as soon as he saw Vora they jumped into each other's arms.

Gerald politely coughed.

"Sorry, this map is the key to what they are doing here. They are looking for something," Gordon sheepishly explained. "I sent a message through the CTC to get reinforcements, but I don't know how long that will take."

Gio touched the CTC but nothing happened. "They must have it blocked so we can't escape." Gerald thought about it. "We bring this place down then. They can't communicate with their side so whatever they have here is it," Gerald said.

"They have at least two teams of damned souls and two fallen angels," David said.

Gordon nodded and looked over at Bariel.

"We need to revive him," Gerald said. They all looked at Gerald, they all felt the strain of using their powers. Reviving an angel was very difficult when being able to call on your abilities to begin with.

"Going to be tough, boss," Gio said as he approached Bariel who was conscious but bleeding badly from his wings.

"Don grab the weapons from those Daemons. We'll need them," Gerald commanded. The rest of The Chosen Dead went up to Bariel, who was grimly staring at them with his one good eye.

"Do not be foolish. The toll it will take is too much. Leave me, save yourselves I shall make a good account of myself before the end." Bariel tried to get up but the missing muscle tissue in his back began to bleed and prevented him from rising.

"No one gets left behind" Gerald signaled everyone, and they all laid hands on Bariel and focused. The process was slow, too slow. His back was knitting up but they had to stop from the strain of the monolith's influence.

"Is too much. We surround and we kill all," Vora breathed. Gordon held her by her waist. There was a rushing tide heading towards them. They all could hear the mass of Daemons and God knows what else nearing the CTC chamber.

Bariel, who was still missing his eye, grabbed Gerald's arm. "The monolith," Bariel wheezed. Gerald didn't understand what he meant. "It is a different kind of energy, use it as a transfer."

Gerald's eyes widened in understanding. The effect that the monolith emitted and caused it to not be seen by any scan was a powerful energy that caused issues with the souls using their power. It didn't seem to affect the angels, though. The roaring tide drew closer as Gerald kneeled and laid both arms on Bariel. "Give me as much time as you can," Gerald told The Chosen Dead who went into a defensive formation armed with the Daemon weapons. Don held a mace in each hand, David a morning star. Vora and Gio grabbed swords, and Gordon a large club.

Gerald left them to it as he heard the initial tide of stinking filth crash down on their tiny line. He needed to focus on the nature of the energy he was dealing with. The energy the monolith emitted was similar in certain ways to the energy that Gordon had shown him so he could cloak himself as well but also very different. This energy flowed like quicksilver and was slippery; it didn't resist him so much as slip out of his control.

Gerald heard the fighting and screaming as The Chosen Dead held off the tide of Daemons bearing down. He focused on getting control of this too fluid energy, but he did see a connection between this energy and Bariel. Gerald focused on the link and started on Bariel's side so that he was able to carefully handle it without it slipping from his control.

Gerald grunted as a Daemon that looked like a giant praying

mantis dropped down from the ceiling below and slashed him in the back.

Gio sent energy through the sword and burned it to ash. "The metal in the sword makes it easier, I think it's copper," Gio yelled and fired additional blasts of energy up above. "Keep going, I got you!"

Gerald closed his eyes and focused back on Bariel but then stopped again. "I need a weapon, something small will do!" he yelled. A few seconds later, a mace bent in half landed at his feet. "Good enough," he said and stuck the mace handle under Bariel's shoulder while holding on to the dented mace head covered in black blood.

Gerald blocked out the noise and a close-sounding explosion and found Bariel's energy again. He was able to delicately guide it to the metal on the mace where it began to slide all around it and flow up and down the handle. Once it touched the metal, it stayed on there and swirled about. In his mind's eye, the energy was silver and was rotating about on the shaft handle. Gerald then reached out for the energy of the monolith which would not let him do anything with it. It would slip out of his control and move all about. It was very frustrating and the saying herding cats popped into his mind.

Gerald thought about that, herding cats; you could still herd them. Instead of trying to control the monolith's energy, he worked on directing it to the mace handle. He didn't try to grasp it but instead blocked it off from where it wanted to go and just tried to get it to go in the general direction of the mace handle. Thankfully it worked. It was slow going and Gerald almost lost his focus on what he was doing when a sharp pain erupted on his shoulder. He counted on his people to take care of him, which they did as the pain from whatever had pierced him was removed.

Vora's scream echoed as if she was far away. The world

dropped away, and Gerald imagined creating a funnel to direct the energy which didn't work. He remembered an old movie called The Good Earth where there was a drought and when it rained, they tried to funnel the water down to the crops and one man threw his body at a bend in the stream to block off the water which then flowed down to the crops. Up until now, he always thought that what that man did in the movie was completely ridiculous. He tried it anyway.

He spread himself out and pushed, directed, and blocked the energy from sliding away from him. He was able to finally get a small piece to flow onto the metal handle. The effect was instantaneous. The monolith's energy synced up with Bariel's without Gerald having to do anything.

Gerald slowly released his hand as Bariel began to glow, becoming brighter and brighter until he was a mini sun burning on the ground. Squeals of fear and pain were heard as the Daemons could not look upon that burning light. Bariel's hands spasmed and his mouth opened wide in a rictus of pain.

Gerald grabbed the mace head to pull it away but was thrown back by the energy itself. The light began to pulse and Bariel disappeared into the light of the mini sun. The pulsing began to beat in rhythm, slowly at first then faster and faster. Gerald could see what would happen next.

"Take cover!" he screamed as the glowing orb that was Bariel detonated.

44

PAYBACK PART 2

The ensuing explosion threw everyone within a two-hundred-meter radius around like rag dolls. Stillness replaced the cacophony of noise from the fighting and Daemons screeching. The CTC was untouched by the blast but anything built by the enemy had been vaporized along with the enemy.

Thousands of Daemons had been in that chamber when Bariel detonated, and they were all gone as if they never existed. The Chosen Dead had been scattered all over the chamber and wearily picked themselves up. Their attention was drawn to Bariel. It was him and not him. He hadn't exploded as they all expected but was completely healed, and he seemed larger and more robust. This version had a lion's head and four large wings to go with four arms. The version that is most associated with angels was of a humanoid with wings but the reality was that angels were not human. This was his true self, and the monolith's energy revealed it.

Bariel closed his eyes and the overlaid image faded. The energy used to heal him topped him off like a full gas tank and left him pulsing with power. The mace used as a conduit to transfer the energy was a nub of molten slag stuck to Bariel's shoulder, which he pulled off and dropped to the ground. The wound immediately closed up while his eyes glowed like a pair of headlamps. There was dead silence as the Chosen Dead approached Bariel.

"Bariel, are you alright?" Gerald called. At first, it didn't seem like Bariel had heard Gerald "Bariel?" he said again.

Bariel turned his burning eyes on Gerald. "We should all be dead," he said.

"You're welcome," Gerald said.

Bariel nodded, and raised his hand, and Gerald's world turned to fiery pain. When Bariel lowered his hand, Gerald and the rest of the Chosen Dead gasped. Bariel had done it to all of them.

"What the hell, man!" Gio exclaimed as he rubbed the back of his neck and then his stomach. Where there had been skin barely healed, it was now fully healed. "Shit," Gio said softly.

Bariel lifted his head and inhaled, his expression changed to one of pure rage. "My fallen brethren come. See to your escape but I cannot leave while they live." Bariel made to leap up into the air and was fired upon by a team of damned souls led by Judas Iscariot. Bariel dropped back down and materialized his flaming sword.

The Chosen Dead jumped into action. "Formation!" Gerald yelled. Vora saw Judas and went to go after him, their eyes locked "Formation, now!" Gerald yelled. She bared her teeth but did as commanded. The Chosen Dead faced off against the damned souls.

"Get him free!" Gerald ordered and they began firing at the damned souls along with a force shield which knocked them back long enough for Bariel to speed away.

Moments later, a roar echoed through the monolith which was returned with two more roars in reply. Angels were about to die.

The damned souls recovered quickly and began attacking The Chosen Dead by firing energy blasts at them while moving in closer.

Judas pulled the long flaying knife out and materialized a long whip with wicked barbs along the length of it. He lashed out with the whip towards Gerald who blocked it with an energy shield and blasted Judas in the legs, which caught him unawares and he fell forward onto his face.

Gordon, who was closest, jumped on top of Judas and began stabbing him with a rusty Daemon knife he had picked up, and they then rolled on the ground like rabid animals.

Vora assaulted the damned souls with a smaller lightning storm that seemed to be working but with the restrictions placed on them by the monolith's effect she couldn't create a full storm.

Don stayed at normal size, David didn't change into his wolf hybrid form, and Gio followed behind and stayed flanking Gerald so that they could attack the damned souls the old-fashioned way with their fists and weapons.

Vora couldn't get a clean shot at Judas, so she left Gordon to go one on one with him while she came around and attacked the damned souls from another angle. The fighting was furious. Daemons were trying to pen them in and harass them.

The damned souls couldn't keep using their powers either due to the monolith's repressive aura. The damned souls outnumbered The Chosen Dead two to one. Though they didn't have any one person nearly as powerful as any of The Chosen Dead, they were smart and attacked like a pack of hyenas closing on lions: never straight ahead and always distracting from the sides using the daemons. The Chosen Dead were surrounded and were being packed in tight. The sheer weight of numbers would eventually wear them down.

Gerald ordered The Chosen Dead to circle up and keep an

eye out for Gordon who he could hear was still brawling with Judas. Vora saw an opening. She rose and fired off a wave of lightning that connected with Judas who had been able to throw Gordon off of him. The lightning blasted Judas backward, and the CTC flickered, then started to glow. Judas stood back up and closed a fist, and the CTC went dark again. He then lashed out with his whip towards Vora who raised her arm to ward it off, but the whip pushed through her weak shield and wrapped around her forearm. Vora immediately screamed in pain as he yanked her towards him.

Gordon had come up behind Judas and speared him through the back. The point of the spear came out through Judas' chest and he dropped the whip, which disappeared.

Vora was lying facedown when a group of Daemons attacked her and started stabbing and slashing her.

"On me!" Gerald roared and The Chosen Dead followed him as he cut a bloody path through Daemons and a few damned souls who tried to fire energy at them. One tried to push him with their mind and was instead repelled by Gerald, at some cost due to the effort.

They reached Vora and killed all the Daemons surrounding her and got her upright. A roar went up and Gordon came flying through the air ass over end and plowed through a group of daemons on his way down.

The CTC began to glow again as they watched Judas who had been lit on fire with the spear Gordon had plunged into him. Judas gritted his teeth and quelled the fires inside his chest. His beard was partially burnt off and his hands had no skin or muscle on them as he pulled the spear out of him. The CTC went dark again as he regained control. The amount of power Judas was displaying by being able to fight and also block the CTC was incredible.

Gordon was back on his feet, and they realized they needed

to take Judas out long enough to give them a chance. Judas must have read the look on their faces. "I can go all night!" he chirped at them.

The Chosen Dead fought through the damned souls and a legion of Daemons to try and make their way towards Judas. For his part, he didn't stay still but instead kept moving away from them, forcing them to use their abilities by trying to reach him.

It was a war of attrition, and they were losing. They would push the Daemons and souls back using a shield barricade, but even combined, it was having the effect Judas wanted which was to wear them down. They all had multiple wounds which they chose not to heal because it would take too much energy.

The one positive was that Judas was finally showing fatigue. He was bent over and a damned soul was helping him to keep moving. The chamber was now almost full of Daemons who were pressing The Chosen Dead in. Soon they would be suffocated under the stinking, crushing weight of daemons.

Gerald watched as the damned soul turned his back to them as Judas turned towards the entranceway. The press of Daemons was hindering them, too, even with him screaming at them to move out of his way. Gerald took his shot and mentally pulled a dozen bladed weapons out of Daemons' claws and sent them flying towards the damned soul. Judas didn't see it till it was too late to stop it and the blades sliced the damned soul to pieces. Most of the blades passed through and connected to Judas, who blocked a blade with his arm that had beheaded the damned soul holding him up. Judas lost that arm mid-bicep. The damned soul, with his head severed from his body, emitted a black light just as blinding as a white light which then turned into black ashes.

Judas's roar was an inhuman hissing like a giant serpent. His control of the CTC fractured, and it began to glow even brighter. Suddenly, it went dark again. At this, Judas looked around to see where it was coming from when he was struck with half the torso of a fallen angel. The torso was sliced diagonally in half and the impacted Judas was flung through a crowd of Daemons.

A roar like multiple lions came rushing down the hallway like a tidal wave, followed by Bariel fighting mid-air with the second fallen angel. Gerald followed the flight used his other senses and saw the connection from the second fallen angel to the CTC. The fallen angel didn't appear to feel the effects of the monolith the way Judas or any other soul, damned or not.

Gerald was struck in the face by a large, muscular Daemon that had pushed through the small barricade The Chosen Dead erected. The Daemon tried to follow up with a sword, but Gerald grabbed the daemon by its wrist and tore it off, and then picked up the Daemon and threw it into the mass of seething vermin trying to get at him. Gerald picked up the sword and began slashing and thrusting into the mass, but fatigue was starting to show.

Gordon and David held up Vora on either side of her. Don looked worse than when he was being tortured by Judas. His body was pierced in so many places it was hard to see any skin. Gio was clutching his chest and wheezing like he was having a heart attack. He had a spear that he was using to thrust into Daemon's flesh, yank it out, and move.

"Gio, the spear!" Gerald threw Gio his sword and, at the same time, Gio tossed Gerald his spear. Gio caught the sword and began to thrust and parry with it, but he didn't have long. Gerald fought off multiple attacks and used precious energy to blast a circle around him. Once he had the space, he tracked the fallen angel who was in hand-to-hand with Bariel now. The savagery these two demigods fought with was incredible.

"Bariel!" Gerald yelled out as he threw the spear right at the fallen angel, hoping he didn't hit Bariel. What happened next was something none would soon forget. The fallen angel saw the spear coming and shifted over to the side so that the spear passed by inches from him. Bariel lashed out and grabbed the spear mid shaft and then thrust the back of the wooden spear shaft into the chest of the fallen angel. Blood spurted from the fallen angel's mouth. Bariel snapped the spear in two with his other hand and then took the spear point and drove it through the fallen angel's eye so far that the entire spear point came out of the other side of his head. The CTC immediately began glowing but nothing appeared.

Down below, Gerald was knocked to the ground and stabbed multiple times with long spears. He rolled on the ground, snapping spear shafts as he went trying to get to his feet.

Vora was fighting back-to-back with Gordon as he also tried to keep David on his feet. They were all exhausted, and the constant fighting had left them all gritting their teeth in pain as the pressure built in their chests from the strain.

Gio was able to slash his way to the team but was knocked down and pinned through by a spear thrust into him by the damned soul with the zig-zag scar on his head and the collar. The damned soul picked up a Daemon and threw it at Vora and it connected, sending her crashing down in a heap along with David.

Gordon turned around and was stabbed in the chest with a long dagger the damned soul held who then blasted Gordon in the knees with energy. Gordon lost consciousness but the damned soul didn't finish Gordon off. Instead, he grabbed the scroll map still attached to his back and ran off.

Don tried to stop him but the damned soul blasted Don as well. He was soon lost in a crowd of daemons.

Bariel came crashing down like a comet and swatted the Daemons closest to Gerald who had been crushed down to the ground by a mob of daemons, grabbed him, and went over to The Chosen Dead.

Gordon was woozy but awake, and the rest of the team was dead on their feet. "He took it," he said drowsily.

"One problem at a time," Gerald said. The Daemons, who now filled the entirety of the chamber, held back not out of fear but anticipation. Down here, where The Chosen Dead couldn't use their full abilities, they knew they could savor the prey. An angel had a chance, but that was if he would fly off and not stay and fight. Enough of them could eventually drown Bariel.

"I cannot kill them all, most yes but not all," Bariel said.

"I wish I had your confidence," Gio gasped out and spat out blood.

The CTC, which had been glowing for over a minute, now began to flicker and then glow brightly again. The Daemons closest to them began snickering and encroaching on their position.

The Chosen Dead had gone past their limits but they continued to fight.

"Protect his six!" Gerald ordered and pointed at Bariel. They complied as quickly as they could with their ravaged bodies. Gerald stood next to Bariel and spoke to him. "You should fly out of here, bring back others."

Bariel looked over at Gerald "Tactically you are correct," After minutes of intense fighting and the daemon horde was winning, The Chosen Dead were shoulder to shoulder with each other and Bariel. Even with their best efforts, Daemons kept grabbing at his wings to pull him down.

"Leave now!" Gerald yelled at Bariel.

Bariel roared in response. He moved out and slashed with the flaming sword and used his wings to sweep Daemons away left and right. He slaughtered hundreds but thousands more came.

Gerald kept fighting even as he was struck in the side of the head and went down. The bodies were packed so tightly that even the Daemons trying to kill him were being interfered with by their brethren. The rest of The Chosen Dead were now dragged down and pummeled.

Bariel was still sweeping his wings back and forth as Daemons jumped on his back to try to use their numbers to bring him down. The end had come. Bariel had finally been brought down to the ground. The Chosen Dead feebly fought but they saw the end closing upon them. Gerald thought about his family and his team and how he had failed them.

A horn sounded and shook the inside of the chamber. Another horn sounded in response and then another. The Eloyie cavalry appeared next to the CTC and blasted the Daemons who had grouped around it. Oriel and Reloa were in full armor astride their horses of seafoam green and purple. Two thousand strong Eloyie made their charge and mowed down a thousand Daemons before they knew what hit them.

Bariel used the distraction, rose up, and fought like a berserker and flung Daemons far and wide. The cavalry not only used the charge but their magic, and they blasted the Daemons surrounding Bariel and made their way toward The Chosen Dead. The size of the horses belied the power they held as they ran down far larger creatures as if they were nothing. They pierced Daemons with their lances and when they were used up pulled glimmering swords from their sheaths and sliced their way to The Chosen Dead and Bariel.

Reloa pointed his sword at Gordon. "We got your message." The Eloyie smiled.

Oriel smirked and spoke to Bariel. "They had the CTC blocked We would have come sooner."

Bariel nodded and asked, "Where are the others?"

Oriel slashed off the stinger of a large Daemon that looked like a scorpion with three massive legs. "On their way. They should be here shortly. Rest as we clean up." He raised his sword and the cavalry lined back up and began sweeping through the chamber slaughtering the daemons.

Gordon limped up to Gerald "They took the map I stole," he said before adding, "That is the key to them being here. They are looking for something."

Gerald looked around the cavern. There were still too many Daemons to get past. Whoever took it didn't take the CTC, so they must have headed up and out of there. They got far enough to use the valley mist to escape.

"Reloa!" Gerald called. Reloa heard and wheeled back around. His horse took flight and landed next to Gerald. "Can you help us get out of here? A damned soul has stolen a map connected to what they are doing here."

Reloa scanned the area and made two shrill whistles. An Eloyie with wings on his helm, dark brown eyes, and riding a lemon-colored horse sped towards Reloa. "Take command. I am helping him" A quickly raised arm, and the other Eloyie was off and barking commands.

Oriel turned to Gerald and extended his arm. "Come, you should let them rest and, in a few minutes, I can have more men bring them up to you once they clear more of the chamber," he said to Gerald, who looked over at his battered and torn team. "Take a few minutes to rest up then his men will bring you up."

The Chosen Dead wearily looked up and nodded, and Vora gave a thumbs up. Gerald turned and they were off.

"Galadan, up!" Reloa ordered his horse. Galadan bunched his muscles, took a few strides, and flew off the ground. Galadan accelerated at a frightening velocity.

Gerald and Reloa were carried through the interior of the monolith at such a high rate of speed that the walls blurred. In only a few minutes they saw light approaching. The entranceway to the monolith closed on them so quickly that you could feel the pressure change when they hit the outside of the monolith. With a sense of vertigo, they accelerated further and flew into the mist that had prevented The Chosen Dead from using their abilities. Gerald could feel the mist weaken him further. He became very dizzy, and his vision started to close in on him. Gerald let go of Reloa's shoulder and felt himself falling into space. With incredible agility, Reloa leaned back in his saddle and grabbed Gerald. Reloa twisted in mid-air and pushed off the saddle edge to get the speed he needed to grab onto Gerald's elbow.

Galadan subtly moved so that Reloa's other foot held him in place by catching on the other edge of the saddle. They flew through the rest of the mist in this way with Reloa holding onto Gerald with both hands now and he got his other foot to hold on. The moment they broke through into the open air, Gerald woke up and his eyes widened to see Reloa holding him the way he was. Gerald focused and was able to heal himself with some effort but nothing like being inside the monolith.

Reloa watched with a smirk on his face "Feeling better, I see."

Gerald smiled back. "You need help getting back in the saddle?" he asked Reloa who instantly looked offended. Reloa let go of Gerald and backflipped back onto Galadan. Gerald, now flying alongside Reloa, shook his head. "Nobody likes a showoff," Gerald said as he scanned the area for any trace of Judas or the damned soul that had the map. "I can't pick anything up," he said to Reloa who also seemed to be searching.

After a few moments, Reloa closed his eyes and sniffed the air like a hound. "Got him," he said and veered to the west and sped up even more. Gerald was now able to keep up with Reloa, and they moved at speed to catch up with Judas.

"How did you pick him up?" Gerald asked Reloa who tapped his nose to show it was the scent. Gerald had tried that and didn't pick up anything but nonetheless was impressed by the

Eloyie's sense of smell. They sped along for a few minutes. Gerald felt better the further away from the monolith he got. He pulled energy into himself to prepare for the coming conflict. He wanted to make Judas pay for what he had done to The Chosen Dead. Gerald always hated bullies. Judas would pay for trying to humiliate Vora and then celebrate over the captured members of the Chosen Dead. Gerald hated Judas most for the impotent feeling he and the rest felt for not being able to do anything to help each other, especially Vora. Gerald and the others may have been old fashioned, but to see a woman demeaned and victimized by a monster who enjoyed doing it.... He gritted his teeth. Gerald would kill Judas. If not him, then Vora or Gordon. *That dance card got full quick* he thought with a smirk.

They spotted a group of four figures off in the distance moving at high speed. Almost immediately the figures sensed Gerald and Reloa. One of them broke off and flew away.

"Go after him!" Gerald told Reloa who raised an eyebrow. "You alright taking three if them on?" Gerald nodded. "My team should be trailing us so I just need to hold them off till the cavalry comes." Reloa nodded in return and zoomed off after the lone damned soul.

Gerald felt a sense of trepidation. He wanted a piece of Judas and anyone else associated with him, but this was more than a calculated risk. Judas showed great power keeping the CTC blocked for as long as he did. "Stupid," Gerald said to himself as he approached the three damned souls who had spread out to try and encircle him.

Judas stopped moving and floated in midair with his black robe fluttering in the wind. His eyes glowed brightly and his neck was a bright crimson. It looked incredibly painful, Good, Gerald thought.

The two damned souls trying to flank him started firing upon him one with energy blasts, the other with fire. Gerald veered to avoid being hit and placed a shield up when the flames tried to engulf him. Nothing was able to hit him. Judas just stood where he was and watched. Gerald turned to his left and went after a damned soul with sandy brown hair and two wooden splinters in place of his eyes that made him weep bloody tears nonstop. With the soul's hood down, Gerald could see this one wore a collar around his neck, not a dampener. It was colored like the egg thrown at The chosen Dead and disabled them.

Gerald fired upon Splinter Eyes and knocked him back. The shield Splinter Eyes put up was pretty strong, and if Gerald had time he could break through and cause some serious damage, but that was not to be as the second damned soul who also had his hood down rushed in from the other side.

This second damned soul had a round face and was completely hairless, no eyebrows either. He looked like a giant, angry, evil baby. Evil Baby took a swipe at Gerald with a jet-black sword. Gerald blocked it with a shield he quickly put up and almost had his head taken off by Splinter Eyes who came from behind and tried to blast his head off with a pole ax made of dark energy. Gerald ducked under it and sent a shaft of energy right into Splinter Eyes's chest that punched through his hastily erected shield and went all the way through his back where it stuck. Gerald ignited it and the damned soul caught fire from within.

Splinter Eyes was out of commission for the moment and Gerald turned his attention back to Evil Baby, who tossed an egg at Gerald. He quickly cloaked himself and flew behind the Evil Baby at Mach speed. Evil Baby opened his mouth in surprise as the eye in the middle of the egg fixed its rheumy gaze on him and exploded. Gerald was far enough away for the blast to not affect him, so he turned around and watched Evil Baby drop like a stone from the sky.

Judas was now frantically looking for Gerald. Judas erected a shield around him as he rotated around trying to sense Gerald. Judas didn't even bother about Evil Baby or Splinter Eyes. His shifting green eyes were searching in every direction. Judas tried his scanning as well but to no avail.

Gerald went further back to give himself more momentum and then hurled himself straight at Judas. In a blink, Gerald blew through Judas's shield and straight through Judas himself. Gerald tore Judas Iscariot in half. The trauma of such an act would have debilitated any other soul. It wouldn't kill them, but they would be as good as dead from trying to defend themselves after that.

Due to the thousands of years of torment, Judas Iscariot had developed a pain tolerance that was beyond comprehension. Judas fixed Gerald with a predatory grin while his bottom half stopped falling and then shot back up and reformed to the rest of his body. "Good effort," Judas said to him and then sent a shockwave that blew out Gerald's eardrums and disoriented him.

Gerald was falling through the air and felt a sharp pain as one of his legs was cut off above the knee. He hastily erected a shield that barely held, but it did hold as it deflected an attack to the side opposite of the cut off leg. Gerald quickly healed himself and stopped falling.

Judas was in front of him with that false smile. "You survived my finishing move. Guess I'll have to take you seriously." The damned soul materialized his whip and a long, black blade. Gerald materialized a silver sword with a matching dagger. Judas flicked the whip so fast that Gerald barely caught it with the dagger and the whip wrapped around it. Judas pulled the dagger out of his hand. Gerald detonated the dagger which blasted the surrounding whip to shreds. Rather than disappear, the pieces of the whip flew at Gerald and before he could burn all the pieces away or block them with a shield, some of them sunk into him, and caused a burning pain. The pieces seemed to be alive and began to dig into his body which caused even more burning pain as they pumped poison into him.

Gerald burned all the pieces away before they sunk in too far. The whip, which seemed to have a mind of its own, reformed then swayed like a snake and Gerald had to block multiple strikes from it as well as block sword strikes from Judas who got in close to try and take Gerald's head off. He almost succeeded as the whip struck when the sword came down.

The shield Gerald erected fractured as the whip wrapped itself around his calf and immediately burning fire erupted. The barbs were pumping poison into him that weakened him. The distraction almost doomed him, but Gerald was able to move his body up enough so the black sword cut off his left arm instead of taking his head. Gerald lashed out with an energy blast. It didn't do much damage but allowed him to get some distance.

Judas pulled back with the whip which was still wrapped around Gerald's calf, upended him, and allowed the damned soul to strike his midsection with his sword. Gerald saw the blow coming and allowed gravity to take him so that the blow just cut off an ear. He blasted at Judas's leg which in turn caused him to lose his balance and allowed Gerald to burn the whip off him. The flames spread right up Judas's arm and he screamed before he put the flames out. The side of Judas's arm was black and the whip reappeared, but this time was much smaller and thinner.

"You fuck!" Judas screamed. "Oh, you're gonna pay!" Judas spat at Gerald with acid which he deflected. The whip, upon closer inspection, was the same greenish scale as the collar and the egg so it was sentient. Gerald burned the whip again and could hear the distinct squeal along with the stink of Daemon. This caused Judas to go berserk, and he flew right into Gerald's chest and tried to bite and stab him with the flaying knife he had used on The Chosen Dead. The strength Judas exerted was incredible.

With the poison still causing pain and weakness, Gerald did all he could do to survive it. He knew martial arts and how to use an opponent's strength against them, but everything he tried didn't work. Gerald blasted Judas square in the face and burned off his skin, so Gerald was now fighting a burned skinless maniac who was pushing them down toward the ground.

He tried to blast him and burn him again, but Judas just accelerated them both faster and faster into the ground. Gerald realized he was going to hit the ground, so he stopped fighting and began to stab Judas, who stabbed him in return. They brutalized each other as they both fell. When they finally hit the ground, the impact caused a crater half a mile wide and a quarter mile deep.

It caused Gerald to black out for a few seconds. When he woke, Judas was groggily trying to stand above him. His face was still burned and his side where he impacted was flattened and a bloody mess, but on the other hand, he held the black sword. Gerald tried to fire a blast at Judas, but he was pummeled with another shockwave. The damage disorientated him enough for Judas to swipe down and cut off Gerald's head.

Halfway down, Judas' arm was blown off and then he was blasted away from Gerald with multiple energy blasts. Gerald turned and saw The Chosen Dead rushing towards them both.

Judas stood up and sent another shockwave at the Chosen Dead, pulled out a bag of the mist, threw it at them, and then took off at high speed. The mist billowed. Gordon and David went after Judas but came back after giving chase. "He must have used another bag of mist to cover his tracks," Gordon informed them. Gerald had healed up by now and looked up to see Reloa joining them.

When he landed, he looked worse for wear. His armor was

scorched and broken off on the side, one of his arms was bent at a bad angle, and Galadan had his right front leg curled up as if injured. They all rushed over to Reloa who grimly smiled. "He got away from me," he griped.

"Can we heal you?" Gerald asked. Reloa nodded and Vora, David, and Gordon laid hands on Reloa, and Gerald, Don, and Gio laid hands on Galahad. After thirty seconds or so, both horse and rider were fully healed.

"He had the map," Reloa said to them.

45

POST OP THE THIRD

By the time The Chosen Dead and Reloa returned to the monolith, things had changed considerably. It took them some time to walk down through the mist but not nearly as long as the last time. Reloa and Galadan could still use their powers, but they were limited. They could see a giant column of smoke as they made their approach from the main road towards the monolith. The giant column of foul-smelling smoke originated at a massive fire where the bodies of the Daemons were being thrown. After a short period of time, their bodies turned to sludge, so it was understandable they didn't want to have hundreds of thousands of Daemon carcasses melting on them.

A couple of hundred souls and at least an additional two thousand Eloyie were part of the Heavenly host going in and out of the monolith entranceway. Within an hour of when they left and returned there were two rail lines laid down and in operation. Gerald noticed the coloring of parts of the rail lines were the same as the giant vehicles that had been zooming in and around the monolith. The Eloyie were directing the efforts and using their magic strategically, brought out another of the massive vehicles. Together, they used their powers to disassemble the vehicle into its parts and reshape it into long stretches of new rail lines.

As they approached the entranceway they were greeted by Oriel, Commander Ho, and Bariel. After trading pleasantries, Gerald and Gordon were ordered up to see command. "Aren't you in command, Commander Ho?" Gerald asked.

Commander Ho thinly smiled and looked uncomfortable as he answered, "I take orders like everyone else. Best not to keep him waiting" He nodded towards the entranceway.

"I'll take them," Bariel offered. "Chosen Dead, we have quarters for you, we will reunite later," Bariel said.

As Gerald, Bariel, and Gordon headed into the monolith there was tension and even worry exuding from Bariel. It made both Gerald and Gordon nervous.

Gerald turned to Bariel and stepped in front of him. "Who is in command?" he asked Bariel. What worried Gerald more was the range of emotions from surprise, anger, and finally, concern that swept over the angel's face in a fraction of a second. Bariel straightened up and looked up into the mist that covered the sky from here. Finally, he answered, "It is not my place for introductions."

Gerald looked over at Gordon who raised his eyebrows "Why are you so worried, are we going to be punished?"

Bariel was taken aback by that "Punished? No, that is not what I am worried about..." He stopped himself from talking as Gerald and Gordon waited for him to continue. "All I can tell you is...he is one who you should always be wary of." Bariel offered nothing else.

They walked until they came to the ramp area which had a road that twisted all the way to the top of the monolith. Two industrial-sized elevators were being built on each side, bypassing the twisting roadway. The elevator lines were built almost as a vertical rail line with no cable. This allowed for a much higher weight capacity and greater speed. The elevators themselves were in the process of being built, so Bariel stepped close to Gerald and Gordon.

"I will carry you both up." Bariel knelt and cradled both Gerald and Gordon as if they were toddlers and flew straight up toward the top of the monolith. In a matter of seconds, they arrived, and Bariel placed them both down. They all headed into the chamber at the top of the monolith.

They passed by the old and rotting relics and artifacts. The smell of age clung to the air. The main change to the room was the center altar visible from a distance was now cleared. There were three souls and four angels looking down at the altar at what appeared to be an old map. All three knew instantly who was in charge.

As they made their final approach, they saw an angel who was much larger than anyone else in the room, a head taller than Bariel. He had dark curly hair and wore light brown robes. The aura of power that radiated off him distorted the air. He shone in a red light with what appeared to be bursts of electrical charges running through it. This angel stared intently at the map on the altar until all three had reached the steps. When he turned his gaze upon them, Gerald and Gordon understood Bariel's concern. Bursts of electrical discharge played across his eyes and sparks floated up into the air. His face was a frozen mask. They all understood how a small animal felt when locked onto by a superior predator, an apex predator.

The angel slowly turned his gaze upon Bariel. "You may leave, brother." The angel spoke so deeply that it sounded like a thunderstorm had learned to speak.

Bariel bowed and went to turn, stopped himself, and spoke to the angel. "Perhaps I should stay and provide my input as well." The angel's face didn't change but a pulse of electrical discharge showed his displeasure at not being obeyed immediately. "I will call upon you," the angel finished. Bariel bowed again and left.

The angel turned his lightning gaze upon Gerald and Gordon. "Approach," the angel said and waited for both of them. When they stopped in front of the angel, they could see the map on the altar was like the map Gordon had stolen from him. It was very old, but the colors of the map were different shades of brown and gold with some pale green for the mega ocean that encompassed the planet.

"Greetings, Gerald Argyll and Gordon Red Feather. I am glad to see you both have survived your interaction with the being known as Judas Iscariot." Gerald and Gordon gave each other a look. Interaction was definitely not the word they would use regarding Judas Iscariot. "I am Uriel the Archangel. I have been placed in charge of this mission. I require your input into the events that have occurred on this world."

Neither Gerald nor Gordon said a word. There were only seven archangels in existence, and Uriel was considered the fourth most powerful. He was called the wisdom of God. It made sense why Uriel was sent here to take command. If anyone knew what was going on, he would.

Gordon went first and recounted all the events he went through once he followed the damned soul, lost him, brought the Chosen Dead into the jungle, found the monolith, and enacted the rescue.

When he was finished, Uriel nodded and with a slight upward turn of his mouth to indicate a smile he spoke to Gordon. "I understand the dead Daemon you sent through the CTC caused quite the stir. Well done. The coordinates you attached to the body as well as the numbers were invaluable," Uriel said.

Gerald looked over at Gordon and smiled, and Gordon shrugged.

"You may leave, Gordon Red Feather. I must speak with your Jarl."

Gordon bowed as Bariel had done to Uriel, nodded to Gerald, and left.

"We have much to discuss. " Uriel said to Gerald as he turned and extended his arm so Gerald could follow him. The see-through walls of the top floor chamber were impressive, and the technology to create such a thing was incredible considering how old it was. All around the mist lay like a Christmas skirt under a tree. It was so thick you could not see below. Around the monolith, roiling turbulence emitted more mist out of the massive structure.

"It is coming from the monolith," Uriel admitted to Gerald. "The monolith itself is made of material long forgotten, a porous stone that does not erode, even after billions of years." Gerald was shocked. He knew the monolith was ancient. Still, billions of years were beyond his ken.

He stopped Uriel. "Billions of years old porous stone that hasn't worn itself down to a nub after all this time. Hard to believe."

Uriel's expression did not change but he extended both arms to illustrate his point that whatever Gerald may have thought the reality was clearly saying something else.

"Touche," Gerald said and let Uriel continue.

"The mist is an after-effect of the true purpose of the monolith which is to conceal this place."

Gerald let that sink in and then offered his thoughts. "Conceal this place, or conceal something in particular?"

Electrical discharge crackled along the surface of Uriel's eyes in acknowledgment of Gerald's statement. "Go on."

Gerald nodded. "From what Gordon detailed, there were other maps and information but the only thing left was the map that was stolen back from Gerald by Iscariot." His gaze fell upon the placeholder where the map was sitting prior to being taken, and he could see a soft white glow of energy radiating from it. Only another placeholder had any spark left as its glow was barely perceptible anymore. "Whatever that map leads to is the real prize." Gerald walked over to the altar and looked down at the map.

The sun was at the altar and over to the left of the monument. The picture of the object shining was beneath the monolith on the map. In the air around it were the same creatures Gordon had described: a lion-like animal, some sort of flock of flying birds as well as a long serpent-like creature. None of The Chosen Dead had seen anything as large as what these creatures were depicted to be. The largest was a canine creature that appeared to be about a hundred pounds. "You know what they are looking for?" Gerald asked.

Uriel fixed him with a glare from his lightning eyes. Gerald didn't think Uriel would respond but after a few awkward seconds, he answered, "I have an idea."

Gerald nodded. "You don't know where it is," Uriel nodded in agreement. "Are you willing to share what you think it is?" Gerald pushed. He never liked it when anyone wasn't transparent, and from what he could see of Uriel, he was as transparent as a stone wall.

Uriel fixed him with another electric glare, "No I am not," he said flatly.

Gerald thought for a moment before saying anything. "Judas said that when they got what they came for he was going to pay a visit to Heaven. Does that make any difference?"

Electrical discharge played across the angel's body now as he loomed larger than before, and his eyes burned. "He said this?" Uriel hissed and smoke leaked out of his mouth.

Gerald's eyes went wide and instinctively backed into the altar trying to create space with Uriel, but the angel grabbed Gerald's

ERIC MALDONADO

arm and burned him with an electrical discharge. Gerald gritted his teeth and tried to pull away, but Uriel's grip was like iron.

To his credit, Uriel regained control and released Gerald. He reverted to his normal size and inclined his head towards Gerald. "My apologies, that was unseemly."

Gerald nodded. "I take it that whatever it is can do something like that?"

"If it is what I think, then it should not exist" This time it was Gerald who extended his arms as if to reinforce the point made earlier about the reality of the situation.

Uriel grunted in amusement. "I am not authorized to share this information with you...yet, but that does not change the fact that we must find it before the enemy does. Are we in agreement?" Gerald nodded. "You and your Chosen Dead have proved invaluable in finding this place. I require your assistance with finding this object. If you find where this object is, I will tell you what it is. Does that seem fair to you?"

Gerald nodded. "That would be nice, but I know how to follow orders."

Uriel nodded to Gerald. "About your predicament. I and others gave much thought as to how best to handle you and ensure you do not get yourself killed." Uriel's tone was lighter as he steered away from the prior topic. "The Souleater and Judas Iscariot were unable to kill you."

Gerald grinned. "Not for lack of trying. I thought I was a goner a few times."

Uriel's eyes flickered. "Yes, a goner. as you say. Yet here you are. Very much present. I have encountered The Souleater, you know." Gerald cocked his eyebrows."That creature was one of the most dangerous beings I have encountered in my long existence. To think such a young soul as you not only survived the encounter but bested that beast is remarkable."

Outside the chamber, a sudden humming filled the air as the elevators went online. They made very little noise for such large devices. "Any advice?" Gerald asked.

"Yes." Uriel turned toward Gerald and placed his arms on Gerald's shoulders. "Don't get killed" He removed his hands from Gerald, smiled for the first time, and continued. "You're very perceptive. Your mind is your best weapon. I have heard you are a natural leader, and you care for your team. All excellent qualities." Uriel was looking out of the see-through wall now. "You need time to grow and learn. Don't do anything too foolhardy. I would like to see you fulfill your potential."

Gerald nodded and said. "So, don't get killed." Without looking at Gerald, the angel raised one finger to affirm that Gerald was correct.

"Dismissed," Uriel said without turning around.

Gerald bowed and departed. What Uriel had told him was similar to what Miller, Porter, and Bariel had said. It was frustrating that there wasn't anything more useful he could follow except, "don't be stupid and die " advice but still, it wasn't a bad place to start. More concerning was that Uriel was worried about whatever this object or artifact was. Whatever it took, he would make sure Judas didn't get it.

Gerald exited the chamber as one of the elevators stopped close by. The Chosen Dead and Bariel came out and rushed toward him. Gerald was afraid something had happened and was instantly on the defensive. "What's wrong?" he barked at them.

They all skidded to a halt. Even Bariel looked nervous. "What is it?"

They all looked at each other, and Vora stepped up to Gerald.

The normal brash, vivacious woman he knew was gone and

replaced by a woman wringing her hands together and smiling nervously. "Your wife is here."

The End

The series continues with Book 2
The Path of Heaven

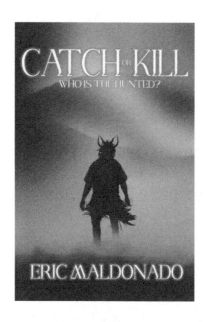

Get The Last Days Saga Prequel
Catch Or Kill

FOR FREE

Sign up for the no-spam newsletter and get Eric Maldonado's
exclusive give away, absolutely free.

Go To
www.ericmaldonadoauthor.com
And Sign Up!

THE PATH OF HEAVEN ~ SNEAK PREVIEW

THE LAST DAYS SAGA ~ BOOK TWO

Chapter 1: LOVE STRUCK

On a bright sunny summer day, ten-year-old Gerald is sitting with his father Ralph and brother Chance in the family car while Kathryn his mother is bringing their cousin Melinda to the car as they head out for church.

"Hurry up, it's hot in here!" Chance yells out the window to his mother and Melinda as they make their way to the car. "Hold your Horses," Kathryn yells back as she makes it to the car and Melinda climbs in the back with the boys and finally settles in next to Ralph up front.

"You look pretty," Chance says to Melinda who smiles in response and says "Thank you, cuz"

They accelerate onto the main road and Chance who has been fidgeting in the back seat pulls himself up so he can be closer to his father.

"Church is so boring, Dad, why can't we go fishing instead?"

"Uh huh," Ralph says in response

"God won't mind if we miss church on a nice day right?"

"Uh huh," Ralph responds again. Chance sets his mouth in a grimace and leans closer to his father

"Dad you hear anything I said?" Chance asks in a huff.

"Of course I did," Ralph says. Chance raises his hands to say well? Ralph glances over at Chance and with a smirk says "You'll understand when you're older and you bring your kids to church." He finishes. Chance does not seem convinced and before he can say anything else Ralph cuts him off. "Also, you don't have a choice so suck it up." Kathryn turns to Chance and cocks her eyebrow at him and also at Gerald and Melinda who both just shrug their shoulders, resigned to their fate. Chance leans back in a huff. knowing better than to push it any further. They arrive at First Baptist Church and as the family gets out of the car and starts walking toward the front of the church a honk turns their attention toward the street. Charlie Haddon, Gerald's best friend is dropped off by his mother Mildred who throws Charlie a kiss, waves to the Argyll family, and takes off without turning around. As Charlie slowly makes his way towards the Argylls Gerald looks up at his father who shakes his head. Mildred hadn't been the same since Winston her husband and Charlie's father died suddenly of a stroke. Since then, Mildred has been more concerned about running around with various men than raising her son Charlie. They all meet up at the steps to the church and Charlie glumly greets everyone. His serious face belied a wicked sense of humor, at this moment there was no humor to be found.

"Your ma seemed in a real huff," Ralph said to Charlie as he laid his hand on his thin shoulders. Charlie nods and says "She is heading up north to Charlotte for a few days so..." Kathryn cuts him off "You're always welcome in our house Charlie. You never have to ask, you stay as long as you like sweetheart." She finished with a reassuring smile and a light tap on his cheek. Charlie flashed them a brief smile and they all headed inside.

Ralph and Kathryn share a concerned glance. After Church, which Chance somehow managed to survive, the crowd is on the street of Savannah talking when Thurston Windicutt, his wife Gloria, and his son Simon approach. Thurston Windicutt is an old money family and Grand Dragon of the local KKK Chapter. He was a tall serious man who was always clean-shaven and never smiled He had his hands in everything locally and liked to flash what local power he had every chance he got. Gloria was a former runner-up, twice she would add, to being Miss Georgia, she had jumped on Thurston's bandwagon years before, recognizing he would be the biggest wig in the area. His son Simon had his mother's pageant looks and his father's sour attitude. Something dark lay within him as well, a cruel boy. Pushing Melinda down the stairs at the hardware didn't help his reputation either. Fortunately, Ralph's father had started a business in farming supply. Once Kathryn began working with Ralph their business grew as they purchased smaller businesses during the Depression. Due to the connections, he made after the Great War and in the Legion, Ralph frequently traveled up north to work with his buddies who had come stateside and settled in the northeast. Thurston approached and began asking how Ralph was doing and making small talk which he was ill-suited for. The real reason he came to speak with Ralph became apparent when Thurston asked his thoughts on him running for office and if he could count on his support. Ralph hated Thurston but couldn't verbalize it since he did hold sway and had a small army of KKK zealots backing him. Ralph, could feel Kathryn watching the exchange from the side and felt her tension from where he was standing. Ralph answered that since he has been friends with Daulton Cray since he was knee high then respectfully no.

"We're tight, you know that" Ralph explained. Thurston already knew their relationship went back to when they were both boys. Thurston liked to try and hide his brutishness behind a veneer of civility. Kathryn had once said "It's like trying to watch a gorilla tap dance" Ralph smirked at recalling her saying that. Thurston picked up on the smirk and cocked his head to the side trying to understand the humor in their conversation.

"That is disappointing." He sighed then continued. "With your moxie and connections, we could do some good in this town. Maybe next time then." Thurston finished and he and Gloria said their farewells to the Argylls.

"Come along Simon," Thurston said. Simon the whole time the adults had been speaking, had been waving at Melinda who wouldn't make eye contact with him, and walked up next to Charlie whom she loved to protect her. Chance raised his hand into a fist and made the throat-cutting gesture at Simon who sneered in return. Chance was itching to get some licks in after the stairs incident with Melinda. He was still upset with his mother for stopping him from turning his lights out. The families separated and pretended to ignore their children.

"One day I am going to knock him into next week," Chance said as the Windicutts walked off. "I have a feeling you're going to have to wait in line son," Ralph said and then asked if they minded walking down to the Second Baptist church. He had to pick up paperwork from John Barnaux for the spring crop order.

"He the colored man with the blue eyes?" Charlie asked. "Yep, known him longer than you have been alive," Ralph replied. "Seems like a good man," Charlie finished. Ralph looked down and smiled at Charlie. "He sure is, as solid as they come"

The sun and breeze accompanied them on their walk on such a beautiful day. When they got close to the Second church, the singing floated from inside the church and captured the attention of the bystanders on the street with its joy and devotion. Chance was bobbing his head and clapping his hands. He told everyone how much he loved the music and singing.

"Why don't we go here? I wouldn't be bored" Chance asked as he continued to bob his head to the music. Ralph and Kathryn just smiled at Chance and then they all smiled and enjoyed the music and the day together. Across the street was a bakery, one whiff, and Gerald asked if he could get some pastries while they waited. Ralph reached into his pocket and handed Gerald some money. Chance and Melinda who had joined him by swaying to the music weren't going to move from their spot so just Charlie and Gerald went across the street, heard the bell as they opened the door, and waited in line for a moment. Once Church let out, the line would be around the corner so they were lucky to take advantage of the timing. The boys ordered black and white cookies and some French pastries in a box. Gerald paid, dropped the change into his pocket, and they left the bakery. Gerald stepped outside, it had quieted down, and the black people who attended church there were walking out speaking to each other on the street. Gerald was looking for his family and saw the most beautiful girl he had ever seen. A young girl about Gerald's age was across the street standing next to John Barnaux. She had long straight black hair and had a native Indian look to her with stormy grey eyes, she looked exactly like the woman standing next to John Barnaux. She locked eyes with Gerald and he felt an electricity run through him. All thought left him and he just walked straight to her. This sudden urge made the world disappear, and all he saw was her. All he knew was that he had to get to her. The loud blaring of a horn sounded and he was grabbed from behind by Charlie who pulled him back before a car could hit Gerald. Spell broken the world came flooding back. The box of pastries was thankfully safe as Charlie had been holding them the whole time.

"Watch yourself. You can't talk to her if you get squashed." Charlie said to Gerald who nodded absently and patted his arm. The girl wouldn't make eye contact with Gerald again but he had caught the attention of the woman who had to be her mother. She watched Gerald closely and smiled when he noticed her.

"You dingbat you almost got hit by a car!" Chance yelled at Gerald. They both safely made it across the street. Kathryn had a knowing smile on her face and Ralph a smirk. He looked over at John who also smirked and shook his head.

"First off, thank you Charlie for saving my son from being road kill. Second, Gerald and Charlie, this is John and Lucy Barnaux, and their daughter Lia." Ralph finished. Gerald felt very self-conscious now but still hoped for a peak back from Lia.

"Hello," Lia greeted them in a low tone without making eye contact with any of them but to Gerald, the sun shone brighter when she said it. The electricity came back and he hoped she would speak again so he could hear that voice.

Lucy stared intently at Gerald who realized she was looking at him again. "Hello, young man, you must be more careful crossing the street." Gerald nodded and said, "Yes ma'am." Lucy smiled and said to Kathryn "They are fine boys and a pretty young girl" Melinda blushed, and said thank you to Lucy. "Three brothers," Lucy added. Charlie replied, "I am not related ma'am" Lucy smiled at Charlie and said to them "Does that make a difference?" Ralph placed his hand on Charlie's shoulder in response. John let Lucy know they needed to head home. She nodded to her husband and looked right at Gerald. "I have a feeling we'll meet again young man, make sure you look both ways"

John grabbed Lucy's hand and they said their farewells. Lia said a quick farewell to everyone and as the Barneux family walked away Gerald waited. *Just turn so I can see you one last time* he said to himself. He began to lose hope as the family turned to the next street Right as she went out of view she turned, they locked eyes, and she smiled at him before disappearing around the corner. He would remember that smile for the rest of his life. "She is pretty," Melinda said. Charlie chimed in. "The little fat baby with the wings hit you right between the eyes." Chance started laughing and patted Gerald on the back. His mother later said he practically floated home.

WOULD YOU LIKE TO READ ON?
www.ericmaldonadoauthor.com

Edited by Megan Harris

Made in the USA
Middletown, DE
06 June 2024